# THE COURIER

## Tony Paull

# THE COURIER

Copyright © 2024 Tony Paull

## All rights reserved.


ISBN: 978-1-0672315-6-9

**ACKNOWLEDGMENT**

My thanks to the Nelson Mandela Foundation for permission to use Mr. Mandela's name in this work of fiction. Should you wish to know more about the foundation, please visit their website at https://www.nelsonmandela.org/

**NOTE TO THE READER**

This book is a figment of my imagination, and the concept and story were entirely devised and written by me. With the exception of the cover art, no Ai was used in the writing of this book.

# Tuesday, January 30th, 1990

AN ABRUPT CLICK ENDED the call, leaving Roux staring at the receiver, a question echoing in the silence. He leaned back in his antique chair, behind his equally old desk. The call was as bizarre as it was inexplicable. The old man never called him at work, and the question about SONA was a surprise. Rising from his chair, he stretched his six-foot frame, stifling a yawn. With one hand in his pocket and the other tugging at an abundant mustache, he began pacing, his mind still grappling with the cryptic call. A gentle tap on the door interrupted his thoughts. His assistant, short and plump with a shock of gray hair, stood expectantly in the doorway.

"Morning, Colonel."

Four years ago, newly promoted to colonel in the South African Police, he stepped into his role as Officer Commanding Logistics for the Western Cape region, based at Cape Province Command headquarters in Compton Square, Cape Town. The Province, covering nearly two-thirds of the country, was subdivided for command-and-control purposes into regions. His area of responsibility, the western Cape region, encompassed the vibrant city of Cape Town and the diverse rural, farming, and coastal communities surrounding it.

The shift from investigator to administrator proved more daunting than expected. Thankfully, Gerda, his wise and competent assistant, stepped in, easing his transition. Their working relationship blossomed with the caveat he curbed his colorful language. Over those challenging early years, he developed a deep appreciation for Gerda, not only as a skilled aide but also as a friend who brightened his days with humor and good nature.

"Morning Gerda," he said with a welcoming smile. "Come on in."

They both spoke in Afrikaans, a language evolved from the Dutch vernacular and introduced in the main by Dutch settlers to South Africa in the 17th century. Although one of two official languages in the country, English being the other, Afrikaans, was the written and spoken means of communication within all government structures.

She strolled over to the in-tray on his desk and began scratching through an assortment of files and papers, her pudgy fingers making quick work of the pile.

"How's Mel, and that handsome son of yours?" she said, as she probed.

He sighed. "My brilliant wife is great, but Rian needs to focus more on academia than sport if he intends to have a future."

Gerda's smile faded as she glared down at the tray. "Where are the letters? You still haven't signed them. Personnel needs to attach the increase letters to the month end payslips, and your department is the only one outstanding."

He smiled to himself. Dear old Gerda, all brusqueness on the outside but soft as melting ice cream on the inside.

"I have the month-end report to read and sign off, and then finish checking the vehicle logs, but you'll have them before lunch."

"Now, when did I hear that one before?" she said, gazing up at the ceiling, a finger tapping her lips. "Ah yes! Yesterday, and the day before, and I'm still waiting, *Colonel!*"

He pretended to cringe.

She scowled at him for a moment before her look softened.

"You OK Marius? Something worrying you?"

Sauntering over to his desk, he collapsed into the chair behind his desk, which groaned and creaked in complaint, leaned back and placed his intertwined hands on what was fast becoming a growing paunch.

"My pa called, and asked if I knew anything about a special announcement at the upcoming State of the Nation Address. Couldn't help him. How the heck would I know what will happen at SONA? He never talks to me unless he's after something."

"That's not true," she scolded. "He's very fond of you."

"Oh sure, in a drill sergeant sort of way," he mumbled under his breath.

She stood gazing down at the desk, her brow creasing—a sign she had something on her mind. "You got a minute?"

"Sure." He waved her toward a chair.

Easing herself into the chair she began twirling her wedding ring as she glanced at the picture of President F.W. de Klerk on the wall behind him. "Will South West gaining independence affect us?"

"Who knows," he said, tired of all the talk about South West Africa. Since 1966, the People's Liberation Army of

Namibia (PLAN) had waged a bitter struggle for independence, culminating in South Africa agreeing, in terms of United Nations Resolution 435, to end its illegal occupation of what was to become Namibia on March 21st, 1990. A war which cost the lives of thousands of young White South Africans, and got the country embroiled in the Angolan Civil War in its efforts to interdict PLAN's supply lines to South West. While many welcomed the end of hostilities, the media, and segments of the business community, were raising legitimate concerns about South Africa's long-term survival. Four recently liberated countries, all vociferous supporters of the anti-apartheid struggle—a support somewhat tempered by their economic reliance on the Pretoria regime—would encircle the land borders. Throw in the devastating effects of international sanctions, and the future looked bleak unless de Klerk ushered in meaningful transformation to gain international backing.

She changed the topic without preamble. "What will happen at SONA?"

"Wait and see, I suppose."

"It's just with all this talk on TV about changes, and with de Klerk saying we should be ready to compromise as things can't stay the way they are, I'm worried Marius," she said, placing a fist on his desk, her brow wrinkled. "The ladies at the church are becoming anxious about the calls to release the terrorists from Robben Island, especially Mandela. I mean, a year ago you got locked up for saying so, but now everyone is talking about it! I just can't believe how fast things have changed."

Opening her hand, she ran it across the desk several times, like she was clearing away dust. Her eyes narrowed.

"What do you think will happen, Marius? Will de Klerk release the terrorists?"

Roux scoffed, flicking a dismissive hand. "I doubt it. The ANC must renounce their armed struggle before any consideration will be given to releasing terrorists, and I can't see them agreeing. True, de Klerk is stirring the pot, but he needs to be careful. Remember the last election? The government needs to tread warily before it makes commitments to free Mandela and negotiate with the Blacks." He sat back, satisfied with his summation of current political affairs in the country. Pa would be impressed.

"But Marius," she shot back, "according to the papers, most Whites are growing tired of the strikes, the sanctions, the riots. Some ladies at the church are even talking about emigrating."

"By most, you mean the anti-government English newspapers. Don't believe everything you read in the papers, or what you hear on TV, Gerda. Trust me, de Klerk won't just hand over everything to the Blacks. If the economy and security aren't in White hands, the country will collapse."

She stood up, straightening her dress, looking unconvinced. "What does your father think about it?"

Roux gave a wry chuckle. "Put it this way. Pa voted for the conservatives in the last election."

"And you?" she said, a faint smile tickling the corners of her mouth.

"Now, now Gerda, we don't ask people who they voted for."

She sniffed. "You're no help, are you? Well, I suppose we'll just have to wait 'til Friday, then. Time to get back to work." She pointed an accusing finger. "Don't forget my letters."

The phone buzzed, showing an internal call. Roux grimaced but made no effort to answer it.

"Don't exert yourself, Colonel, *I'll get it*," said Gerda.

"Colonel Roux's office, Mrs. Steyn speaking. How may I help you?" she intoned. "Oh! Hello Marie, how are you?"

Roux watched her, corners of his mouth turned down, waiting for the conversation to progress into an analysis of last night's episode of Dallas before the real purpose of the call revealed itself. His thoughts returned to his father's call. What was he hoping to find out?

But Gerda only listened, frowning. "Now? OK. Thanks, Marie, he's right here. Meet you for lunch?"

Roux snapped back to the present. This was about him.

"The general wants to see you *now*," she said, putting down the phone, "and Marie says he's not in the best of moods, so I suggest you hurry along."

Roux sat bolt upright. "*The* general? Why does he want to see me?"

"How many generals do you know, Marius? Of course it's *the* general."

*Quite a few, courtesy of my pa,* he thought. "Did she say why?" he said, leaping to his feet, knocking over his pen and pencil holder set, sending the contents flying. "Damn," he muttered as he straightened his tunic.

"No. But Marie said it wasn't a request. Maybe he'll demote you for not signing the letters." She waved her hand. "Leave it, I'll pick them up."

"Thanks. I just hope Kloppers is there." Brigadier Kloppers, who, as Officer Commanding Finance and Administration, which included logistics, reported to *the* general, and was Roux's immediate superior.

He chewed at the inside of his mouth.

"Relax, you'll be fine."

"Talk later, assuming I survive," he said, taking his peaked cap off the top of a filing cabinet and heading out of the office. He took the elevator up to the top floor of the four-story building and hurried into Marie's office.

"Go in Colonel, the general is expecting you."

"Thanks". He made his way to the open door, hesitated, took a deep breath, and marched into the room, tucking his cap under his left arm before snapping to attention.

This was his first sight of the CO's office. By government standards, it was large but austere. An oversized desk, two chairs, and two filing cabinets left plenty of open space. Four massive windows faced out onto the open park of Compton Square. Along the wall to his right hung the ubiquitous, enlarged pictures of the president and the commissioner of police. Maps of the Western Cape, including Cape Town, covered most of the wall to his left.

Major General Warmer, the aging Commanding Officer of the Western Cape region, stood peering at something of interest on a map, which Roux guessed was the area around the Black locations. These squalid and over-crowded housing estates, sometimes referred to as townships, were the primary focus of the police's efforts in suppressing the rising anti-government protests.

But it was the second man, seated at a small round table to his left, who caught Roux's attention. Bespectacled and in a brown suit, he was studying Roux through hooded eyes. The recognition was almost instantaneous. Major General du Plessis, commander of the Security Branch.

"Roux. Morning. Sit," the man said, removing his glasses and using them to point at a vacant chair at the table. "You know who I am?"

He had never met du Plessis but was aware of his reputation for abruptness and intolerance of incompetents. His small stature and grandfatherly appearance belied his ruthlessness, lulling many a subordinate and senior officer into a state of complacency in his presence, only to be decimated by his foul temper and cutting tongue. His rise through the ranks had been meteoric after gaining prominence during the brutal suppression of the student uprisings in 1976. As chief of the nation's secret police, he was a powerful man, and at one time, which seemed a lifetime ago, Roux's indirect boss.

Roux sat down, straight-backed, in a chair opposite du Plessis. Seeing him up close for the first time, he understood why first impressions could deceive. In his mid-fifties, with a full head of brown hair edging towards gray around the temples, an open face with chubby cheeks, and a body Mel would have referred to as "cuddly," the man did look like someone's grandfather. But the cold eyes gave a distinct impression. They would scare the proverbial out of any kids. He gnawed at the inside of his mouth, aggravating a partially healed lesion.

"Morning General, yes I do."

Du Plessis stared at Roux for a minute, then called over his left shoulder, "Hennie, would you like to join us? It's important you are aware of the changes."

Warmer sauntered over to the table and sat down, leaned back, stuck a finger in his ear, wiggled it about for a moment, as though adjusting a lever in his brain, and then stared up at the ceiling.

"I take it you heard about van Rensburg?" du Plessis said, lifting his glasses to the overhead light as though checking on the cleanliness of the lenses before putting them on.

Roux couldn't discern whether his reference to van Rensburg's health, whoever he was, was ambivalence or disinterest. "Uh . . . no General, I haven't." He was powerless to stop the tremor in his voice.

"Bugger had a heart attack. Last week. Didn't even ask permission. Just fell over at home."

Roux realized with a start the offender was none other than Brigadier *Slang*—meaning snake—van Rensburg, the head of Security Branch for the Western Cape.

"Is he dead?" queried Roux, uncertain what emotion he was required to display.

"No," replied du Plessis, "in Groote Schuur, ICU."

Roux got the impression the general was not altogether enamored the man had survived.

Du Plessis grunted. "I doubt he'll be back, considering he has only two years to retirement, and his convalescence period will take him close to that date, so I need to replace him. Swanepoel, the number two, is running the unit for now, but he is almost as old as van Rensburg, and so unsuitable as a permanent replacement. The other officers lack the seniority for the position."

"Yes, General," said Roux dutifully. He had no idea why he was being told about Security Branch's staff changes. Maybe du Plessis wasn't aware he was in the Finance Department.

"A situation which leaves me with somewhat of a dilemma," du Plessis continued. "Move one of the operational brigadiers from Pretoria down here, or look for a local candidate." He ran two fingers along the bridge of his nose, then out across his hairless upper lip.

"However, I have been, how shall I put this, coerced into revising my plans? Yesterday I received a call from Personnel, General Niemandt. Any idea why?" He paused, his eyes penetrating Roux's.

*How the hell would I know, you old fart,* thought Roux, but said, "I'm sorry, no idea General," straining to keep the sarcasm from his voice.

"He suggested it should be you."

Roux sat motionless for a time, staring back wide-eyed.

"M-mm-me?"

"Ye-ye-yes, you Roux," mimicked du Plessis.

"General, with . . . with all due respect," squeaked Roux, "I am not the man for the job. I've been in logistics for the last four years."

"I couldn't agree more," said du Plessis, leaning back in his chair, folding his arms across his chest.

Roux felt a touch offended. The man could have at least been less direct, but he knew any commander worth his salt did not want "sponsored" subordinates foisted on them by outsiders.

"In all fairness, Niemandt raised several salient points. Ten years in SB, with three stints on the border in South West. You're here and know the area, and his praise for your involvement in the rescue operation of that Recce operative, what was his name, Rickerts or something, was glowing. He claims it was only your insistence the bugger was still alive saved him."

"Roberts, but that was more my father's doing than mine."

"Quite so, but he believes you were the star performer." Du Plessis raised his hands. "And who am I to disagree?" The tone in his voice made it clear he did. "But, bringing someone from Pretoria who needs time to acclimate before SONA makes no sense."

Roux stared down at his hands. Returning to SB meant sacrificing his comfortable nine-to-five, his weekends at home—all because some old fart had a heart attack. Mel wouldn't be thrilled. He'd left SB for a reason, with a solemn vow never to return. His skin prickled as though a thousand tiny needles were dancing across his back. Yet, amidst the trepidation, a long-forgotten sensation stirred within him—excitement. The monotonous logistics job was wearing him down, turning him into a moody, irritable shell of his former self, much to Mel's dismay. But back to SB? She'd go ballistic. So, in deference to his wife, he was about to object vehemently when he caught the general's baleful glare and instinctively toned down his protest.

"General, I'm not sure I am the most suitable choice. Surely, there must be someone within SB who would be more suitable?"

Frowning, Du Plessis ran a hand through his hair, coming to rest behind his neck. "I must work with what I have, Colonel, and I need someone settled in before SONA. Besides, the move is temporary until I decide what to do next. Any other problems?"

*I tried Mel.* "No General,"

"Good. Settled then. Right, let me explain what I want from you." He coughed to clear his throat, thought for a minute, and then said. "The intelligence boys have been picking up talk in several locations across the country of possible unrest being orchestrated by the ANC and UDF. Reports suggest the UDF is to instigate nationwide strikes and school boycotts during the latter part of February, which will coincide with violent uprisings in the Cape Town locations, courtesy of the ANC. Much of the intel is unsubstantiated at this stage, but your priority is to establish whether there is any foundation to these rumors, and put a stop to any plans the UDF and ANC may be cooking up?" He paused. "What concerns me is this office is unaware of the rumors. Seems to me they have lost control in the locations."

Roux noticed General Warmer, whose sole interest so far had been the state of his hands, sit upright, looking apoplectic. "I beg your pardon, but we have not lost control! I'll have you know—"

Du Plessis raised his hand. "Relax Hennie, no one is criticizing you."

Warmer, looking relieved, sat back in his chair.

"This unit is a disaster," du Plessis said with disgust. "Swanepoel, who's responsible for interrogations and Desk C, runs the unit like his own private army, with van Rensburg's tacit approval. His proclivity for using torture on suspects, which even I find extreme, has produced little in the way of tangible results. The man is old, a drunkard, and incompetent. He needs to go, asap. Move Captain Meiring to Desk C. He's diligent, trustworthy, and, above all, loyal."

Roux recognized the reference to one of SB's seven designated areas of responsibility. Desk C, or Section C as it was also known, was tasked with monitoring the country's major banned political organizations, including the African National Congress (ANC), the Pan Africanist Congress of Azania (PAC), and its more militant offshoot, the Azanian People's Liberation Army (APLA). These liberation movements, along with the non-militant United Democratic Front (UDF), formed in 1983, constituted the primary source of the country's unrest. Unlike the other two, the UDF was a non-racial coalition of civic and church leaders, students, workers and other organizations who relied on rent boycotts, school protests, and worker stay-aways rather than violence. This made Desk C the most active desk within SB.

"Move him where?"

"No idea. It's your problem. As I was saying. SONA is on Friday and, considering the changes our new president seems hell-bent on implementing, anything could happen. What they will be, Heaven alone knows. We are just as much in the dark as you are, but one possibility is the release of Mandela, although doubtful. But, if it happens, it'll throw the locations into joyful pandemonium. You need to be prepared."

Roux had a frightening image of a Black tsunami crashing into the White-only suburbs. Was Mandela's release what his father was trying to find out?

"Irrespective of what comes out at SONA, I need you to ensure we regain control in the locations, keep the lid on any sudden spurts of violence, and confirm whether these rumors are true."

He glanced over at Warmer. "Anything you want to add, Hennie?"

Warmer was staring at du Plessis, open-mouthed. The mention of Mandela's possible release appeared to be news to him.

"Oh. Yes. I see. OK, well, Kobus, I mean Brigadier van Rensburg, ran a tight ship. Splendid chap, a good man. I would go so far as—"

There was an irritable wave of a hand. "Bullshit!," snapped du Plessis, glaring at Warmer.

Roux's jaw dropped.

Warmer seemed to shrivel in his chair, his neck turning a deep purple. His mouth clamped shut.

"There is one issue you need to be aware of," said du Plessis, looking back at Roux. "The commissioner has decided, given the government's new approach, it is time for us to reconsider our methods of dealing with the terrorist organizations. He is adamant about limiting unwarranted police violence or aggression in the locations, especially here with SONA coming. Cape Town is going to be bulging with journalists, many foreign, so he wants to avoid any adverse publicity over the next few weeks." He shifted in his chair.

"So, what this means, in simple terms, is he does not want mass detentions, unexplained disappearances of high profile ANC and UDF members, and no, I repeat, no shoot-outs in public places. Clear?"

Roux couldn't believe his ears. SB's strong-arm tactics and disregard for human rights and international borders when arresting or eliminating what it considered legitimate targets were legend.

"Clear, General, but it could make my job a lot more difficult. How are we to confirm the rumors without detentions?"

"I understand," said du Plessis. "But you still have the powers the State of Emergency provides. However, be subtle about how you use them. No tortured bodies turning up in the *veld* or back streets, eh! But from what I hear from your ex-colleagues in South West, your reticence to bang a few heads during interrogations may benefit us right now. Minimal violence is the order of the day, Roux, so monitor your men."

*Talk about a contradiction. Regain control of the locations but be subtle about it? Nuts!* Roux sighed and nodded. "Yes, General."

"Good. I'll be briefing all SB Cape regional commanders here on upcoming events within the next few days. So until then, you need to get familiar with the unit, and the current game. One more thing. You report to me, and you take instructions from only me."

Warmer squirmed in his seat and cleared his throat.

"You will, of course, keep the general here appraised of your operations. We may require backup from his uniform men from time to time," said du Plessis, rolling his eyes.

Warmer beamed, as though it was his idea.

"Questions?" said du Plessis.

"No, General, I think I understand what's needed. When do I move?"

"Today. I'm curious to see if you're as good as Niemandt believes." Du Plessis stared at him for several moments.

"Get order restored and keep control of the locations, Roux, and this could be a permanent transfer, with the commensurate promotion, which should please your father and," he paused, "that *liberal* wife of yours, hey!"

Roux flinched. What was the man implying? He assumed the whole UNICEF fiasco was dead and buried.

Du Plessis stood up and walked across to Warmer's desk where he picked up the phone, punched in a string of numbers, spoke in a hushed voice for several minutes, then dropped the instrument onto its cradle with a bang, and returned to the table.

"Right. Personnel in Pretoria will implement the transfer and also notify Swanepoel of the change," he said, then looked at Warmer. "I assume you'll arrange for Roux to hand over to someone." It wasn't a request.

He nodded at Roux. "You better get packing. You can use van Rensburg's office, and oh, take your fat admin assistant with you. You'll need her."

Roux tossed his cap onto the filing cabinet as he entered his office and then leaned against the corner of his desk, sucking the inside of his cheek. This day had taken an unexpected turn. While he welcomed the move back to SB, Mel certainly wouldn't. The thought of explaining the temporary transfer to her sent shivers down his spine. He had to craft his explanation carefully before telling her.

The door opened, and Gerda peeked in, a broad smile on her face.

"You still with us, or the general kick your rear end for you?"

Roux laughed. "Yes, I'm still employed, but not at logistics, thank heaven."

"What?" she wasn't smiling anymore.

"It wasn't Warmer who wanted to see me. It was du Plessis, the CO of SB, who flew down from Pretoria to talk to little old me. Seems van Rensburg had a heart attack without his permission," he said, grinning.

"Yes, I heard. Quite serious, almost died. What's that got to do with you?"

"I'm taking over from him. You're looking at the new head of SB, Western Cape, my dear, although only temporary for now."

"Oh, no!" said Gerda, "You can't go. I'll miss you. When does this happen?"

"With immediate effect, dear Gerda, and guess what?"

She raised a quizzical eyebrow.

"You, Mrs. Steyn, are transferring with me. Tomorrow morning."

"Oh, shit!" was what he thought he heard her mutter under her breath, but on reflection, discounted it. After all, Gerda never swore.

WITHIN THE HOUR, HE was summoned to Klopper's office to hand over to his replacement. It took all of thirty minutes. After a quick lunch, he wandered up to the Personnel Department to look at the personnel folders for each of the senior officers at SB. It did not take long. The files told him little other than there were five senior officers, who he assumed ran the seven Desks between them. The files of Swanepoel and two of the captains, Grobler and Haveman, revealed men of average intelligence and ability until they arrived in Cape Town. Overnight, the three had become star performers. Swanepoel, in particular, received two promotions in six years. Either van Rensburg was an exceptional man-manager or those two had a history. A long one. To his surprise, he discovered one of the so-called senior officers was a Lieutenant Els, twenty-seven with most of his career in uniform branch, only transferring to SB two years ago. How an officer so young commanded a Desk became clear when he read the man was van Rensburg's son-in-law.

Of the remaining two officers, Captain Jansen, a recent addition to the unit, appeared to have potential, but Captain Eugene Meiring was somewhat of an enigma. Thirty-four years of age, he had moved from SB Johannesburg to Western Cape Command four years before. Prior to his arrival, all of his superiors had considered Meiring's performance exemplary, with two commendations for bravery during his year with the South West Africa Police special anti-terrorism unit, *Koevoet*. As with Haveman and Grobler, things changed after he arrived in Cape Town, but in his case, for the worse. According to Swanepoel, Meiring's performance was lackluster, which was in stark contrast to past assessments and du Plessis' opinion of the man. Meiring was no ordinary cop. His record showed two university degrees. Either he joined the force at a late stage in life or he'd studied part-time—which took some doing. Roux sat back, rubbing his chin. Why work long, dangerous hours for a pittance with those qualifications?

There was, however, one piece of information continuing to trouble him as he made his way to his office. Du Plessis' had failed to mention—either unwittingly, or more likely deliberate that Swanepoel was a colonel, and based on length of service in the rank, senior to him. Yes, officially he was the new acting CO, but in reality, Swanepoel held all the cards. He was senior, knew the men, the job, and the area, most of which were new to Roux.

As he neared his ground-floor office, he thought he could hear what to him sounded like the wailing of his neighbor's cat. He quickened his pace and plunged into his office where he found a humming Gerda busy moving his personal effects from his desk to a small, rather tattered-looking box. A lone folder lay on the desk.

"You OK?" he said.

Her hand stopped in mid-air, giving him a puzzled look.

"It's just I heard a noise, and I thought someone was in pain, but—" He realized his mistake. "Oh!"

She glared at him. "Marius Roux, there's no need to be rude. I was singing a hymn. The church choir members find my voice soothing." She hesitated, looking bemused. "For some reason, my husband doesn't agree."

Roux could guess why but just mumbled an apology.

She waved the incident away. "Right. Your packing is almost done, but you need to sign those letters," she said, pointing at the folder on the desk before folding her arms across an ample chest. "I've promised Personnel I'll drop them off on my way home," her authoritative tone leaving little room for negotiation.

He huffed in a weak show of defiance but pulled out his chair and got to the business of completing his last task in the Logistics Department. It felt good to be moving on.

"By the way, I took a peek at my new office at SB."

This snippet of information brought Roux's eyebrows up. "And? Do they know about the change?"

"Seems so, but I'm afraid they are not happy campers up there," her eyes rolled upwards. "Mr. Swanepoel was shouting about the 'effing bastards' upstairs, stabbing him in the back. He is such a horrid man. But, the good news is I'll be leaving my bug-infested, dingy cubbyhole of an office for another, larger bug-infested, dingy cubbyhole, but this one has windows facing onto the square!"

"Whoopee!" Roux mumbled, but hearing of the aggressive reaction from Swanepoel, and the apparent unhappiness of the rest of SB, worried him. Any thoughts of introducing himself to the men today vanished. Walking into an agitated bee hive was not his idea of how best to end a day. He signed the last letter, closed the file, and handed it to her, then glanced at his watch. It was just after four.

"Done," he said, standing up. "No point in me hanging around any longer. My replacement is up to speed, so I'm heading for home. I need to break the news to Mel and Rian."

She chuckled. "Good luck with that. No problem, I'll finish up with the packing."

He thanked her and headed for the underground parking, cap, and briefcase in hand.

INSTEAD OF RETURNING HOME, he drove to *his* sanctuary, a secluded stretch of beach on the city's west coast, known as the "Currents" because of its perilous undercurrents making swimming impossible. Here, fanned by the fresh Atlantic breeze, he sought solace from his monotonous workdays. But this evening, a storm of thoughts swirled within him, centered on how to inform Mel of his transfer. The return to SB would bring its share of challenges, but after four years in the shadows, he felt a renewed sense of belonging. He would again be part of the fight against terrorism. All of which was great—for him, but Mel would remind him of his promise to forgo fieldwork, get a quiet desk job, and to focus, for the first time in a long while, on their marriage and the family. The only consolation was the move was temporary, but if he was honest with himself, the thought of going back to any administrative job gave him a painful knot in his guts. For almost an hour, he explored his options. Blurt it out, or ease into the subject, emphasizing the eventual move back to logistics? He opted for the latter and headed home.

Chicken for dinner, his nose informed him as he made his way through the kitchen to the lounge. Dropping his briefcase in a corner, he tossed his cap onto the sideboard with the realization he wouldn't be wearing it for some time. SB required civilian dress.

"Hey Mel?" he called out, catching a faint whiff of the not-uncommon smell of stables.

Melanie Roux came out of their bedroom and marched down the short hallway. Her auburn, shoulder-length hair bobbed in time with her somewhat masculine gait, worn riding boots clicking on the tiled surface. A wide grin was spreading across her grime-covered face. Although not a head turner, her pug nose, large, hazel eyes, and freckles on her cheeks and nose—which seemed to shrink and grow with the change in seasons—still captivated him. At forty-five, and a year younger than him, her once curvy figure now hinted at middle age, yet her hair remained stubbornly youthful, devoid of a single gray strand. Although right now, there appeared to be strands of grass sticking out the back. A gray tee shirt, once white, hung loosely over faded black jeans covered in dust and dark stains. Stains which he hoped were mud. She stood up on her toes, hand on his arm, to give him a peck on the mouth.

"You stink," he said, pulling back.

"And I love you too," she said and winked. "We took the Down syndrome kids to the riding school again. It's unbelievable the way those kids and the horses relate, so therapeutic. They love it, and seems to work wonders for them. How was your day, big man?"

"Erm . . . bit out of the ordinary, to be honest." He'd switched to English without hesitation. "Are those the Black and Colored kids you take?" he said, maintaining a neutral expression as he collapsed into his favorite armchair. "Any chance of a drink?"

She stood a moment, staring at him quizzically, and then dipped her head. "OK, no problem, but unusual for you, isn't it, considering it's a workday?" She headed for the fridge in the kitchen, talking over her shoulder.

"By the way, I have a new boss. He arrived from the London office yesterday. Professor Jonas Kani. He seems nice. Spent some time in the US before returning to London and now here. And before you ask, yes, he is a Black South African. Born near Port Elizabeth. And yes, it was *those* kids, so don't pretend you're interested."

He huffed. *You're not the only one with a new boss*, he thought. "I'm sorry, but it's been one hell of a day. Where's Rian?"

Mel retrieved a beer from the fridge, removing the cap as she returned to the lounge. "He stayed for extra studies at school, but he should be home soon."

He took the beer from her, examined the bottle as though he had never seen one before, and without drinking, scratched at the label.

She sat on the armrest and tousled his short, black hair. "And . . .?"

Roux continued to scratch at the label, dropping the pieces on the carpet. After several seconds, he slid down in the chair, looking up at the ceiling as though hoping for divine intervention in his hour of need.

"They're making some changes at HQ," he said, surprised at how steady his voice sounded.

Mel got up. "Carry on, I need to check on dinner. Will it affect you?"

"Um . . . Appears so."

"Really? How?" her voice was clear above the clatter of pots and utensils.

"Mmm. Well . . ." He wasn't sure if he should wait until she returned, but decided to join her and levered himself out of the chair, feeling as though he was sixty and life had not been kind to him. Walking into the kitchen, he placed the full beer on a counter.

"It seems the head of the Security Branch here, Brigadier van Rensburg, had a heart attack a week ago."

"Shame," she said with what sounded like genuine concern, "Is he alright?"

"Yes, but he's in ICU. The problem is, he's only two years off retirement, so he won't return to work according to his boss." He leaned against the counter, trying to appear as nonchalant as possible.

Mel glanced up from the bowl of potatoes she was mashing together with chunks of butter. "So how's this affect you?"

How best to respond to that question had occupied Roux's thoughts all the way home. "I'm being transferred out of Logistics to Security Branch, in charge of the Western Cape region," he blurted out and then cursed under his breath. So much for easing into the subject.

Her hand went still. "Marius. No."

Shoving the bowl away and throwing the spoon into the sink, she turned and glared at him. "You promised you were finished with SB." Her voice was low but angry. "Your father organized this job so you would spend more time at home with us. After all the years of absolute hell I had to endure while you satisfied your father's wishes, we finally have a life, a family life, and now you want to destroy it and go back to playing policeman?"

He raised his hands. "Hey! Relax, Mel, it's only temporary until they find a permanent replacement."

She gave him a measured look. "How long is temporary?"

He shrugged, not meeting her eyes. "Three months, give or take. It all depends, but I can't see it being much longer," he said, hoping he sounded more confident about his predictions than he felt.

"And then back to your usual job?"

"Without a doubt, and as soon as Rian matriculates at the end of the year, I'll apply for the instructor's job at the college in Pretoria. Although I will miss living here," he said with a sheepish smile, trying his best to appear reassuring.

His wife stared long and hard at him, as though trying to unmask his real thoughts. "Is this going to interfere with my work in the townships?"

"No, no, not at all. If your working at The Foundation was still a problem, they'd have found someone else. You carry on doing your thing while I ride out the next three months or so, and then back as we were."

She continued to stare at him, thoughtful, before inclining her head. "OK, but I want you to promise me something. If you are offered a permanent position, you will turn it down. Agreed?"

He squirmed. "Even if it means a promotion?"

Her hesitation was only for a heartbeat. "Even if it means a promotion. Do I have your word?"

"No problem, Pet," he said, knowing he would break his promise, if, or when, du Plessis offered him a permanent position.

"OK," she said, and turned back to preparing the food. "I'll go along with this for now. How come they chose you for the job?"

"Seems I was recommended by the head of Personnel, would you believe, but I think my having being in SB, and the fact I'm here with SONA coming on Friday influenced their decision. Makes sense, I suppose, but have to admit it came as a bolt out of the blue."

"Sounds more like your father pulling strings again," she said, looking skeptical.

"Why would Pa want me back in SB?" he said. "I don't think he really cares what I'm up to these days, although surprise, surprise, he called me today. Asked if I knew what de Klerk will say at SONA. Like I would know. He seems to have forgotten I'm in logistics."

"Perhaps he already knew about the move."

"How could—" He stopped. Was it possible? Had his father engineered the transfer, and if so, why?

"No way," he said, shaking his head. He picked up his beer and strolled back to the lounge.

"Who's your new boss? I take it you no longer work for that chauvinist, Kloppers?" she called after him.

Roux slumped into his armchair, heaved a deep sigh, took a long swallow, and belched. It had not gone as bad as he expected. Sure, Mel was unimpressed, but he got the impression she was more worried than angry. But her reaction was understandable. During his previous stint in SB, the extended periods away from home had strained their relationship and deprived him of being the father he'd longed to be. But fate stepped in. His injury during his last tour in South West brought things to a head. Mel demanded he seek his father's help and transfer out of SB. The move to Cape Town had offered both a chance to make up for his many absences and save their marriage. In the beginning, he had struggled with the change but finally settled into a routine, spending more time with the family. Time at the beach, at school events, on Sunday drives, and just talking, began to mend broken bridges. Their house, in a decent, middle-class, Whites only suburb, courtesy of Mel's parents, became a home. A safe and comfortable home. It was everything he had ever hoped for and promised her. But he would need to prove to Mel and Rian he was still a family man, even in the Branch, if he had any hope of making the transfer permanent.

"General du Plessis, in Pretoria, he's head of SB."

Mel joined him in the lounge, collapsing onto the couch, leaning back, and stretching her legs out, with one ankle over the other. "And what does *he* think de Klerk will say?"

"I've only had the one meeting with him, but they are expecting some changes to be announced," he said, waiting for her response, but when none came, he plowed on.

"Pet, any changes de Klerk announces at SONA will take months to be implemented, by which time a replacement for me will be found. Until then, we'll be monitoring the locations to ensure things stay the same." The ease with which he slipped back into his SB-honed tactics of deceit and misinformation to achieve his goals surprised him.

"I hope they release Mandela, then things will change for the better," she said, standing up. "I'm going for a bath. Dinner is ready. You and Rian can help yourselves, and you can give him the *good* news."

"Now why doesn't that surprise me?" he muttered as he heaved himself up out of the chair.

# Wednesday, January 31st, 1990

ALTHOUGH TIRED AND IRRITABLE after a sleepless night, he perked up when he saw Gerda waiting for him at the ground floor reception.

"I came in early to get your new office cleaned and ready for you," she said, looking him up and down. "You're more handsome in uniform. The suit does you no favors."

He pretended not to hear.

Together, they took the elevator ride to the third floor for his first visit to the SB offices. Stepping out into a hallway lit by several fluorescent ceiling lights and looking like every other hallway in the building, he counted five doors to his left and four to his right.

"Let me show you around," said Gerda, opening the first door to his left.

"This is for the senior Desk officers. Colonel Swanepoel's office is next door, followed by another room for junior White officers. The Blacks and Coloreds are in the annex building across the courtyard. The last two rooms are filing and storage. Our offices are the first two doors on the right, and a small conference room is at the end. The steel door is the armory."

Roux peered in. It was a long, narrow room divided into five small cubicles, each separated with head-high movable partitions covered in dirty green cloth. An assortment of files and boxes lay stacked at the far end alongside an old coffee maker. The place reeked of stale tobacco smoke. He flinched, stepping back into the hallway.

"I know, it stinks," said Gerda, "even with the windows open." She crossed the hallway and opened a door. "My office with a connecting door to yours." She left the door open and walked a few paces towards a door labeled Brigadier van Rensburg.

*That will have to go*, mused Roux.

Gerda flung the door open. "Ta-da," she sang out, one arm inviting him into his new accommodations.

Stepping across the threshold, he couldn't help but gasp. The office dwarfed his previous workspace. Three expansive windows overlooked the square. To his right, an open door revealed Gerda's office, and on the left, a multitude of maps adorned the wall. Directly in front of him, a substantial L-shaped desk, crafted from a combination of metal and melamine, commanded the room's attention. Positioned behind the desk was a towering, high-backed chair. It wasn't empty.

A man, his legs propped up on the desk, fixed Roux with a piercing stare amid a swirl of tobacco smoke. Struggling against the morning light, Roux's gut churned as he stared at the figure—it had to be Swanepoel.

Bald as a rugby ball save for a tuft of unruly, gray hair above each ear, his pallid complexion, etched with small red veins over sunken cheeks, accentuated the shadowy circles beneath his dark, watery eyes. An old man whose blue suit looked in desperate need of a professional clean. The top button of his off-white shirt was undone, and the necktie pulled down several inches. A cigarette dangled between yellowed fingers. He didn't move, just watched Roux with a predatory glint in his gaze, one corner of his mouth turned up in a sort of cold, crooked half-smile.

Gerda, surprised by Roux's hesitancy, leaned over his shoulder.

"Oh! Colonel Swanepoel. I-I didn't realize you were here." She stepped back.

Swanepoel swung his legs off the desk and stood up, flicking ash onto the carpet and then tossing his cigarette butt out a half-opened window. "So, this is du Plessis' pet monkey."

Bile clawed its way up Roux's throat. He choked it down and opened his mouth, but the words seemed to evaporate off his tongue. He swallowed and tried again, his voice shaky.

"Colonel Swanepoel, morning." He took two hesitant steps into the office. "I came in early, hoping to meet you and introduce myself, and have a chat before the rest of the men came in."

"Is that so? You want to have a chat, eh?" said Swanepoel, with a smirk as he gave a mock bow, arm outstretched. "Well, you better sit down then." He straightened up, using the corner of the desk to steady himself. "Please, sit down and let's chat." The smirk mutated into a sneer. "I'm all ears, Roux."

"Great!" Roux hurried over to the desk, realized Swanepoel would not budge, so edged around him. He dropped his briefcase on the desk and sat down, hoping Swanepoel would do likewise, but the man remained standing, looking down at him through hooded eyes, the tips of his nicotine stained mustache disappearing between tight lips.

*Stuff him.* Roux stood up. As he did so, he glimpsed Gerda still standing in the open doorway. "Thanks Gerda, I'll call you when we finished here. Please close the door."

She closed the office door, then hurried through the office to the inter-leading door, closing it behind her.

Roux looked at Swanepoel, their eyes level, waiting to see who would blink first. Roux baulked. He took a deep breath.

"Colonel, I understand you are not happy with my being here, but I did not ask for this job. General du Plessis has decided otherwise. Now either we do our best to work together for the short time I am here, or we can squabble like children, which will hurt morale, I'm sure." He waited, locking eyes with Swanepoel, chewing at the inside of his mouth.

The man stood motionless for several seconds, then grunted and moved toward the nearest chair, misjudged the distance as he sat down, and ended up sliding over the armrest. Roux's eyebrows shot up. He'd seen eighty-year-olds more steady on their feet.

"Thank you," said Roux, sitting down. "First, let me give you a bit of background. You are probably not aware of it, but in fact I spent—"

Swanepoel held up a hand. "I know all about you, Roux. How you panicked in South West after a little action, and got daddy to get you a safe job here in Cape Town." He laughed, a mocking laugh.

*OK. He returned the favor and looked at my file. At least it saves me some time.*

"I see. Colonel, the fact is, we are stuck together for the next several months, so do you mind if I call you . . ." Damn! He didn't know the man's first name. "By your first name? I'm Marius, by the way." He attempted a reassuring smile, but was sure it appeared as though he was ready to cry.

Swanepoel gave that mocking laugh again. "No. You can't. I'm senior to you, and therefore you will address me as 'colonel.' And, by the way, I had a word with the brigadier and he assures me he will instruct du Plessis to appoint me as his replacement, so I doubt you'll be here very long."

Roux studied the man. *He's lying.* From what Gerda said, van Rensburg was in no position to be talking to anyone about their career prospects, never mind making *demands* of du Plessis. Unless he intended on having a second heart attack.

"I expect the same courtesy when the other men are around. Agreed?"

"Piss off Roux, I'll call you whatever I please."

*OK, If this is how you want to play it, fine by me,* thought Roux. *So here's the bad news.*

"General du Plessis has given me three explicit orders, which are not negotiable. First. I need an update from you as to the current operations you are busy with. Two. A full report on the situation in the locations. The general is of the opinion SB is no longer in control, and finally, an explanation why Pretoria believe this unit is not aware of the rumors of upcoming strikes and violence in the city."

Swanepoel went pale, then his face darkened, his lips working, a vein vibrating at his temple. He stood up and took a step toward Roux, fists clenched.

Roux gulped, pushing himself back in his chair. Shit! Was the man about to attack him? Instead, Swanepoel leaned forward, his hands on the desk. When he spoke, his voice was low, menacing.

"You listen to me, you little bombastic shit. I run this department. I decide what gets done, and I give the orders." His eyes shifted to the right, his voice unsteady. "I'm aware of the rumors, but with the brigadier's illness, I-I just haven't had time to complete the report, but it's on my desk."

Roux stood up, confident no such report existed. "Good. Then you can hand it to me today."

Swanepoel stepped back, eyes wide for a moment, and then his mouth tightened. "No, I won't. Like I said, I run this department. Stay out of my way while you are here and then go back to pushing paper. You do that, and we'll get along just fine. Get in my way, and . . ." He left the threat hanging in the air.

Before Roux could respond, Swanepoel glared at him, shook his head, lifted an arm as though to emphasize something, changed his mind, and stormed out, slamming the door behind him.

Roux stared at the closed door, his breath coming in quick gasps. How was he supposed to deal with this man? Run to du Plessis, like some ten-year-old whining about the school bully? He would be the laughingstock of the station. No. He would have to deal with this himself. "Find his weak point and leverage it until you break the man. You must annihilate him, or he will continue to cause you problems. Show no pity." His father's instructions on how to deal with a troublesome subordinate echoed in his mind. Destroying this man would not be easy. But of one thing, he was sure—he would need to watch his back.

Closing his eyes, he concentrated on getting his heart rate back to something resembling normal.

After regaining a semblance of control, he sat down and swiveled the chair to face the windows, which offered a panoramic view of Compton Square and the city center beyond. He wondered what his father would think. Proud of him, or was Mel correct? Did his father orchestrate everything, and if so, what was the motive? With a sigh, he turned back to his new office, noting the typical VHF radio set on the desk, a small filing cabinet, and a valet stand in the corner. Two beige cloth-covered visitors' chairs stood on the brown carpet in front of the desk. The cream-colored wall on his left, divided by the door to Gerda's office, was bare. A dust-covered four-bladed fan, lazily rotating, hung from the ceiling.

"No photos of our glorious leaders?" he remarked.

He rose, stripped off his jacket, and was about to drape it over the back of the chair when he remembered the valet stand. After hanging up his jacket and loosening his necktie, he sauntered back to his chair and slumped into it, which to his surprise did not creak or groan. He was about to call Gerda when there was a light tap on the inter-leading door.

She peeked around the edge of the door, saw he was alone, and walked in, a pile of brown files in her hands, and dropped them onto his desk.

"What are those?" He snapped. Paperwork was the last thing he needed right now.

"Oh-oh! Bad meeting?" she said, frowning.

*Like she didn't hear all of it*. He leaned back in the comfortable chair, feeling a touch embarrassed by his outburst. "Sorry. Yes, I suppose so. I expected grudging acceptance, and perhaps a little opposition from

Swanepoel, but I didn't expect the vociferous response I got. Sorry if you heard him swearing."

She shrugged. "Never heard a word."

He smiled to himself. *Sure you didn't.* "OK, what are the files for?"

"I pulled four of the thickest files from a cabinet in my office, which appear to be all recent operational stuff. Give you a chance to update yourself on what everyone has been doing." She peered at him for a moment, her face reflecting a mother's concern. "You OK?"

"I'll survive. It's just the man is insufferable. Told me *he's* running the department and I won't be here for long. Can you believe he went and read my service file? The problem is, I'm stuck with him."

Gerda snorted. "He's a pig of a man is all I know."

"That he is. That he is," said Roux, sucking in a good gulp of air. "But, no fear, I'm a big boy, so will just have to take him in my stride."

She nodded, looking unconvinced.

He cocked his head to one side. "Relax, I've got this. Swanepoel is just pis . . . annoyed he didn't get the job. Understandable. But I'll convince him we need to work together so he'll impress the general. He'll come round."

Gerda returned a smile which said, "Nice try, but I'm not convinced you know what you doing." If he was a mind reader, he would have agreed with her.

He planted his forearms on the desk. "Right. Time to work. What I need from you this morning is to keep an eye open for any of the Desk officers. As soon as you spot one, drag him in here, but don't give him a chance to talk to Swanepoel first. I assume you know who they are?"

She grinned. "I do. No problem boss, I'll nab the little runts. Anyone first?"

"Nope, as you spot them, although I am keen to meet Captain Meiring."

"Got it. See what I can do. What do you think of the office?"

"Fancy, but I'll get used to it," he said with a wicked smile.

She grinned. "Coffee and muffin on the way. I'm glad you like the office. You deserve it." She chewed at a finger for a moment. "Sorry, don't want to sound nosy, but how did the family take the move?"

"Mel is reserving judgment at this stage subject to certain conditions being met, i.e. it's only temporary."

"Uh-huh, and is it?"

He winked, waving a hand at her. "Hey! Off with you, woman."

It was late afternoon when he threw down the last in a pile of files, which included those Gerda brought and those he found in the cabinet in his office. He browsed his notes, trying to sum up what he had learned.

There were five so-called "team leaders," each assigned to command one, or more, Desks. Tactics ranged from block searches to night raids to mass arrests and brutal interrogations, yielding minimal results. Recent operations in various locations lacked substantiated informant feedback or proper intelligence gathering, resembling more of a dartboard approach—pick a number, throw, and hope you come up lucky. They had seldom found their mark. No wonder du Plessis was frustrated.

Gerda's attempts to set up meetings with the Desk officers were only partly successful. Swanepoel had left the building to destinations unspecified, Jansen was on leave for a month and Meiring was in court all day. But she collared three of them.

Captain Haveman was the first to step into his office. A middle-aged nondescript pipe smoker who reeked of cheap tobacco and attempted to say as little about his current activities as possible. His responses to Roux's questions were short and bordering on insubordination.

Captain Grobler was nothing other than the dumping ground for anything Swanepoel didn't want to do after he'd assumed the leadership role. A "yes" man who thought Swanepoel and van Rensburg were the next best thing after God.

The young Lieutenant Els, though, turned out to be a surprise. Roux, impressed with the man's enthusiasm and willingness to learn, also got the impression the youngster was adrift without the protection and guidance of his father-in-law.

He ticked off a few more points on his hand-written notes and then turned the page and smiled mischievously. Maybe Swanepoel's "boys" weren't much at gathering intelligence, but his agent, Gerda, was *par excellence*. With her intimate knowledge of everything going on in the building, her insight was invaluable.

According to her, Swanepoel was a confirmed alcoholic and a bully. He seldom appeared at the office, and when he did, he was late and often reeked of alcohol.

"If you need to make an impact here, the man you need on your side is Captain Meiring," Gerda had said. Soft-spoken and although distant and by the book, his colleagues and subordinates liked and trusted him, including the Black and Colored staff, and was the only officer achieving some modicum of success. Her feedback on the other three officers was much in line with his own assessments.

Time to pack up and go home and see if Mel had cooled off somewhat.

# Thursday, February 1st, 1990

HE GREETED THE FIRST rays of sunrise, coffee in hand, seated on the back porch. This time of day held a special charm for him—watching the early morning sunlight confront, and then slowly overwhelm, the night shadows. His quiet time for contemplating the day ahead. Today, his reflections centered on matters at home. Despite Mel's apparent acceptance of his transfer, she was not happy. He clicked his tongue and shifted his focus to work. Du Plessis had kept his promise, organizing a briefing at nine for all the Cape Province regional SB commanders, most of whom had arrived the previous night. It promised to be an interesting day.

Two hours later, seated in his office, he read through the overnight reports from the Desks. It was more of the same—unrest and mayhem in the locations. Will du Plessis announce a new plan to counter the increasing violence? These days, the evening TV news was almost entirely devoted to the growing unrest across the country. The State of Emergency, declared in 1986, only inflamed the violence, to which the government responded by deploying the army to the locations. Attempting to placate the growing international disgust with the apartheid policies, de Klerk's predecessor, the hardliner, P.W. Botha made several concessions, amending or abolishing some of the most oppressive apartheid laws. Neither the liberation movements nor the international community were fooled.

Alarmed by Botha's perceived capitulation, radical factions of the ruling National Party, nicknamed the "Nats" by the media, broke away to establish right-wing parties. Botha, fearing he was losing his grip on the country, swiftly moved to reassure Whites by clamping down further on the Blacks.

Upon assuming office in the previous August, de Klerk promptly signaled a shift. Changes to the current policies were coming, and Whites needed to adapt, he said. To test public support for his approach, he called for a snap election in September. The Nats suffered a significant loss of parliamentary seats at the ballot box, with the right-wing emerging as the official opposition.

Gerda interrupted his thoughts. "Marie just called to tell you to meet in General Warmer's office."

*That was odd*, he thought, checking his watch. It had only just gone eight, an hour early, and why in Warmer's office?

Ushered into the general's office within minutes of arriving, he found du Plessis seated behind Warmer's desk, but no Warmer. There was, however, a squat, brown-haired man, in a dark gray suit, standing at the desk peering down at the contents of a blue folder, which he closed when Roux walked in.

Du Plessis looked up. "Grab a chair," he pointed towards the small table in the corner. "Let's get down to business."

The stranger introduced himself only as Greyling and sat down opposite Roux. Du Plessis joined them.

"Where are the other regional commanders General, I understood this was to be a commander's briefing?" said Roux.

"I shifted the briefing to ten, but you won't need to attend. Right. To business. About a month ago, we received intel from our sources in Lusaka, which told us the ANC leadership was using a courier to get a very important message to Mandela. All we knew is he would fly to Johannesburg and then make his way to Cape Town, where a contact would facilitate his access to Mandela. Greyling here is from NIS and will explain what transpired."

Hearing the man sitting opposite him was with the country's spy organization was not a surprise. The National Intelligence Service and SB had a close relationship, both on internal and external operations.

Greyling leaned in, his expression earnest. "Colonel, for some time now, exploratory talks have been going on between us and the ANC at various levels. These led to a recent meeting between de Klerk and Mandela to explore ways to initiate negotiations on bringing change."

Roux's stomach muscles tightened. *Any more talk of change and I'll throw up, irrespective of whose office it is.*

"Mandela's release will happen." Greyling continued. "The when is the unknown. What we don't understand is why the sudden urgency to get a message to him. Why not wait until his release?"

"I've heard Mandela is being allowed to have visitors since he was moved to Victor Verster Prison," interjected Roux. "So why not use one of them?"

"He is. Which I'm sure they would do if the message is of little importance. The fact they aren't implies it is so secret they can't be trusted, hence the courier. Which also suggests it is for Mandela's eyes only. Are they going to renege on agreements reached so far, or is Mandela being sent information to use prior to his release? We just don't know, so obviously, we would like to see the message *before* it gets to Mandela."

Greyling sat back, arms folded across his chest. "Unfortunately, we received only scant information as to the description of the courier. Other than he was Black, in his fifties, with gray hair and beard, and would arrive on a flight from London sometime between January 26th and 30th, not much else. We followed several Blacks arriving during that period, but only one headed for Cape Town. We thought he would take a connecting flight, but he chose to go by road instead. He was met by two men at the airport, and after an overnight stay, they left in a vehicle heading south. We followed them to Cradock, where an SB team from Port Elizabeth took over. After another overnight stop, they drove to Nyanga, where unfortunately we lost them yesterday morning. We are still watching incoming flights, but this man seems to be the only one heading towards Mandela, so our bet it is him." He nodded at du Plessis, who took up the narrative.

"We need to find this courier as a matter of urgency, and that's where you come in."

Roux chewed at the inside of his cheek. *Second day on the job and I get handed this pile of crap.*

"Did we get any photos of him?"

"We did," said Greyling. "Unfortunately no clear facial shots. But they should give you an idea of what he looks like. They're in the file."

"Any idea who the courier will meet?"

Greyling shrugged his shoulders. "I assume a senior member of the local ANC cell."

"Are the two men escorting him local ANC and are they likely to be armed?"

It was du Plessis' turn to shrug. "No idea."

"Does he have a name?" asked Roux, becoming exasperated.

"Temba Chewitt," replied Greyling.

"Chewitt? It's not a Black name. Is this guy South African?" said Roux.

"British national, so his passport says," replied Greyling. "Unfortunately, we know nothing about him. New name, new face. He is either a Brit ANC supporter or an exile who changed his name."

Roux snorted. "He could be anywhere in the locations, assuming he's still in the locations. This is a needle in a multitude of haystacks."

Du Plessis got up and retrieved the blue folder from Warmer's desk. "Here is all the info we have on him and his escorts," he said, handing it to Roux. "Descriptions, what they were wearing, vehicle details, and where they were last seen. Nyanga has a strong ANC support base, so I doubt he will leave it. My guess is he will make contact with someone there."

"And if I find him, what then? On what pretext do I arrest him? He's here legally, and a Brit national to boot. The Brits will have a fit. It will also alert the ANC, and if the two men with him *are* armed, they may resist. Do we take them out?"

"The two men with him are almost certainly ANC, although unconfirmed as yet. When you arrest him, they *will* be armed, won't they, Colonel? Association with two armed terrorists from a banned organization is enough to detain him. We'll take it from there," said du Plessis.

Roux remained silent as the import of what du Plessis had just implied sank in.

"General, are you suggesting if they are not armed, I should—"

"We do what we have to, Roux," cut in Greyling. "We need to know what this message is." He sighed. "I know it's a tricky one, Colonel, and to make it even more difficult, you will need to do it quietly without attracting attention. If the ANC reports him missing to the local UK High Commission, we can feign surprise at his presence. We'll deal with the UK Government if, or when, it is required. That's not your problem. Your job is to find him and grab him without anyone the wiser."

"Colonel, I know this is one hell of an operation to hand to you so soon, and I understand your predicament, but we need to get this individual. Urgently," said du Plessis. "Greyling and I will provide any support or information you may need, but with all the international media expected here for SONA, you will need to be extra careful. Keeping this low key means limiting the information you share with your men, and being very selective as to who you use. I suggest you use Captain Meiring and his men. Top-notch. He also has contact with the vigilante group we used before. I forget their names, but they wore white scarves. He'll know who I mean."

Du Plessis paused, pushing his glasses up his nose. "You keep me advised at all times. Questions?"

*About a hundred* thought Roux but said. "And Colonel Swanepoel? How does he fit into this? He has refused to accept the change and the senior Desk officers are in sympathy, making getting things done difficult. He also has seniority over me. With the urgency of this op, I don't have the time to be monitoring the colonel."

The look on du Plessis' face made it clear he didn't believe a single word about Roux not having time but had more to do with him lacking a certain part of his anatomy, and it wasn't his backbone which came to mind.

"As I said, use Meiring, but be clever about how you do it, and then deal with Swanepoel. You're in charge, Roux, so take charge. I'm not your nanny. Anything else?"

"No, General." He rose and left the office.


A GLANCE AT HIS wristwatch when he entered Gerda's office told him the meeting had taken less than an hour.

"Please make a copy of this folder, but be careful. It's highly confidential. Once you have, return them to me and then find Meiring. Tell him I need to see him now." He turned to leave but stopped. "Is Swanepoel here?"

Gerda shook her head.

"OK. Thanks."

Once he had read through the folder twice, he extracted a single sheet of paper from the copied version, attached the best of the photos, and placed it face down on his desk. He began to marshal his thoughts into some plan of action but was interrupted by his phone ringing. It was an external call.

"Roux."

"Man, you're a hard bugger to find," said a voice in English. "I called your office and was told you now head up

SB. What's happened to that fine institution if they put you in charge?"

Roux laughed, switching to English with ease. "Phil. Christ, it's been a while. How are you? Where are you?"

"I'm jolly old boy," replied Philip Roberts in a poor imitation of an upper-class English accent. "And would you believe I'm right here in the mother city?"

"Cape Town? You on leave?"

"No," chuckled Roberts. "I've been transferred here. I'm in Operations Command now, so no more fieldwork, but it's not bad."

Roux frowned. "I didn't realize you sneak and peek boys worked this far south."

"We've been here for years, but always kept a low profile. But listen, why don't we catch up over a few beers?"

"Great, when and where?" Then Roux had a thought. "Hey! Why don't you come round for a *braai* Saturday afternoon? I'll get my old man over, and I'm sure Mel and Rian would love to see you again."

"Smart idea, old boy. You still in the same house?"

"We are. Say about four when it's cooling down a bit?

"I'll see you then. Love to Mel." Roberts rang off.

A quick call to Mel to tell her of Phil's arrival in Cape Town and the arrangements for Saturday elicited first surprise, and then enthusiasm.

Ten minutes later, there was a firm knock on his door. "Come," he called out. In his old office, his normal voice sufficed, but now he discovered shouting to be more appropriate. He bellowed the command a second time.

"Captain Meiring? Morning, grab a chair," he said as a younger man, dressed in a blue suit with short light-brown hair, a slim build, and an inch or two shorter than him, strolled confidently into his office. The set of his jaw spoke of determination, but the deep-set, intense brown eyes gave Roux the impression of a young man who had perhaps seen too much of life's miseries.

"Apologies for the sudden summons, but we need to get an operation going and I want you to drive it."

"No problem, Colonel."

"Good, but first, there is something I would like your opinion on."

A half-frown creased the captain's face. "About what?" The voice was flat.

"I have decided, with the approval of General du Plessis, to whom I report directly, to move you across to Desk C with immediate effect. Swane—Colonel Swanepoel will remain responsible for interrogations and assigned other duties. How do you feel about it?"

Meiring seemed unimpressed. "I'm already at Desk C."

He did not see that one coming. "You are? Since when?"

"After the brigadier took sick, Colonel Swanepoel took over command and moved me to Desk C full time. I'd been working with him for several months already, so it made sense."

Roux could have kissed the man—well, not actually kissed him, but it was as if he'd just pulled his head out of a dark hole. The day seemed brighter. One of du Plessis' orders was fulfilled without even having to confront Swanepoel.

"Well, that solves some problems, and If you are already on Desk C then you may be able to answer a question General du Plessis has." Roux explained about the rumors.

"Yes, we did pick up on them about a week ago but in my opinion, they are nothing but that. Rumors. I informed Colonel Swanepoel twice and I assumed he'd sent the info to Pretoria."

*Which just confirms the colonel is a liar*, thought Roux with satisfaction.

"Thank you. I'll make sure the general knows. But back to the operation. I've just come from a briefing with General du Plessis and NIS, the details of which are confidential at this stage, but I will explain more as we proceed. But for the moment, I urgently need you to find three men last seen in Nyanga yesterday. The leader is a man in his fifties, with gray hair and beard, and is not a local Black. Here are their full descriptions, some photos, and where they were last seen." He handed Meiring the one sheet of paper on his desk.

"Colonel," said Meiring, avoiding taking the piece of paper, "shouldn't you be sharing this with Colonel Swanepoel?"

Roux was becoming irritated. "Captain. Irrespective of whether the colonel, or any of you men, is comfortable with it, I am now in charge and therefore will decide who gets briefed when. You head up Desk C, this is your area."

Meiring's eyes widened. "It's your prerogative who you share the information with, Colonel."

Roux held up a hand.

"My apologies. I am not trying to put you in an uncomfortable position with a superior officer. Can we move on?"

Meiring nodded, face blank again. This time, he took the piece of paper and scanned it, gave the photos a cursory glance, and said, "So. Just another car with three guys in it somewhere in a maze of houses, shops, shacks, and open *veld*. A location with thousands of people who will happily give their lives to protect anyone opposed to the government. Assuming they stayed in Nyanga. But his name is going to attract attention, especially if he is not South African. That help you?"

"That bit I'm able to work out for myself. Thank you, Captain. What I am trying to establish is how effective your informant network is. How soon can you activate them to start the search, and who the hell are the vigilantes in white scarves General du Plessis referred to?"

Meiring shifted in his chair. "They called themselves the *Witdoeke* on account of their members wearing white cloths on their heads or arms as identification." He stood up, walked over to the map on the wall, and pointed to an area near the city airport. "Crossroads. An informal shanty town of filth and hovels which sprang up in the early seventies when Blacks were removed to create White farming areas. In the eighties, there was a dispute amongst rival factions over the allocation of land, and one of these factions, headed by a pro-government gent, formed the *Witdoeke*. As always with Blacks, they resort to violence to resolve their differences, and the UDF and other leftist groups became their prime targets. SB sort of gave them a hand, suggesting individuals they should have a chat with. All of which helped undermine the UDF. Although now disbanded, I made contact with the old leadership, and have stayed in touch with them. They have plenty of eyes on the ground in Nyanga, but keeping them on our side costs us big time, but worth it." He returned to his chair.

"OK, but how soon can you get your men working their sources?"

"Today."

"Good. The next problem. Due to the need to keep this operation low-key and its sensitive nature, those in the know must be kept to an absolute minimum. Only the most trusted men can be used. Your thoughts?"

Meiring pondered his response for several moments. "I trust my team implicitly, but I have serious doubts about some of the other teams. I wouldn't use them for the moment."

"Then this stays between us, for now."

"What about Colonel Swanepoel? He'll ask me what I'm doing."

Roux hesitated. This was now becoming swampy ground. "Captain, Colonel Swanepoel and I are having our differences, and I have concerns about his commitment at the moment, but that is my problem. If questioned, you refer him to me."

"He was on Desk C for years, knows the locations well, and has a large informant network," said Meiring, looking decidedly ill at ease. "Colonel, it won't be easy to find these guys. All the folder tells me is where they lost them, not much else besides the vehicle details. They could be anywhere by now. Are you able to tell me why they're here? I take it they new to the area?"

"Captain, all I can tell you is their presence has something to do with Mandela. But all your men need to know is we are looking for three suspected terrorists. Nothing more."

"O-kay," said Meiring, with a glint of excitement in his eyes.

*Maybe if I give him an inside view, it could push him off the fence onto my side.* Roux cleared his throat. "One other thing, which goes no further than this office. Understood?"

"Understood."

"We suspect the leader of this group is a courier sent from the ANC leadership with instructions to contact Mandela. We need to know why, so catching him in one piece is imperative. That help you, Captain?" he said with a grin, unable to restrain himself.

To his relief, Meiring's mouth curved upwards. *So, he can smile.*

"It does. I'll get moving with my team today. "

"Thank you. Please keep me informed the minute you unearth any information. As to Colonel Swanepoel, you are right. We need access to his resources and knowledge. Any idea where he is?"

Meiring grimaced. "Bar?" then held up his hands. "Sorry."

Roux looked down at the folder on his desk. A way to bypass Swanepoel was beginning to take shape in his mind. "I'm afraid," he said without looking up, "this is going to sound like me handing you a grenade with the pin pulled, but I need your help. Colonel Swanepoel will not allow me to have a rational discussion with him on this, and there isn't time for us to resolve our personal differences. That means I have to ask you to brief him and suck him dry on everything you can that will help find this group. But share no more information than you give your men. Everything else remains between us. Can you do that?" He looked up.

Meiring was studying him through hooded eyes but said nothing. Then he stood up.

"Understandable."

Roux felt like crawling under his desk, but repeated confrontations with Swanepoel would achieve little other than side-tracking the operation, but he now had a long way to go to earn Meiring's trust and respect.

"Thank you. Seems General du Plessis' high opinion of you is warranted."

"With all due respect to you and the general," said Meiring with a look of disdain. "I have to work in this environment every day and don't have time for personality clashes. I keep my head down, try my best to get the job done, and couldn't care less what you, or the general, think of me. Judge me on my results. I have no interest in office politics." He turned on his heel and walked out.

Roux watched him leave, scratching his head. "With an honest attitude like that young man," he said softly, "you ain't going nowhere in SB."

IT HAD BEEN A day steeped in frustration. Knowing he must rely on Swanepoel and Meiring, his inability to contribute had him mauling the inside of his mouth. The hours had crawled by, filled with alternating bouts of map-gazing, restless pacing, and irritating Gerda with pointless questions and incessant coffee requests. A hushed message from her after midday informed him that Swanepoel had returned to his office, soon followed by Meiring. He returned to his desk, expecting Swanepoel to burst in and unleash another barrage of abuse for not working through him. But, to his eternal gratitude, nothing, and relaxed when he noticed both men were out. Glancing at his watch for the umpteenth time, he strode over to the map, hands shoved deep into his pockets.

"Where are you?" he said out loud, staring at the map, his focus centered on Nyanga and the surrounding areas, including several White suburbs. "You could be anywhere in the damn locations." He caught himself—with all the changes coming, township was more appropriate, he decided. Deep in thought, role-playing a range of scenarios, when he was startled by Swanepoel barging into his office.

"I've found them!"

Roux spun around. "Where?"

Swanepoel came over to the map, pushing Roux to one side, almost knocking him over. He ran a finger over an area in the north of Nyanga and then stopped and circled a small section of crisscrossing streets.

"They're hiding in a shack behind a small tavern, NY113." He was referring to the government's street naming designations—Native Yard number 113. "We've got the Black turds," he snarled.

The nauseating odor of alcohol and tobacco caused Roux to temper his initial exuberance.

"Well done, man," he said with a measure of caution, "how many of them, and do we know if they are the group we looking for?"

Swanepoel stepped back from the map, looking uncertain. "Um . . . I'm not sure . . . uh, let me call Meiring." He stood in the doorway and shouted.

Roux studied the man. Was he nothing other than the bearer of glad tidings?

Minutes later, Meiring sauntered up. "You called?"

Roux motioned to him, "Come in Captain, am I right in assuming your informants came through?"

"*My* informants," snapped Swanepoel, scowling at Meiring as he followed him into the office.

The man's not only a drunk, he's a fraud, thought Roux. In his current state, it was doubtful he could find his zipper, never mind three well-trained terrs in the townships.

"Yes, Colonel," said Meiring. "My *Witdoeke* contact was of great help. Seems a *friend* of his was at the Yard Tavern, at NY113, yesterday evening when he saw three men and a boy enter through a back gate at the bottom of the property. Two of the men were dressed in dark clothes with floppy hats and very large rucksacks. The third man was a short, fat, elderly guy with gray hair and beard, and wearing a red jacket, like a windbreaker. Seems he was leaning on the boy for support, which suggests he's injured. They went into a small shack at the back of the property, which sounds like a storeroom or something similar, and were still there when my informant left about ten. I informed Colonel Swanepoel, who instructed me to go have a look."

"I was going to go with," interrupted Swanepoel, sounding flustered while exposing Roux to another lung full of alcohol-laden air, "but it's better I control the op from here, you know . . ."

Meiring glanced sideways at Swanepoel, then back at Roux, and rolled his eyes.

Roux inclined his head. He'd got the message. "Carry on Captain."

"As the bloody locals know every vehicle we use, I kept to the side streets to avoid attracting attention and alerting the men in the shack. One of my men, Sergeant Ndlovu, took a walk around the back and said the side and back walls are high, brick, old but solid, with glass shards cemented into the top of the walls. There's a metal gate, locked and maybe with a bar behind it, so he wasn't able to see into the property. But he did see the roof of a structure just inside the back wall. I left him at the place and sent two constables to back him up. He's in radio contact if needed."

Roux grinned. Things were going well so far. But was this the group they were looking for? He needed to brief du Plessis and get direction.

"Gentlemen, thank you for the hard work, but is this the group we are looking for?

"From the informants' descriptions, I reckon so," said Meiring.

Swanepoel mumbled something in apparent agreement.

"OK, I need to brief the general and get direction on whether we take a chance and pick them up, or observe them until we are positive it's the group."

Swanepoel grunted and walked out.

Meiring raised an eyebrow and then shrugged. "If OK with you, Colonel, I'm going to head out and check in with my informant. If the courier is going to contact someone in the ANC, he needs to go to one of the safe houses and my guy has eyes on almost all of them. I'll be in radio contact."

Roux glanced down at his watch. Well after five. He grabbed a pen and a notepad from his desk and scribbled a number. "This is my home number, in case I'm not here. I'll let you and Colonel Swanepoel know what the general decides."

After Meiring left, he dialed du Plessis' number and was surprised when the man answered after the second ring. Two minutes later, he put down the phone. Both Swanepoel and Meiring's phones were unanswered. He pulled out the internal phone directory, scrolled through the Es, and dialed Els. Now armed with the individual call signs for each of the SB members, he picked up the radio.

After trying Swanepoel repeatedly, he gave up and called Meiring, who, after several agonizing minutes, responded.

At last. "Captain, I can't raise Bravo One, but we are to observe for the moment until we can confirm the target is legit."

"Copy that," Meiring responded. "I'll let Bravo One know."

"Thanks. Let me know if they start moving."

Meiring hit the transmit button twice, which Roux took to mean he understood. Time to head home and get some food. He suspected it was going to be a long night.

To his relief, he found a note in the kitchen from Mel. She was attending a welcome function for her new boss and wouldn't be home 'til late. Rian was staying over at a friend's. All of which were ideal. He was not in the mood for company. Although tense, he felt excited. This is what he had missed for four years. The hunt for the quarry. The thrill of the chase and the feeling of accomplishment when the arrest was made. He made himself a sandwich and coffee and headed for the lounge to watch TV, but unable to concentrate on anything, he stretched out on the couch and closed his eyes. It felt like only minutes before he was woken up by the shrill tones of the phone. He dragged himself up and wobbled over to the phone. The wall clock told him it was just before midnight. He'd been asleep for over three hours.

"Roux."

"Meiring here, Colonel. Sorry, but a bit of bad news. Our target has flown the coupe."

"Christ! Where are you?"

"Compton."

"Wait in my office. I'll join you there."

# Friday, February 2nd, 1990

HE MARCHED INTO HIS office to find Meiring pacing, looking apprehensive. "What's happened? From the beginning," he barked. His earlier excitement was replaced by disappointment and annoyance.

Meiring sighed and collapsed into a chair, forearms on his knees. "While we were watching the back gate, we saw the old guy leave the property just after nine and walk to a house about ten minutes away. After about five minutes, he came out with a guy Ndlovu recognized as someone we know to be ANC and on our watch list. They chatted for about ten minutes, and then he returned to the tavern. In the meantime, I got a radio call from Colonel Swanepoel asking for an update. I told him we were to observe only, but all he said was . . . 'Bullshit' and went silent. I came back here. Somewhere between ten thirty and eleven, I got a frantic call from Ndlovu telling me to get to the tavern asap. When I got there, I found him and Gainsford, together with the owner, outside the front of the tavern,"

He sighed again and shook his head. "It appears that after the tavern closed, Ndlovu and his constable, who were watching the back entrance, heard a vehicle screech to a halt at the front, followed by a flurry of torchlights and shouting. Running to the front, they saw a figure scaling the front wall and dropping into the yard. There was a series of crashes and shouting, followed by gunshots from the property's rear. Then they heard someone screaming, 'I'm being murdered!' Gainsford leaped onto the wall, opened fire, and plunged into the yard. Ndlovu followed.

"To cut a long story short, what he found was one dead guy with a Tokarev pistol and the back gate open. They checked the shack and found two packs and a kid hiding under a bed. Turns out, Colonel Swanepoel jumped over the wall and landed amongst some trash cans, alerting everyone in the shack. It was him they heard screaming. The dead guy came out shooting and Gainsford shot him. But by then it was too late. The target and a second guy had bolted out the back gate." He looked crestfallen. "Sorry."

Roux felt like crying. "Where's Swanepoel? And the boy and the dead guy?"

"The colonel had a superficial wound to his leg from falling amongst the trash cans, so I arranged for him to be taken home and the kid brought here and detained. I called CID and told them we had carried out a raid on a suspected arms cache, but turned up nothing but the dead guy. They're at the scene now, and the body will be moved to our morgue. One of my team will go with to make sure it's fingerprinted."

"What were Swanepoel and Gainsford doing there? Had they been drinking?"

"Gainsford seemed fine when I asked him why he was there," said Meiring. "Following orders, he claimed. The colonel, on the other hand, reeked of alcohol, and his speech was slurred. Told me he did not have to explain his actions to a captain, and it was none of my damn business, anyway."

"Where's the boy and the packs?"

"Gainsford is interrogating the kid and the packs are on my desk. Just clothes. Nothing else in the shack."

"What age is this boy, and how good is Gainsford at interrogations? He may know where the old guy went."

Meiring rubbed his palms down the side of his trousers. "About sixteen. Gainsford is very effective. I don't agree with his methods, but he will get results."

"OK. Tell Gainsford I want to see the boy in one piece and coherent later this morning. While I understand the need for urgent information, he's a child who will admit to anything to avoid the pain, which is of no help."

"Will do." Meiring looked exhausted.

"Go home, Captain, and get some rest. We'll talk again later. This wasn't your fault, by the way."

After Meiring left, he sat for several minutes, wondering how to explain this to du Plessis. The upside was Swanepoel would have a problem justifying his role in this fiasco, and there was no way he, Roux, intended to take the blame. Maybe no need for a confrontation, just apply pressure by warning the idiot if he didn't back down du Plessis would hear the facts.

Blackmail? Absolutely. He left for home ten minutes later.


AFTER A LONG SHOWER, a change of clothes, and a light breakfast, he was back at the station by six, with a premonition today was going to be a bad one. Du Plessis and Warmer needed updating, and then, of course, there was the State of the Nation Address.

He went straight to the detention cells housed in the building's basement. The cell block was as he expected: dank, dark, and foul-smelling. Inquiries as to the whereabouts of the boy led him to the furthest section at the end of a dimly lit corridor, designated for SB use only. The duty constable unlocked a door and let him in.

The room, brightly lit by a massive overhead bulb, was about ten square feet and devoid of any furnishings save for a waste bucket in a corner. He gagged at the overpowering stench of sweat, feces, and urine. The boy lay huddled in the corner either asleep or unconscious, Roux couldn't tell, but from the dried blood around his mouth and eyes and the state of his clothes, it was clear Gainsford had not held back.

The constable walked over to the boy and kicked him in the stomach. "Hey! Wake up, boy, the boss is here to see you," he said, following the kick with further nudges with the toe of his boot.

The boy's one eye opened, the other, swollen and bruised, remained shut. Struggling up on one elbow, he whimpered as he levered himself into a sitting position in the corner, one arm raised in front of his face, either to shield his eyes from the light or fearful of a further beating. Although no stranger to the physical abuse metered out to terrorists during interrogations, Roux detested it.

"Ask him his name and age," he said to the constable.

"We booked him in as—"

"That's not what I asked you, man. I want to hear it from him!"

The constable walked over to the boy and kicked his foot, raised his hand as though to strike, and spoke to the boy in what Roux knew to be Xhosa.

The boy glared at Roux through one bloodshot eye, his arm still raised. "My name is Isaac, and I'm eighteen," he said in English.

Roux shook his head and glared at the constable. "Get him checked by the duty doctor and moved to a better cell, and you," he pointed a finger at the man, "make sure he gets food and water, now!" He turned on his heel and marched out.

Gerda was bashing away on her newly acquired computer when he stuck his head into her office. "Any chance of organizing a TV for my office for SONA?"

"I'll see what I can do, boss. Coffee on its way."

"Thanks, I could do with it. Please find out who heads up CID these days and get him on the line, it's urgent." He went into his office and closed the door. Minutes later, his phone buzzed, and a Brigadier Martins from the Criminal Investigation Department introduced himself.

The CID chief, knowing not to ask too many questions, eliminated one of Roux's nagging concerns. No, there had been no media interest in last night's incident. They were too busy speculating on what the president would announce at SONA to be interested in the death of some Black "gangster" in Nyanga.

Next came du Plessis. He checked his notes from Meiring's report back. Short and to the point seemed the best option, and then hunker down for the inevitable angry outburst and transfer back into uniform, which was bound to follow. To his surprise, headquarters in Pretoria informed him du Plessis was in Cape Town to attend SONA, but his current whereabouts were unknown.

Gerda came in bearing a mug of steaming coffee.

"Thanks. Do me a favor. Can you call around and see if General du Plessis is in the building? I need to see him asap."

Her knowing look made him suspect she knew something was on the go, but he said nothing. Instead, he chewed on the inside of his cheek; instant pain and blood filled his mouth. He had to kill this habit before he ended up with a serious mouth ulcer. Where the hell is du Plessis? The screw-up last night was bad enough, but if du Plessis was to hear about it from anyone other than himself, it would be the final nail in an already-closing coffin lid.

He would need to compile a report on last night's incident, but before he started, he wanted another one-on-one with Meiring. Swanepoel's drunken behavior, and disregard for a direct order, might give him the evidence he needed to suspend him. His train of thought raised a question. He picked up his phone and buzzed Gerda.

"Gerda, has Colonel Swanepoel come in this morning?"

"Oh, sorry Marius, I forgot. His wife called in to say he had gone to hospital. Something about a very serious leg injury he got last night, so won't be in today. Sorry, boss."

He thanked her and put the phone down. The lying bastard, he fumed, from the way Meiring described it last night, the injury was just a scratch. Well, just more ammo for the firing squad, he decided. So absorbed in his scheming, he failed to hear the door open.

"So, our courier has taken to the wind." General du Plessis stood in the doorway and Roux could sense the man's anger. "What went wrong?" he said, closing the door. "Just a summary. I'm in a hurry."

Roux emphasized the relevant details in minutes, making sure he embellished Swanepoel's questionable bravado. Du Plessis listened without comment until Roux ran out of explanations.

"Did you give Swanepoel an order to observe only?"

"No, General," Roux replied, his voice cracking a touch, "I tried calling the colonel several times on the radio without success, so Captain Meiring passed it on to him." He waited.

Du Plessis ran his hand through his hair and gave Roux a hard look. "Hmm. So, we have one dead terr, a teenager, probably their runner, and the old guy with one other terr, loose in the township. How sure are you now he is the courier?"

*Townships, eh! No longer locations. Even he was moving with the changes.*

"From the description, his contact with someone who is ANC, and their flight from the tavern, I'm convinced he is our man. I'll have it all in my report."

"Forget the report, waste of time. Focus on finding the old bugger. It's priority, Roux, and even more so after this afternoon." He sucked on his teeth and turned to leave, but stopped in the doorway. "Were Swanepoel and Gainsford drunk?"

"According to Meiring, Gainsford appeared fine, but the colonel reeked of alcohol and his speech was slurred. It may account for his accident with the trash cans." Roux felt like a snitch, but if he was to resolve his Swanepoel problem; help from any quarter was welcome.

"Roux, you need to take command." Du Plessis' tone was gentle but insistent. "I appreciate the difficulty with Swanepoel being senior to you, but we can't ignore his incompetence. Time is of the essence, and you need to sort him out and focus on the task at hand. Do I make myself clear?"

"Yes General," said Roux to his departing back.

He stared at the open door for a moment, stroking his mustache. He was surprised. The reaction was not what he had expected. He still had a job. Maybe the man had a human side after all.

He was about to call Meiring when Gerda slipped into the office. "Is everything OK? I couldn't help but overhear. The inter-leading door wasn't closed. You still having problems with Swanepoel?"

"I am, but he may have resolved my problem for me. By the way, who is Gainsford?"

"Sergeant Gainsford. One of Colonel Swanepoel's favorites. I've never met him, but I hear he's a brute of a man with a pea-sized brain. But don't change the subject. General du Plessis put you in charge, and Swanepoel knows it." She sat down. "The longer you allow him to push you around, the worse it's going to get."

"I know. But, after his behavior last night, I may have enough to suspend him. I just need to think it through. Problem is, he knows I'm here temporarily, so he's riding his luck 'til I go."

"If you ask me," Gerda said, getting up, "and from what Marie says, the general sees you as permanent, and I think you, and Mel, better get used to the idea. So, young man, grow a pair and deal with this arsehole. Time to take charge!".

Roux almost fell off his chair. That was the last thing he expected to hear from dear old Gerda, but she, and du Plessis, seemed in agreement about certain shortcomings in his anatomy.

"Gerda. Language!"

She giggled and turned to leave.

Still in shock, he called after her. "Please keep an eye out for Meiring. I need to see him."

"He is already here," said Gerda. "I'll call him."

Minutes later Meiring sat opposite him.

"I went to check on the boy earlier," said Roux, "and left instructions for him to be fed and seen by the duty doctor. He's eighteen and looked awful. Gainsford's work I assume?"

"So did I," replied Meiring. "Seems Gainsford got very little from him. He claims he's living in the shack until his father returns from Joburg, and denies knowing who the terrs were, saying they burst in earlier that night forcing him to remain in the shack, which we know is a lie. Tough little bugger."

"I want him moved to a better cell and made comfortable, Captain. Tell Gainsford to back off until I inform him otherwise, and if he has a problem, tell him to take it up with me. Once the boy's patched up, and had some food and rest, I want you and Ndhlovu to have a friendly chat with him, and I mean friendly, no more beatings."

"You think he can tell us anything?"

"I do, and don't ask me why, just a gut feeling. There were youngsters like him in South West who were acting as runners and lookouts for SWAPO, and if handled right, and with a bit of patience, it was surprising just how much they could tell you."

"Hope you know what you doing Colonel, we don't have a lot of time."

"I'm very aware, Meiring, and don't need reminding."

WITHIN MINUTES, THE PRESIDENT, F.W. de Klerk, would begin his State of the Nation address to a country waiting on tenterhooks, irrespective of their ethnicity. To his eternal gratitude, Gerda had coerced Els into hooking up a somewhat antiquated but serviceable TV in his office, eliminating the need for him to watch in the conference room surrounded by Swanepoel's sycophants.

"It'll only have a bunny ear aerial, but that *young cutie* assures me the picture will be fine," she enthused. Roux, in horror, just grunted under his breath.

He sat quietly at his desk, going over in his mind the events of the last twelve months. 1989 had been a tumultuous year. The country was in the grip of international economic sanctions. Attacks on police in the townships had escalated. In February, de Klerk's predecessor, P. W. Botha, had stepped down first, as leader of the ruling Party, and later, because of internal pressure, as president. In August, de Klerk was inaugurated as the ninth State President of the country. The move towards political change began. The more he speculated on de Klerk's stated intentions and actions, the more he realized his worst fears were becoming reality; change was coming, but how far de Klerk would go remained to be seen.

Just before two, Gerda joined him in the office and tuned the TV to the South African Broadcasting Corporation TV station just as the opening proceedings started. They sat waiting anxiously while they nibbled on snacks and treats she had weaseled out of the canteen. The rest of the unit was nowhere to be seen.

As was customary, the address opened with a prayer; Gerda bowed her head during the delivery. Then the nation's president, and leader of White South Africa, dressed in a dark suit, made his way to the podium. Bespectacled and almost entirely bald, he gazed out over the National Assembly. His party members sat to his right with the opposition parties, both moderate and extreme right-wing to his left. Ambassadors, foreign political representatives, and other dignitaries packed the gallery above the chamber. A deathly hush pervaded the house.

"*Mr. Speaker, Members of Parliament,*" he began.

Roux leaned forward in his chair, every fiber in his being attuned to what the president would say. He knew the speech would be delivered in equal parts in both official languages: English and Afrikaans, but he suspected those parts of the speech announcing any changes would be in English for the benefit of the international community.

"*The General election on September the 6th, 1989, placed our country irrevocably on the road of drastic change,*" said the president, his voice clear and strong. "*Underlying this is the growing realization by an increasing number of South Africans that only a negotiated understanding among the representative leaders of the entire population is able to ensure lasting peace.*"

He continued. "*The alternative is growing violence, tension and conflict. That is unacceptable and in nobody's interest.*"

"Depends on who you ask," said Gerda.

De Klerk highlighted the changes in eastern Europe, the fall of the Berlin Wall, the collapse of communism, and the change in ideologies on the African continent. He expanded on human rights issues, the work of the Law Commission on protecting individual and minority rights, and then dropped a mini-bomb shell—the reform of the current death penalty laws. Being convicted of terrorism or attempting to unseat the government by violent means resulted in only one outcome—death by hanging.

Gerda sat bolt upright. "Has he just abolished the death penalty?"

"No," responded Roux, "but it looks like he's opening the way for it. Convicted terrorists can now appeal the death sentence."

It got worse, in Roux's opinion, when de Klerk announced the repeal during this Session of Parliament, of the Separate Amenities Act.

Gerda gasped. "Does this mean they can go to the beaches and parks, or the movies, and come into our restaurants?" she blurted out, wringing her hands. "Whites won't allow this," she said, shaking her head. "I won't sit next to them in a movie or have them stinking out our restaurants."

Roux could think of nothing to say. First the death penalty and now allowing Blacks and Coloreds—the government's racial classification for people of mixed race—free access to White only areas. The man had gone nuts!

He leaned over to the desk and helped himself to another *koeksister*—a traditional Afrikaner confectionery made of fried dough dripping in syrup or honey. "I think there's more to come, so buckle up."

The tension in the room eased a little as the president focused on the plans to rectify the ailing economy and rescue it from its current state of deep recession. Roux was not a convert of the accepted opinion sanctions had brought the country to its knees. Sure, some international brands had disappeared from the supermarket shelves along with some imported cars, but local innovation and ingenuity had supplemented many of these in quick time.

A shining example was the arms industry. The country was designing and manufacturing world-class weapons and, with a bit of sanctions busting here and there, exporting the technology. He shared his father's belief that much of the doom and gloom espoused by the business sector was mere propaganda emanating from the English-speaking elite.

*Other than the death penalty and the Amenities Act, not much new so far*, thought Roux. What did concern him was whether this would mean Blacks would go to White schools, which was a lot harder to stomach.

De Klerk's sudden switch to English should have been a warning; but neither picked up on it.

*"In conclusion, I wish to focus the spotlight on the process of negotiation and related issues. The focus, now, has to fall on negotiation. Practically every leader agrees that negotiation is the key to reconciliation, peace and a new and just dispensation."*

"Here it comes," said Roux, his voice flat.

*"I wish to urge every political and community leader, in and outside Parliament, to approach the new opportunities which are being created constructively. There is no time left for advancing all manner of new conditions that will delay the negotiating process. The steps that have been decided are the following:*

*The prohibition of the African National Congress, the Pan Africanist Congress, the South African Communist Party and a number of subsidiary organizations is being rescinded—"*

He continued to announce further unbannings, but Roux never heard them. He and Gerda gaped at each other as the consequences of the announcement materialized in their minds. The gasps, shouts and groans from members of the right-wing opposition parties in parliament, many of whom were standing up and walking out of the chambers, echoed their own disbelief,

Roux could not believe what he had just heard. It felt as though his entire world had just crashed down around his head. He continued to stare open-mouthed at the screen, hearing very little of what followed, until—

*"In this connection, Mr. Nelson Mandela could play an important part. The Government has noted that he has declared himself to be willing to make a constructive contribution to the peaceful political process in South Africa.*

*"I wish to put it plainly that the Government has taken a firm decision to release Mr. Mandela unconditionally. I am serious about bringing this matter to finality without delay. The Government will take a decision soon on the date of his release. Unfortunately, a further short passage of time is unavoidable—"*

They sat speechless until the end of the address. He heard Gerda sniff and saw her dabbing at her eyes with a tissue.

"Hey! It'll be OK," he said, placing a hand on her arm. But he knew it was going to be anything but OK. The problem was; what was it going to be?

"I need to call my hubby," she said, rising slowly.

"Good idea," Roux responded, needing to be alone.

Gerda left, closing the door behind her. Moments later there was a light tap, and the door opened, revealing Meiring, looking pensive.

"Got a minute, Colonel?"

Roux nodded and motioned him to a chair.

"I assume you heard all of it?" said Meiring. "The question is, with the terrorists now unbanned, where does that leave us with this op and finding the courier? Is he still relevant?"

Roux had to clear his throat several times before he could talk. The words still catching in his throat. "To be honest, I don't have any idea. I'll need to talk to du Plessis and find out." He felt drained and dispirited. What was the point to anything anymore, he wondered, staring down at the carpet.

"Colonel, I had a disturbing thought earlier."

Roux looked up. There was a worried look on Meiring's face.

"Considering the way the right-wing parties reacted to the announcements, what if someone, or some group, takes out Mandela when he's released? It would bring the negotiations to an end and start a civil war."

Roux burst out laughing. "What a clanger," he said. "All the talk of a negotiated peace, and some smart arse blows the shit out of him. It'll screw up de Klerk's bright ideas." He stopped. The implications of such an event dawned on him. The prospect no longer seemed funny.

"Who the hell would want to take him out?" he asked.


SMALL WAVES FROM THE unusually calm Atlantic Ocean teased the edge of the all but deserted beach. Off in the distance were several Colored fishermen casting lines into the surf from the beach and he wondered if they were aware of the enormity of what had happened just hours ago. When he arrived at his spot, it piqued him to discover a Black man seated on "his" bench. His frustration exploded. Without pause, he pointed at the faded "WHITES ONLY" sign, painted in black, on the backrest of the bench, and vehemently ordered the man to move. It took the threat of an arrest before the man angrily got up and shuffled off down the beach. Roux sat on the opposite side of the bench.

The SONA speech had taken a little over thirty minutes, but the impact on the men and women in the headquarters building was devastating. People with worried looks congregated in small groups in offices and hallways, discussing the announcements with obvious concern, and in some cases, loud opposition. Gerda half-heartedly began clearing up his office, although it was obvious her thoughts were elsewhere. It was as though keeping busy would somehow diminish the import of what had just happened.

The rest of the afternoon passed in a haze interrupted only by a call from du Plessis informing him he would stay in Cape Town until Mandela's release, and yes, the courier needed to be found, the urgency of the operation increasing tenfold as Mandela's release could be imminent. Roux was to make sure he was contactable over the weekend, and be available to meet first thing Monday morning.

He'd locked his office door at four and left the building.

Now he stared out over the water, struggling to marshal his thoughts into some form of logical reaction to the president's announcements. The potential effect of the imminent changes was still not clear in his mind. All the terrorist organizations were unbanned and, therefore, as he now assumed, arresting them for being members no longer applied. Three hours ago, they were the enemy, but was that still the case?

But if he was honest, pretending he wasn't aware change was coming would have been childish and pure self-denial. All the signs had been there ever since de

Klerk took office. Daily, the media theorized about how far the government would go, its actions and announcements all pointing to a dramatic shift in policies, but he had ignored the signs hoping Afrikaner strength, and the will to survive, would prevail. Massive White opposition would force de Klerk to capitulate and the government would have to enforce separate development. Or so he hoped. He was comfortable granting Blacks some political freedoms and economic access in their own homelands, but what de Klerk intended was a direct assault on the very foundation of apartheid. An assault which could either be surrendered to or challenged.

Where was this whole mess going to end up? His thoughts immediately turned to Rian and Mel, and their safety. It was time to get home in case the entire city went berserk with celebrating Blacks and Coloreds. But more importantly, he needed to talk to his father.

As he stood up to make his way to his car, he caught sight of a plastic bag being coaxed across the sand by the mild sea breeze. "The winds of change," he said out loud, a wry smile on his face, "are going to blow us all to hell."


TO HIS DISMAY, HE found Mel and Rian sitting in front of the TV watching a panel of journalists and political commentators, debating the potential changes that would, or could, happen over the days, months, and perhaps even years to come. He threw his jacket over the back of a chair and sat down next to them on the couch.

"Do we need to be hearing more of the same?"

"Shush," said Mel. "This is important." Her enthusiastic response he expected, but Rian's obvious interest for what was unfolding troubled him.

Irritated, he got up and went into the kitchen and helped himself to a beer from the fridge, screwed off the cap and took a deep swallow. The voices of the TV commentators, emphasizing the inevitability of change, sent a spasm of nausea through his gut. He gulped another mouthful.

"Here's hoping there is a civil war, and we can take out these bastards and maybe include de Klerk and his sidekicks," he muttered. "Mandela and his Blacks need to bloody well tow the line and accept separate development, then we can all get on with our lives." He was mulling over how the security forces could maintain control when Mel and Rian came into the kitchen.

"What do you think, Dad?" said his son, a smile lighting up his face.

*What the hell do I think?* He couldn't believe his own flesh and blood had just asked him that. He was a security policeman, spending his days doing whatever it took to keep White South Africans safe in their homes, and his son wants to know what he thinks of their entire world being turned upside down? Maybe he should have done what he assumed almost everyone at headquarters had done after work: gone to the bar and got drunk. He drained the beer and walked over to the waste bin and dropped it in. He was conscious of Mel studying him.

"What I think is de Klerk has sold out the Afrikaners. He's going to give the country to the Blacks. They will take our house, our jobs, send you to school in the locations so their children can take over our schools and universities and force us to leave the country. Assuming they don't kill us all first." He immediately regretted his outburst when he saw the look of fear on his son's face.

"Rubbish," said Mel harshly, folding her arms and leaning back against a counter, glaring at her husband. "Your father knows that is absolute nonsense." Her eyes shifted to Rian. "The government has simply opened the door to negotiation, and got rid of petty laws that do nothing other than foster hatred. Any idiot knows the army and police are still going to control the country, and I have to admit I'm surprised at your father's churlish attitude, being a policeman and supposedly in the know." There was more than a look of surprise on her face. She glared at him as she stormed out of the kitchen, followed by a shocked-looking Rian.

They ate dinner in silence, an oddity in the Roux household, and it wasn't long before Rian excused himself to head for the sanctuary of his room. Mel washed up the dinner dishes and then headed for a bath without a word. Roux, waiting until she was asleep, tried calling his father several times with no success.

# Saturday, February 3rd, 1990

HE BOUNDED OUT THE front door the minute he heard the car pull up in the driveway. "Christ! Phil. It really is good to see you again," he exclaimed in English.

He was greeted with a lopsided grin and an outstretched hand. Roux grasped the hand and threw his other arm around the man.

"Jeez Phil! It's been ages man, how the hell are you? The last I heard, you were running around in Botswana, or some other godforsaken place." He stepped back, sizing up his friend of over twenty years. He had changed little since their last encounter. Blond hair neatly trimmed, but way too long for the regulation army cut, and with looks, women drooled over. Blue-green eyes, constantly on the move, were now appraising him in return.

"Got a little porky there, my man," said Philip Roberts, patting Roux's stomach and feigning concern.

Roux could not respond in kind. His friend looked as fit and well-proportioned as always. No wonder women couldn't resist the bugger. But where was the full beard, an almost prerequisite for special forces operatives?

"Hey, gorgeous," Roberts called out as Mel came out the front door. They hugged, her face flushed. "You still pissing off the authorities working at that Foundation?"

She giggled, a hand touching her hair, face still flushed. "I am, much to my husband's annoyance, but I find it invigorating and rewarding."

"Good for you, old girl," said Roberts. "Now, where's your young man."

"Rian," Mel shouted over her shoulder, "Your uncle Phil is here."

Their son met them as the three made their way into the lounge.

"Hi, uncle Phil, it's fantastic to see you."

Roberts gave him a bear hug and, despite Rian's size, lifted him off his feet. "Good to see you, too." He dropped Rian back on his feet and ran an eye over the boy. "Definite Recce potential Marius. Let me know when he gets his call-up and I'll pull some strings."

"Hey! A desk job for him is the best I'm going to allow," laughed Roux. "Come on, let's crack a beer in the garden. I've set everything up for a *braai* and Pa should be here soon. So, you still with the Recces?" said Roux, running a hand over his chin and raising an eyebrow. He had used the colloquial name for the various reconnaissance units that made up the army's elite special forces. "Lost the beard I see."

"Yip. But in HQ now, and as the ladies prefer me without the extra hair, I decided to oblige."

Beer in hand, they settled into the beach chairs around the brick fireplace in the back garden. Roberts unscrewed the cap off his beer and tossed it onto the table.

"So, what do you think of yesterday? De Klerk really blew the lid off things," he said, his brow creased. "I didn't think he would go that far."

"Madness," said Roux, as he poked at several smoldering pieces of charcoal in the fireplace. "Releasing Mandela was half expected, but unbanning the ANC and PAC without a commitment to stop their terrorism just makes little sense to me, and Whites will not be happy." He dropped the meat tongs over a hook on the corner of the brick fireplace and sagged back into his chair shaded by a large beach umbrella. It was one of three spread around the table in the corner of the back garden. "How are we supposed to deal with these bastards if they are now free to do what they want? It's tough enough keeping a lid on the violence as it is. But now, how do we stop it?"

Roberts chuckled, stretching his legs out in front of him. "Relax old boy. I can't believe de Klerk is doing this on a whim. I'm sure there is a plan behind the apparent madness. But, it's going to take time. We still control the security forces and the generals will not allow de Klerk to go off half-cocked." He was dressed as most white South Africans would be on a hot weekend. Open neck short-sleeve shirt, shorts and toe thong sandals, or flip-flops, as they were better known.

"With a bit of luck, the ANC will focus on the talks and create less mayhem in the locations. The reality is we are in the toilet, economically, that is. You don't need to be a banker to realize sanctions are killing us. Something, sometime, was going to break. Rather this than open civil war."

Roux gazed at his friend, somewhat taken aback. For a man who had spent his adult life committed to fighting terrorism and communism, his apparent blasé response was a surprise. He stifled a yawn. Little sleep and an early morning walk to think things through had left him sweaty, tired and irritable, and no wiser as to what the future held. The cold shower on his return eased some of the weariness, but he still felt wound up and uneasy.

Mel disrupted their conversation by calling from the back patio, where she stood with a platter of assorted meats in her hands. "Marius, do you want to start cooking the meat? The salads will be ready in about twenty minutes, and your pa and Sonja will be here soon." She looked stunning today, the loose-fitting green top accentuating her auburn hair and the drizzle of freckles across her nose and cheeks.

Roberts leaped to his feet and jogged over to the patio.

"Honestly, Mel, what the hell does your husband know about *braaing*, other than turning the meat into burned offerings to some unknown cooking God? Better I cook or we'll end up with takeaways," he said, taking the platter.

"Go on then," said Mel, nudging him off the patio with a look of a girl who'd just experienced her first kiss. "Show him how it's done."

Roux grinned. If his friend wanted to take over the cooking responsibilities, all the better. He hated it. Cooking meat over open coals did not appeal to him, considering the modern appliances available to achieve the same result. But he kept his distaste for one of White South Africa's decades-old traditions to himself. As Roberts approached the fire, he noticed Mel still standing on the patio watching them, a faraway look on her face as though reminiscing on some long-forgotten pleasure. After a moment, she turned and went back into the lounge.

Roberts began laying out the meat on the grill. "Cheer up, old chap. Things are not as bad as you think," he said, reaching for his beer. "Nothing is going to change overnight." Satisfied the meat was placed as it should be, he returned to his chair.

Roux shook his head. "Phil, you don't have kids. I'm worried about Rian being able to complete his matric. If they start flooding schools with Black kids, education will go down the drain."

"Can't see it happening. Negotiations will take years and until then, status quo. Anyway, enough of Mandela. So, the terror of a sister of yours coming? I don't mind admitting she scares the living bejesus out of me, Marius."

"You're not alone. Many a braver soul than you or I have tried their luck and got smacked down. She changed after Kenny crashed—for the worse."

Roberts laughed. "The man flew his helicopter into a mountain in the middle of the day for God's sake, killed half his crew and four army kids."

Roux eyed his friend. Subtlety was not one of Roberts' positive traits. "You know she still believes the official version he was shot down?"

"Don't worry, I won't spoil her day. If she wants to believe the idiot was a hero, I won't disillusion her."

They sat for a while, staring into the fire.

"Been a while since you saw the old man. South West if I remember."

Roberts averted his eyes, shifting in his chair. "Um, yes. Be good to see the general again." Despite the affection his father had showered on his friend from the day they met—treating him much like one of his own—Roberts always referred to him as "The general."

Moments later, they heard Rian announcing his grandfather's arrival. Roux grimaced, then took a swallow of beer. "Come on," he said to Roberts as he got up. "I'm sure the old man will be glad to see you."

They both made their way over the patio into the lounge, arriving just as his father, accompanied by his sister, were being welcomed by Mel and Rian.

"Hello, Pa," he greeted his father with the customary handshake leaving his fingers feeling like they'd been through a wringer. Father and son bore little resemblance, save for their shared height and black hair. Roux, unlike his sister, had inherited his mother's softer, gentler features. He knew little of his father's upbringing, apart from the occasional tidbit his mother had shared. Hailing from three generations of farmers and deeply religious stock, his father's childhood had been harsh. His parents, struggling to scrape a living from a dying plot of land, toiled themselves into early graves, providing the bare necessities for their seven children. He had never met his grandparents or his father's siblings, of whom his father never spoke, which his mother attributed to a lack of familial ties and family discord. His father's hard features and unforgiving demeanor mirrored his upbringing.

"Son," was all his father said, handing him a bottle. As always, he was immaculate, in gray flannels, cream shirt, and dark blue sports jacket, his gray tinged black hair noticeably longer than the usual short-back-and-sides he favored. Although almost seventy, his father carried little excess weight.

Taking the bottle, Roux smiled at his sister, never sure of her mood these days. "Sonja, good to see you again."

She ignored him and, taking Mel by the arm, pulled her towards the kitchen, where she placed a large carry bag on a counter with a loud clink of glass on glass.

"I made a trifle for afterward," she said to Mel, "you know how pa loves my trifles."

His sister was three years younger than him, but looked ten years older. Dressed in a faded brown top and black slacks in desperate need of an iron, her unkempt long brown hair framed a thin, drawn face which had not seen makeup since the death of her husband. She unzipped the bag and removed a glass topped bowl.

"Place it in the fridge, please," she instructed, passing the trifle to Rian. Two brandy bottles, one full, the other two-thirds empty, followed the dessert. Mel scurried to the cupboard for a glass while Rian carefully stowed the trifle in the fridge. Sonja's trifles were not a Roux family favorite due to the copious amounts of liquor drenching the fruit, custard, and other ingredients. Depending on her drink of choice during preparation, the alcohol could range from brandy to sherry to port, or a combination thereof. But he knew between his father, sister, and Roberts, the bowl would be empty before nightfall.

His father held up two fingers. "You know the way I like it. Ah! There's the Recce man," he said, looking around and spotting Roberts. The two men shook hands, embracing briefly. Roux watched, puzzled. As far as he knew, they had not seen each other in four years, and knowing how close they were, the greeting seemed perfunctory. *Odd*, he thought as he watched them walk out of the lounge and into the garden, talking in Afrikaans and laughing.

"Give this man the same," his father shouted over his shoulder.

Roux poured an estimate of what he thought was a measure of two fingers of the gold liquid from the bottle his father had given him into two glasses, adding blocks of ice to each glass. His father was not a big drinker, but when he did partake, the most expensive brandy available was his drink of choice.

His sister, drink in hand—a half-filled glass of cheap brandy, several ice cubes and topped off with a dash of tap water—sat on the counter watching Mel prepare the last of the salads, but making no effort to help. They conversed in English, which always surprised Roux. Unlike his father, who never spoke English unless ordered to do so, Sonja was content to switch, seeming to understand from the moment they first met that although reasonably conversant in Afrikaans, Mel was more comfortable in her mother tongue.

He left the women in the kitchen and, taking both glasses, walked out into the garden, passing his son going in the opposite direction. Rian, like all sensible teenagers, had decided an afternoon at the movies was likely to be far more entertaining than listening to the old fogies waffle on about politics, the economy, and other topics of little interest to him. So after a hug for grandpa and a quick handshake with "uncle" Philip, he was heading out.

Roux handed the two men their drinks before retrieving his beer and sitting down opposite them. Toying with the bottle, he watched his friend tending to the meat while engrossed in conversation with his father, explaining the reasons for his own father's recent retirement from commercial farming.

It was during their second year of studies at separate universities in Johannesburg, when he first met Philip Roberts, and his girlfriend, a shy, almost timid auburn-haired girl who left a lasting impression on him. They could not have been more different in background and outlook. Roux, serious-minded and reserved, hailed from a staunch Afrikaans Calvinistic upbringing and was educated in the government's public school system. Being a schoolteacher was his sole ambition. In contrast, the flamboyant, outgoing Roberts, a political sciences student, was a product of the "private" English schools system, an education affordable only by the very wealthy. His parents, sugar cane plantation owners, ensured they gave him access to the very best, a situation, in all fairness to the man, he never flaunted. To the amazement of everyone who knew them, they developed a friendship and rapport which lasted until Roberts changed courses. Without explanation, he announced he was off to study a degree in military science at a different university. They remained in touch and after completing his degree, Phil signed up for officer training in the army, much to Roux's surprise. It was the start of a brilliant military career, enhanced by his joining the special forces. They had stayed in contact over the years and worked together once in South West, but as time passed, the demands of their respective professions interfered with their regular contact.

His nostalgic reverie was cut short by Mel's call for help in transporting a multitude of salads, plates, and utensils from the kitchen. He walked over to provide an extra pair of hands. After placing the food and plates on the table, the two women joined them. It was not long before Phil announced the meat was cooked to his satisfaction and, on his insistence, it was time to eat. Mel, addressing her father-in-law in heavily accented Afrikaans, offered to dish up for him. Although grammatically incorrect, the meaning of her offer would have been obvious to any Afrikaner; but not to his father.

He sneered, glancing at his son. "When are you going to teach your woman to speak Afrikaans?"

Roux felt his face redden. He was about to blurt out that the old shit could get his own food, but he bit his tongue and said nothing. To challenge his father was sacrilege and would lead to an instantaneous and very unpleasant end to the visit. Mel's face was turning a color matching her hair and Roux had a terrifying moment, fearing how she might react, but to his relief she stood up, announcing she needed to fetch the mustard and stormed off to the house.

"I'll get your lunch Pa," said Sonja, standing up, and in the process spilling some of what appeared to be at least her second brandy. She threw a look at Roux, which plainly instructed him to hold his tongue.

Roberts was looking uncomfortable. "Can I get you another drink, General? I'm due one," he said, rising.

"Ja, why not my boy," the older man said, handing his empty glass to Roberts.

"And for me," said Sonja, downing what was left in her glass and handing it over.

Phil winked at Roux and made his way to the house.

His father sat back in his chair, a smug look on his face. He wants me to challenge him, Roux said to himself, but I will not bite this time, old man, but my opportunity will come.

Roux got up and joined Sonja at the table where she was busy adding a selection of meats and salads to a plate. "Why do you always do that?" he whispered. "He can feed himself. He's not a cripple. Mother treated him like God, and look what it did to her, and now you're doing the same thing."

She paused and glared at him. There was no sisterly love in her expression. "Because I love and respect him, unlike you. He was there for me after Kenny. Where were you?" She had whispered, but Roux knew his father heard every word. The smirk on the man's face confirmed his suspicions.

He decided to wait for Mel before eating, so helped himself to another beer, watching Sonja hand their father a full plate of food, who cut off a sizable chunk of steak and stuffed it into his mouth.

"Philip knows how to cook meat," he said as he chewed, more to himself than anyone else. Still chewing, he looked across at his son.

"So, tell me, what's du Plessis think of de Klerk's speech?"

Roux stared at his father. Since the morning of the phone call, they had not spoken, yet the question implied he knew du Plessis was Roux's boss. Was Mel right? Had he engineered the whole thing?

"I spoke to him after the speech, but said nothing, other than there is a meeting scheduled for Monday."

"De Klerk has sold us down the drain," grumbled Sonja. "Ever since he took over from PW, he's just been giving the Blacks whatever they want and bugger us Whites." She was looking longingly at the house.

"I tried to call you last night," said Roux. "I wanted to hear what you thought. If all the terrorist groups are unbanned, does it mean we are no longer at war? Someone needs to tell us what they expect us to do."

"Sorry, I had a busy night." His father paused. "There are many conflicting opinions, as I'm sure you understand.

Not everyone is celebrating what has happened. But, as I understand it, nothing has changed for the moment. De Klerk is perhaps overstepping his authority, unbanning the terrorist groups, releasing Mandela, pulling the army out of the locations, and talking of negotiations with the Blacks. Negotiating for what? To hand over the country to them? I believe de Klerk will be forced to moderate his approach in the coming months, and the pace of any change will be managed correctly. There won't be any sudden hand over." His father dropped his plate of half finished food on the grass and pointed a finger at Roux. "The conservatives and the real Afrikaners are gathering support daily. You saw what happened in the last election."

His father's negative reaction to SONA did not surprise Roux. Ever since he could remember, his father held to what he claimed was one incontrovertible truth; the African countries which achieved independence over the last thirty years were failed states. Therefore, they were proof Blacks were simply incapable of running anything efficiently. An opinion Roux agreed with, and which supported his own personal standpoint, that the homelands were the answer. Leave the Blacks to their own devices in their own countries and let the Whites live in peace in South Africa. But was his father now suggesting de Klerk's moves could lead to violence between opposing views in the White communities?

"Are you suggesting Whites will turn on one another?"

His father was about to respond when he checked himself and leaned back in his chair and went silent for a while. Then he said, "No, of course not. I believe the conservatives in parliament will force the government to tone down their proposed changes. There's a lot of prominent Afrikaners running businesses now, including the mines, and they won't just lie down and hand it all over."

He looked at Roux and chuckled, placing a hand on Sonja's arm. "Don't worry, things will not go as bad as you think. Someone will bring de Klerk to his senses sooner rather than later, and tell Mandela what he can and can't have. Probably expand the homelands and the whole separate development program."

In the early days of apartheid, the government, seeking to attain a White demographic majority and to bolster their justification that apartheid meant "separate but equal," established Bantustans, later renamed homelands. These ethnic and linguistically distinct homelands were touted as the "original homes" of South Africa's Black populace, each destined for political autonomy and economic prosperity. These "independent states" would then coexist harmoniously within White South Africa. Or so the theory went. Since the sixties, the government had created ten homelands, forcibly relocating millions of Blacks. For White South Africans, this meant Blacks would reside in their designated states while providing cheap, migrant labor to White-owned farms and industries without receiving South African citizenship. Surplus labor was expected to find employment within their respective homelands. While internationally condemned, this policy remained widely supported among White South Africans, who seemed oblivious to the reality that nearly sixty percent of the Black population lived in townships and informal settlements within and around South Africa's urban and industrial centers.

Each to their own, his father had taught him and hadn't God ordained that men of different ethnicities should not intermingle? He used his own interpretation of several scriptures to justify why Blacks and Whites could not co-exist in one land. This same dogma was preached in schools and, until recently, by the Afrikaans churches. His father's logic was hard to argue against, and who was Roux to challenge the laws of the Almighty?

The return of Mel and Roberts interrupted the conversation. Roux could see Mel had been crying, but now she looked defiant. She walked to the table and began dishing up for herself. Roberts handed out the drinks he had replenished and sat down. Roux noticed a small damp patch on his shirt just below the shoulder, but his friend ignored his inquiring look.

Roux got up and joined Mel at the table. "You OK?"

She shrugged. "Why wouldn't I be? Your father treats me like dirt, and you sit there and allow it to happen."

"I'm sorry, but you know what he's like, and if I say something, it'll end in one of his tantrums."

"So what's changed?" Her plate full, she returned to her chair.

Roux had no answer. His father did not approve of the marriage, and that was that. Antagonizing him further by questioning his aggressiveness toward Mel would sour his own relationship with his father, a tenuous one at best.

Roberts and Sonja joined him at the table, and moments later, everyone was seated, eating. The meal was accompanied by desultory conversation, after which Sonja helped Mel carry the dishes through to the kitchen, accompanied by Roberts on another "top-up" mission. Roux remained in his chair. The incident between his father and Mel had, as always, left him ashamed and cursing his inadequacies.

The three returned from the kitchen with dessert and refreshed drinks. Mel suggested everyone help themselves and sat back, sipping a beer. Mel rarely drank alcohol, a fact which should have alerted Roux to possible upcoming trouble. But it didn't. Sonja filled a small bowl with a large helping of trifle and handed it to her father. Roberts waved off the invite.

"So, daughter-in-law," his father said, "what do you English people think of the SONA speech?"

"Well, Pa," Mel said in English, "I wasn't able to understand all the speech, just the English parts, and I have to be honest I was discombobulated when he spoke about unbanning the different parties." Her face was the epitome of child-like innocence.

Sonja giggled and then hiccuped. Roberts covered his mouth with his hand, his eyes screwed shut, his whole body shaking.

His father's drink stopped midway to his mouth, his brow furrowed. "Ah." He paused, not sure whether to take a drink or put his glass down. "Yes . . . I'm sure . . . I suppose that . . . well . . . women don't understand politics. . ." He looked at Roux for help.

You are on your own, old man. He had no clue what "discombobulated" meant, but what he knew was his wife's tone was deliberate; she was taunting the old man, and when Mel went on the offensive, anything could happen, and usually did.

"No, we don't," she said, all sweetness. "We have to rely on our menfolk to explain, but then it appears, other than being scared shitless, they don't understand the implications, and are struggling to come to grips with the realities of change."

Roux shook his head and glared at her, hoping she would get the message. Back off, woman, before the old man explodes.

Mel was about to continue when Roberts interrupted her. "Hey! Let's relax, see what tomorrow and next week bring. Everyone from the extreme left to the extreme right is going to have something to say about SONA, so let them blow off steam, or rejoice, whichever takes their fancy, and then wait to see what de Klerk does next." He drained his drink. "Trifle time," he said rising, and dished up an extraordinary large helping of the dessert. Sonja followed suit, already looking unsteady on her feet, her face flushed.

His father sat motionless, staring at Mel with a look all too familiar to Roux. It was the way he had looked at his mother when she dared to challenge or oppose him, the consequences of which were severe. He had loved his mother. But he also despised her. His father belittled and mistreated her, disappointing and infuriating Roux. Despite this, she always defended his actions, justifying it by blaming herself for not being a good wife. Their regimented and emotionless home life had become worse after his father's expectation of promotion to police commissioner failed to materialize. A policeman all his adult life, he was devastated and Roux watched helplessly as his mother's life became even more unbearable as the man vented his frustration on her. The doctors said the cancer was widespread, and had killed her quickly, but Roux suspected she had mentally given up and welcomed the release from her existence.

His father glanced at his watch and stood up. "Come daughter," he said, looking disapprovingly at Sonja, "I have calls to make so time to leave."

Sonja grumbled something about spoiling the party but started gathering up her things. Mel stood and began clearing away the dirty dishes.

Roberts seemed disappointed, but rose and shook the old man's hand. "Til me meet again," he said.

Roux stood, watching the two men. The absence of the usual back-slapping, teasing and loud recollections of their exploits in South West, which epitomized their reunions, still flummoxed him. It was as though they had seen one another the day before!

But the day was over. His father, after nodding a farewell to Roux, walked to the house, followed by everyone else. Once inside, his father headed for his car, leaving the rest of them in the kitchen. Sonja began packing her carry bag, bemoaning the fact she was just beginning to enjoy herself and now he wanted to leave.

Roberts smiled at Mel. "You sure gave it to the old man." She laughed, and they hugged. "Look after yourself, little one," he said before turning to Roux, concern on his face. "Take care out there, brother. Things could get rough. Talk soon." He gripped Roux's hand, and then accompanied by Mel, walked to his car where they hugged again before Mel turned to come back inside.

"You realize she fancies him, don't you?" Sonja whispered into his ear.

Roux turned to face her. "Mel, and Phil? You must be joking? Sure, they dated at 'varsity, but they've only been friends since, besides you've had one, or three, too many, again." His smile was gentle as he took her into his arms, their embrace tender. In his own strange way, he loved her.

She kissed him on the cheek and winked at him. "None so blind as those who will not see. Bye, big brother." She weaved her way to their father's car and got into the passenger seat.

After a wave to his sister and a mock salute for Roberts, he shook his head as he closed the front door and walked into the kitchen, where Mel was busy loading the dishwasher.

"Were you try—"

"No, I don't have to explain my actions to you Marius, but it's time you appreciate I will no longer allow your father to intimidate me. If he has a problem with me, he can stay away." She hadn't looked up. "Why don't you go clear up outside?"

Roux took another beer from the cooler box and sat down, sipping slowly. Another family disaster, he groaned. Mel and his father had never liked each other, but the animosity had grown after the Foundation inquiry, and neither of them were making any effort to even try at cordiality. He just wished she would ignore the old man's idiosyncrasies and be nice. Surely not that hard? He put the beer down and began gathering up the glasses and other dishes half-heartedly, regretting the missed opportunity to gain a deeper insight as to his father's interpretation of de Klerk's speech and how it would affect the way the police were operating. But the nauseous feeling he experienced every time he thought of SONA had more to do with how the change would affect his family rather than his job. Could Mel stay safe in the townships and could Rian be sent to a Black school? He needed to have a long and honest conversation with his family about their future, but tonight was not the time.

Glasses and plates in hand, he made his way to the kitchen, arriving just as the telephone rang. Mel grabbed the phone off the wall and answered.

"It's a Captain Meiring," she said, passing him the phone.

"Meiring," said Roux.

"Sorry to worry this late in the day, Colonel, but I think we need to meet."

"Can you meet me at Compton?" Roux responded without hesitation.

"I'm already here," Meiring shot back.

"See you in my office."

"I need to go to work," he shouted to Mel, grabbing his car keys and heading for the garage.


TWENTY MINUTES LATER, HE sat opposite Meiring in his office. The captain, wearing denims and a short-sleeve shirt, looked quite human. "OK, what's the emergency?"

Meiring took a moment to collect his thoughts and then leaned forward. "Had a long chat with the kid this afternoon, along with Ndlovu. Seems you were right. With some coaxing and patience, he opened up." He reached into his shirt pocket and pulled out a well-worn notebook, flicking it open.

"The two men with the courier are ANC. Seems the kid was the designated runner for them but won't tell us who put him in touch with the group. The kid described the old guy as mid to late fifties, with gray hair and a beard which ties in with our description. He described his clothing as dark, maybe brown or black trousers and a zip up jacket. Red with yellow stripes on the cuffs. Sounds to me like a bomber jacket. It also had what he called a football badge on the left breast, a logo, I assume. He also said he was not well, having problems breathing."

Roux studied the man as he recited the information. *Does this man have a life outside of work?* "Did he describe this logo?"

"Said it was round, yellow with a picture of a black face, side on, with what he thinks was long hair hanging down."

"Could be anything," said Roux. "Get Els to ask around and make some calls. See if he can come up with anything that fits. Check all the football club logos."

Meiring leaned across Roux's desk, helping himself to a pen, scribbled a note and then flipped to another page. "Two things stick out about this old guy. First. He only spoke English. None of the Black languages, so sounds like he's not South African. Second, the kid overheard him tell the others he had to, as the kid puts it, 'get Mandela' as soon as possible, but Ndlovu thinks it could also mean 'get to' Mandela."

Roux chewed on his inner lip. "If he's having health issues, it will slow him down. Besides, walking around in a red jacket isn't what I would call inconspicuous. Do you think the boy can tell us anymore or has any idea where he went after he ran?"

"Other than who his handler is, I doubt it," said Meiring. "But there is something else which came in this afternoon."

"Related to the courier?"

Meiring looked uneasy. "Maybe, but does point to a potential threat, and it's the reason I suggested we meet. One of Ndlovu's informants, who is a relative which makes it easy for them to meet, told him this afternoon of a group of four APLA men who arrived overnight from Johannesburg. The informant started asking around, and it seems the group, led by Che Tau, has moved into an old PAC safe house in Langa." He frowned. "But what is worrying is they were asking at some of the *shebeens*"—the township word used to describe a drinking tavern—"if anyone knew of a recent arrival of an ANC man from Lusaka. The courier?"

Roux scratched his head. "That name sounds familiar."

"Tau is well known in Soweto and other Joburg locations," responded Meiring. "We were looking for him when I was stationed there. Left the country after the seventy-six riots and joined APLA and did some training in Libya before he got involved with their faction battles in Tanzania. Appears he returned to the country in the mid eighties and started his own branch of APLA. It's believed he planned several attacks in the Johannesburg area but nothing came of them, but his vocalized hatred of Whites and alleged summary executions of so-called apartheid spies gave him a mythical like status in certain areas in the north."

"This is not good news," said Roux. "How does he know about the courier? Makes you wonder who else knows?"

Meiring shook his head. "No idea. But the PAC is against any talk of negotiated settlements. Black rule through the barrel of a gun is their way of changing things."

Roux snorted. "So, seems we are not the only ones looking for this courier. If APLA know then the PAC must know about him, and I assume they want to stop him reaching Mandela for the same reasons we do. Doesn't say much about the ANC keeping his arrival secret."

A moment's silence followed. Roux ran a thumb and forefinger across his mustache while he stared at the map on the wall. "Did the informant have any idea why they here?"

"Nothing, but he and Ndlovu are going to take a look at the house this evening, and with a bit of luck, might pick up on what is happening."

"Could Tau be here to try to stop the release?"

Meiring thought for a moment. "I know it sounds ridiculous, but with him, we can't rule out the possibility."

*Why don't they just leave Mandela in Verster until we find this courier? It'll make things a lot easier,* wondered Roux. But the arrival of Tau may provide him with the justification to raise the question with du Plessis.

"The PAC don't have a big following here, so he's going to struggle to get any support or information from the locals, and if all we have are rumors and innuendo about his activities in the past, there's nothing we can arrest him for. So unless he does something blatantly illegal, we can't *touch him, thanks to ou*r president."

"Fun and games," said Meiring.

"OK. Let's see what Ndlovu gets and then I'll update du Plessis. Anything else?"

Meiring flipped to another page in his notebook.

"Sergeant Conradie called in to say he attended a meeting last night in Mitchell's Plain, which, as you know, is largely Colored. Seems a group of hotheads, Coloreds and Blacks, were making a lot of noise about Mandela being the puppet of the de Klerk government, and intends giving away their rights in exchange for his freedom. The meeting got rowdy, with some serious threats made about stopping Mandela's release." He turned over the page. "They call themselves The Movement for Black Liberation, or MBL."

Roux sat up. "The who? Where the hell did they spring up from? I've never heard of them, have you?"

Meiring shook his head. "Nope."

"What else did he say?"

"Not much, but seems the main mouthpiece was a Black guy called . . .," he eyed his notes again. "Elias Khumalo. I've never heard of him and neither have my men. There were also two Coloreds, Phineas Davids and a guy who called himself Akmet, who seem to be his big supporters."

Roux's face went blank. "Who they when at home?"

"I know a bit about Davids," said Meiring. "Businessman, but also involved in drugs, prostitution, buying and selling firearms and owns a couple of *shebeens*. Nasty character. He's been trying to worm his way into a senior position with the local ANC, but not even they are interested. Maybe he's now trying to make a name by hooking up with this Khumalo. The only other name Conradie mentioned, which I recognize, is a thug called Gumbo, a gang name. Leads the Crossroads gang. Twisted psycho who kills for fun. Why he was there is beyond me, maybe just supplying muscle in case the crowd got out of hand."

"Christ!" said Roux. "We got some old guy trying to get a secret message to Mandela, a group of fanatics talking about opposing Mandela, and to top it all, four APLA terrorists led by Tau arrive in Langa also looking for the courier and planning who knows what else."

He slumped back in his chair, chewing at the inside of his mouth. "Eugene, I know this sounds dumb, but I'm not sure how we prioritize all of this."

Meiring hesitated. Roux, realizing the man was uneasy at the use of his first name, was about to apologize when Meiring interrupted him.

"No problem, Colonel, Eugene is fine." He paused, looking down at his notebook again. "I'll get hold of my contacts at the old *Witdoeke* again, see if they can find out more about Tau and this MBL crowd. But it's going to cost."

"Do it," said Roux. "Money is not an issue at this stage. I'm sure I can get du Plessis to sign off on what you need. Talking about du Plessis, I'm going to wait till you and Ndlovu have checked things out and we have something concrete, then I'll brief him."

"Colonel, I suggest you inform him about APLA as soon as you can. If this blows up and he is caught unawares?" He left the question hanging in the air.

"Don't worry, I know the man. If I bug him with unsubstantiated intel, which is all we have at the moment, he'll just tell me to get the answers."

Meiring looked worried for a second, but seemed to brush aside whatever was troubling him. "With some luck, I should have a better feel of what's happening on the ground by tonight or tomorrow. I'll call you as soon as I know anything."

Both men stood and made their way to the door. Roux stopped.

"By the way, how did Conradie get invited to the meeting?"

"He told me a couple of weeks ago he became suspicious of his brother when he started asking questions about our operations, particularly the planned raids in the locations. I suggested he play along, see what he could find out. He told his brother he hated the way he was being treated and wanted to leave the police and join the ANC. My guess is his brother bought into the act. Conradie can be very convincing, even more so when he's lying. Anyway, his brother invited him to go along to this MBL meeting."

Roux shook his head in amazement. "Unbelievable. OK. Keep Conradie on this MBL crowd and let's see if they just another overnight wonder or whether they are a potential threat."

"Will do."

Roux returned to his chair. Three possibilities. Were they all three trying to achieve the same thing? Were they in contact with one another? Did APLA intend stopping the release? Answers eluded him for the moment. He stroked his mustache and thought back to another problem gnawing away at the back of his mind. Sonja's comment about Mel and Phil, but he pushed it away. Time to get home.

# Sunday, February 4th, 1990

DU PLESSIS BROUGHT ROUX'S traditional Sunday morning lie-in to a premature end. He sat up bleary-eyed and reached for the bedside extension. "Roux," he squawked. A quick glance at his watch told him it was just past seven.

"Du Plessis. I need you in your office together with Captain Meiring at oh-nine-hundred. Don't be late." The line went dead.

He was about to reach over to nudge Mel awake when she opened an eye. "You going to work?"

"Du Plessis wants to meet. Not sure when I'll be back."

"Good," was all she said before rolling over and pulling the duvet over her shoulder. He stared at her for a moment, shook his head, and dragged himself out of bed.

After a hurried shower, a brief phone call to Meiring, burned toast and a coffee, he was on the road. He felt relieved to be out of the house. Having to tiptoe around a moody wife all day did not appeal to him. With the usual scarcity of traffic on a Sunday, he was behind his desk just after eight-thirty. Meiring strolled in ten minutes later dressed in jacket and tie, which made Roux feel underdressed in his open-neck shirt and denims.

"Morning Eugene," he said. "Do me a favor and lose the jacket and tie, you making me feel uncomfortable."

Meiring obliged, hanging both items of clothing over the valet stand.

"Any idea why du Plessis wants to see us?" he said, sitting in one of the visitor's chairs.

"No idea. But I have to assume it's about the SONA speech. Maybe he knows more about Mandela's release, although the bastard can stay where he is as far as I am concerned."

Meiring grimaced. "Maybe. On another issue, Ndlovu confirmed the APLA guys are staying at the house in Langa I mentioned , but my informants couldn't confirm if Tau is one of them," he said. "But we also have another serious problem."

"OK, hold it for du Plessis. We can update him on everything we have so far, but in the meantime, tell me what the mood of the people is like in the townships since SONA?"

Meiring rubbed the side of his face, looking thoughtful. "Going from what Ndlovu tells me, it seems to be mixed. The older generation is positive and believe the negotiations will lead to a free election, your one man, one vote scenario. On the other hand, the younger crowd is optimistic but cautious, 'I'll believe it when I see it' reaction. The more militant elements are worried too many concessions will be made to Whites. But it's still early days. Once the actual release date is announced, we will get a better feel."

"And our guys?"

"Its what I need to share with you. We may have a problem."

Du Plessis strolled into the office, armed with a cup of coffee, and Roux was pleased to see, dressed as casually as himself. He waved them back to their chairs before seating himself in the other visitor's chair.

"Morning gentlemen," he said. "I'm meeting Greyling later, so I need to know where we are with this courier. Security at Verster will intercept any parcels or letters going to the man. Visitors will be searched, and all conversations recorded, but it's no guarantee we'll pick up on anything." He yawned, making no effort to cover his mouth, then glanced from Roux to Meiring and back at Roux. "Any progress?"

Roux coughed into his hand, cleared this throat and said, "We have some information on the courier but not much. Eugene?"

Meiring pulled out his notebook and summarized page by page the information about the courier he had shared the previous evening, and then paused for a moment before continuing. "The problem is, he could be anywhere. But on the positive side, between the kid, the photos and my informants, we have a reasonable description of the man."

Du Plessis stared at Meiring a moment, then addressed Roux. "OK. I assume you still have legs out looking for him?"

"We do," said Roux, "but there are two other issues which we only found out about yesterday. The first is the emergence of some radical group called the Movement for Black Liberation, which seems to have only formed after SONA, but I don't give it much credence. Mostly local thugs and hot heads claiming Mandela is working with the government. The other bit of news is of more concern. There is an unconfirmed report of Che Tau being in Langa, but—"

"Tau! Here in Cape Town?" Du Plessis had shot upright in his chair, eyes wide, his voice raised. "Why wasn't I told?"

"At this stage, we don't know if it is him," said Roux before nodding at Meiring.

"Initial intel confirms four APLA guys, including Tau, arrived in Langa on Friday night," said Meiring. "They are staying at an old PAC safe house, but my informants have not yet confirmed if Tau is with them. I should have some feedback later today. The problem is trying to verify if it is him. All we know about him is he's tall, just under two meters, well built, around forty-ish with a facial scar and enormous ears, but nothing more."

Roux chipped in. "What worries me is they have been asking around about any recent ANC arrivals from Lusaka. It sounds like they are looking for the courier. How does the PAC know about him?"

Du Plessis glared at Roux, his jaw clenched, his face taut. "Why didn't you inform me of this last night?"

"My apologies, General. I intended to brief you as soon as we had verified it was him," said Roux, shifting in his chair.

The man growled. "I need to know about these things, Colonel, as they happen. As for the PAC knowing about the courier, I'm not surprised. With everyone spying on everyone else in Lusaka, it was bound to come out. But it means we need to keep a close eye on them and find the courier first. What else don't I know about?"

Meiring spoke. "General, we have another problem, a serious one."

Du Plessis gave him a brusque nod. "Uh-huh? Tell me."

"With all the talk of changes coming many of our informers are not showing up for meetings, which means we'll lose our coverage at the popular hang-outs like *shebeens*." said Meiring. "My guess is the last thing they want now is to be identified as an *impimpi* and get themselves necklaced."

Roux went cold at the image. Informers, or *impimpi* as they were called in the townships, were an essential source of intelligence to SB, but were in constant danger of being exposed. If identified, they qualified for special retribution by the "comrades" in the terrorist organizations. Necklacing meant being bound hand and foot, a rubber tire, filled with petrol placed around the upper arms, and then set alight. An excruciating and slow death. He could find only one word in his vocabulary to describe it: barbaric.

"This is compounded by some of our Black and Colored officers worried about how they will be treated if the ANC gets into power," continued Meiring. "I'm not sure we can trust most of them anymore, and I'm worried some of them may play both sides of the fence, trying to curry favor with the ANC."

Du Plessis sat back in his chair, scratching his unshaven jaw. "I can empathize. How trustworthy are Ndlovu and his guys?"

"I would trust him and his team with my life. My concern is some of those on the other Desks."

"Understood. Gentlemen, we can't afford leaks of any sort, which means you use only those you can trust implicitly."

"That creates a problem," said Roux. "If informants are going underground, our sources of reliable information will fast dry up. Our guys, those we can trust, are known, making their ability to infiltrate limited, which exacerbates the situation. We need unfamiliar faces who we can use to get close to the APLA guys and the most militant activists—"

Du Plessis held up a hand. "In hand. Major Uys from PE, whose guys followed the courier from Cradock, will arrive on an air force cargo flight tomorrow morning along with his best and most reliable Blacks and Coloreds. They'll be in a better position to operate freely amongst the population. Use your men to work the informants and act as guides for Uys' team."

"I can arrange that," said Meiring.

Du Plessis sat forward in the chair, elbows on his knees, hands clasped. "OK. What do we have at the moment?" He stared down at the carpet for a while, then sat back, crossed his legs, and raised a fist with the thumb outstretched.

"One. We have some old guy we call the courier, running around in the townships, trying to get a message of sorts to Mandela. What are the chances of him achieving his goal?"

"There are only two ways he can get any message to Mandela," said Roux, staring off into the distance. "First, he meets with Mandela, and is unlikely if access is being controlled. Second, he passes the message to someone who already has access to Mandela, but if all the conversations at Verster are being monitored, we should hear it. However, if the message is about upcoming negotiations, there's no urgency in getting it to Mandela. The courier can wait until the man is free and then meet him. But if it's to reach him *before* the release, it is going to be difficult for them. "

"My guess is Mandela will want to address a rally or crowd after his release," interjected Meiring, "and if the message refers to something he must announce at the rally, he'll need it before his release."

"Which is my belief as it supports the courier's sudden arrival," said du Plessis. "However, Greyling is not convinced. He still believes it's more to do with negotiation tactics. But let's look at the other problems." He raised his index finger.

"Sorry," said Meiring, raising a hand. "Who is Greyling?"

"NIS, and that's all you need to know," said du Plessis, appearing annoyed at the interruption.

"Oh," said Meiring, and sat back in his chair.

"Two. There are a bunch of locals banging on about Mandela being in cahoots with the government. Nothing new there."

He raised his middle finger.

"Tau, and three other APLA men arrive just after the announcing of Mandela's release. Tau is no mug. If he is here to find the courier or to try to interfere with Mandela's release, he is a serious threat indeed. One we would be fools to disregard. Have I covered it?"

"I think so, General," said Roux. "Of course, we still need to confirm it actually is Tau, but I'm sure we'll know either way today. But I'm curious. Would the PAC be stupid enough to try to derail the negotiations?"

"They run a massive risk of being ostracized if found out. But with Tau, you never know, so finding out what he is up to is your number one priority. We can't allow him to find the courier first, but as important is my worry he could be a genuine threat to the talks, and even Mandela himself. Greyling has been talking to the PAC leadership about negotiations and he can ask them why Tau is here. The commissioner will also need to be updated."

Roux glanced at Meiring, who, seeming to know what was about to come, gave an almost imperceptible shake of his head, but he ignored it, weighing his next words with care.

"General, I understand the urgency in all of this considering the release has been committed to and announced, but wouldn't a delay in the process be less devastating than some violent intervention by APLA? Until we find the courier and pin Tau down, if it is him, or Greyling gets answers from the PAC, we're chasing ghosts. Another week or two won't make much difference, considering the man has been in prison for twenty-odd years. The government will still honor its commitment, and if starting the negotiations is so urgent, why can't it begin at Verster?"

Du Plessis was shaking his head even before Roux finished.

"Secret talks have been going on for months, but the president wants to bring the process out into the open for the world to see just how serious the government is about change. Holding Mandela in prison is going to raise questions. The release will happen, probably within the next few days."

He waited for several moments, and then continued.

"The president is no fool. He knows there are people out there who oppose what is happening, and not all of them are Black. But, he is relying on us to do our job, which is to ensure the release goes off with no risk to Mandela. No, we need to do this as quietly as possible. If there is a threat to Mandela's release, stop it in its tracks, with no one the wiser."

Roux threw up his hands. "I hear you, but it doesn't change my opinion. If we get this wrong, and someone gets to Mandela, all hell is going to break loose," he knew his voice, along with his anger, was rising. "I know how to do my job, but you're telling me to find out if any of the threats are real, but to go easy on the terrorists, no unnecessary raids or arrests. *Subtlety* was the word used, if I remember. Knocking on people's doors and asking if they just happened to have overheard a discussion at the local tavern or beer hall about killing Mandela is unlikely to go well."

"I appreciate your concerns," said du Plessis, but the set of his face made it clear he didn't, "and the enormity of the problem, but you will have additional resources tomorrow to cover more ground."

The general continued, his tone making it clear this was not a negotiation. "What I need from you is to stay focused on the primary targets, Tau, and the courier. Find this old guy and if Tau is here, pick him up and have a chat with him. It may rattle him and force him to go back to Joburg." He held up a hand before Roux could protest. "I know, difficult, but find a way."

He stood up, looking tired. "The State of Emergency still applies and therefore we are free to operate within its directives. But," he paused for emphasis, "only when you are sure of positive results. I don't want a repeat of Thursday night." He took a deep breath and exhaled slowly. "Couple of things you need to know. The government today ordered the army back from the townships, although they will be ready to react if needed."

Roux sat back and stared at du Plessis. His father had said the same thing. How did he know yesterday?

Du Plessis continued. "We have, in addition, put STG on immediate standby. Colonel Heyns assures me he has teams ready to deploy at short notice. I've asked him to liaise with you so you know what is available and where." The acronym stood for the Special Task Group, a police unit specialized in counter-insurgency operations in both rural and urban settings.

"The Air wing is at full strength and available whenever needed. They will also support the STG."

He stood up and made his way to the door. "I need to see Greyling. As of now, you keep me updated with anything you get, no matter the hours. I'll decide if it needs verification before we act." In the doorway, he turned and looked back at the two men. "When you locate the courier, no more observing. Arrest him on suspicion of being associated with armed terrorists." He paused. "One last thing, Swanepoel will not be returning to the unit. He is on medical leave and will then transfer to the Criminal Investigation Department, that makes you the number two Meiring. Make the most of the opportunity."

FOR SOME REASON HE was unable to fathom, he felt depressed as he made his way through the kitchen to the lounge. After kicking the problems around for several minutes, he and Meiring had realized they were getting nowhere, and needing to escape the station's stifling environment, called it a night.

He was about to call out to Mel when he noticed she was sitting on the couch in the lounge, looking at him. She wasn't alone. In a chair alongside her was a man, gray hair and dressed in a light colored suit with matching shirt and tie. Roux had never seen him before. But that wasn't what caused his mouth to drop open. It was the fact the man was Black, which left him speechless.

"Hi, love," said Mel as she hurriedly rose from the couch, "This is Professor Jonas Kani, the new CEO of the Foundation. Remember, I told you about him. He needs some help, so I suggested he came round to meet you to see if there was anything you could do for him."

The man rose from his chair, his right hand extended. He was almost of Roux's height and looked like any other old Black man, except . . . there was something in the dark eyes that belied the man's apparent senior years. They were bright, intelligent and did not avoid Roux's stare, as many Blacks would do, especially in the house of a White man, and a security policeman to boot. But there was no sign of discomfort or, as Roux would have expected, fear.

*He's a confident bugger*, thought Roux, which made him suspicious. He dropped his jacket on a chair and grasped the man's outstretched hand. The grip was dry and firm.

"A pleasure, Colonel. My apologies for the unannounced intrusion on your evening," he said, grinning. "Your wife was kind enough to invite me for an excellent cup of tea and a chance to meet her 'better half' as she calls you. I was hoping you could help with a, rather . . . shall we say . . . delicate matter?" There was no trace of a Black accent in his English. Roux would have described it as a "British accent."

His immediate instinct after releasing the man's hand was to wipe it on his trouser leg, but he caught himself in time.

Kani remained standing, waiting.

"How can I help  . . . er . . . Mr. Kani?"

"It's a small matter, and I know you are a very busy man, Colonel, especially after Friday. But a young man, a relative of a friend of mine, seems to have disappeared from his lodgings. His friends tell me he has been arrested. I was hoping you could find out where he is being detained and on what charges. He may need legal support, which, as you know, the Foundation provides when necessary."

Roux knew only too well the "support" the Foundation provided. It was the red flag which led to the investigation into the actual activities going on in the halls of the institution.

"Could be difficult," he said. "He could be at any of the stations in the Cape Town area. I would need more information, like his name. Where was he picked up, and was it uniform or detectives who arrested him?"

"His name is Vuyo. I've been given an address where he was last seen, but how accurate it is I cannot attest to, other than it is in Nyanga township, or location, as you call it. The officers were in civilian dress, so I assume it was security policemen. As to the crime? None I can ascertain." There was a fleeting look of anger in Kani's eyes, but his face remained neutral, no inflection in his voice. He handed Roux a folded slip of paper. "My secretary typed up a list of additional information which may be of help. Age, description, where he was last seen, clothes he was wearing, that sort of thing, but please, do not hesitate to call me if you need any further information, although I am not sure I could add anything."

Roux pocketed the slip of paper. He needed him out of the house before some neighbor started rumor mongering. "OK, I'll see what I can do."

After a moment of embarrassed silence, Kani smiled, walked over to Mel, taking her hand in both of his. "Thank you, my dear, for the introduction. You have removed a big worry from my mind. I'll see you in the morning?"

"Of course, professor, bright and early as usual. Let me see you out."

Kani shook Roux's hand again, grinning. "You may now go wash your hand if you need to, Colonel. Don't worry, it does not offend me. I have witnessed it many times before." There was no malice in his tone.

Mel, looking a touch embarrassed, accompanied him to the front door.

Roux stood, cemented to the spot, his face beginning to redden. He stared down at his hand and shoved it into his trouser pocket, instinctively wiping it against the inside of the pocket. He resisted the urge to head for the bathroom.

"Thanks, my love," said Mel, walking back into the lounge and picking up the tea tray. "I wasn't sure you could help, but I'm happy you can. He is a gentleman, in the old-fashioned British manner, if you know what I mean," she said with a giggle, and headed for the kitchen.

Roux didn't. He slumped into his chair. "Not as easy as it sounds. He could be anywhere, but I'll ask Gerda to check tomorrow. You are going to wash his cup separately from ours, I hope? And Mel, please warn me before you invite Blacks into our house, especially from the Foundation."

Mel, returning to the lounge, kissed the top of his head. "I know, sorry. Inviting him just sought of came out after he told me about his problem. I'd told him you were in the force, and it just seemed natural for you two to meet to see if you could help. But I'll check in with you first next time." She paused. "You know the polite way to address him is 'Professor.'"

"Professor my arse," said Roux, irritation in his voice, "he's lucky I didn't chuck him out."

He looked up at Mel. There was a look of contempt on her face as she turned and walked away.

# Monday, February 5th, 1990

THE DAY HAD DAWNED muggy and wet, with little prospect of changing. On time, Gerda marched into the office with the usual mug of coffee in one hand and a scone on a plate.

"Strawberry jam, for a change, but no butter. Bad for your cholesterol."

"There's nothing wrong with my cholesterol," said Roux. "We are doing just fine."

"Mel says you putting on weight, and I agree," retorted Gerda. "You were so slim and fit when you arrived here. Some girls in the typing pool quite fancied you, but you've got pudgy over the years."

Roux winced. Early morning lectures on the state of his health and physical appearance were above Gerda's pay grade, he reflected, despite being accurate. But he knew she meant well.

"I need you to look for a Black boy for me," explaining the unwanted visitor of the previous evening, and handing her the slip of paper from Kani. He hadn't bothered to read it. "Here is some info on him. Please see what you can find out."

"Where do I start?" she said, her brow lined.

"Start with the Charge Office down stairs, see if uniforms detained anyone on that night. Also CID. You may need to check with some of the other stations, but there's an address where he was last seen, which should narrow it down."

"OK," she said, sounding dubious, "see what I can do."

Just as she left, Meiring appeared at his door, and Roux waved him in.

"Some good news for a change," said Meiring, stifling a yawn as he sat down.

"Oh?"

"Ndlovu has been watching the PAC house, and he is positive he saw Tau. The guy fitted the description we have of him. They mostly keeping to themselves, but the neighbors told him they had been meeting with people and asking a lot of questions about the courier. To be honest, Colonel, this crowd worries me. The consensus of the SB guys in Johannesburg is he's a psychopath."

"Brilliant! At least we know it's him. I'll let du Plessis know," said Roux. "Ndlovu still watching them?"

"No, I sent him and his guys home to get some sleep, but I've got two other constables watching the place."

"Great. OK, the PE men should be here today, so we need to decide on how to use them," said Roux, "and Eugene let's drop the colonel crap when it's just us. Marius is fine."

"Oh. OK," said Meiring, looking a touch uneasy.

Several combinations were examined before they agreed Meiring's men would stay focused on APLA and the courier, and the incoming men would be used in Langa and Nyanga to keep an eye on known trouble makers and mingle with the crowds at popular gathering spots.

"We'll need two or three of our guys to work with each of the incoming team," said Meiring. "There are some guys on the other Desks who are reliable, but I know Grobler and Haveman will not be happy about losing them. They're already muttering about all the secrecy, and why aren't they involved?"

Roux groaned. Picking up the phone, he called each of the two captains. Their unhappy responses were much as he expected.

"Done. Select the men you want from the other Desks and make it happen," said Roux.

"I would also like to keep Conradie on the MBL," said Meiring. "I know they pose little risk but best to know what they up to."

"Agreed."

"Have you met Uys before?"

Roux shook his head. "You?"

"No, I haven't, but I'm keen to see how involved he wants to get."

Gerda interrupted them just before lunch with a tray of sandwiches, biscuits and coffee, but before they could finish she buzzed Roux to inform him a Major Uys was waiting to see him. Moments later, a red faced, blond-haired man beaming from ear-to-ear filled the door frame. "Uys, Cornelius Uys, best damn SB man south of the Limpopo River. You must be Roux, or is it Colonel Roux?"

Roux liked the man from the minute he saw him. "Marius, please. This is Eugene Meiring, my number two. Welcome to Cape Town." The three men shook hands and sat down.

"So, Marius, what have you done with my car load of communists since I left them in your care? Du Plessis tells me you shot one bugger, but seem to have misplaced some old guy he called a courier," said Uys, with a glint in his eye. "Good thing I came back to find him for you, eh!" His booming laughter filled the room.

Roux smiled. "That we have Cornelius, but we are making some progress on it. Couple of other events have us a bit sidetracked at the moment."

"So. Tell me. What's the buzz?"

It took ten minutes for them to bring Uys up to speed, highlighting Tau's presence.

Uys whistled through his teeth. "Ouch, he's a mean bitch is Tau. You think he's trying to stop the courier from getting to Mandela?"

Roux nodded. "They certainly looking for him, and Du Plessis is concerned they may try to derail the negotiations by pulling off some stupid stunt at Mandela's release. We are waiting on NIS to check in with the leadership of the PAC to find out what game they playing, but we have eyes on Tau at the moment."

"Sounds like you got things under control. What do you need from my men?"

Meiring stood up. "I'm going to get Els while you update Cornelius. We'll need him to arrange radios, call signs and vehicles," he said.

Roux was explaining to Uys how they proposed deploying the teams when they were interrupted by the return of Meiring, accompanied by Lieutenant Els. It didn't take long for the final allocation of men to each of the teams, their responsibilities, and a reporting structure to be finalized.

"Right, gentlemen," said Roux, "let's get things moving."

Els left to organize additional radio handsets and transport for the teams while Uys and Meiring agreed to meet at six in the basement to divide the men into their respective teams, brief them, and issue orders. All three men would meet again at seven in the morning. With nothing further to discuss, Uys departed to find suitable lodgings for himself.

Roux collapsed into his chair and heaved a sigh. "Finally, we are getting organized. You know, the youngster has potential."

"You mean Els? He does, especially now Swanepoel is not riding him," replied Meiring.

As if on cue, the door to Gerda's office flew open and Colonel Swanepoel staggered into the room. Gerda followed, looking flustered and shaken.

"I'm sorry Marius, but he just barged in, I—"

Roux and Meiring both stood. "It's OK, Gerda. Please close the door," said Roux, walking around his desk to confront the man.

Swanepoel beat her to it, slamming the door in her face.

"You little bastard," he screamed. "Running to du Plessis because you don't have the balls to face me." The smell of alcohol and sweat radiated through the room. "This is my unit and . . . and . . ." He stared around the room for a moment, as though not sure where he was, then he appeared to compose himself, his eyes becoming slits. He stepped forward, pointing a finger at Roux.

"You think this is over, Roux? You know nothing about me. I am going to cause you a lot of pain, you little shit!" Spittle flew into Roux's face. "I know where you and that wog-banging wife of yours live, and you'll never see me com—"

Roux pushed off the desk, lunging at Swanepoel, but found his attack blocked by Meiring, who grabbed his arm a heartbeat before Roux could get his hands around Swanepoel's neck.

"Don't Colonel, he's not worth it!" .

Roux stood motionless, his breath coming in gasps, his whole body shaking. Violence was not in his nature, but right now all he wanted was to see Swanepoel's face a bloody ruin, but he knew Meiring was right. He stepped back, gulping in air, trying to regain control.

"Go home, Colonel," he breathed. "You're making an arse of yourself. You are an embarrassment, so get out of my office before I have you arrested and thrown into the cells."

Swanepoel's eyes widened, and he opened his mouth to say something, but then thought better of it. His face purple, he retreated to the door then turned on Meiring. "You too Meiring, You are next . . . you bastards!" He teetered on his feet, but turned around and fumbled for the door lever. Meiring leaned around him, grasped the lever, opened the door and, holding Swanepoel by the shirt collar, propelled him through the doorway. The man stumbled several steps, righted himself, and then pushed his way through the men gathered in the hallway, all curious as to the cause of the fracas.

"Back to work," shouted Meiring. "Shows over."

Roux leaned against his desk, heart racing, a throbbing pain invading his temples. He clenched his fists to stop them shaking.

"Marius, I don't want to alarm you, but you need to be careful."

This is all he needed. "How dangerous is he?"

"Very," said Meiring. "I can get some of my . . . uh . . . friends, to keep an eye on you, and the family if you'd like?"

After a moment's hesitation, and several deep breaths, he shook his head. "Thanks, but I'm sure I'll be OK."

"Wasn't you I was thinking of," replied Meiring, "but if you worried, let me know."

Roux's phone interrupted them.

"And how is the boss of SB today?" said Phil Roberts.

Roux's face cracked into a smile as he sucked in large gulps of air. "Hey there, how are you doing? Sorry Saturday turned into a bit of a disaster, but you should know my old man by now."

"Mel gave him some lip. Good for her." Roberts laughed. "The general's face was a cracker. Any chance of having a few beers this evening?" Roberts continued in English.

Roux hesitated. With the briefing at six, and the deployment of the teams for their first night, sitting in a bar did not seem appropriate, but then, what the hell? There was not much for him to add to the operation for now, so a few beers and a good night's rest might be good for him.

"Sure. When and where?"

Roberts gave him the name of a bar on the city waterfront and they agreed on six o'clock.

"Old 'varisty buddy of mine," he said to Meiring as he replaced the phone. "Regular army. Recces."

Meiring grinned, "Good friends to have." He checked his watch. "I need to organize a reliable vehicle for Ndlovu's guys, which is not already used in Langa. Oh! For your info, I'm going to join him tonight. Try to get a firsthand look at this house, and our Mister Tau, if I can spot him."

"Assuming you can recognize him," said Roux.

Meiring laughed and stuck his hands behind his ears, pushing them forward. "The ears man, look for the ears," he said. "I'll let you know if there are any dramatic developments." He stared at Roux for an instant, his eyes earnest. "Marius, try to get some rest this evening. You need to put Swanepoel out of your mind or he's going to cloud your judgment. We're all tired as it is. Worrying about what he said, or might do, will not help." He gave Roux one last worried look and left.

ROUX SAT AT HIS desk, staring at the wall map, mauling the inside of his cheek. Despite his attempts at bravado, Swanepoel's vicious verbal attack had left him shaken and concerned. His only consolation was the man was on sick leave and then off to CID. *With a bit of luck, I never see the animal again.*

He rose and ambled over to the win"ow, 'eering out at the park below. The square and the surrounding streets were emptying as the day surrendered to evening. The familiar sounds of traffic rose from below, the all too familiar noise of cars, trucks, and buses battling their way through the rush hour gridlock. He watched the late leavers scurry along the sidewalks, looking relieved to be heading home. Watching them, he let out a humorless chuckle. If only they knew how their ordinary, comfortable lives were about to be forever changed. His eyes drifted to the plethora of posters plastered on lampposts and propped against trees, each a testament to the varying media responses to SONA. The liberal press expressing enthusiastic praise for the government's bold initiatives, while the more cautious Afrikaans media called for clarity and a measured approach to the upcoming negotiations.

He returned to his desk and sat down, his thoughts drifting back to Tau. What if he found the courier before SB? Was he planning to kill him once he'd extracted the contents of the message? Was the courier his only objective, or was there a more sinister motive for the unannounced arrival? Targeting Mandela? But he agreed with du Plessis. Any attempt to derail the negotiations or interfere with Mandela's release would be tantamount to giving the world the middle finger. The PAC would never recover. But then, if Mandela was killed, and de Klerk could prove to the world his security apparatus was not responsible, the backlash would be catastrophic for all the terrorist movements. Mandela getting killed by his own people would just prove Blacks were untrustworthy. Not hesitating to turn on anyone, even their own leaders. Maybe then the world would come to its senses and allow South Africa to pursue separate development. He stopped. Is that what he was hoping for? A dead Mandela? He pushed the thought away. His heart"told'him all this change was wrong. Whites and Blacks could never live together in harmony. But a small voice in his head, ignoring his attempts to banish it, kept prompting the same question. Was he such a fool as to believe apartheid could survive? He picked up his jacket, locked his office door behind him, and headed for the basement parking area.

He arrived just before six to find Roberts already seated at the bar, which, with the attached restaurant, was a popular spot for locals, and the occasional international tourist or business executive. It was brightly lit and, for the moment, smoke free. After shaking hands, Roberts indicated a vacant table in a corner before ordering two beers. They exchanged pleasantries for several minutes until their drinks arrived.

"So. You no longer doing ops?"

Roberts' smile showed little pleasure. "Nah! Brass reckoned I'm getting too old, so they moved me to operations. Not too bad, I suppose. I get to plan the ops and monitor the progress." He paused, looking wistfully out a window. "Better than nothing, I suppose. At least I'm in on the action, even if from a distance. But enough about me. How you handling the move back to SB? Mel can't be impressed."

"She's not, but the move is temporary until they find the right man but my sources,"—he meant Gerda—"tell me it'll be permanent, not that I'm complaining. Damned admin job was driving me up the bloody wall. Mel won't like it, but if I can keep weekends free for the family, we should be able to make it work."

"Don't know how you handled four years behind a desk. Would drive me nuts," said Roberts. He leaned in closer to Roux and lowered his voice. "I hear you guys had some action the other night?"

Roux took a long pull on his beer, exhaling loudly. "What have you heard?"

"There was a NIS guy at our morning briefing," said Roberts, "and mentioned there was a manhunt on for a guy he called the courier, which was taking priority over all other SB operations. I also heard you'd done a raid in Nyanga last week. Wondered if they were linked."

"They are."

Roberts sat watching him, an expression on his face which said, "Tell me more."

Roux wondered just how much he should share. But he'd known Phil almost all of his adult life and there wasn't another man alive he trusted more. Besides, if you can't trust the Recces, who can you trust? Keeping his voice low, he gave his friend an outline of who the courier was.

"We picked up their location last Wednesday and hit them the same night. He had two armed terrs with him and we killed one, but the old bugger escaped."

"You've no idea where he is at the moment?"

"Nope, but we'll keep scouring the townships 'til we get him. Won't be long," said Roux, taking a long drink and smacking his lips. "But something a bit more worrying has cropped up."

Roberts, drink in hand, raised an eyebrow. "What?"

"You know the name Che Tau, APLA killer?"

Roberts' face went serious. "Is he here?"

Roux stared down at his beer glass, sliding it around the tabletop. "He is, with three other guys. Arrived on Saturday and from what our informants tell us, they looking for the courier. Weird thing is they making no attempt to hide their presence, and bugger all we can do about them since the unbanning."

Roberts studied Roux for several moments. "You reckon the courier is the only reason they are here? The PAC is anti any form of negotiations, and Tau is a snake. He could be up to anything."

"Du Plessis concurs."

"I'd say you have a problem, old boy."

Roux sighed, shaking his head. "I don't know why they just don't leave Mandela in Verster until we know more. Simple solution to me." Roux finished his drink and raised a hand to attract a waiter. "One more then I must be off.

I'm expecting some feedback later tonight from the guys watching Tau. So, who's the current lady in your life?"

Roberts laughed. "Air hostess by the name of Linda, but just a fling. Nothing serious, thank goodness."

Their drinks arrived, and this time Roux paid. "Ah, just a passing shadow in the night," he said, trying to sound mysterious. "Sounds like our MBL crowd."

His friend stiffened in his chair. "Who?"

"Nothing serious. Just some gangster crowd in Mitchell's Plain mouthing off about Mandela being a White man's puppet and needs stopping. Led by some loud-mouth called Khumalo, who claims they are anti-negotiations, but we don't think there's much more than hot air there."

Roberts' eyes shifted away. "Plenty of that in the locations, I would imagine."

He sipped his beer for a moment and then suddenly glanced at his watch. "Crap. Didn't realize the time." He stood up, extending his hand. "Sorry to run, but I've just remembered I need to get some guys organized at the barracks—work thing, you know."

Roux couldn't hide his surprise. "Oh, OK, no problem. I should head off home, anyway."

They shook hands and Roberts left without looking back. Roux watched him through the bar window, thoughtful.

# Tuesday, February 6th, 1990

HE PARKED UNDERGROUND AT Compton, clambered out, jacket and briefcase in hand, and slammed the car door behind him. Feeling out of sorts after another sleepless night, he marched to the elevator door, ignoring the cheerful greeting of a passerby.

"Come on, come on," he growled, banging his finger against the button, trying to will the solid silver door to open. He was going to be late for his morning session with Uys. "Great way to start our first day," he growled.

Although late, Uys, waiting in Roux's office, either didn't notice or didn't care. He was browsing through one of the many morning news editions.

"Morning Cornelius. How was your first night?"

Uys folded the paper and tossed it onto the desk. "Quiet. We got all the teams deployed by eight with no serious problems. The kid of yours, Els, came through with everything he promised. I'm quite impressed with the little bugger. Any chance I can take him back with me?" he said with a hint of a smile.

Roux chuckled. "No chance Major. He stays here where I can keep a fatherly eye on him." He hung up his jacket, loosened his necktie, and sat at his desk as Meiring ambled in. "Morning, Eugene."

"Morning," grunted Uys. "Did you get any sleep last night? You said you were going out with the men."

"I did, much to the relief of my wife."

"Good," said Roux. "So. What can you tell me after your midnight sojourn? Any news on our mysterious courier, and what's happening with APLA?"

Meiring exhaled with some force, collapsing into a chair. "Nothing on the courier as yet. I spent some time with Ndlovu at the house, but not a lot happening. Some people in and out, male and female, many dressed in bad rip-offs of green combat fatigues, caps and boots. I got a call from Ndlovu ten minutes ago," he said, looking bemused. "A guy brought them coffee and toast at about five. So much for clandestine observations. The only thing of interest is he reported that around two this morning a panel van arrived and offloaded a bunch of boxes, and what appeared to be four very large, army style duffel bags. Took two guys to carry one."

Roux was making brief notes as Meiring spoke. He looked up. "Could be weapons. Do we know if Tau is there?"

Meiring threw up his hands. "Not a hundred percent sure. I was there for about two hours and thought I saw him, but the light was crappy, so can't be sure. Du Plessis said to pick him up to find out why he's here, but on what pretext do we go barging in there to grab him?"

Uys slapped the desk with an open hand. "Bloody hell! Last week we could have just grabbed the lot of them. No reasons given. Now we need a reason, a legal one, to do our job. Can you believe it? What's this bloody world coming to?"

"Couldn't agree more," said Roux, tugging at his mustache, "but Eugene is right. Add the commissioner's instructions to avoid unnecessary confrontation, and we have ourselves a headache. We need to get creative here."

"Anything from the other teams?" Meiring said.

Uys shook his head.

"I was giving this whole mess some thought last night, and I'm not convinced we are handling this the right way," said Roux.

"What do you mean?" said Meiring. Both he and Uys leaned forward in their chairs.

"From what we know, the courier appears to offer no threat, and I can't believe he is here to tell Mandela to withdraw from the negotiations," said Roux. "The ANC in Zambia would have already denounced the talks, but there's been nothing, which implies their approval. We know Tau is looking for the courier, but is he planning something else? The boxes and bags may suggest he is, but until he makes an illegal move, we've got nothing. All we can do is sit with our thumbs up our arses and watch."

"So what do we do?" said Meiring. "We can't just ignore what we know, and *assume* all will go well."

"Agreed. But we need time. Time we don't have, Eugene. Despite what du Plessis thinks, I'm still not convinced there is any sinister plot out there to disrupt the release or harm Mandela. Everyone who is vocalizing their opposition to the release is just too obvious about it."

Meiring gave Roux a quizzical look. "The ones we know about, anyway. You still pushing for a delay in the release date?"

"I need to persuade du Plessis to postpone the release until we can assert with ninety-nine percent certainty there are no threats or we have identified a potential threat and removed it. Mandela needs to stay where he is until then."

Uys shook his head. "Marius, forget it. Not going to happen. Can you imagine, one day the president announces the release, and the next he says, oops, sorry, he needs to stay where he is because we *think* there is a threat to his release? No way will the government allow that. Besides, we'll have riots across the country. Personally, I think we need to come up with a plan, now, to get Tau and his gang off the streets, and find this courier, in that order."

Roux slumped back in his chair, his shoulders sagged. He knew deep down Uys was right. The president was in too deep to retract his promise now. It was so frustrating. "So how do we deal with Tau?"

"We kick in the front door to the house," said Uys, "and round up everyone, and detain them under the Emergency Powers on the basis Tau is wanted in connection with crimes committed in Soweto, and hold them until Mandela is free and tucked up with his ANC buddies."

"You have a point there, Cornelius," said Roux. "Eugene, can you call your mates in SB Joburg and check if there is sufficient evidence to make an arrest? I assume du Plessis has told them he's here."

"Will do," said Meiring, heading for the door.

Roux stood up and walked to the map, chewing on his inner lip, running thumb and forefinger across his mustache. "Ndlovu and his team are compromised. Coffee and toast. Shit! How embarrassing." He strolled back to his desk, sat down and swiveled his chair to stare out the window, and then turned to face Uys.

"Assuming there's insufficient evidence to arrest him, we'll need to force Tau's hand. Make him play his cards, and react in a way which gives us reasonable cause to nail him. What if we do this differently?"

"How different?" said Uys, his eyebrows arching.

"Maybe we need to do things in the spirit of de Klerk's desire for negotiated change."

The major snorted.

"Instead of doing what we know best, bashing down doors and hurling people into the back of our vans, we knock on the door and ask to see Mr. Tau."

Uys smiled. "Ooh, I like this one," he said.

"I thought you might, but let's test my theory," said Roux, leaning forward, placing his elbows on the desk. "First thing we need to do is swap out Ndlovu and his team with two of your guys. They're new in the area, so less prone to be identified. Ndlovu can go back to looking for the courier."

"Second, you and Eugene go to the house as soon as your guys are in place and ask to see Mr. Tau. Whether we talk to the other three is irrelevant at this stage. It's Tau we need to interrogate."

"OK, so we introduce ourselves and say what?"

"We invite him for tea, here, in the spirit of negotiation and change, courtesy of President de Klerk. No arrest, no snatch, just an amicable request to have a chat since we noted his arrival from Joburg."

"And if he refuses?"

"Somehow, I don't think he will. From all accounts, he's an arrogant bastard. What better way to give us the middle finger than to do it in SB headquarters? It'll also improve his standing with the party. But if he refuses, we will know what he looks like, and makes a snatch easier if we have to. Your only problem is you will need to make sure it's Tau you meet, not some stand in."

Uys sat back in his chair, a broad smile inching its way across his face. "You're hoping with a soft-handed approach it may throw him, disarm him. He could lose face if he refuses?"

"My hope, Cornelius. My guess is they expecting a raid which is borne out by their blatant display of militancy but making sure they don't cross the line. They want us to be our usual aggressive selves, and if we oblige, you can bet the press will be there to film it."

"What if he says he wants to meet at their house?"

"Politely decline. Too many people, not private. Highlight the fact it may damage their image if the people in Langa see them entertaining the police of the hated regime. No. it's critical he comes here of his own accord. Give him some bullshit about a very senior member of the police who wants to meet him.

"And he gets here and there's no one to meet him but us?"

"We'll deal with that when he gets here," Roux said, looking at Uys enquiringly.

The man chuckled. "OK, worth a try."

Their discussion was interrupted by the return of Meiring. "OK," he said, sitting down. "Appears all Joburg have is hearsay and rumors, nothing concrete. Their opinion, given the current political climate, is to avoid a confrontation which could embarrass us."

"I was afraid it may be the case," said Roux. "Cornelius, and I have been exploring an alternative." He explained their idea to Meiring.

"Great! At least we doing something, not just being reactive. I'm in," responded an enthusiastic Meiring.

Uys slapped Meiring on the shoulder. "Let's get the two teams swapped out and be on our way to Langa."

Roux stood as the two men left. His heart was racing. Was he overplaying his hand? But he had committed himself now, so all he could do was wait and see if it all went as he hoped. Gnawing at the inside of his mouth, he wondered how Uys would get on at the APLA house, considering his aggressive approach. It was anyone's guess how Tau would react. But maybe a senior SB officer requesting a meeting, as opposed to the usual door splintering entry the township residents were more accustomed to, would have the desired effect of convincing Tau there was no threat to his person.

He tried to focus on the pile of documents in his in-tray, hoping to kill time, but it was not helping. Gerda's arrival clasping something resembling a sandwich on a plate made him realize he was hungry.

"Lunch time already?" he said, relieved at the interruption.

Gerda put the plate on his desk. He studied the dry, curling bread with suspicion. There appeared to be two slices, but he was at a loss what lurked between them.

"Ham and tomato," she said, "you owe me seven rand."

"You paid seven rand for this?" he mocked. "You got ripped off, but thanks. Draw it from the office petty cash account."

"Sure," she said disbelieving, and marched out.

Roux tossed the mess into the trash bin.

"Bravo, this is Uniform one, do you read?"

Roux grabbed the radio handset, almost dropping it in his haste. "Go ahead Uniform One."

"Tango will see us at three."

"Thank you. How was the reception at the house? Over."

A long moment of silence.

"Arrogant." replied Uys, sounding annoyed.

Roux closed his eyes and offered up a silent prayer of thanks.

He thumbed the transmit button. "I'll meet you back here. Out."

Replacing the handset, he wondered how du Plessis was going to react to this somewhat unorthodox approach. Well, time will tell.


UYS, HIS FACE A dark red with beads of perspiration on his forehead and upper lip, barged into his office, followed by Meiring.

"How did it go?"

"Bloody bastard!" said Uys, throwing his jacket over the back of a chair. "Next time I see the arsehole, I'll rip his balls off."

Behind Uys, Meiring winked at Roux, the corners of his mouth turned up.

"Not go well then?" said Roux, frowning.

"Black bastard," said Uys. He ran a hand through his hair. "I know what I'd like to do with the cocky bastard, and it won't involve talking. Shit Marius, I don't see how you think you're going to get him to tell you anything about why he's here. He needs a few serious *klaps* round the head to get him talking."

"Slapping him around is what he expects us to do, Cornelius. I hope to rattle his confidence by not doing what he expects. From the little info we have on this guy, my suspicion is he won't be able to resist the opportunity to belittle and needle us. In fact, I'm counting on it. The more he mouths off, the more he's likely to share. We just need to ask the right questions. Perhaps borrow a page from the Brit police, eh! Be gentlemen."

He looked at Meiring. "How certain can you be it was Tau you were talking to?"

"When I asked him, he laughed and showed me his PAC membership card. I was hoping it might reveal his real name, but no, just Tau. Add the scar, and those bat-ears, and I'm satisfied it was him," said Meiring, "Although he looks a lot older than we thought. He's arrogant, but there's more to it than that. We don't scare him."

Uys gave Roux a concerned look. "Does General du Plessis know what you are planning?"

"No, he doesn't, and I would appreciate it if we could keep it that way until I've met Tau. We'll know soon enough if I'm on the right track, but I'll update him after I meet with Tau, and let's hope with something of interest to tell him."

"OK, fine with me," said Uys. "Let's hear what the bugger has to say. You need me at the meeting?"

Roux shook his head. "You were the senior representative. Now he can deal with the plebs. It will confuse him if he's expecting the commissioner or head of Security Branch. The more we can disorientate him, the better. I also don't think it would be appropriate to have you castrating the man when he arrives."

"He might just get up and walk out," retorted Uys.

"He might," Roux replied, "but I don't think so. If APLA is planning to disrupt the release, he will suspect we know something, hence our approach. He'll want to know what we know. Where we meeting him?" he said to Meiring.

"Training room three on the ground floor. It's small. Both Els and Gainsford will be close to hand. No microphones or cameras in the room, but I'll be wearing a mic so Ndlovu can listen in and translate later if need be."

"Excellent," said Roux. He stood up and extended a hand to Uys. "Thanks for your support."

Uys appeared undecided for a moment, then nodded, shook hands, and left.

"Looks like it's you and me, Eugene. Let's talk through how we approach this man."

On the assumption Tau would be late, just to prove a point, the two men remained in Roux's office until Sergeant Ndlovu radioed from the car park to announce Tau's arrival.

Roux reached for the radio. "Thanks Sergeant, give us five minutes to get to Training room three and then bring him in. Anyone with him?"

"Just one other."

All the furniture except a rectangular metal table and three chairs had been removed. Roux and Meiring occupied the two chairs facing the door. Minutes later, there was a single knock, and Ndlovu opened the door. He waved a hand at the two men standing behind him.

Che Tau, or whatever his real name was, slowly entered the room. He was not what Roux expected. Slightly shorter than him, he was dressed in a green military style shirt and khaki trousers with large pockets on both legs, and black, well-worn boots. His clothes snug on a lean frame. Long hair and a thick, wiry beard which reminded Roux of a steel wool pad covered the lower half of his leathery face, but it did little to hide the wide, rough edged scar that went from beneath his left eye down to his chin. Roux placed his age as mid forties.

Tau stood for several moments in the doorway. His alert eyes surveyed the room, taking in the furniture, the ceiling, hovering at the corners.

Roux stood. "You can relax, Mr. Tau. There are no hidden microphones or cameras, but you are more than welcome to look under the table and chairs if you're worried. This is a meeting, not an interrogation. You are free to leave whenever it suits you." He wiped his clammy right hand on the seat of his trousers, and extended it toward Tau. "I am Colonel Marius Roux of Security Branch. I think you have already met Captain Meiring." He could feel a trickle of sweat inching its way down his spine, and more gathering under his armpits, thankful for his jacket.

Tau ignored the hand and motioned to his companion. A tall, broad-shouldered man entered the room, dressed in similar attire but with a Fidel cap, closed the door behind him, and stood, arms folded across his chest, blocking the entrance.

Roux gestured to the remaining chair as he sat down. "Please, take a seat."

Tau took his time. He sat down, rocking back in the chair. "So, *boer*, what do you want to talk about?"

Roux disregarded the insult—the word meant *farmer* in Afrikaans, but had taken on a derogatory meaning amongst the terrorist groups. Settler, in the PAC slogan 'One Settler, one Bullet,' often replaced with the word '*boer*.' He leaned forward, making eye-contact with the one time adversary.

"Perhaps we could start by you revealing a bit about yourself, such as your real name, background, that sort of thing. You know we have been keen to have a chat with you for the last few years, but you've been a difficult man to find."

Tau gave a derisive snort. "You couldn't find me because you have no influence in the townships. The people hate you, and your informants really work for us."

Roux had to admit the man was probably right.

"My name is not important. The reason for this meeting is." The voice was gruff, the accent pronounced.

*This is going to be like pulling teeth*, Roux thought.

"OK, then let's get to the point. Why are you here in Cape Town? It's not your area of operations? This is ANC and UDF territory. The PAC holds no sway here. I would imagine the ANC are asking the same question, considering the in-fighting between you two. So what brings you here?" He sat back and waited for a moment, but Tau stared back at him, the lips pursed.

"We heard the minute you arrived. So, maybe our informants are not so loyal to you after all." He hoped his comment would make life difficult for any informants who were playing both sides of the fence. "We've been watching you people since you arrived, but then you know that, and by the way, thank you for the coffee and toast you offered my men. Very thoughtful of you." Roux allowed a smile to cross his face.

Tau stopped rocking his chair, looking a little uneasy. "Where is the senior *boer,* the commissioner, or at least du Plessis? Why just a small man like you?"

Roux suppressed his surprise at the use of the general's name. "It will please General du Plessis to know you are aware of his senior position, but both gentlemen are otherwise engaged. This *small man* is head of Security Branch in Cape Town, which means I'm responsible for what goes on here, and a known terrorist in my jurisdiction interests me, even if your organization is now unbanned. I have to wonder if your visit was planned to coincide with Mandela's release, or are you here just to visit the tourist attractions?" He waited for a response. When none came, he pressed on.

"Let me be frank, Mr. Tau. There is talk in the townships of plans to disrupt Mandela's release, and they seemed to have started after your arrival," he lied. "We've seen the bags and boxes delivered to the house in the middle of the night, and we know you are looking for an ANC man who you claim is here from Lusaka. Do the ANC know you are looking for one of their people? I'm happy to let them know."

Tau's smile did not reach his eyes, but realizing it was on the wrong face, slipped away in a hurry. But the momentary glint of concern in the eyes at the mention of the courier had not gone unnoticed.

"Mr. Mandela has been in prison for a long time. We are here to celebrate with the people. What is in the bags is for the people," said Tau, then paused. "We are not looking for anyone, so there is nothing to tell the ANC."

"I'll decide if we need to," said Roux, trying to sound amicable, but could feel his anger rising. "The PAC has made its position on negotiations very clear, so why is APLA celebrating his release? If there are negotiations which lead to an election, you will not get much support. The PAC, and especially you guys in APLA, are not a threat, just an inconvenience. You talk big, but you do little."

Roux knew he was goading the man, but he needed a reaction, a violent reaction, a threat, something to explain why he was in Cape Town.

"By the way, do the PAC leadership know you here celebrating Mandela, or you acting on your own? One of the senior men in our National Intelligence Service, you know, the NIS, will meet with them to ask what they know about your visit."

Tau stood up, his dark eyes flared. "I don't need the leadership's approval," but Roux noted the nervousness in his voice. *He's gone maverick. That makes it easier for us.*

"The ANC may want to talk with the oppressor, like the cowards they are, but APLA knows you *boere* understand only one thing. The bullet." His tone was bitter. "The fight is not over. We don't negotiate, we take."

Roux forced himself to remain calm, keeping his clenched fists below the table. He glanced furtively at Meiring, who appeared unfazed. He stood up, fighting to keep his face and voice devoid of emotion.

"And you need to understand, Tau, the Emergency Powers are still in force, which means you are not beyond my reach. If I suspect in any way you are plotting terrorism acts or are a threat to Mandela, you will watch his release from inside a prison cell. You people are a joke. If you think parading around Langa in children's uniforms is going to impress us, you are mistaken."

Che Tau spat on the floor. Turned around and walked out, his brute right on his heels.

"That went well," said Meiring with a humorless chuckle. "Didn't tell us anything, but he remains my first choice as the problem."

"I agree, but now he knows we are going to be watching his every move, but what was of interest was how he referred to APLA only, not the PAC. I think he's here without the leadership's approval. Time to update du Plessis. Let's do it in my office with Cornelius there." He gestured towards a wet spot on the floor. "Better get that cleaned up."

Fifteen minutes later, du Plessis walked into Roux's office, swinging his glasses around in circles with one hand. Roux took all of five minutes to update him.

The general gave him a surprised look and then turned to the other two men. "What do you two think of this approach?"

"Worth the effort, even if he revealed little, other than he's operating without party approval. But he's dangerous. I would look for a reason, any reason, to pick him up," said Uys without hesitation.

Du Plessis looked at Roux with what some would consider a smile, but with him, you could never be sure. "Ballsy Colonel. But I like it. As you said, he now knows we are on to him, so he'll need to be careful about what he does and says. If we can keep him under surveillance as long as he's here, it'll make it difficult for him to do anything other than watch the release on TV."

Roux thrust his hands into his trouser pockets. "General," he said, "The MBL are too vocal about their opposition, and just too obvious, so I don't see them as a threat to the release. Tau seems more interested in finding the courier, and I'm not sure how much damage four men could do to stop the release. They won't get much help from the local communities either. However, if there is a plan to disrupt the release, APLA is the primary risk. But if he is planning anything, he knows we are watching them, which may cause him to do something rash, or more likely, pack up and go back to Joburg."

Du Plessis nodded slowly. "So, you don't think there is any real threat? Interesting." His gaze shifted to Uys. "Your thoughts?"

Uys waited for several seconds before speaking. "General, to be honest, I have no idea. But if there is a threat, Tau is my choice."

"Thanks. Captain?"

Meiring shifted from one foot to the other, looking down at his hands, and then up at du Plessis. "My gut instinct tells me there is more going on than just looking for the courier. My sources are acting weird. There is something in the wind." He glanced at Roux, who gave him a disapproving look. "But I can't prove it at the moment. We need time, as the Colonel has already alluded to."

"Time we don't have, gentlemen. OK Colonel, it's your op. What's next?"

"We increase our surveillance. He doesn't know when we will release Mandela. So, if he is planning something, he will need to prepare to move at short notice when it's announced, and get people and weapons in place now. Either at the entrance to the prison or wherever Mandela is likely to go after his release. Those preparations are what we need to see. It will provide sufficient cause to detain him."

"Agreed. Use as many men as you need, even if it means reducing our other activities," said du Plessis. "They will allow Mandela to make a speech somewhere, but at the moment, I'm not sure where. Could be a stadium in one of the townships, but I should know within the next few days. In the meantime, we'll be meeting several local ANC representatives to discuss what happens on the day of Mandela's release. The area around the prison is going to be mobbed, so we need to be ready to spot any potential sources of trouble, but it's Warmer's concern, not yours. I'll let you know if anything of interest comes out of it." He chewed on the end of the stem of his glasses for a moment. "I'll chase up Greyling about meeting with the PAC leadership."

"It would be a great help," said Roux. "If he's acting under orders, it may place the leadership in the spotlight, which I'm sure they'll want to avoid. If he's gone maverick, they may rein him in. One last thing. If Tau moves, we will need to strike and pull him in. I may not have time to clear it with you."

"Do what you think is necessary. Any news on the courier?"

Roux shook his head.

Du Plessis said nothing, but turned to Uys. "I think you need to return to PE. You may have your hands full there when the release happens, but leave your men here reporting directly to Roux. Thanks for the prompt reaction and your help." He turned without another word and left the office.

"Huh!" said Uys. "I was looking forward to catching Tau doing something and busting his head, but he's right. Anything could happen when Mandela goes free. But bit late to leave now so will hit the road early tomorrow. Right now I'm going for a shower and a few stiff brandies with some mates." He stuck out a beefy hand. "Its been a pleasure Marius. I hope all goes well. Eugene has a list of all my guys. Sergeant Dick is the senior man, and he's trustworthy and reliable." He gave Meiring a playful punch on the shoulder on his way out.

Roux turned to face Meiring, annoyance in his voice. "So, you believe there is more going on than we are aware of? Where did that come from, *Captain?* If you are having doubts or concerns about the way I'm handling this, please raise them with me before sharing them with people like du Plessis."

Meiring glared back. "Colonel, if you had taken the time to ask for my opinion, you would have heard it before du Plessis asked. If I'm asked for my opinion, I would like to think I have your support in voicing it. If we're to find out what is going on, then every opinion, thought or suspicion needs to be vented and explored. Surely?"

Roux sighed, his initial anger at what he considered a betrayal by Meiring, evaporated. "Sorry Eugene, you're right, but some prior warning next time?"

"Will do."

But Roux wondered, for a moment, if he still had Meiring's support.

An uncomfortable silence hung between the two men. Roux cleared his throat.

"OK. Back to business, I suppose. By the way, this Sergeant Dick? Is he White?"

"No," laughed Meiring, "Colored, but he's a good guy. Him and Ndlovu have hit it off, which helps."

"Poor man, with a name like that," said Roux.

Minutes later Meiring departed, leaving Roux to go over the day's events. His phone rang, interrupting his thought pattern.

"It's your father," said Gerda.

He closed his eyes. *What does he want now?*

"Thanks, put him through."

"Hello Pa. How are you?"

His father ignored the salutation. "Son, there is someone important I need you to meet."

"Pa, I'm really busy at the moment. Can't it wait 'til the weekend?"

"No," came the harsh reply. "Have you got a pen and paper?"

Roux scratched around on his desk. "Yes."

His father rattled off an address. "It's the house of Felix Fouché, and I'm sure even you know who he is. He needs some help, and I told him you will provide it. Don't let me down. Be there at six sharp." His father cut the call.

"I'm fine Marius, how are you, and the family?" said Roux into the dead phone.

"Great Pa, Mel and Rian are doing well."

He slammed the receiver down. *Bastard! He talks to me like I'm one of his constables, not his son. Maybe I should just ignore him and go home.* But instead he buzzed Gerda, asking her to let Mel know he would be late.


DRIVING THROUGH WHAT CAPETONIANS referred to as their equivalent of a "Millionaires mile" on the lower slopes of Table Mountain was breathtaking. The two and three story mansions, set in grounds which the farming community would call smallholdings, were an eyeopener. After having to ask for directions several times, he at last pulled up in front of two huge, ornate steel gates, with the Fouché family crescent brazenly displayed in intricate detail in the steelwork.

As he came to a stop, a security guard appeared from a guardhouse and walked up to the juncture of the two gates. "Evening sir, can I help you?" he shouted.

"Colonel Roux. Police. Here to see Mr. Fouché," Roux shouted back.

The guard immediately pushed a button on the fob hanging from his belt, and the gates swung open. As he pulled level with the guard, he was told to follow the road up to the front of the house where he would be met. He drove slowly, marveling at the manicured lawns and mind numbing masses of flowers in every color imaginable.

When he first saw the house, he was surprised at its size. Built in the old Cape Dutch style, with its whitewashed walls, thatched roof, large wooden sash cottage panes with external wood shutters, and Dormer windows on the second floor, it was dwarfed by its neighbors. *Big money, small house. Odd.* After pulling up in front of a magnificent front door and alighting from his car, he was approached by a man dressed in what he could only describe as an English butler's uniform.

The man inclined his head and said, "Colonel, welcome. Mr. Fouché is waiting for you in his study. Please follow me." Despite his senior years, the man took off at a pace Roux struggled to keep up with. After walking through several rooms, with paneled walls and stuffed full of exquisite antique furniture and ornaments, and light fittings he could only imagine dated back to the early 19th century, they came to a stop outside a closed door. The butler, as Roux now thought of him, knocked once.

"Come," came a voice from inside. The butler opened the door, motioning for Roux to enter.

The study struck Roux as English in both style and furnishings, even a fireplace. With one exception: there was no large book case or collection of reading matter, which surprised him. He assumed a man who had achieved so much would be an avid reader. The late afternoon sun was still bright in the sky, but the room was in almost total darkness, with heavy drapes pulled to cover the windows. A green banker's lamp was the only item on an otherwise clear, oversize oak desk. It threw a faint shaft of green, almost ghoulish light, across the room, offset by the golden glow from a tall bronze lamp standing in the corner.

Felix Fouché, who Roux knew to be in his mid seventies, rose sprightly from an antique beige and brown Baroque style chair and approached him with an outstretched hand. The full head of silver hair topped a hard face. The discriminating brown eyes looking up at Roux seemed to bore into his soul.

"Marius, may I call you that? It is a pleasure to meet you. Please, sit. Can I offer you a drink?"

Roux noted he spoke in Afrikaans, which surprised him knowing Fouché's home language was English. He also knew the man's recently deceased wife was born in England.

"Mr. Fouché," said Roux. "My honor, sir." For some inexplicable reason, he disliked the man the instant he shook the limp hand. "No, thank you. I'm on call. "

"Understandable. Coffee, tea, a soft drink perhaps?"

Roux shook his head. "Honestly, sir, I'm fine." He found the nearest chair and sat down. "If it is easier for you, I am more than happy to converse in English. My wife is English speaking, so I'm comfortable in either language. "

Fouché returned to his chair, picking up a drink from a side table.

"Felix, please. No need for formalities here, Marius, and Afrikaans is fine. I need the practice." He eyed Roux for a minute. "Your father speaks often, and in glowing terms, about his only son. He has nothing but praise for you and your advancements in the Security Branch. Congratulations on the promotion."

*Not only is he a smarmy character, he's a bullshitter as well*, thought Roux, as he studied the man. "Just a temporary transfer back. No promotion."

"I'm sure it will come."

"How do you know my father, if I may ask?"

Fouché was silent for a moment, then spoke in a businesslike manner. "I needed several security audits done on some of my companies, the mines in particular. An associate recommended your father. I was most impressed with his dedication and the quality of his reports, and we have stayed in touch as and when similar needs arose."

"I see." Roux cleared his throat. "My father said it was important I should meet with you, as there was something you may need help with. How can I be of service?"

"Ah, yes. Straight to the point. I like that in a man. Like father, like son." He took a moment to stare down at the drink in his hand, as though fascinated by the clinking of the ice cubes against the glass as he twirled it.

"I, along with some of my, shall we call them, associates, have been watching developments since de Klerk took office with some trepidation. No, don't get me wrong, we all recognize the current system is no longer viable, and change is needed. It will mean the end of sanctions and the opening up of international markets, which will energize our economy. But what is of some concern is the *degree and pace* of change envisaged by the government." He took a sip from his drink and leaned forward in his chair.

Roux was confused. With his reputation and influence, why didn't the man pick up the phone and ask de Klerk himself?

As though reading his mind, Fouché said, "Obviously, I have spoken to friends and colleagues in government and cabinet, even tried to arrange a face-to-face with de Klerk, who begs off because of his tight schedule, but little in the way of meaningful information on what is envisaged is forthcoming. But that is the strategic view. Right now, I am more interested in what is happening on the ground. The mood in the locations. Expectations. Fears. What the terrorists are up to, and of any potential threats to Mr. Mandela's safety. Your father suggested you could enlighten me, being at the rock-face, so to speak. But please, it is a request for general information, nothing secret or confidential. It's not my intention to jeopardize the work of the security forces or to compromise your position in the force. But it would be of great help to us."

*Who is the "us"* wondered Roux. What he felt like doing was ramming the man's patronizing attitude down his throat, followed by a roll of razor wire.

"Sir, with all due respect, with the contacts both you and my father have, anything I may share with you would be of little value, and old news. I do not make the decisions, just follow orders from Pretoria."

Fouché's smile faded. "I've already explained myself. The country is in a state of flux, with little clear direction being given at the moment. Many people, even in high places both within government and business, are in . . . a state of shock? The president's announcements were far-reaching, to say the least. It has made people nervous at voicing opinions or sharing what they feel may incriminate them." He took another sip of his drink and placed it on the table beside him.

"Son, relax. I am not asking for state secrets, just an occasional update on what is going on in the locations. I'm sure you can appreciate our interest in the country's future."

Roux contemplated refusing to say anything and leave, if only to embarrass his father, but then thought better of it. Fouché was a powerful man, and his "associates" probably included the likes of the Minister of Police and the commissioner, so pissing him off may not be such a good idea.

He repeated Meiring's assessment of the mood in the townships, but said nothing about APLA. There was nothing of real importance in Meiring's information. All you had to do was ask the first Black or Colored you met on the streets of Cape Town and you would get the feedback you needed.

Fouché listened intently, sitting back in his chair. "Thank you. Most informative. Just the feedback I need." He paused, looking off into the distance, before his penetrating eyes locked with Roux's. "And any developments on locating this mysterious messenger from Lusaka?"

Roux shifted uncomfortably in his chair. Du Plessis would remove an important part of his anatomy if it came out he'd been sharing information on the courier with a civilian, even if that civilian was Fouché.

"Sir, unfortunately, that is information I cannot give you. It is confidential and part of an operation currently underway. Maybe the commissioner or General du Plessis could help you?"

"I see," said Fouché, a momentary look of annoyance on his face. "And Mandela? When do you expect he will be released?"

Ah! Now we get the real reason. It also explained his father's call last week. Roux's first reaction was to tell the man to take a long walk off a short plank, but again, he hesitated. Would it be so risky to keep Fouché in the picture? Maybe he could bring a halt to the whole negotiations nonsense? But then he thought of du Plessis' reaction if he found out. Was there a way to play the middle ground?

"Mr. Fouché," he said, "I'm more than happy to provide you with what information I can regarding the mood in the townships, and flare-ups which may occur when Mandela is released, but as to the details about his release, I'm afraid I am as much in the dark as you are. In fact, not even my boss knows when the release will be." Which was true.

Fouché stared at him for several seconds, and from the expression on the man's face, Roux's response had not met his expectations. "Unfortunate. Never mind. But thank you for sharing what you have. Any insight you can provide us over the coming weeks will be appreciated, especially about the release and the reaction in the locations." He stood. "Thank you for seeing me at such short notice, Marius, but I am sure you need to get back to your duties. Give my regards to your father. Conrad will show you out."

*There's the "us" again. Who are these people?* But it was obvious the meeting was over, and his host was not too pleased with the outcome. *Pa will not be impressed either. But I have a job and family to protect, so it's the best I can offer.*

The two men shook hands, and Roux was met by the butler as he opened the study door.

"Oh! One last thing, Marius. I don't think it would be a good idea to mention our little chat to du Plessis. It could create an embarrassing situation. For *him*, and we both would hate that to happen. Just a suggestion, no threat intended," he finished offhandedly.

Roux sat in his car for several minutes, reflecting on Fouché's parting comment. From the tone and look on the man's face, it was exactly that, a threat. As he pulled away, his mind tracked back to a question which Fouché had asked. One now waving a red flag in his head. How did he know about the courier?

MEL, SITTING ON THE couch with her legs tucked up beneath her reading, looked up as he came through the kitchen door into the lounge.

"How'd it go?"

"Not sure," he said, dropping into a chair. "Went to see Felix Fouché, would you believe? Pa seemed to think I could help him with a couple of things. You should see those houses up on the hill. Absolutely mind blowing."

"The millionaire?" she replied, astonished. "What could he possibly want from you?"

"Wants me to keep him informed on what's going on in the townships. Mood of the people, any terrorist activity, and also when Mandela is being released."

Her eyes narrowed. "What is your father up to? Why send you to Fouché? Why doesn't he just ask you himself and pass it on to Fouché? Sounds like he's putting you in the firing line by having you acting as a spy for someone."

"I'm not spying for anyone," he snapped back. "All I told him was how the Blacks are reacting to SONA. I don't know when Mandela is going to be released. Not even du Plessis knows, and I told Fouché that. Also told him I can't share any classified information, so I'm not betraying anyone, and I'm disappointed you think I would."

She gave a short, derisive laugh. "Marius, when it comes to your father, you will do anything to appease him, so drop the holier-than-thou crap."

*Why was she being like this?*

"You're not being fair, Mel. I told Fouché I can't help him. Sure, he wasn't pleased, and no doubt he'll tell Pa, but tough shit, I'm not their lackey boy."

The lingering look she gave him made it clear she didn't believe him. "Your dinner is in the oven. You'll need to warm it up."

"Thanks." To avoid any further disparaging remarks about his relationship with his father, he changed tact. "How are your boss and your colleagues at the Foundation reacting to the speech?"

"Excited," she said with a smile. "Jonas believes it's a step in the right direction, albeit a little late. But he's cautious. Wants to see how the president moves forward on his promises. How is everyone at Compton taking it?"

"Not well, but I get the impression no one seems to know how to react."

She frowned. "And how do you think they should react?"

"To be honest, I'm not sure myself. Our Blacks and Coloreds are jumpy about where this is all going. What will happen to them if a Black government takes over? Meiring, who's my new right-hand man, seems almost neutral."

"Really? I thought you would at least have an opinion. But I see you still sitting on the fence. Not to worry, but tell me, how will Mandela's release affect you and this temporary transfer?"

His eyes shifted upward to the right. "Um, not much, really. We'll just go on watching what happens in the townships and see how the Blacks react to the release. You know, all the usual stuff."

"I most certainly do," she said, mockery in her tone. "Can you help Jonas?" The sudden change of topic caught Roux unawares.

"Huh? . . . Oh yes, Gerda's trying to find the boy, but he didn't give me much, so going to take a while. I've made a note to check with her in the morning," he lied. He had completely forgotten, but he reasoned there were more pressing priorities than finding some Black guy's kid, but he made a mental note to ask Gerda in the morning.

"Find him and get him released. Jonas is a good man, Marius, and from what he told me, so is the child. Do something right for once in your police career. And without your father's permission."

Ouch! That stung. She really was in a foul mood, and he had no idea why. Although she had agreed to go along with the "temporary" move to SB, something had changed in her. Or was it still his silent resentment of her work at the Foundation?

After university, Roux bowed to his father's incessant pressure to abandon his desire to become a teacher, and follow in his footsteps. Mel was not happy but agreed to a brief career in the police, to satisfy his father, after which he would look for teaching opportunities. They were married soon after he completed training, and Rian's arrival two years later was the pinnacle of their relationship. But it came with devastating consequences. His traumatic entry into the world left Mel unable to bear more children, robbing them of their wish to have at least a football team size family. With the best psychiatric help, her own determination, his devotion to her, and the love and support of her family, she slowly recovered from months of postnatal depression.

Years of happiness in their small, middle-class suburban house in Johannesburg, bought by her parents, followed. Life was good until his father wielded his influence and announced his move to Security Branch. "It's how you get ahead in this force. Look what it did for me," was how he justified it. A brief spell at SB in Johannesburg was followed by years of rural postings. Mel found herself living in old, broken-down police accommodations as they moved from town to town in areas close to the borders of the country. His long work hours, aggravated by attending Officer Training courses to improve his chances of promotion, meant Mel was left alone with Rian for extended periods of time. Rifts appeared in the relationship and widened with the one year posting to South West. But the eventual move to Cape Town had changed everything.

Until she joined the Foundation for Child Welfare. With her degree in child psychology, she started working with Black and Colored children in the townships, particularly those with disabilities. Roux opposed it from the beginning, for sound reasons, in his judgment. Then came the raid based on SB's suspicions the Foundation was harboring ANC cadres entering the Cape Town area. But being UNICEF funded, it was not simply a case of storming the castle and hanging the defenders. SB needed to tread warily, which they did until they believed they were ready to pounce. To the embarrassment of the top brass, a massive night raid produced nothing to incriminate the Foundation. But to Roux's dismay, the TV news on the morning after the raid broadcast the chairman, accompanied by a furious Mel, denouncing the actions of the police and the racist regime. Threats of legal action from UNICEF, and condemnation by the US government, forced SB to back down. But the damage was done. He became ostracized at work, belittled by colleagues and superiors. Over time, the atmosphere at work and home improved as other news occupied the headlines, but Mel remained unapologetic.

She continued before he could respond to her scathing remark.

"So, business as usual? No threats to his safety? Everyone in SB relaxed about the way things are going?"

"There are some folks mouthing off in bars and *shebeens* about being anti the changes, but nothing . . . you know . . . serious. Just bar talk." He gave a nervous giggle. "All normal, no need to worry, I promise you." He swallowed hard.

"Sure, heard that one before, like in South West." She closed her book, dropping it onto the couch beside her, and folding her arms across her chest, staring at him expressionless. Mel had something to say, and was going to say it whether or not he liked it. He cringed, gnawing away at the inside of his cheek.

*What was her problem?*

"Stop that!" She snapped. "You're going to eat yourself from the inside out, besides it's a disgusting habit. And while you're at it, please shave off that ridiculous mustache. It doesn't suit you. Makes you look like every other policeman, stupid. Besides, it feels like I'm kissing a hole in a carpet."

He just stared at her, mouth gaping. She'd never complained before. Why now? He ran his fingers across his upper lip. He couldn't remember a time without his mustache.

"OK, if it'll make you happy," he whispered, then paused for several moments. "What's really the matter, Pet?"

She got up and walked over to the open doors facing onto the patio, staring out across the backyard for several moments before speaking.

"Rian spoke to me this morning. He and his friends have decided they do not want to do their call-up next year. They are going to proclaim themselves conscientious objectors on the grounds they, like me, oppose apartheid." The tone in her low voice was determined. "And I support him."

He stared at her for a moment, speechless, eyes wide. "Mel, are yo-you crazy?" he stammered. "He can't! What the hell does the child think he's doing? He'll go to prison for years. For what? Just to prove a point? Do you know what the inside of those places are like? It would kill him." Rising from his chair, he walked over and stood behind her, placing a hand on her shoulder, gently trying to turn her around.

"Mel, please, think this through, talk some sense into him. He needs to do his bit like all the other White kids. Defend his country. It's his duty. You need to make him understand. He won't make 'varsity, so no deferment, and I can't see them stopping National Service until the government knows how the terrorists will respond to the negotiations. It's just a case of wait and see."

She turned and faced him, with a look he had never seen before. It was filled with loathing.

"That's exactly how I told Rian you would react. What *I'm* thinking of is our son, Rian, remember him? What if he gets killed while we wait for the government to decide? Can you live with it? I certainly can not, and Marius, I won't. He doesn't want to go, and I support him. My dad says he'll hire the best legal team to fight it in court. Delay it for years if need be. Maybe by then Mandela will be in charge and there won't be conscription. But if need be, I'll find some way for him to go overseas to study, or play rugby, or whatever he wants to do."

He knew her parents had the contacts and wherewithal to help her with either option.

She jabbed a finger against his chest. "This is not up for discussion, Marius," she said in a low voice. "He is not going to the army!"

He recoiled. The temper, eyes spitting fire, teeth bared was what he was used to, but this? A calm, but cold and calculating Mel, was something new.

"Mel, no . . . please . . . not this. Listen to me." He tried to reach out, but she knocked his hand away. "There's no more South West. The National Service guys are doing their time in the townships, all low-key stuff. He'll be safe, I promise you."

She snorted. The look on her face was as though she had just tasted something foul. "Marius, your promises are worth shit. Maybe if you people stop killing innocent Blacks and Coloreds, there won't be a need for an army. You've made your opinions on what de Klerk is trying to do very clear, to me, and to your son. We don't agree with you. In fact, the reality is I'm not afraid of how the Blacks will react, but *I am* terrified of how Afrikaners, like you, and the arrogant arsehole you call a father, will react. You hear the news this afternoon? The shootings in Pretoria?"

He shook his head, dumbfounded. "No," he squeaked.

"Some stupid Afrikaans kid shot three Blacks, and injured I don't know how many. Right in the center of Pretoria. Apparently, because they are Black, no other reason, just because of their color." She punched his chest, the pitch in her voice rising with each word. The Mel he recognized. "That's what I'm terrified of, Marius. You

Afrikaners are going to start a civil war because of your narrow-mindedness, your blind faith in an unjust and cruel system, your ridiculous devotion to duty, to your heritage, to . . . to . . ." She waved her arms in the air, and shouted, "to being Afrikaners. Damn you people! You'll end up destroying this country, for everyone. But I won't let you destroy Rian's life just to satisfy your ego. He will not be a part of it. Discussion over." She turned on her heels and stormed out of the lounge. The front door slammed.

He didn't move, unable to grasp what was happening. How could she send his son away? Not now. He needed his family here, supporting him. Didn't she realize what pressure and strain he was under with this whole Mandela business? How could she be so selfish? He walked to the kitchen and yanked open the fridge door, scratched around inside until he found a beer, took it out, hesitated, and reached back in and found two more. Unscrewing the cap off one, he hurled it across the room, and stormed back to the lounge.

No way could his son become a conscientious objector. The country's tiny regular defense force relied on conscription to combat the ever-increasing threat of terrorism, but as the number of young men dying on the borders escalated, the End Conscription Campaign organization, formed in 1983 to support the growing number of conscientious objectors, attempted to challenge conscription. It got itself banned five years later, but it did not stop the growing opposition to the war.

He dropped into his chair and downed the beer in one long swallow, tossing the bottle onto the carpet and uncapping another. A blinding pain stabbed him in the gut. *What the hell is happening to us?*

# *Wednesday, February 7th, 1990*

AN APPARENT POWER FAILURE throughout the city center, and the resultant traffic congestion, did little to help his black mood. A late phone call the previous evening told him Mel and Rian were spending the night at a friend's place, which meant another sleepless night for him. But he did as she asked, removing his mustache. He rubbed at his gritty eyes, sucked at his teeth and blasted the horn several times out of sheer frustration, knowing it would make little difference. His mind wandered back to last night's argument. Mel's concerns about Rian's future echoed his own, although his related more to Blacks swamping the White schools, and lowering the standards of education. Almost all school-leaving White males were eligible for call-up, and in his opinion, a couple of years in the army would make a man of the child, and hopefully wean him off his reliance on his mother. Claiming to be a conscientious objector would have disastrous outcomes for Rian. The only hope for a deferment to his call-up would be attending university, but his mediocre academic results eliminated that option. Would Mel be able to convince him to knuckle down and study? But he was running out of time with only ten months to go until he matriculated.

The morning news on the radio brought him back to the present. It was more of the same, with the shooting in Pretoria being prominent. In addition, Whites wearing military-style clothing had come close to beating a Black petrol attendant to death, while the police, according to eyewitness reports, stood by and watched. Earlier in the day, a group of Black youths assaulted a White couple outside a department store in the country's east, while in some rural town a restaurant owner had opened his facility to all races. The authorities quickly shut him down. What the hell was he thinking? After five minutes of more doom and gloom, he switched it off.

Gerda greeted him with the usual cup of coffee as he threw his briefcase onto the desk and took off his jacket.

"Oh-oh," she said, "bad night?"

He shook his head. "Mel's worried about Rian's call-up next year and terrified by the way us *Afrikaners* are reacting to Mandela's release."

"That surprises me," said Gerda, "I'm more worried about how the Blacks are going to react. My hubby says they are going to go on the rampage and attack us in our homes. He's taken the morning off to go shopping for food and water to stock up in case we can't go out." She stared closely at his face for a moment and then touched her top lip, eyebrow raised.

"Yip! Gone. Appears Mel hated it, which is the first I hear of it. But, anything for happy families." He sat down and peered at her. "Your husband really out shopping for food?"

"He is. Says he's going to get things like batteries and bottled water. Don't mind admitting it, I'm worried Marius, what's going to happen?"

His unshakable assistant was rattled and nervous, but people rushing out to stockpile food and essentials came as a real shock to him. Maybe it was time to pay more attention to what was happening in the White communities, as opposed to what he expected from the townships.

A knock on the open door interrupted them.

"Got a minute?" said Meiring.

Seeing Meiring with a huge grin on his face was a surprise, but no more so than the man's appearance. Tousled hair, the lower half of his face speckled with stubble and black cream, and dressed in a brown bush jacket and green cargo pants, held up by a webbing belt to which was clipped a sidearm.

Roux raised an eyebrow. "You must have caused quite a stir coming to the office dressed like that. Were you on an overnight raid on some ANC camp in the Cape I don't know about?"

"Better than that." Meiring's grin seemed to have taken up semi-permanent residence on his face. "Any chance of a coffee, Gerda?"

"Of course, Captain, be right back," she said, patting him on the arm as she left.

Meiring collapsed into a chair. "Seems we have put a rat up Tau's arse." He now had Roux's full attention. "Got a call from Dick just after midnight.

Roux suppressed a smile at the mention of the sergeant's name. "And?"

Meiring leaned forward in his chair, "Shortly after dark, there was an increase in people and vehicle activity at the house, and around eleven, a convoy of cars and light pickups arrived. The people at the house started loading boxes, cases, crates and the duffel bags into them. He said Tau seemed agitated, shouting and shoving guys around trying to get them to speed things up."

Gerda arrived with the coffee, and Meiring took several sips before continuing.

"As I was saying. Dick told me the convoy was ready to move and he would follow. About an hour later, he radioed to tell me he was in section four of Langa. I drove out and joined him, along with Ndlovu."

Roux raised a hand. "Section four means nothing to me. Where is it?"

Meiring motioned for him to join him at the wall map. He ran his finger along the northern reaches of the township and then stopped on a spot hemmed in by three roads. It was a distorted rectangular shape shaded in green except for a small white square in the lower right corner bordering the bottom road.

"Here."

"It's open *veld*, nothing there," said Roux, looking confused, "except for the white square, and surrounded by what I assume are houses and shacks."

"It is, mostly thick vegetation with some trees, and lots of broken ground. Looks like it's used as a dumping site. But," he pointed at the white square, "this area contains several old buildings." He ran a hand over the map in a circular motion. "Houses on three sides, with about half a kilometer of open bush behind the old buildings, which leads up to the main road which bypasses the location."

They returned to their chairs.

"According to Ndlovu, it was a school built in the fifties by a missionary crowd, but was looted and destroyed in the seventy-six riots and never repaired. He chased some suspects in there about a year ago, so got a good look at the place. At the time, it housed squatters, but now it's nothing but an empty shell, all the windows, doors, and anything of value, stripped out." He paused for effect. "Except someone's cleaned up several of the rooms."

Roux's hand went to stroke his mustache. He grimaced, running a finger over the sensitive upper lip instead. "Cleaned it up how?"

Meiring squinted at Roux's mouth.

"The wife," grunted Roux, "says it's like kissing a hole in the carpet."

The captain laughed. "No comment. Can't say I've ever kissed a woman with a mustache." His eyes shifted off to the left, as though recalling some long-forgotten memory. "I tried to grow one in college, but irritated the shit out of me. Any way, where was I?"

"The cleaned up rooms," said Roux.

"Ah! Yes. It appears to be occupied, and not by squatters. Someone has refurbished some rooms and cleared away all the crap around the front of the place, including any small bushes and long grass." He stuck a hand into the pocket of his trousers and extracted a folded piece of yellow graph paper, which he flattened out on the desk.

Roux stood to get a better view of a drawing on the paper. Along the bottom and the two sides were three pairs of two lines marked "roads." In the lower right corner was a long rectangular shape, with a second, smaller rectangle at right angles to the first, forming an L-shape. To the left of the longer arm of the L, a square had been drawn, and in the area facing the L-shape were a row of dotted lines.

"Is this the area?"

"It is. As you can see, there are two main buildings." Meiring rose from his chair. "This one," he said, pointing at the longer rectangle, "has, from what I could see, five, possibly six doors, all equidistant from each other, so my guess is class rooms. This one," he said, running a finger over the small rectangle, "has three doors. Ndlovu wasn't sure, but thinks the squatters were occupying a much larger room in this building, which to me sounds like an assembly hall. The last office was probably the principal's."

Roux chewed on his inner cheek, then stopped, feeling guilty. He pointed at the small square. "And this?"

"Toilets by the look of it," replied Meiring, "and the dotted lines are foundations only, for what I guess were temporary structures. There are the remnants of a dirt track leading off the road to the buildings."

"OK. You said some rooms have been refurbished."

Meiring nodded. "Yes. This block," he pointed to the short rectangle. "New doors, which look metal, not wood as you would expect, and new windows with not only glass in them, but burglar bars as well. They obviously want the rooms protected." He sat down.

"When I got there, they were busy offloading the last of the gear and carrying it into a room, which, from what Ndlovu said, I'm calling the assembly hall. Problem is, we couldn't get close, so we had to park some way off and leg it to a bushy area closer to the school, but still some distance away. This time, everything was done with as little noise and light as possible. Tau supervised the entire operation. Most of the men left at about four this morning. Five or six stayed behind, but I couldn't see if Tau was one of them."

Roux eased himself back into his chair. "Sneaky bastard." He scratched his head. "They must know we are watching them. I think I made it clear at the meeting."

"My thoughts as well, so I asked Dick about it," said Meiring.

It was on the tip of Roux's tongue to ask "yours or his" but thought better of spoiling Meiring's moment.

"And?"

"They were aware we may have eyes on them. Before the vehicles arrived at the PAC house, Dick saw a group of men, armed with *pangas* and *knobkerries,* gather outside the house. He and his guys ducked into an alleyway between some shacks and hid. The bastards did a sweep of the road, and the interconnecting streets checking empty cars and chasing the odd passer-by away, but missed Dick."

Both the *panga*, or machete, and the *knobkerrie,* a wooden stick with a knob on the end, were traditional weapons used by both rural and urban Blacks to settle individual or group disputes. In the hands of a skilled fighter, which they often were, the weapons, if not lethal, caused devastating injuries.

"Does Sergeant Dick have a first, or other name?"

Meiring looked perplexed. "Don't know, to be honest, never thought to ask. Why?"

"Never mind. So, can we assume Tau thinks they got away with their midnight dash?"

"Appears so," said Meiring.

Roux tried to picture the old buildings and the surrounding open *veld* as he stared down at the drawing.

"We've got him now," said Meiring, leaning back in the chair looking very pleased with himself.

Roux continued to mull over the drawing. Meiring had done well, but he wasn't sure there was a legitimate reason to raid the place. He glanced up at Meiring.

"Maybe, but they've done nothing to warrant a raid. So they surreptitiously moved stuff from one location to another. So what? It's not illegal, not until we can find out what's in those boxes and duffel bags, which at our meeting Tau said were for the people. From the way you describe the place, it will not be easy to catch them by surprise."

"Marius, there's something being planned," said Meiring, sounding frustrated. "If the contents of those bags and boxes are so innocent, why wait till the dead of night to move them? Why not just do it in the day, as they did when they delivered the stuff to the house? My gut tells me those bags contain more than just goodies for the celebrations. My hunch is there are weapons and maybe even explosives in some of them. We can't sit around watching and waiting for him to make a move!"

Roux could feel his frustration beginning to match Meiring's. "I hear you, but act on what? Some bags and boxes which may contain weapons and explosives? Anyway, how the hell do we even get close to the place? Any smart ideas?" His frustration was turning to anger. It was fine for everyone to tell him to act, be decisive, but what if there was nothing incriminating in those boxes and bags? If APLA were planning their own operation, a pointless raid would just send them underground. But, on the flip side, what if Meiring's hunch was right? If he did nothing, and the worst happens, they would accuse him of acting independently of advice given to him by the man on the ground. An experienced man familiar with the area. But still.

"Eugene, I'm not comfortable we would achieve anything by going now without more info."

Meiring felt annoyed and did not try to hide it. He stood up. "So, we sit on our hands waiting for Tau to hit us, then we clean up the mess. Is that what you suggesting? Colonel, I need to know if I'm wasting my time working my arse off if you're just going to sit on *your* arse and wait for more *info.*"

Meiring's outburst momentarily caught Roux off-guard. "Captain, *sit down*," he said. "Arguing amongst ourselves will achieve shit," he said firmly, but without raising his voice. "Let's just try thinking of a way through this."

Meiring sat down on the edge of his chair. "Can I make a suggestion?"

"By all means," said Roux.

"Let's get Colonel Heyns from STG in and ask him what he thinks could be done."

Roux shook his head. "He will tell us nothing other than how his men will carry out what we decide to do. We . . . I . . . have to decide if we are going to do anything. I need to think. Go home, Eugene, and get cleaned up. Come see me when you get back. We'll take it from there."

Meiring shook his head and walked out.

*Damn. He's the last person I need to be arguing with,* thought Roux. He flipped over the drawing, and grabbing a pen, drew a line down the center. At the top of the left column, he wrote "YES," and "NO" at the top of the right side. In his mind, he sifted through the reasons to act, and those which called for a delay.

Three hours later, Meiring knocked on the open door. He was back in jacket and tie, shaved and looking less aggravated. He sat down, hands in his lap, looking expectant.

"We go. I spoke to Heyns, and he'll be joining us soon."

No sooner had he spoken when Gerda buzzed him. "A Colonel Heyns downstairs to see you," she said.

"Thanks Gerda, will you bring him up?" He replaced the phone and looked at Meiring, who let out a massive sigh. "Let's see what Heyns suggests."

Meiring was now all enthusiasm. "What made you decide, Marius?"

Roux flipped over the yellow page in front of him. Other than the two words he'd written, the columns were blank. "Simple," he said. "I'm damned if I do nothing, and Tau kills Mandela or blows up a police station, and I'm damned if we do the raid, find nothing, and the PAC go public. So, I might as well go out with a bang!"

Meiring laughed. "Don't worry, it'll pan out. You've made the right decision."

Colonel Heyns of the Special Task Group marched into the office, not waiting to be announced. "Heyns," he said, thrusting out his hand.

Heyns, dressed in Disruptive Pattern Material fatigues, or camouflage as it was more commonly known—which in this case comprised grass green and russet foliage shapes on a khaki background—appeared to Roux to be in his early sixties. Cropped, but sparse, white hair crowned a pinched face.

"Morning Colonel, this is Captain Meiring, our man on the ground." The men perfunctorily shook hands.

"So, you men got something on the go. Good. My boys are tiring of all this training. We need some live targets to practice on. Fill me in." Heyns sat down.

"Thanks for coming at such short notice. I'll let Captain Meiring give you the background."

Meiring walked over to the map, drawing in hand, and in as few words as needed, briefed the STG commander.

Heyns got up and strode over to the map, fishing a well-used pipe out of his back pocket and stuffing it into his mouth without lighting it, much to Roux's relief. He peered closely at the green area and surrounding township, took the drawing from Meiring, peering down at it.

"See what you mean." He crunched on the stem of his pipe, appearing to be deep in thought, or so Roux hoped. "Going to be a bastard getting in close without them knowing we coming." After more crunching and running his fingers around the green area, he stepped back. "But we can do it, no problem."

"You can?" said an astonished Roux. Meiring seemed skeptical.

"*Ja*, we just have to be smart, Colonel, but then these Blacks aren't that clever, so nothing elaborate." He ran the tip of the pipe stem along a road to the west, or left, of the green area, leaving a thin streak of spit on the plastic. He tapped the tip on what Roux assumed was a residential area bordering the three roads. "I take it these are huts, with people in them?" His question was addressed to Meiring.

"Yes Colonel," said Meiring, "*houses*, all old, with shacks scattered between them, but all of them occupied. There's also a *shebeen* on the corner of that road, and the one that passes the front of the school."

"Excellent," said Heyns, for no apparent reason.

"What you thinking?" asked Roux.

"Right," said Heyns, "I have four teams on standby. We wait for early hours of the morning, and surround the place with three teams, one in a car, in case we need to chase anyone and me, with the fourth team in Betsy, go in and grab them," he said grinning. "The old girl is a sixties Cortina. Only has one head light, makes a hell of a noise, and looks completely buggered, like every other car in the locations, but goes like a rocket. Fools them every time. We drive straight up to the buildings and storm them, flash bang grenades, forced entry, that sort of thing." He said in a tone and pace which suggested his two listeners were slow on the uptake.

*What century is this guy in*? wondered Roux. "Won't any guards they have posted hear the vehicle?"

"No," chuckled Heyns, "We'll use the old chopper trick." He said it as if both Roux and Meiring were knowledgeable as to the mechanics of this "trick."

"What trick?" said Meiring, trying to sound patient.

"We put up a couple of choppers over the area to the west. Make a lot of noise, use their spotlights, like we already doing an op in the area. During all the noise, we slip in with our teams."

"Colonel," interrupted Meiring. "With the curfew in place, the entire area will be like a graveyard. All the noise will wake up everyone in the location, including the guards at the school. They'll be expecting us, surely?"

"Nonsense man," said Heyns, dismissing Meiring's question with a casual wave of his hand. "Done this plenty of times." He looked at Roux. "I'll take a fly over the site with Prinsloo when I get back to the office, and then send him over to bring you up to speed on details. Anything else Colonel?"

"Where do you want us?"

Heyns gave him a look which implied at home tucked up in bed in his mother's care. But said, "I hear you new here Roux, so let me explain the procedure. You boys find the intel, and we do the killing. So stay here 'til we finish." He ended with a smug grin.

"OK, thank you. We'll do it. I will discuss the pertinent details with your man when he gets here later. But, Colonel, let me make something clear. There'll be no shootout. I have orders from General du Plessis of Security Branch, endorsed by the commissioner, that any operation is to be low key. The suspects are to be taken alive. Non-negotiable."

"Alive?" said Heyns with an exasperated look. "*Ag no man*". He grumbled, his head drooping as he walked from the office.

Meiring, to Roux's amazement, was smiling.

"I'll talk to Prinsloo. Chris Prinsloo. Worked with him before. Experienced operator who runs a professional outfit. He's the brains and ignores anything Heyns tells him. The old man's never heard a shot fired in anger, sits in the control room during the ops while Chris does the work."

"What a relief," said Roux.


HIS CALL TO MEL to explain he would be late getting home elicited an "OK, see you when I do," response before she ended the call. He sat at his desk, feeling despondent. Maybe it was time to explain to his wife what was going on, and why his work was occupying so much of his time, and remind her the assignment was only temporary. But could he trust her to keep it confidential? The realization their relationship had deteriorated to such a degree terrified him.

Several minutes later, the radio in the charger came to life. It was Meiring, who was with Prinsloo in the parking basement. *Why the basement?* Roux wondered as he made his way down in the elevator. Once he met up with the two men, he understood why. Captain Prinsloo was fully kitted out for deployment. His camo fatigues, and an assortment of weapons and additional equipment strapped to his body, reminded Roux of the SWOT teams he had seen on American TV shows. Prinsloo was a very different individual to Heyns. Of similar height to Roux, a chiseled but handsome face topped a wiry body. His deep blue eyes studied Roux for a minute before he introduced himself. Appearing satisfied with his appraisal, he wasted no time getting to the purpose of the meeting. He spread a map over the hood of his Land Cruiser and, in a low voice, explained his proposal to Roux.

The outline of the plan was still in line with that suggested by his superior. With one significant change. He agreed with Meiring. Going into the townships in the early hours of the morning would doom the operation to failure from the outset. The agreed time was now just after dark. With the extended summer daylight hours, they would time the operation for around nine, which would be the last hour before curfew. Civilians would still be out and about, but not in the numbers associated with the early evening hustle and bustle of township life. He believed the helicopters would create a diversion, but despite his recommendations to approach the buildings on foot, Heyns' insisted Betsy was still the primary mode of entry. His hope was the guards would interpret a lone vehicle driving towards the buildings, even if only momentarily, as someone trying to evade the "raid" by the helicopters. This would give the team precious seconds of extra time, but would also attract the attention of the guards, allowing one ground-based team to move in and incapacitate them.

He, together with the occupants of the car, would then storm the buildings backed up by the same team. Each team would be equipped with NVDs or Night Vision Devices, giving them an added advantage over the guards whose night vision would be impaired by the effect of the helicopter's bright lights. Once they gained access, the helicopters would position themselves over the school to provide extra support and flood the area with light. Despite the many assumptions, Prinsloo was confident there would still be an element of surprise.

In response to Roux's question, the captain confirmed he would lead the ground operation, but Heyns, in a helicopter overhead, would have overall command.

Prinsloo waited for Roux to react.

"OK, Captain, sounds good to me. You seem to know what you are doing. You have my vote."

Meiring smiled.

"Thank you, Colonel, but I have one request."

"And that is?"

"With your permission, I'd like Eugene to accompany me in the Cortina. His knowledge of the immediate area around the school and what the buildings look like will be invaluable. I've only seen the site from the air, which is not adequate."

Roux knew they out-gunned him. Besides, the man deserved to be in on the arrest. "Agreed. Where do I go?"

"Colonel, I've suggested you, together with Ndlovu and Dick, wait in a car near the turnoff to the school. Once Chris and his guys have control of the situation, you would join us," said Meiring.

*Damn right*, thought Roux. *This time, I intend to be on the spot.* There was going to be no repeat of the Swanepoel fiasco.

"We move at eight," said Prinsloo. "I've asked for a final fly over just before dark to see if there are any lights burning in the school. If there is, it should give a clearer idea which rooms are being used." He looked at Meiring. "I understand your men are at the site and will stay there up to the launch and confirm any new arrivals or late departures?"

Meiring nodded. "Two of our guys squatting by the side of the road, but in radio contact. I checked in with them about an hour ago and all was quiet at the school. Two or three people moving around the place but no activity of concern."

"Great," said Prinsloo. "Now all we need to do is to get you some decent gear. Tie and jacket will just get in the way."

"No problem, my gear is in my car."

Roux left the two men in the parking garage and returned to his office. He sat down at his desk and pulled over a pen and pad, and began jotting down the main points of the op while they were clear in his head. He reasoned du Plessis will need a full report on what they planned, and the outcome.

He was reading through his summary when Meiring entered, carrying a camouflage jacket and a wide-brimmed bush hat which he dumped on the desk. "I thought you might need this. It should fit."

"Crap, thanks Eugene. I didn't even think of that." Roux was grateful for Meiring's blank face as he strained and grunted his way into the tight-fitting jacket. Gerda was right, he was getting fat. He took it off, glancing at his watch. "Eugene, you better get off home and try to get some sleep," he said. "I'll meet you here just before eight for a last check in with your guys at the school."

WHEN HE ENTERED THE kitchen, he was surprised to see Phil Roberts and Mel in deep conversation, with his hand on her upper arm. She took a step back as he entered.

"Oh, Marius, you're home?" she said with a nervous giggle. "I didn't hear the car. Phil just popped in to see how I . . . we are doing. I thought you were going to be late tonight?"

Roux studied the two for a moment, not sure what he was witnessing, but if nothing else, last night's hostility toward him appeared to have gone. Maybe spending time with her friend overnight calmed her down and helped her see reason.

"I will be. Just popped in for a quick sandwich if you can manage it."

"Of course," said Mel. "Ham and tomato?"

"Sure. Hi Phil, what brings you here?"

"In need of a beer on the way home, old boy," said Roberts, helping himself to two beers from the fridge. He unscrewed the cap off one and handed the other to Roux. "Relax, just a social call."

He declined the proffered beer, dumped his briefcase and jacket on a kitchen counter and pointed towards the lounge. "I'm working tonight. Let's take a pew."

Roberts fell onto the couch as Roux sat down in his usual chair. He took a long swallow, exhaling loudly, then squinted at Roux's mouth. An eyebrow went up.

"Mel doesn't like it apparently," Roux whispered, cocking his head in the direction of the kitchen.

"Oh. OK. Bit of a surprise, but then who knows with women. So, what's happening in the secret world of SB?"

"Real interesting couple of days. Had a one-on-one with our friend Tau. Arrogant bastard, but we're convinced they're up to something." Roux furtively checked if Mel was still in the kitchen before lowering his voice. "We are going to spring a little surprise on them tonight. Seems my meeting with him rattled them."

Mel walked in with a plate of sandwiches and a mug of coffee. "You sure this is enough for you?"

"Be fine, Pet, thanks, looks good."

She touched her upper lip. "Thank you," she said softly before returning to the kitchen as he tucked into the food.

Still chewing, he spoke to his friend. "You guys still not deployed? Someone forget to tell me the war's over?"

"Sounds like it with de Klerk's announcement," said Roberts, gulping down what was left in the bottle. "We ain't got nobody to shoot massa," he said, in a bad American accent.

Phil's total disregard for the feelings of the women he dated, his propensity to talk too much, and his ludicrous attempts at imitating accents had all annoyed him in the early years, but Phil was a good friend, so he learned to live with the man's idiosyncrasies.

"Hey! Here's a thought. Why don't you ask du Plessis if I can join you guys tonight?"

Roux stared at him, incredulous.

"Seriously? I can't see du Plessis buying into the idea," but he hurriedly added, "not that I would mind. I just don't see du Plessis agreeing, considering the commissioner's orders against aggressive actions. We are to be more subtle in our dealings with the Blacks."

Roberts laughed. "You have got to be joking? Subtle! Christ! Shoot all the APLA and ANC terrs we can find, then tell Mandela we are ready to hear his story." He finished his beer in one long swallow and looked longingly at the small liquor cabinet in the lounge corner. "You got anything meaner?"

"Help yourself," said Roux.

Roberts returned with a full glass of brandy and perched on an armrest of the couch. "Tell me about Tau."

Roux relayed the previous day's events, including details of the upcoming raid. "I'm hoping we've scared him enough into doing something rash. Give us an excuse to pick him up under the Emergency Powers."

"Makes sense." Roberts took a mouth full of brandy. "Any more news on the other crowd you mentioned, some liberation movement you said?"

Roux grinned. "The Movement for Black Liberation? Bunch of hot heads. We've got a guy inside monitoring them, but don't see any threat."

Roberts' eyes widened. "One of your guys or an informant?"

"One of our Colored sergeants."

"Shit. Could be risky if he's discovered."

"He's fine. His brother is involved with the group, and they know he's a cop. He's playing along, but nothing substantial coming out of it. Real amateurs."

"Sounds like it," said Roberts, draining his glass. "And the courier?"

"Still looking, but Tau is the priority now."

"OK, my friend, I'll leave you to your grub and tonight's fun. I'm rather jealous, old boy. Hey gorgeous, I'm leaving," Phil shouted in the kitchen's direction.

Mel came hurrying through. "So soon? Marius boring you?" she said, with a small laugh.

"Can't keep Christine waiting. You know how women are about being home on time," he winked at Roux.

"Oh!" said Mel.

"Christine? What happened to Linda?" said Roux.

"Training course in Joburg, its what air hostesses do."

Roux shook his head and accompanied his friend to the front door to see him off.


SERGEANT NDLOVU PULLED UP in a small side street facing the school and killed the engine. It was just before nine. Roux hunkered down in the back seat of the Toyota SUV, his face almost shielded by the borrowed balaclava, which stank of tobacco and bad breath. He had swapped out his jacket and tie for a dark-colored zip up track top, but still wore his suit trousers and work shirt. The familiar sound of the whoop-whoop of helicopter blades, which had just arrived overhead, their spotlights beaming across large swaths of houses and shacks, drowned out all other noises.

Ndlovu spoke out of the side of his mouth without turning his head. "The school is straight in front of us. You can see the two buildings."

Roux lifted his head enough to see through the gap in the front seats, spotting the school. It was more ramshackle than he had imagined, but he could see the faint glow of lights from the corner of the L-shaped block. Excellent. Prinsloo could tell which rooms were occupied, but the fact APLA was comfortable lighting up the school was a surprise to him. Wouldn't they want a total black out? He picked up his binoculars, adjusted the focus, and scanned the area to the west of the center. The residents, some caught in the glare of the helicopter spotlights, were heading indoors or walking away as fast as would appear natural. No one ran. Running from a police or army operation was not something you did unless you wanted a bullet in the back. He swung the glasses to his right, sweeping across the school, and along the road that fronted it. He was looking for the Cortina, but nothing matching the description caught his eye. How long was Prinsloo going to wait? He looked out the back window at the sky. It was as black as it was ever going to get.

"There they go," shouted Sergeant Dick from the front passenger seat.

Roux didn't need the glasses. He could see a vehicle speeding up the dirt track, its taillights barely visible through the clouds of dust as it streaked towards the school. How long should he wait? Meiring said he would radio as soon as the rooms were secure, but he needed to be there, to see for himself what was happening. He chewed on his lip. The wait was going to kill him.

The driver of the Cortina killed its single headlamp as it pulled up in front of the buildings and the occupants de-bussed. There was a flurry of activity as members of the ground teams took up their positions. Without warning, the area lit up in a blaze of light, as though someone had turned on a bank of spotlights, which it was. Two of the helicopters were now circling overhead, their powerful lights focused on the school. He watched as a third chopper hovered outside the school, throwing up dust and debris as it settled on the ground. Someone in the doorway jumped out before the bird lifted off again. Heyns no doubt.

"Put on your lights and go," he shouted at Ndlovu, pushing the man's shoulder while he reached for his radio with the other hand. "Bravo Two this is Bravo, I'm on my way in now."

"Copy. You will want to see this, Colonel," came back Meiring's voice.

Much to his annoyance, Ndlovu drove as though on a Sunday outing while Roux fidgeted with anything he could get his hands on, chewing the inside of his lower lip raw. They parked alongside the Cortina and Roux leaped from the back seat, spotting Meiring coming towards him. His heart sank when he saw the leaden look on Meiring's face.

"And?"

"Tau and five of his men were sitting at a table inside, drinking beers when we burst in. All very relaxed. They were expecting us, Marius."

Roux stared at him. "Someone leak the raid?"

"Must have. How else would they have known we were coming? We've searched all of them. Nothing. Prinsloo's men are going through all the boxes and bags, but nothing so far. Just clothes, tinned food and PAC pamphlets and flags." Meiring spoke softly, voice flat and even.

Roux walked into the room designated as the assembly hall. The light in the room came from three paraffin lamps and several candles on the table. Tau was seated at the head of an old wooden table looking relaxed, a thin smile on his face. His companions sat on either side of him, their hands on the table, probably on the orders of the STG team. Two armed men stood behind them. Others were working their way through a pile of boxes, cases and duffel bags which lay against two of the walls. Heyns stood just inside the door, a smirk on his face.

"Where the terrs Roux? Nothing here but these bastards, and plenty of nothing else." His tone was accusatory.

Before he could answer, Tau, laughter in his voice, spoke,. "Ah, Colonel Roux, good of you to join us. I'd offer you a beer, but I can see you are on duty." His English was impeccable, with none of the heavy accent from the previous meeting. He still wore the APLA "uniform," but his beard and hair were trimmed, which made him look younger, but emphasized the size of his ears. "How can we help you?"

Roux felt a wave of nausea overwhelm him. He opened his mouth and then shut it. There was nothing to say.

Tau laughed. A deep, raucous laugh.

"Come, Colonel, don't look so down. You came, you saw, we conquered." His companions joined in the laughter.

He heard Heyns mutter something behind him which sounded much like "shoot the buggers." Roux turned to him. "Thank you, Colonel, for your help." The last thing he needed was Heyns going on a vengeance spree to make up for the mess.

The laughter died down. Tau turned in his chair to face the STG man behind him. "May I stand up, *boss*?" The man looked at Roux, who nodded. Tau stood and walked over to Roux, smiling as he placed a hand on Roux's shoulder. "I was going to invite you to search the building, but it seems your men decided not to wait for my invitation." His smile faded, and he dropped his hand. "I hope, Colonel, that I can trust you to ensure your men do not help themselves to our property. The clothes and food are for the starving people in the locations."

"We are not petty thieves like you people," said Roux, sounding petty, and knew it, but he couldn't think of anything to say or do which would put Tau on the back foot. Someone within his unit had betrayed them.

A hand touched his elbow. It was Prinsloo. "Nothing, Colonel, in both rooms. We've also been through the rest of the buildings and zero. I would suggest you get the ground around here searched tomorrow morning. They may have had time to dump or bury any stuff they didn't want us to see." He didn't seem to care if Tau heard him.

"Gentlemen," said Tau, "there are no weapons or explosives or any other such material here, or anywhere else, but please, dig up the place. It could do with some landscaping." He laughed again.

Meiring walked up beside Roux. "What do you want us to do with this lot?" he said, gesturing towards the APLA men.

"Arrest them," snarled Roux, "chuck them in the cells at Compton. They can spend the night, and we'll let Gainsford have a chat to them in the morning."

His hope that Tau would protest his order was destroyed when the man, holding out his hands in front of him, said. "Please do. The international press will enjoy this one." But there was less bravado in his tone. "I hope the food has improved in prison." The other men looked uneasy, their smiles gone.

Ndlovu and Dick herded the six men toward the door.

"Chris, I see your Caspers have arrived," said Meiring, referring to the STG mine-proofed troop carriers. "Any chance you can take this lot to Compton?"

"No problem," replied Prinsloo.

"Oh, Colonel," said Tau from the doorway. "If you're worried one of your men is an informant, you needn't. We spotted the somewhat amateurish attempt to observe us last night. Honestly, Colonel, if your men need training in covert surveillance, you only have to ask. I knew you would come, and by the way, the helicopter thing is becoming a touch tiresome." He looked at Heyns. "Still using the Cortina, I see. You may want to get the other headlight fixed." All six of them were talking and laughing as they left the building. Heyns' face was dark red.

"Shit," was all Prinsloo said as he walked off, signaling to his men to follow.

"I'm going to take my guys and check out the PAC house. See if there's anything there," said Meiring, looking shattered.

"Right thing to do. Don't worry, it'll all pan out, is what I think you said," scoffed Roux.

# *Thursday, February 8th, 1990*

WITH THE HEELS OF his palms, he rubbed his itchy eyes, imagining what they looked like. Getting home just before midnight, he'd sat in the darkened lounge nursing a beer, mulling over the events of the previous hours. First, he blamed Meiring for the disaster, then Heyns. But after a heartrending self-examination, himself. Tau had played him, of that there was little doubt. The man needled him during the the meeting, and instead of remaining calm and revealing as little of his intentions as possible, he'd made it obvious SB would watch him. APLA was expecting the usual heavy-handed approach from the police, despite his claims he would do it otherwise. Do a de Klerk on them, negotiate, he recalled saying. What a balls-up. This was his second failure in a week. The general would not tolerate it. After several hours of fitful sleep on the couch, he headed for the office as the first rays of sunlight filtered through the partially closed lounge curtains.

He now sat in his office staring, bleary-eyed, at nothing, unsure of his next move. With the APLA men incarcerated, had he eliminated the only viable threat? It would depend on du Plessis' interpretation of events.

At a little past eight, Gerda poked her head into his office. Took one look at him and disappeared, returning a short time later with a huge mug of coffee and two heated muffins dripping with butter.

"You look awful Marius, you OK?" she said with a worried look.

"No," he grunted. Feeling famished, he grabbed the coffee and muffins. "But you're a lifesaver, as usual, Gerda. Thank you."

She frowned. "I know it's not my place, but everything is alright with Mel, isn't it?"

"Not Mel." He grunted through a mouthful of muffin. "We did a raid last night, which went terribly wrong. Du Plessis is probably going to sack me."

He knew sharing operational details with admin staff was against the rules, but he reasoned she knew almost as much about SB's activities as he did, and right now, he needed a sympathetic ear, something he knew he would not have got at home.

"Real disaster. I ended up looking like a real pr . . . uh . . . peach!"

"I think you mean like a real prick," said Gerda without batting an eyelid. "Happens to the best of us, Marius. You can't always be right. Mistakes are going to be made, and Du Plessis should know that. From what I've heard, he's made a few lulus in his time."

Roux just sat staring at her. Who was this impostor and what had she done with his sweet mouthed Aunty Gerda? He was brought back to his senses when there was a light tap on his door revealing Meiring in the doorway.

"Morning Colonel, got a minute?" He was back in his habitual suit and tie, but his drawn features told Roux the man felt as fragile and despondent as he did.

"Morning, Captain Meiring, some coffee?" said Gerda, all smiles again.

"Thanks Gerda." After she left, he slid into a chair. They both remained silent for some time, staring at the map on the wall.

"I still think we did the right thing," Meiring said, leaning forward in his chair, elbows on his knees. "What do we do with Tau and his boys?"

Roux switched his gaze to stare out the window. Without looking at Meiring, he said, "Stuff it. Detain them under the Emergency Powers, and ship them off to the worst prison you can think of. List it as an investigation into firearms possession. I doubt anyone will question it."

Gerda returned with a coffee which Meiring gratefully accepted.

"Two weeks ago, I would have agreed with you," he said. "Now, I'm not so sure."

A thought flashed through Roux's mind. "Prinsloo's suggestion about checking out the entire area in daylight. We need—"

Meiring stuck up a hand. "Already on the go. I got Ndlovu and Dick, and every sick, lame and lazy pair of legs on station, along with a handful of uniforms out there this morning. Told them I want every inch of those buildings and every blade of grass searched. We might just find something. At least support the weapons or explosives claim. I also ripped the PAC house apart. Nothing besides pamphlets and some PAC tee shirts."

"Oh well, we tried," said Roux, sounding resigned. "Now I need to update our glorious leader. He's going to blow a gasket!"

Meiring gave him a look which said, "I'm so pleased it isn't me."

Roux reached for his phone and dialed Gerda. "Please call Marie and see if I can meet with General du Plessis, asap. Thanks."

It was not long before his phone buzzed. "Thanks Gerda," he said without enthusiasm. "The general is waiting in Warmer's office for both of us." Meiring now looked as nervous as he felt. That'll teach the smug bastard, he thought, smiling to himself.

Ten minutes later, they sat at the small table in Warmer's office. Both generals staring at them. The silence was deafening. Warmer smirked, obviously enjoying SB's embarrassment. But to Roux's surprise, du Plessis was smiling, or as close to what could be called a smile from the man.

"I had Heyns in my office at the crack of dawn," said du Plessis, "complaining about your operation. Although he bitched about time wasted, I got the impression he was more pissed about Tau tearing apart his helicopter and car 'tricks'. Got his blood pressure up. Time he retired, and let Prinsloo take over." He placed his clasped hands on the table. "Want to tell me your version?"

Roux tried to be as concise as possible as he outlined the plan and the subsequent action. His monotone voice sounded as though he were reporting a routine bumper-bashing on the freeway. Du Plessis gave the odd nod, raised eyebrow or grunt, but said nothing. He finished with a mention of the sweep of the entire area and the empty PAC house.

"What you doing with Tau?" said Warmer.

"My thought is to detain him under the Emergency Powers. Let's hold him for hundred and eighty days before putting him in front of a magistrate, assuming we find something at the site. If not, we wait 'til Mandela is released, and then boot his backside back to Joburg." Roux was looking at du Plessis as he spoke.

"Agreed, but I wouldn't wait much beyond Mandela's release. Greyling spoke to the PAC this morning, and they are mighty upset about Tau's detention, but, in Greyling's opinion, they knew nothing about him being in Cape Town. He got them to hold off on talking to the media for the next few days, but by then, we need to decide what we do with him."

"We should know if there's anything at the site by lunchtime, but even if nothing is found, Tau or the PAC leadership don't need to know that," said Meiring. "We can imply we have found suspicious items and are investigating further. I'm convinced those boxes and duffel bags did not contain food and clothes yesterday morning."

"Good point, Captain. It would allow us to keep him off the streets until boss boy Mandela is out of Verster," du Plessis said, addressing Roux.

"With APLA now out of the running, who else could pose a threat? What's happening with the MBL crowd and the courier?"

Roux looked at Meiring, who responded.

"Nothing much. No more meetings or gatherings, and we're still looking for the courier. Sorry, but to get back to Tau. What bothers me is why go to all the effort of sneaking around in the middle of the night to move nothing but food and clothing? It makes little sense."

Roux stared at Meiring. Dammit, the man had a point. Why hadn't he thought of it?

"Valid question, and the first one which popped into my head. My guess is it was a dry run, a false flag, if you will," said du Plessis. "Make their move, see if we react and if not, then move whatever it is they were hoping to stash there. But you ruined the plan by arresting them. I don't think they counted on that happening. With them inside and unable to contact their cohorts or look for the courier, the exercise ends. Once we ship him back to Joburg, risk averted. Good thinking Roux." He sat back in his chair, folding his arms. "So, with APLA sorted, all quite on the western front, then?"

Praise was not on Roux's list of likely reactions from Du Plessis, and it came as a surprise, albeit a pleasant one. His thoughts began scouting around the events at Fouché's house. He cleared his throat.

"General, I know this is going to sound ridiculous, but I'm just wondering if . . . there . . . if there is any possibility that someone, maybe in Pretoria or at NIS, has mentioned the courier to . . . um . . . A civilian? He expected a flat denial from du Plessis. But the man took a moment, deep in thought, by his expression.

"No one, as far as I'm aware. We've kept a tight lid on his presence," said du Plessis.

"Fine. I was just wondering," said Roux, squirming in his chair.

There was a questioning look forming on du Plessis' face. "Do you know something I should know, Colonel?" Although a question, it sounded to Roux more like an accusation. Did he know about his meeting with Fouché?

"Nothing specific. It's a worry the APLA knew about him. I wondered who else does."

Du Plessis inclined his head, continuing to stare at Roux through slitted eyes.

Roux shifted in his seat. This was getting uncomfortable. Time to exit.

"General, we will keep our ears to the ground, and let you know if anything crops up. In the meantime, we'll keep watching the MBL, and anyone else who makes threatening noises." He was about to again voice his doubts about any actual plot, but dropped it. He wanted out of this room, now.

"OK," said du Plessis. "Thanks for the feedback."


MEIRING YAWNED, A HAND covering his mouth, as they seated themselves back in Roux's office. "Suppose I better get hold of Ndlovu, find out if they've discovered anything." He pushed himself up with a tired sigh and headed for the door.

"Wait," said Roux, motioning Meiring to return to the chair. "Something I have been meaning to ask you. It won't take long."

Meiring gave him an inquiring look, but said, "OK," and sat down.

Roux got up and stretched his back. "I'm curious. You have said nothing about what you thought of SONA. Your opinion on where things are going?"

Meiring gazed out the windows for several seconds.

"My honest opinion?"

"Of course, speak freely."

He took several moments, seeming to weigh up his options. "I think it's a good thing." His voice lingered in the quiet office.

"Huh?" said Roux. It was not the answer he was expecting.

"I know, not what you were expecting. But if this country has any hope of avoiding a bloody and destructive civil war, we all need to cool off, put our radical beliefs in our pockets and be prepared to compromise. If we don't, all of us will end up with nothing. Let's face it. Sanctions are strangling this country. Foreign investment has dried up and businesses are pulling out. The entire world has labeled us a pariah state, and other than the UK, with its neutral policy, and the odd country sanction busting for us, we're on our own. Add the fact many highly skilled Whites are leaving, tired of the violence and uncertainty, and you have disintegration, slow but inevitable." He paused for breath.

Roux cut in. "So, you think separate development is a pipe dream?"

"Let's look at this unemotionally, remove the blinkers, examine the facts," said Meiring. "We have an economy on its knees. It is labor intensive and we rely on the very people we are desperate to suppress and ship off to non-productive, so-called homelands, in the hope they will stay out of our cities and keep to themselves. The reality is our economy would collapse overnight if we did not employ Blacks. If we employ them, they need to live near their places of employment. So the locations, and the growing number of squatter camps, are here to stay. Either we have a viable economy, in which everyone shares the benefits, or we have economic ruin. We need the labor to survive. But you can't expect people to work and live in almost slave-like conditions without becoming discontent. We are the last White bastion in Africa. It can't last. De Klerk and his supporters have realized it. Business knows it."

"Wow, Eugene, I didn't realize you felt this way," said Roux, scorn in his voice. "I take it then you're happy to see our kids sent to the township schools, or our houses and jobs taken from us. If you believe everything you've just said, how can you stay in the police?"

"First off, I don't believe it will happen," replied Meiring. "Mandela is no fool. The economy is still in the hands of Whites, so unless they try nationalize everything, which has failed everywhere else, including Russia, they need a negotiated settlement. The ANC doesn't want a shooting contest because they know they won't win it. They must know of the rumors doing the rounds of this country's chemical warfare and nuclear capability. The ANC needs a peaceful settlement as much as we do."

Roux sat speechless.

"I'm sorry Marius, but you asked for my honest opinion," said Meiring, looking conflicted.

"As for my job, to be honest, I'm struggling with it. And the reason the wife and I agreed I'll resign as soon as we put this whole Mandela issue to bed. My conscience doesn't allow me to stay. But until then, you have my guarantee you will get every ounce of loyalty from me until the operation is complete, then I'm out of here. I want to make the most of my degrees, start over in civvy street." He stood.

"Sorry to end so abruptly. But I need to find out if Ndlovu has picked up anything." Meiring turned to leave, but stopped in the doorway. "Colonel, if you believe, based on what I've just said, I should pull out of the operation, just say so. I would prefer to see it through, and be there when Mandela walks free, but I understand you may have doubts." He waited for Roux to respond. But when only silence followed, he left.

"Shit, shit, shit!" said Roux, banging his fist on the desk, and then waving his hand around in the air, trying to numb the pain. He walked to a window and opened it. The noise from the streets below wafted in, accompanied by a cool breeze. He stuck his throbbing hand in his pocket while stroking his smooth upper lip with thumb and forefinger of the other hand. Bugger Mel and her hole in the carpet crap. He missed his mustache. *Time to let it grow back, and if she doesn't like it, she can go kiss the neighbor's dog for all I care.*

His thoughts wandered back to his discussion with Fouchè. The fact of the matter was they were much in line with his own; deep concern about the future. But who was the "us" the man kept referring to? The lack of an answer to that question still troubled him. *But then Meiring thinks the change is the only way Whites will survive. Is he right? Is apartheid a dinosaur in its final death throes?* Lincoln's famous quote came to mind. "A house divided against itself cannot stand." *Is that what we're becoming? A divided White nation?*

Feelings of frustration and helplessness overwhelmed him. There seemed to be no logical answers, just more confusion and—what was it? Fear? He also knew deep down the unit, without Meiring, was not where he wanted to be. He checked his watch. Lunch time. Maybe a stroll in the square, and a hamburger at the new grill on the corner will clear his head. Putting on his jacket, he walked out, locking the door behind him.

By the time he got back, his mood had further darkened, his thoughts were more confused than before. The more he mulled over SONA, Fouché, Rian's future, the country's future; the more depressed he became. Despite soap and water, his hands still smelled of hamburger grease, and the onset of a bout of indigestion was threatening. He slumped in his chair, pushed some files and papers around, but knew any attempt at being productive was a waste of time.

Things got worse.

Meiring radioed to tell him every inch of the buildings and surrounding plot at the school had been searched twice. Nothing. *But, as Meiring suggested, Mr. Tau doesn't need to know we found nothing. Maybe time in the cells will knock some of the arrogance out of the shit.*

His somber thoughts were interrupted by a tentative knock on his door as Gerda sidled in, holding a piece of paper. "Sorry Marius, I don't mean to disturb, but there's something," she waved the piece of paper at him, "I need to tell you."

He attempted a polite smile but failed. "Yes."

"Well . . . it's about . . . well . . . you see," Gerda said, looking concerned.

He flashed her a look he hoped she read as, "if you don't get on with it I'm going to be guilty of staff abuse."

She didn't.

"I'm not sure . . . if . . . well . . ."

"Gerda! If you say 'well' one more time, I'm going to throw you out." He felt irritated, and he was pleased to note he sounded it.

She waved the paper frantically in the air. "Sorry, sorry. It's just I thought you need to know about . . ." She waved her hand around again, as though looking for a place to offload the offending piece of paper.

"Ger-da!"

"OK, OK! It's just I thought you would be cross if I told you. It's about the boy."

"What boy?"

"The one you asked me to find, for Mel's boss," she said, looking a little peeved at his apparent ignorance.

"I don't know about any—" He caught himself. Oops! He'd forgotten about that. Making a poor attempt at nonchalance, he said, "And?"

Gerda more confident now walked up to his desk. "I contacted everyone you suggested, and a few others, but it was one of the sergeants at the front desk, such a lovely boy. You know his mother—"

"Woman!" pleaded Roux, exasperated. "Just tell me."

"Humph," said Gerda. "That's rude. Anyway, seems the boy the professor is looking for is the one Captain Meiring arrested last week. The one in the cells at the moment. He lied about his name when he was arrested, but gave it to the sweet sergeant at the front desk—his mother—" She put up her hand. "Sorry, sorry. The boy admitted to the sergeant his real name is Vuyo, the name on the piece of paper you gave me. I asked Konrad, that's the cute sergeant by the way—"

The look on Roux's face brought her quickly back to the topic at hand.

She cleared her throat. "To check whether this Vuyo knows Professor Kani. He does. Turns out it's his uncle."

"Well, well, well. Seems I need to have a quiet chat with our professor friend." The man had said the missing boy was a relative of a friend, Roux reflected.

"Do me a favor, get hold of Mr. Kani at the Foundation and tell him to get his backside over here." He held up a hand. "No, wait. I'll pay him a visit. Make his staff wonder why the police are back again. Shake them up a little.

Don't accept any excuses. Tell him it's police business, and I will see him at five. Please also let Mel know I'll be home a bit late. Again. Well done, Gerda."

She grinned and strutted out.

Roux smiled to himself. The conniving bastard. Going to be a shocker for Mel when she finds out he'd lied to the police. Maybe the day was improving.

He was wrong.

Moments later, his phone rang. "Roux."

Back came the all too familiar voice. "Find anything at the site?"

Roux was caught off-guard for a moment, but then dived in. "No General, nothing. We flooded the area with men, searched it twice."

"Release him."

"What?" was all Roux could muster.

"Tau, release him. The PAC is making a lot of noise, public noise. Greyling says it's just a cover. He still believes they were as surprised as we were by his appearance here, but the commissioner wants him out if we have nothing to hold him on."

"But General—"

"Today Colonel. Make it clear we'll be watching him night and day. Suggest he gets his arse back to Joburg. The PAC has agreed to pressure him as well. If he doesn't take the hint, make things difficult for him, but get him out of Cape Town." The line went dead.

Roux closed his eyes and said a silent prayer. "Hey! If you're listening up there, how about a break, just one?"

No one was listening.

*Damned if I'm going to give Tau the pleasure of gloating at me*. He picked up the radio handset and called Meiring, who was just as confounded. "Get Gainsford to release him," he instructed. Meiring responded in the affirmative, sounding relieved. *Bastard gives Gainsford any lip he'll get a rifle butt in his mouth.* A malicious grin creased his face at the prospect.


THE NARROW STREET WAS flanked by massive white karee trees, providing abundant shade to the sidewalks. The houses, to his left and right, were almost all identical, small by South African standards: two, and possibly three bedroomed, single carport and small, but neat yards, each separated by low mesh fences. Garish round and rectangular flower pots guarded narrow porches. It reminded him of a military base, or a mining village. He peered through the windshield, looking for number twenty-six. Assuming Kani, as CEO of the Foundation, would live in something more ostentatious, it surprised him to see the house coming in to view on his right, looked the same as all the others. He drove through the open gate and stopped behind a small Toyota parked in the short driveway. *Small house, compact car. Where's the benefit of being CEO?* He still could not fathom why the professor opted to meet at his residence as opposed to his office, but either way, he did not care. Right now, all he wanted was to nail the bastard to the nearest door. He climbed out.

As soon as he closed his car door, the front door of the house opened, and Jonas Kani emerged, dressed in brown slacks and a charcoal colored smoking jacket, topped by a cravat.

*He's more colonial than I am*, mused Roux.

The professor waited for him on the narrow porch, extending his hand as Roux reached him.

"Colonel, good to see you, although I am surprised by your visit. I would have been more than happy to meet in your office." They shook hands. "Please, after you," said Kani, gesturing toward the open doorway.

Roux entered what turned out to be an open plan lounge with kitchenette. Two simple, blue, two-seater couches and a single chair, on a faded beige carpet, faced each other, with spindle legged side tables next to each. There was little space for anything else. A three shelf bookcase stuffed to capacity with hardcover books stood against the wall to his left. He selected the chair and sat down.

"A drink Colonel, non-alcoholic I'm afraid, as I don't imbibe," said Kani, a faint smile on his lips but the dark eyes were intent and suspicious.

"No, thanks Mr. Kani. I won't take up much of your time. I just require clarification on a statement you gave us," said Roux, feeling somewhat out of place. He wasn't accustomed to interviewing suspects in their homes, or calling them mister.

"Oh," said Kani, sitting down on one of the couches, "I wasn't aware I had given the police a formal statement." The smile widened. "I'm afraid you will need to enlighten me, Colonel."

*I intend to; you conniving bastard. Wipe the smile off your face.*

"It's about the boy you asked me to find. Vuyo, who, incidentally, gave us a false name. We arrested him for assisting armed terrorists and an elderly individual who is of extreme interest to us, but seems to have disappeared. It appears they were in the country intending to interfere with Mandela's release." Roux waited, eager to see how Kani would react to the implied accusation.

"To interfere with Mr. Mandela's release? That is a concern. Did you arrest any of these men, and if so, have they admitted to their involvement?"

Roux hesitated. The entire Nyanga would know no one had been arrested in the raid other than the boy. Pretending otherwise would sound lame.

"Well, other than the boy . . . not exactly."

"I see. And has the young man provided you with any uncoerced information which would support your hypothesis?"

Roux felt a touch cornered. This wasn't going the way he planned. "He claims they forced him to assist them, but that is not the issue, Mr. Kani. The reason I am here is to establish why you lied to me?"

The eyes widened. "I lied? About what, if I may ask?"

Roux leaned forward in his chair, pointing a finger at Kani. "You told me the boy was a relative of a friend of yours, correct? But in fact, he is your nephew. Why did you deliberately hide the information?" *Let's see him squirm out of this one.*

To Roux's horror, Kani threw back his head with a resounding guffaw. It took him several seconds to regain his composure. He straitened the front of his smoking jacket before raising both arms.

"You have me Colonel, I surrender. No need for the electric prods or water torture, I confess."

Roux just stared at him, thrown by the man's flippant reaction.

"Mind if I get a cup of tea? Sure you won't join me?"

Roux gave a quick nod, followed by a longer shake of his head.

Kani got up, walked over to the kitchen, and flipped the switch on a bright red kettle. "You are correct, of course. I lied, or more accurately, misled you, but not with any nefarious intentions, I assure you. He is my nephew, and as family, I was trying to be of some help. Perhaps naïve, but I thought by not disclosing my family link I would avoid any suggestion I was using my position at the Foundation to pressure the authorities to prioritize my inquiry. I do sincerely apologize, Colonel. I hope my childish mistake did not inconvenience your men. It was not my intention."

A whistle from the kettle interrupted the silence in the room, followed by a loud click as it switched itself off. Kani reached up to a wall mounted cupboard, retrieved a cup and saucer, and placed them on the counter. He fished a tea bag out of a round tin and dropped the bag into the cup, ensuring the label hung over the side. He looked back at Roux as he filled the cup with steaming water.

"But my concern for the boy is genuine. If he was involved with these armed men, I am convinced it was not of his own volition." He dropped the used tea bag in a bin and walked back to his chair.

"Then why did he lie to us about his name? The fact is, he was in the company of terrorists."

Kani sat forward in his chair. "His lie was probably an attempt to protect me." His face hardened. "The majority of the youth in this country are angry and embittered by the injustices of the apartheid system. You saw the depth of this hatred in seventy-six. They make no excuse for supporting the liberation movements however they can. But there are some who want nothing more than to lead as normal a life as the misery in the townships allow. Get a basic education and try to make something of their lives. I know my nephew to be one of them, who without a choice, has been caught up in the violence and hatred by being forced to assist a group of armed men. Can you blame him for what he did?" He clasped his hands under his chin, elbows on his knees. A look of deep sadness crossed his face.

"Colonel, the profound commitments President de Klerk made last Friday shocked not only the White population, it did much the same within the liberation movements. No one, irrespective of their color or beliefs, is sure what will come next. It is a very confusing time, but until we know what is to happen, life, as we know it, will go on. The liberation movements will continue the struggle, and the security establishment will do their utmost to prevent it. All we can hope for is our leaders agree an end to the violence is the only solution, and engage in meaningful discussions."

Roux snorted. The man seemed to have an answer for everything and he was becoming irritated. His mouth engaged with no prior consultation with his brain. His tone aggressive.

"And what do you suppose all the talking will produce? Tambo, Mandela, and the ANC taking over the country? As my father says, countries in Africa who have gained independence are a mess. Most of them have let the Russians and Chinese in because they are incapable of running their own countries, and are now subservient to the communists," he barked. "One-party states with the people still starving. Is that the African style of democracy we are supposed to welcome with open arms?"

A look of surprise was Kani's response. "I see." He paused, apparently taken aback by the vociferous reaction. "Granted, some of them seem to be incapable of moving from a liberation movement to a governing party. But they are in their infancy and time, and support from the west is needed. The Berlin wall is down, the old USSR is becoming a thing of the past. Communism failed. Africa will soon discover the Russians and Chinese do not offer their services and finances without strings attached. But they need to learn it in their own time."

Roux grunted. "My father often refers to the corruption and incompetence which is rife across Africa. Mozambique is falling apart, and Angola is so wrapped up in civil wars it's ceased functioning. 'Failed states' he calls them."

"You seem very influenced by the opinions of your father," said Kani. "Do you have any of your own?"

"Uh . . . yes . . . of course, they just happen to be the same as my father's, and South Africans," said Roux, running his fingers along the inside of his shirt collar, feeling the need to get more air into his lungs.

"I assume you mean White South Africans? I am sure there are those who would agree with you, but there is a growing call by many Whites for an end to the pointless bloodshed and a return to normalcy. To be part of the world again. To travel, play international sport, and trade without the racist stigma. Even *some* Afrikaners I would venture."

*I can think of one*, thought Roux.

Kani continued. "We want nothing more than what you want. The right to govern ourselves, free elections, and equal access to quality education, and job opportunities. Forcibly moving people to so-called ethnic 'homelands,' where the land is unproductive and business opportunities non-existent, and pretending they will be independent states, is a ludicrous notion. However, I concede there is much skepticism and concern amongst Whites about how the potential changes could affect them.

Their children. Their future in a country ruled by the majority. Most people find any form of change unsettling, so their worries are understandable. But let me ask you this. Have you read the ANC's Freedom Charter? I am sure the Security Branch must have a copy somewhere. It may be worth your while."

Every police officer knew about the Charter, a banned document, drafted by the ANC in 1955, laying out their vision for a free South Africa. Roux felt a slight embarrassment as he shook his head.

"No, I haven't, but I am told on good authority it is filled with nothing but militant threats and communist propaganda."

Kani sighed, as though he had heard this all before. "With all due respect to your good authority, the document is anything but that. But please, do not take my word for it. Read it and judge for yourself, but I beg you to have the courage to do so with an open mind." He paused.

"Colonel, no one is going to come marching into your house and throw you out, or send your son to a rural school. There will be no wholesale slaughter of Whites. Tambo and Mandela are intelligent men, with a good team behind them. There is a genuine determination to abide by the Charter's principles and create a free, but equal, South Africa. For all races. They too have seen the errors made by countries to the north and I am sure are determined not to make the same mistakes. But Whites will need to understand the ways of the past can no longer hold."

He waved a hand. "But enough of my opinions, and back to my nephew." The voice was now determined, with what sounded to Roux like a touch of anger.

"To punish a young man for the rest of his life for a single moment of submissiveness brought about by a threat to his life is unjust. But then we live in an unjust society, don't we, Colonel? I implore you not to charge my nephew. He has already spent days in the brutal care of the security police. Let it be his punishment. If you agree to release him, I assure you, I will have severe words for him, and will take greater care in monitoring his comings and goings." He paused. His tone softened.

"Allow me to ask a simple question. Let's do some role playing for a moment." He held up a hand, dipping his head. "I appreciate the scenario I am about to create may be impossible for you to imagine, but try. Imagine our lives reversed. Whites living in the townships, in the broken-down houses and shacks, in constant fear of harassment and brutality by Black policemen. How would Rian react if a group of armed men belonging to a White liberation movement ordered him to do their bidding? Do you honestly believe he would refuse, sacrificing his life for a cause he may not support? Would you idly sit by, allowing it to happen?"

There was a prolonged silence, broken only by the sounds of birds calling outside the lounge window. Roux stared down at his hands, unable to answer. The man's comparison to Rian had hit home with an element of realism, considering his son's recent decision to become a conscientious objector. Logic was telling him one thing, his heart another. He looked up.

"I . . . I don't know," he said in a limp voice, shaking his head. "But put like that, I suppose I would do whatever is necessary." This was becoming uncomfortable, and feeling cornered, he rose to his feet.

"I need to think this through, but I promise I will give your request serious thought, and you'll know my decision by early tomorrow. Thank you for your time."

Kani stood up, nodded once, and led Roux to the front door. As they passed the bookcase, Roux stopped and peered at a small framed photograph on the top shelf.

"I take it that's you?" he pointed at the Black man standing next to a White man in a suit. It was the zip up jacket worn by the Black man which caught his attention.

"Yes," said Kani, picking up the photo. "Taken two years ago while I was at the Washington office. That's Ed Kaminsky, a senior executive at the Washington Redskins."

"The Redskins?"

"The Washington Football team, American football, not British football. Americans call the British version soccer. You would most likely compare it to rugby. The Foundation donates to the team every year, and as it was my turn to hand over the check, they gave me the jacket at the handover ceremony."

Roux examined the jacket. The color was what he would call maroon. There were yellow stripes on the cuffs and collar. It was typical of a jacket worn by club supporters all over the world, but it was the logo on the left breast which made him catch his breath. It was the side-on face of a Native American with two feathers hanging down from the back of the head. A yellow circle surrounded the face, with a further two feathers attached to the outer circle on the left side, also pointing downward. He tapped the jacket.

"You still have it?"

"No, I am no sports lover. I gave it to my brother in London, a die hard Redskins fan."

"Oh. OK," said Roux, trying to imprint an image of the logo on his mind. "I'll be off, thank you." The two men shook hands in silence.

After exiting the Foundation gate, he pulled over and closed his eyes. The thought of going back to the office gave him a headache. He rammed the car into first gear and headed for his spot. This time, however, he remained in the car. He wound down the window, parked an elbow on the window frame, and rested his head against his hand. He felt sick. Rian's desperate face, with a gun to his head and his eyes pleading for his father's help, had been haunting his thoughts since he left Kani. Damn the man. Damn his impertinence, and the stupid, unrealistic picture he tried to paint. Whites in the townships? Never! *We would never have allowed it to happen. If the Blacks tried to suppress us, we would . . .*

He stared out at the darkening sky, felt the wind beginning to increase in speed, stirring up white caps across the graying Atlantic.

*We would fight. Of course we would. No way would Whites allow themselves to be oppressed by others, no nation would accept that. We would fight for what is rightfully ours, just like—*He stopped. *Just like they were doing.*

He punched the dashboard. "Shit!" He shouted at the wind. Closing his eyes, he ran a hand through his hair, tugging at it as though if he pulled it out, the tumult in his head would ease. As the fear in his gut subsided, a soft whimper escaped from tight lips. Maybe Meiring was right. Change was inexorable. But could he live with it? Mel and Meiring seemed to think it would be OK. But his father?

"Christ Almighty, what am I supposed to do?" he screamed out loud. But before anyone, Devine or otherwise, could respond, the radio clipped to his belt squawked. It was Meiring.

He unclipped the radio and depressed the transmit button. "Go ahead, Bravo two."

"Colonel," said Meiring. "We have a problem."

*Seriously*, sneered Roux, *just one*? "What is it?"

"Conradie's brother was found dead, and the sergeant hasn't been home in almost two days. Seems he's gone missing."


THEY SAT ON EITHER side of the bench in the square, their backs to the Compton building. Roux took a deep swallow of the cool evening air, relishing the freshness after the piercing heat of the day. He almost fancied he could smell salt in the air, but considering the distance to the closest beach, he knew it was pure fantasy. He stretched his legs out in front of him, his arms limp at his sides. His jacket and tie hung over the back of the bench, shirt sleeves rolled up.

During the drive over, he had mulled over Kani's request and the pros and cons of releasing the boy. Despite his best efforts to shut it out, the image of Rian and an AK kept intruding. It made his gut heave. He had calmed down and was feeling embarrassed by the way he had aggressively challenged Kani on what, truthfully, was a trivial issue. Kani's explanation was plausible, and it made Roux feel even more uncomfortable. By the time he parked his car in its allotted bay, he knew what needed to be done.

The tension between the two men when they met in the parking basement was palpable and, at Roux's suggestion, opted to leave the stuffy building and enjoy the open air. They now sat alongside each other in the growing shadows of the late afternoon sun.

"So, Conradie's brother is dead, and he's missing. What's the story?"

Meiring turned to face him, resting an arm along the back of the bench. "Uniforms found the brother with his throat slashed at around three this morning. Took some time to get the body identified, but once they did, it didn't take them long to confirm he had a brother in the force. Ndlovu went to see the mother this afternoon, but she says she hasn't seen him for almost two days. No idea where he is or where he was last seen. Girlfriend confirms the story. She hasn't seen him since Tuesday night, and has been asking around at his usual drinking haunts with no joy. Ndlovu is trying to piece together his movements over the last few days as best he can, but proving difficult."

"When did he last check in with you or Ndlovu?"

"Three days ago. Seemed fine."

"What's your take on this?"

"Not sure until we can find him or someone who saw him in the last two days. But I'm assuming the worst."

"Why?"

Meiring removed a small plastic bag from his jacket inside pocket and handed it to Roux. It contained a blood soaked hand-written note with just one word on it. The letters all capitalized. "IMPIMPI." Roux turned it over, nothing on the back.

"This is more ANC or APLA's style. You think the MBL would resort to killing one of their members, considering they know he's the brother of a police officer?" Roux said, sounding doubtful.

"Looks like it, especially if they thought the brother or Conradie were informers."

"OK. Let's assume they did. But it doesn't mean they also killed your sergeant."

"Agree, but remember, his brother introduced Conradie to the group. What if he had one drink too many, and started asking the wrong questions, arousing their suspicions about his commitment? Either that or he stumbled onto something the MBL doesn't want us to know about and they found out. His brother brought him into the group, so would be held responsible for his snooping. So remove both problems. If I'm right, our Sergeant Conradie is buried somewhere with his throat cut." Meiring's tone was flat, as though commenting on some distant tribal dispute in the rural areas.

Roux found Meiring's apparent disinterest confusing. "Hell, Eugene, he's one of ours. You may not think much of the man, but we owe him, his family, and the rest of the unit, to find him, or his body, and nail whoever did it. Who's dealing with it?"

"Van der Merwe at Murder and Robbery. Brusque individual but damn good at his job," said Meiring. "Got a good number of informants, and a good arrest record. I suggest we leave it with him for a couple of days and not go butting in with nothing valuable to add. As instructed, Conradie was out there operating on his own. Only Ndlovu knew where he was or what he was doing. Let van der Merwe do his job and get his informants asking around."

"My gut feel is your second scenario is accurate," he said. "If the MBL took out both of them, it was not because Conradie was a police officer. They knew that already. So the possibility he uncovered something is more plausible. But, so far all they've done is bang on about their claim Mandela is a puppet of de Klerk's. Nothing illegal about that. So why kill a SB officer if your motivations are strictly political? No one is that stupid. Unless—"

"—your intentions are not purely political," said Meiring, snapping his head round to face Roux.

"Exactly. Could be they are not as harmless as we assumed. Does Ndlovu know where these guys hang out?"

Meiring stood. "I'm meeting him after this, so will find out what he's uncovered."

Roux held up a hand.

"Eugene, one other thing. My wife asked me to help her boss, a Professor Kani, the new CEO at the Children Foundation, find a missing boy. Gerda did some checking for me, and it turns out the missing boy is the one you arrested during the tavern raid. When I first spoke to Kani, he told me it was a relative of a friend. He lied. It's his nephew. I went to see him this afternoon to challenge him about it. He came clean, admits he lied but didn't want his inquiry to be perceived as the Foundation applying pressure on us by declaring it was his nephew. I see nothing untoward with the whole thing. I also think the boy has told us as much as he knows, so I'm going to release him."

Meiring nodded, but said nothing.

"One other thing. I need Els to check on something for me." He explained the photo at Kani's house; the Redskins logo on the jacket. "Get Els to find a copy of the logo and show it to the boy before he's released. See if he recognizes it."

The captain eyed him for several seconds with a quizzical look. "OK, I'll get hold of Els from the office. Night." He strolled off in the station's direction.

Roux returned to his office to collect his briefcase. On the way out, he left a scribbled note on Gerda's desk. *"Please ask Records for a copy of the ANC Freedom Charter - Thks."*

# Friday, February 9th, 1990

MEETING DU PLESSIS IN the hallway of the SB office was a surprise. "Your office, and get Meiring," he barked as he walked past.

Minutes later, all three men stood in Roux's office. The general's face was dark. "Cabinet is considering releasing Mandela this weekend. Sunday, most likely, but not confirmed as yet."

Meiring whistled through his teeth. "Wow! That doesn't give us much time to find the courier."

"It doesn't. Where are we with it?"

"We have several teams on the ground still searching for him, General, but the man seems to have disappeared into thin air," said Meiring. "I spoke to the senior officer at Verster on the off-chance they had noticed someone new paying Mandela a visit, but nothing."

Roux gave him a grateful glance.

"If it is Sunday, you have two days to find him, gentlemen, or you'll be explaining your failure to the commissioner in person."

Roux cleared his throat. "We will, General, but something else has come up which may need more urgent attention."

Du Plessis held up a finger. "One more thing. Mandela will address the masses at a public meeting after his release."

"We assumed that," said Meiring, sounding a little irritated as though the news of Mandela, who had been in prison for almost thirty years, was about to make a public address, was commonplace.

"Really?" du Plessis glared at him, sarcasm oozing from his lips. "Well, Captain, what you may not know is the ANC has insisted on City Hall. Slap bang in the middle of Cape Town and the most public place you could think of. Any ideas about how you will keep him safe?"

"Jeez!" Said Roux. "How the hell do we protect him there? But why us? I thought the ANC is responsible for his safety after his release?"

"They are. But City Hall is a public place where thousands of people will gather, which makes it our concern. But for the moment, it is not your problem. Your priority is to find the courier. Has Tau been released?"

"He has, last night. Put on a flight back to Johannesburg," replied Meiring.

"Good." Du Plessis leaned against the desk. "You were going to tell me about another problem."

"It concerns the MBL," said Roux. "Our sergeant who infiltrated the group has disappeared, and his brother, who was his entrance ticket, has been found with his throat cut and 'informer' written on a piece of paper and plastered to his chest. The fear is our man is in a hole somewhere with the same problem. Eugene and his team are trying to establish his last movements and attempt to pick up some kind of trail to help locate him, or at least the body. Murder and Robbery are handling it, and I'm assured the senior investigator is a results man. He's aware of the urgency in solving this."

Du Plessis frowned. "Motive?"

"If the MBL is responsible, it makes them more than just a collection of political hotheads," said Roux. "You don't resort to killing a police officer unless you have something to hide. Something more than calling Mandela a puppet. I'm going to pull back most of the teams on surveillance and get them on the hunt. We need to know today what has happened."

"Damn!" said du Plessis. "As if we don't have enough on our plate as it is. OK, but this doesn't diminish the need to locate the courier. Let's hope like hell we haven't been ignoring the elephant in the room." A brief wave of his hand ended the meeting as he left.

*At least he had the courtesy to refer to "we" and not "you",* Roux noted, as the two men watched him leave.

"I'm going to check if Ndlovu's back." Meiring said, following the general out.

"Bring him back with you if he has," shouted Roux at Meiring's back.

Roux was about to sit down when Gerda's head appeared around the inter-leading door.

"Lieutenant Els is here to see you." Roux sighed and waved him in.

Had it not been for the young man's ears, his smile would have split his face in two. "We found it, Colonel. Took ten minutes once we knew what we were looking for. I've just come from the cells, and the kid confirms it was the picture he saw on the old man's jacket at the tavern. It's the Washington Redskins logo."

Roux felt elated for the first time in a while. "Good work Els. Thanks. Get Charge Office to release the boy, now, no charges. Ask Gerda to call a Mr. Kani at the Foundation to collect him."

Els strutted off.

Meiring and Ndlovu passed him in the doorway.

Meiring sat down, Ndlovu remained standing, but Roux waved him to the spare visitor's chair. "OK, what we got?"

Sergeant Ndlovu spoke. "No sign of Sergeant Conradie, Colonel, but his girlfriend says he was very nervous about the MBL. Told her he was going to a meeting on Wednesday night, and then would come to the station to see the captain."

"At the same house where Friday's meeting took place," chimed in Meiring. "We don't know if he met with them, but it's not coincidental we find his brother's body the next day. Ndlovu checked the house last night. Empty, but definite signs of being occupied, and there was a pool of blood, which looks fresh, on the floor in one room, and blood splatter all over the walls. I've passed all the info to van der Merwe. He's on his way to the house now."

Roux ran a hand through his hair. "Do we know of any other hangouts they use, or was that the only one?"

Meiring shook his head. "No, not at the moment, but I've sent Dick and Gainsford to find Khumalo, Davids and Akmet. I told Gainsford I want info. He just smiled. So, with a bit of luck, we'll have something in the next couple of hours."

"Anything more on the courier?" Roux said to Ndlovu.

"Nothing, Colonel. Sorry."

"Thanks Sergeant, you can go."

"Wait for me at my desk, Ndlovu," said Meiring.

"Marius, if Conradie wanted to meet with me, you can bet he had something. He may be a piss artist, but he knew what he was doing."

"I agree, Eugene. The last people he saw appear to have been from the MBL. That makes them the prime suspects if he is dead. When Gainsford and Dick get back, I want you in on the interrogation."

"OK." Meiring looked unhappy, and Roux could guess why.

"Some good news in all this doom and gloom," said Roux. "Els got hold of a copy of the logo I referred to and showed it to the boy, who confirmed it was what he saw on the jacket the courier was wearing. I know it's not enough to point a finger at Kani, but it raises my suspicions about the professor. I suspect he knows more than he's telling us, but I'll deal with him. We need to focus on Conradie first, and get eyes on the MBL pronto!"

"On it," said Meiring and left.

Roux got up and walked over to the windows, hands in his pockets. *Fine saying I'll deal with Kani, but what is it I'll be dealing with? The boy identified the logo as the one on the jacket worn by the courier. Kani has a brother living in the UK to whom he gave a Redskins jacket.* American football jackets were not common in South Africa. So pure coincidence? Thinking of Kani turned his thoughts to Mel. They needed time to sit down and talk. He walked back to his desk and collapsed into his chair, picking up a pen and chewing on the end.

"You need to eat something more substantial than a pen, young man. You look worn out," said Gerda, waddling into his office. She placed a salad and a mug of coffee on his desk. "Eat." She sat down uninvited. "I know you have your hands full, with whatever, but what else is worrying you Marius? I know when something is worrying you."

Roux let out a slow and loud sigh. "Any idea how a man is supposed to mend bridges with his wife when he can't share what he does all day for a job?"

"Oh! So it's Mel. Talk to me." She sat back, arms folded. Roux knew from experience she wasn't budging until he coughed up.

"She's encouraging Rian to claim he's a conscientious objector to avoid call-up next year, which scares the hell out of me. He could go to prison, but she won't even talk about it. Add the fact she believes us Afrikaners are going to start a civil war. I wouldn't be surprised if she's also worrying about her job, the Foundation kids, and a dozen other things I don't even pretend to know about. Things are getting tense at home. What we need is to sit down and resolve the problems, but I'm never at home," he waved a hand aimlessly in the air, "with this whole Mandela release thing."

"Have you told her why you so busy?" she asked.

"No, but I intend to. Tonight."

"Good. Be honest and get it all into the open, and don't stop talking 'til you sort it out. Now eat." She gave him a matronly smile and left.

It was sometime later when a grim-looking Meiring appeared at his door.

"Mind if I close the door?"

Roux nodded.

"Conradie is dead. We don't have the body, but we've confirmed it. Gainsford and Dick didn't find Khumalo and friends, but arrested two other guys they found at Khumalo's place. One look at Gainsford with his shirt sleeves rolled up and the knuckle dusters got them cooperating. They say Conradie and his brother attended a meeting on Wednesday night at the house where the bloodstains are. After the meeting four guys took them into another room. They accused them of spying for SB. Obviously they denied it at first, but after the living shit was knocked out of them, Conradie confessed he'd been ordered to find out more about the group. Then they shot him. Probably took out the brother at the same time."

"Did they see the shooting?" interjected Roux, his voice rising.

"No, or so they say, but heard one of Gumbo's boys bragging about it later the same night. They hauled the bodies away in the boot of a car, or so the story goes, and dumped them. Could be our man went into the sea. As we suspected, Gumbo's gang are providing the muscle for the MBL, and we know he was at last Friday's meeting, so he's linked to the killings."

Roux felt sick. "OK. They tell you anything else?"

"They did, but all hearsay, and difficult to verify until we can find Khumalo."

"Let's hear it."

"One of them claims to be a friend of Davids and says he was told of a meeting on Tuesday night which both Conradie and his brother attended with about twenty other guys. From some names he gave us, it was the most militant crowd of terrorists in Cape Town, together with a sprinkling of communists."

Roux felt even more sick. "What was discussed?"

"Plans to disrupt Mandela's release. Three of the group were tasked with drawing up specific ideas and to present them to Khumalo on Wednesday night."

Roux frowned. "The Wednesday meeting Conradie mentioned?"

"Sounds like it, and somehow Conradie's cover was blown, either at the meeting or afterwards."

"Can we grab some of them who were there?"

"I've given the list to Dick and sent him with some of my guys to see who they can find, with Khumalo and Davids top of the list, but I doubt they'll have any luck at this stage. They'll know we've found the brother, so will have gone underground. We got the addresses of two other houses they use in the townships and we'll start there. The guy mentioned a third place, but did not know where it was, other than outside of Cape Town." Meiring looked down at his hands for a moment. "There's one other thing worrying me a bit, though."

"Like the other stuff doesn't?" said Roux with a sardonic smile.

"It does, but this could imply a much bigger problem. Khumalo allegedly ended the Tuesday meeting by saying a 'spy' had been sent by the ANC to give a secret message to Mandela. He described the courier exactly and told everyone to get the message out in the locations to find him and kill him."

Roux stared at Meiring, wide-eyed. "How the hell do they know about the courier? First APLA, now them. How legit is this guy?"

"Marius, I'm not sure but my gut tells me this guy wasn't *told* anything. He was at the meeting."

*He's exhausted. Given his intention to resign in the next month, I can't fault his commitment.*

The phone rang, an internal call. Roux was sure who it was, so hit the speaker button. "Roux."

"Can you talk?" said du Plessis.

"Yes General. Meiring is with me, and you're on speaker. The door is closed."

"Right. The release is confirmed for Sunday but no specific time as yet. I'll let you know once I have an exact time. Anything on your side?"

"Ninety-nine percent sure our sergeant is dead, although we don't have a body as yet. We've detained two MBL members, and Meiring's team is out checking on the initial intel we got and trying to find Khumalo and other members of the group. It also appears, from unconfirmed info, the MBL know about the courier and have told their members to find him and kill him. But we'll know more once we have Khumalo."

"How do they know about the courier? You running out of time, Roux, we need answers. Anything I can do?"

Roux looked at Meiring, who scrunched up his nose.

"Nothing for now, but I'll certainly shout if there is." The line went dead.

The two men looked at each other.

"Shit," said Roux. "Tomorrow is Saturday!" He felt bile beginning to edge its way up the back of his throat. "What do we do?"

Rubbing his eyes with a thumb and forefinger, Meiring slumped back in his chair. "Hell Marius, off the top of my head? Panic would be my first choice," he said with a rueful smile. "But I suppose one step at a time."

They discussed the options open to them and concluded there was not a lot they could add until Meiring's team concluded their searches. Roux knew he had to confront Kani, but as Meiring agreed, with what? Realizing it was twenty minutes before six, they opted for a home-cooked dinner and a full night's rest.

HE PARKED THE CAR and rested his head against his hands on the steering wheel. Meiring was close to the end of his tether, but he wasn't feeling too perky either. He wished this whole damn mess would end. If Mandela gets killed, so be it. But now he needed to save his marriage.

He found Mel seated on the couch in the lounge, pecking away at her dinner. She looked up at him. Her eyes were red, underlined by dark smudges.

"Where's Rian?" he said, sitting on the edge of a chair.

"Out." She placed the almost uneaten food on the couch beside her.

"Pet," he said, "we need to talk. It's time I tell you what is happening, work wise. I know I told you this temporary transfer wouldn't entail any field work, but circumstances have changed since SONA. I'm sure you can appreciate that?"

Her head bobbed once, but she said nothing.

He felt drained and mentally at sea. "Something has developed which could have serious consequences if it is not resolved within the next few days. The operation is highly secret. I've been warned by du Plessis not to discuss it with anyone outside of SB, even family. But, being in SB almost destroyed our marriage once before, and I'm not making the same mistake again. However, I need to ask you to be patient with me for just four or five days more, after which the operation will be over."

He got up and walked over to the couch, shoved the plate aside, and sat next to her, taking one hand in his.

"I know, I should have said something earlier, but you know how secretive SB is about everything." He squeezed her hand. "I'm sure once it's over I'll be moved back to uniform, but until then, I have to focus on this operation. It's high risk, and if we get it wrong, the fallout for this country could be catastrophic. But one thing I know for sure, Mel, our marriage, and the happiness of you and Rian, are paramount to me. I will not let the job get in the way again."

"I know," she said, placing her other hand over his. "Not the details, just the fact you were involved in something top secret."

He freed his hands, sitting upright. "How?"

"Phil was here. He left just before you arrived."

"What was Phil doing here, again? He knows how to get hold of me. Why's he coming to see you?"

"To tell me you were working on something secretive and dangerous, and asked me to warn you to be careful. He said he was worried about you, that you were maybe out of your depth. He's a good friend Marius, what's so wrong with that?"

An unbroken stream of images flooded into his brain. He stood up and walked back to his chair, sat down, and stared at her for a moment.

"Mel, what's the story with you and Phil? You two looked very intimate the other night, and you were like a lovesick schoolgirl with him at the *braai*. I'm not blind, so please don't patronize me. I'm getting the impression there's more than just old-time friendship."

He expected a fiery response, but she averted her eyes and spoke in a low voice.

"It's not what you think Marius. I would never be unfaithful to you. I love you, I love Rian, I love what we have, or had, as a family. But the truth is Phil and I go back a long way, as you know. You must understand, he was my first, in many ways, and there will always be a place in my heart for him, but as a friend, nothing more. He taught me a lot, matured me, gave me a voice, a belief in myself.

But being Phil, he couldn't help himself. Once he got what he wanted, he went looking elsewhere for new challenges. When I found out he had cheated on me, on more than one occasion, I left him." She looked at him, wringing her hands in her lap.

"Marius, despite his bravado and intelligence and outgoing demeanor, Phil is a child at heart. He's never satisfied with what he's got, he always wants more. So he discards things and people without a second thought. I was not the only young woman who had her heart broken by him. The tragedy is he doesn't even realize how his immaturity hurts those around him." She took a deep breath.

"No, we have never got together again. South West was the last time I saw him, which you know about. I was just as surprised as you were when you said he was in Cape Town. But yes, over the years we did stay in touch and spoke occasionally on the telephone." She got up, walked over, and knelt in front of him, her arms across his knees.

"Phil has always understood me, Marius, knew how I felt about things, could see when I was worried and upset, and was there for me when things got difficult with you away so often. I know it sounds unfair, as though you weren't there for me. You were, but your devotion to your work and the inability to truly open up and allow me into your life prevented you from being what I desperately needed. A rock on which I could lean. Phil gave me that." She gripped his knees.

"Marius, I am happy in our marriage, and don't want to lose you, but you need to face up to your father, and allow yourself to grow, to take charge of your life, our lives. Whether because of your father's influence, or your time in Security Branch, or both, you have become distant over the years, losing the ability to recognize who you are. The amazing man I fell in love with. The man you have now locked away from me and Rian. We want . . . need . . . you back. Now more than ever." She stared imploringly at him.

He was having difficulty maintaining eye contact. It felt as if something deep down inside him had been ripped away, leaving a void he may never fill.

She shook his legs. "Hey! Please listen to me. Phil is not meddling in our marriage. There was nothing underhand about him coming here. He knows if he talks to you about his concerns you will brush him off, tell him you're handling it. So, he came to me hoping, because you and I are close, I could get through to you." She hesitated for a fraction of a second. "Or were close." She paused. "He's not trying to get back together with me, but he is worried about you, nothing more."

He sat there, stunned, his eyes unfocused, groping around for something to say, but the sound of the doorbell interrupted his efforts.

"Maybe it's Phil back to explain himself," she said, rising and making her way to the front door.

Moments later, he heard the door open and muffled voices.

"Marius, it's Professor Kani, he'd like to talk to you."

Dazed, he stood up and walked to the door.

"Ah, Colonel, sorry to worry, again, but I would like a word with you, if I may. It is important and pertains to your work." Kani made no effort to enter the house.

Roux joined the man, closing the door behind him. "What is so important you need to come to my house?" he did not hide the brusqueness in his voice. This intrusion could not have come at a worse time.

"My apologies I know it is late, so I will be brief. First. Thank you for releasing my nephew. I am most grateful, and in a show of good faith and appreciation, I thought you may wish to know of a property being used by, how shall I put this, a vocal anti-Mandela release movement?"

Roux was blindsided. "Sorry?" he said, trying to cover his astonishment.

"The Movement for Black Liberation." Kani said, searching Roux's eyes with his. "You have an interest in them? If so, you may want to pay them a visit at an abandoned fruit farm called Waterfalls, near a town called The Willows. It's in the Winelands, about an hour from here."

Roux just said "Thanks", dumbfounded.

"My pleasure," said Kani, turning toward his car. "Goodnight Colonel."

Roux watched him for a moment, then called out. "Mr. Kani, a few quick questions, if you don't mind."

Kani stopped and looked back at him.

"Are you a member of the ANC?"

The man laughed. "Oh dear, my cover is blown. Yes, Colonel, I am, but not a high-profile member. In fact, only a very select group of people within the organization know of my existence. If you get a free moment tomorrow, you may wish to return my visit. There's something I'd like you to see, which I believe will answer the question you are about to ask me. Mel has the number for my residence. Call me and let me know when you are on your way, so I can warn the main gate."

He opened his car door. "I bid you a pleasant, but possibly busy, evening, and happy hunting."

Roux watched the car reverse out of the driveway. Kani's remark had taken the question right out of his mouth. A question he wanted answered, but the information was more important. Besides, he would know tomorrow. He walked backed into the lounge. First du Plessis and then Meiring. Kani was right. It was going to be a busy night. Ignoring his wife, he headed for the phone.

Two minutes later, he was in the bedroom hauling down an old trunk from the top of a cupboard. Rummaging around inside until he located a camouflage jacket, brown combat trousers, brown tee shirt, and a brown bush hat. He stripped off his work clothes, and to his amazement, he discovered the jacket still fit. The tee shirt barely covered his stomach and went back into the trunk, followed by the trousers, when he discovered he couldn't button them up. He opted for a dark blue golf shirt and black denim trousers. His transition was completed with a pair of boots more suited to shopping malls than walking through the bush, but they'd have to do. He tucked the hat into a side pocket and headed for the kitchen.

"Marius?" said Mel, still in the lounge.

He stared at her as though she were a stranger. "I need to get back to work."

"But we need to talk this out."

"Maybe a bit late for that," he snarled. "Seems I have been badly treating you all these years. Strange, you now suddenly find the need to tell me about you and Phil. I saved his life in South West, and he knows it. He would never betray me. But you, Mel? Pity you didn't trust me enough to tell me how you felt about Phil before we married. If you didn't trust me then, how can I believe what you tell me now?"

She stared at him, a look of shock on her face. Her hand went to her mouth. "You . . . honestly believe . . . I would cheat on you . . . with *Phil*?"

"I don't know what to believe anymore." He spat back at her. "Maybe you should go lean on your 'rock.'" He turned and stormed out.

AFTER APPRAISING THE TWO men's dress code with an inquiring look, General du Plessis listened as Roux recounted Meiring's update on the MBL and the information from Kani.

"Can we assume the reason Kani is so forthcoming is he, slash the ANC, is aware of an imminent hit by the MBL? But of more interest is why tell us? They are more than capable of dealing with the MBL on their own. Captain, can you go find a map of this place, The Willows?"

While Meiring was out, Roux explained. "He claims as a show of appreciation for releasing his nephew, but my guess is the ANC wants this crowd out of the picture, irrespective of whether they're hot air, or a real risk to Mandela. How better than to get us to do it for them?"

He worried for a moment if du Plessis was going to ask about the nephew but, to his relief, said nothing.

Du Plessis chewed on the stem of his glasses for several seconds, then said, "Could be. Just seems odd. I have to wonder if there is another angle. Maybe something to do with what he wants to show you?"

"Could be. I won't know 'til I see him tomorrow."

Meiring joined them and rolled out a map on the desk. He pointed to a small black dot.

"This is The Willows. About ninety minutes from here. But where exactly the farm is located is anyone's guess.

STG were doing training runs out there last week, so I've left a message for Chris to contact me. Charge Office is trying to find out if the place has a police station, or one close by."

"Main road all the way there," said Roux, tracing a finger along a solid black line on the map, "and should be a clear run. We could be there by ten, latest."

Du Plessis looked up from the map. "I assume from your get-up you want to go have a look?"

"I do. I need to determine if it's occupied, and if so, by whom, and if there is anything of interest going on," he looked at Meiring. "This may be the third house the Colored guy you interrogated was referring to."

"Possible," said Meiring, then held up a hand as his radio crackled. He responded to the caller while walking out of the office.

Du Plessis was staring down at the map, still chewing on the stem of his glasses. "So you go there, get a feel for the place, and then?"

"If the MBL is there, we hit it. Use STG. Round up everyone and shut the place down. The more of these characters we can get off the street, the better I'll feel. If we can get Khumalo, and the other top guys, we'll be able to establish if they are genuinely planning something or not. And get them for Conradie's murder."

Du Plessis remained silent, eyes on the small black dot.

Meiring rejoined them. "That was Chris. He knows the area, wine estates all over the countryside, but never heard of Waterfalls. He says there is no station at The Willows, or much else, other than a small hotel. Suggested we wake the owner and get directions, or ask at the petrol station, which is in the middle of the town. I've told him we going to take a look and maybe a good idea to have his teams on standby."

Roux raised an eyebrow. "Shouldn't you have spoken to Colonel Heyns first?"

"He's taking a break," du Plessis said. "Prinsloo is running the unit in his absence."

"Eugene, think we should go look?"

"Absolutely," grinned Meiring, "I'll drive. Chris gave me a quicker route."

Roux winced. "If you insist, but happy to take my car," he said, but found he was talking to himself. Meiring was gone.

"General. If the MBL occupies the place, and I suspect there is reason to close them down, do I have a green light to proceed?"

Du Plessis twirled his glasses for several moments and then nodded. "Agreed, but let's hope we don't have another APLA story. I'll stay on the radio, but I'm not sure if I'll be in range. Does Meiring have a radio in his car?"

"He does. But if we have a problem getting through to you, we'll go via the main radio room in the Charge Office."

"Good luck, Roux. Let me know what you find."

Thirty minutes later, they were hurtling down roads Roux never knew existed. The dark western Cape countryside flashed past as he alternated between staring at the passing landscape and furtive glances at the speedometer. He'd thought about asking Meiring how he intended on finding the farm, but opted to allow him, in the interests of his own personal safety, to concentrate on his driving. His thoughts went back to the row with Mel.

His anger had dissipated somewhat, but the rancor remained. To find out his wife still harbored feelings, if only as a friend, or so she'd claimed, for a man she dated decades before, was a hard one to come to grips with. Why hadn't she told him about her feelings for Phil before they married? And *she* accuses him of becoming withdrawn and distant. He reflected for a moment. Had he? Is that what South West left him with? An image of his interpreter slumped forward in his safety belt with the top half of his head sprayed across the interior of the Land Rover, brought back a memory he had spent years blocking out.

The early evening ambush in the dry river bed lasted a matter of seconds, and he owed his survival to the reliability of the vehicle, which, although riddled with bullet holes, he'd managed to limp back to base. It was only then he discovered he had been shot through the left shoulder. He blamed himself for the whole bloody mess. The interpreter was dead because of his incompetence. If they'd just left the meeting with the informant half an hour earlier, they'd have been back in base camp long before dark. Hospitalization, followed by two months of convalescence in Windhoek, culminated in his transfer, at his request, and with his father's help, out of SB a month later. They were on their way to Cape Town. His physical wounds healed quickly. But the mental ones remained. He refused counseling, or to discuss it with Mel, preferring to dig a hole in the dark recesses of his mind and bury the experience. Until tonight.

He closed his eyes, and for the first time in four years, looked inward. At himself, and at what he had become. Time had allowed him to surround himself with a high wall, pushing back the memories until, over time, they faded. As his mental health improved, his spirits rose, and he could focus on his marriage and the family. But of late, the desk job had taken its toll, and he'd again retreated behind his wall, becoming withdrawn and depressed. He sucked in a long breath, allowing it to escape slowly through pursed lips. Maybe she was right, he reflected, Marius Roux was not a pleasant individual. No wonder their physical relationship was almost non-existent.

The awareness of the car slowing down brought him back to the present.

"We're here," said Meiring as they entered what Roux assumed was the town or village of The Willows. The few shops and a broken down hotel which made up the center of town were in darkness. Small dirt roads branched off on either side. Meiring veered to the right, crossed the road, and pulled up at the small office of a two-pump gas station. It, too, was in total darkness. Meiring got out and banged on the door until a dull flicker of light appeared inside, followed by a startled Colored face appearing at a small window.

*"Ja baas?"*

"Police," Meiring introduced himself. "Outside," he ordered. Moments later, a man in shorts and vest stood hugging his chest, staring wide-eyed at the unwelcome caller. After several minutes of talking and gesticulations, mainly in the direction from which they'd come, Meiring climbed back in the car.

"Seems we past the turnoff. Don't know how I missed it."

Roux hazarded at a wild guess. Anyone flying past a road sign at something just short of light-speed was bound to miss it.

They'd only been driving for minutes, at a speed Roux was more accustomed to, when Meiring slammed on the brakes.

"There it is, clear as daylight. Can't believe I didn't see it."

Roux peered through the darkness at a sign, which read "Waterfalls," in faded black paint, and reached knee height. It was not bigger than two feet long and about twenty inches high. *Clear as mud*. The sign pointed down a dirt road to their right. Meiring turned and began cruising down the road.

"Shouldn't we put some thought to what we are going to do when we get there?" said Roux.

"Not going to get there by car," replied Meiring as he dimmed the headlights and peered through the windshield into the darkness. "Once we know where it is, we go in on foot. No point in announcing ourselves until we know what's there."

"Really?" retorted Roux, giving Meiring a look which said, "You have to be joking."

"The petrol station guy said it's about a kilometer up this road, and we've gone about eight hundred meters. There's a rise ahead. I suggest we stop this side of it and walk up to the top of the high ground to see what's out there." He grinned mischievously.

Roux squinted into the darkness. There was a slight variance in the dark colors ahead of him which he assumed was where the sky and the rise Meiring referred to met.

"OK," he said, feeling anything but "OK."

The crest of the rise became clearer to him as they neared. Meiring pulled off the road and parked under an enormous umbrella shaped tree, and turned off the motor. He leaned into the back seat and pulled a rucksack onto his lap. From a side pocket, he handed Roux a semi-automatic pistol in a clip-on holster.

"I drew this from the armory for you. I have my own."

Roux stared down at the weapon. He detested firearms, and would happily admit to his inability to use them, a fact borne out by his shooting scores on the range during College Training. During his time in uniform, carrying a sidearm was a requirement, but it always felt as though there was an offensive object attached to his belt. There had been only one occasion in which he needed to draw his, and he'd promptly dropped it, to the utter disgust of his partner.

He eyed the pistol for several moments, and then grudgingly took it, placing it on the seat next to him. Meiring followed this with a pair of binoculars.

"If the place is still operating, it'll be lit up, so you should still be able to see with these. Hang it over your neck *inside* your jacket. I've brought the NVG's which we can use if its in darkness. But first we need to hide the car."

He reversed into the road so he faced the brush alongside the road, turned on the lights and flicked them to bright.

"I need you to walk in front of me so we don't end up in a hole or hit a rock."

Roux obliged but after ten paces into the brush he stopped, but an irritated wave from Meiring sent him further into the long grass. Three stops and three hand gestures later, Meiring turned to the right and parked the car behind a low row of thick thorn trees, switched off, killed the lights and got out holding the rucksack, which he slung on his back.

"Let's go."

They walked back to the road and followed it to the top of the high ground. A valley, which ended against a low range of mountains, lay below them. The black valley floor was interspersed with tiny blobs of lights off in the distance. But below and to their left was an array of lights emanating from several buildings and spotlights much closer than the rest.

"Bingo," said Meiring. "That looks like Waterfalls. But we need to get closer. Doesn't look far. Follow me."

"Some moonlight would help," mumbled Roux, tugging his hat down on his head as they set off. "Why don't we just follow the road?"

"There's a good chance they'll have guards out watching the road, so better we cut through the bush," said Meiring, over his shoulder. "You got your gun?"

"Oh crap," muttered Roux and jogged back to the car. He was puffing when he rejoined Meiring, who gave him a look used when the wearer is in serious doubt as to the competence of his companion.

Shaking his head, Meiring moved off into the darkness, Roux stuffed the weapon into a jacket pocket and stumbled after him, attempting to ward off branches from side swiping him in the face. After several minutes of walking, Meiring stopped.

Roux cannoned into his back, knocking the man forward.

"Oops. Sorry. But you need to get your brake lights fixed," he whispered, hoping his attempt at joviality would deter Meiring from shooting him on the spot.

Meiring turned, his face inches from Roux. "Jeez Marius, are you being tracked by a herd of elephants? Damn well sounds like it," he said in a voice which was more than a whisper.

"Sorry, Eugene, I'm not into this crawling around in the dark business. I can't see a frigging word," he whispered, borrowing one of Mel's favorite quips.

"You want to go back?" Meiring queried in a normal voice.

"No, I'll be careful. Promise. Just walk slower," Roux continued to whisper.

"Why you whispering?"

He was stumped by that one, having to consider the question for a moment.

"I thought it's what you did in a jungle in the middle of the night." This time, he spoke normally.

To his gratitude, Meiring laughed. "We're still a way off Marius, but from here on let's try to keep the talking to a minimum with less noise. OK?"

Roux grunted, hoping Meiring couldn't see his look of disgust with the entire enterprise. After what seemed an eternity of being scratched, slapped and pricked by what he hoped were specimens of the flora variety, they reached a six strand fence. He was sweating, his breath coming in quick gasps.

"Vineyard," said Meiring in a hushed voice. "Wait here and get your breath back. I just want to make sure it's not electrified or alarmed." He disappeared into the black maze.

Roux gulped in the cool air, trying to reduce his panting. He was making positive progress with his control exercises when he yelped at Meiring's sudden appearance next to him.

"Quiet!" Meiring looked determined, and a touch annoyed. "No problems. We can cut through the vineyard towards that glow, which I assume are the main buildings.

Oh, and Marius, watch your step. Cape Cobras hunt in vineyards at night."

Roux went cold. After guns, snakes ranked number two on his hate list. "You're not serious. Are you?" His attempt at a whisper sounded more like a squeak.

Meiring chuckled softly and slid through the strands in the fence. Roux followed as best he knew how. With the relatively clear terrain and aided by the glow of lights, they picked up their pace. Roux's eyes darted continuously between Meiring's back and the ground. Without warning Meiring slowed, so did Roux, just in time to avoid a second collision.

"Gate," he pointed, "probably leads to the buildings."

The gate creaked on old hinges as they swung it open. Once through, Roux gently slid the bolt back into place and crouched down next to Meiring on a well-used path which meandered off toward the buildings, the outlines of which Roux could now see. He unzipped his jacket, pulled out the binoculars and put them to his eyes, adjusting the image before panning across the area ahead of them.

This was no abandoned farm.


FROM WHERE HE CROUCHED, he could see four buildings. The one off to their right was much larger than the rest. Men, carrying boxes, bags and other items, were wandering in and out through a door alongside what looked like a massive roller door. It reminded him of an aircraft hanger. Two smaller buildings angled away from them, restricting their view to side on only. The last and smallest of the four buildings, a house, flanked by a row of small trees, was brightly lit with yellow light emanating from several windows and doorways. It was off to the left and the furthest away. He could see dark shapes milling about amongst the buildings, drifting in and out of the pockets of light cast across the area by floodlights on poles.

He touched Meiring's shoulder and pointed at the house. "That must be where most of the top guys will be."

"Let's move around to the left and see if we can get a look at the front of the house," said Meiring, before creeping off into the darkness.

Roux sucked on his teeth and followed. His mall-friendly boots were making his feet hurt.

There was an expanse of open ground behind the house, which turned out to be a paddock and devoid of any cover, forcing them to loop around it until they discovered a small, overgrown orchard. They moved through the lines of trees until they encountered a broken-down fence. From there, the front of the house was clearly visible, although still a good distance away.

"I suppose this is also cobra hunting grounds?" said Roux.

"Nope. It's an apple orchard. Puff adders like the apples," said Meiring, with what sounded to Roux like a snicker. "But don't worry," he said, slapping his rucksack. "I've got anti-serum. Just don't scream if you are bitten, it'll attract attention."

*Ah! Well, that makes everything better. I'm going to scream bloody murder if I get bitten*, Roux decided, although he had to concede the boy scout thought of everything, which reminded him. Meiring exuded a faintly familiar body odor which he couldn't quite place until he slapped at a mosquito on his cheek.

"Hey!" he whispered, "you got mosquito cream?"

"Shit! Sorry," said Meiring, as he fished out a tube from his top pocket.

As Roux covered his exposed body parts with liberal amounts of the cream, he found the smell both comforting and disturbing, bringing back further memories of South West.

They knelt down behind the fence. Roux lifted his glasses. A floodlight lit up the house, which was no larger than the average suburban two-bedroomed house, with a small porch covered with a tiled overhang fronting it. Bright light shone through the open door and two front windows, illuminating three men standing on the porch. The taller of the three, dressed in a tee shirt and jeans, was waving his arms around in what seemed like an animated discussion. They were too far to hear, but studying the man's face through his glasses revealed a middle-aged Black man with a mustache. The other two were both Coloreds. Panning across the front of the house, he counted three cars and at least five light delivery trucks and SUVs parked in a cluster, around which a group of men were busy unloading boxes, crates, packets, and other items.

Meiring elbowed him and cocked his head towards the dirt road leading up to the house, along which a pair of yellow lights were moving towards them.

"Vehicle coming," he said, using his own binoculars to scan the area to their front. "From what I can see, there is a mix of Blacks and Coloreds going in and out of the other buildings. The three on the porch are probably Khumalo, Davids and Akmet."

He swung the rucksack from his back and laid it in front of him, unzipping a side pocket, he retrieved a handheld radio and a small green bag.

"I'm going to the back of the orchard to see if I can make comms with the station. Time to get Prinsloo and his boys geared up, and ready to go, just in case."

"Will you be able to get the Control Room?" asked Roux.

Meiring tapped the green bag. "Extended aerial," he said, backing into the trees.

Roux turned his glasses on the approaching vehicle. Within minutes, a blue BMW pulled up in front of the house. Two men got out, both wearing dark hoodies, and approached the house. There was something about the driver which caught his attention. The man seemed familiar. Was it the way he walked? The vehicle's occupants walked onto the porch and shook hands with the three men. Adjusting the focus, he trained the glasses on the two newcomers, squinting to get a clearer look at their faces. Definitely both light-skinned. White? He continued to study the driver, desperate to get a glimpse of his face. There definitely was something familiar about him. But what? The problem was he didn't know any Coloreds other than those in his unit.   Could they be . . .? No it couldn't.

He continued to stare, his eyes beginning to water. A sudden movement next to him caused his buttocks to clench, but relax when he saw Meiring. He realized he'd stopped breathing and gulped in a lung full of air before handing the glasses to Meiring.

"The two guys in hoodies just arrived in the BMW. Hard to see their faces, but do they look like Coloreds to you?"

Meiring focused on the gathering on the porch. "Hard to tell," he said, returning the glasses to Roux. "But I would guess they are Coloreds. Why?"

Roux shrugged. "I don't know, it's just the guy in the green pants—"

He was cut off by the sound of a loud clanking, sliding noise coming from the "hanger." He swung the glasses up in time to see the roller door grinding its way upward. A pair of bright lights temporarily blinded him. Cursing, he pulled his head back. Coming out of the doorway was a vehicle, followed at equal intervals by two more. Three compact sedans, clearly visible in the floodlights, exited the building, moving towards the dirt road at a sedate speed. They watched as the vehicles made their way onto the road and then sped off into the night. Meiring was digging around in his rucksack again. This time producing a pen and notebook, which he flipped open and began jotting down something.

"Two Nissans and a Ford," he hissed as he wrote. "Blue, white, and what looked like cream or yellow. Couldn't see the plates, but they're all old models."

"Wonder where they're going?" said Roux. "Could you tell how many occupants?"

"Too dark."

Roux rolled off his knees and sat up, stretching his legs out, the joints popping in protest. A few moments later, a message from his stomach reminded him he was both hungry and thirsty.

"Do you have anything else in your bag of tricks, like some water?"

His companion's hand disappeared into the rucksack, emerging with a small bottle of water. Roux took it without a word and gulped down the contents. He sighed in pleasure, then gave Meiring a hopeful look.

"Don't suppose there's any coffee and something to eat in there?"

Meiring's hand once again delved into the wizard's bag, this time producing first a small flask with a plastic cup screwed onto the top, and then a sandwich, wrapped in brown paper.

"Got them from the canteen before we left. I can't vouch for the sandwich. If you get the squirts, don't come complaining to me." A playful grin creased his face.

Roux unwrapped the sandwiches and got half of one into his mouth with two bites while he busied himself with pouring a coffee. The cheese was stale and almost tasteless, but he relished it.

"We need to shut this operation down," he said through the second half of the sandwich. "Did you get a message to Prinsloo?" he queried, looking across at Meiring, who, to his surprise, was busy drawing a map of the farm in his notebook.

"I did. He's getting his teams formed and will be ready to go within hours." He sat down, facing the house. "I'm going to suggest he move in at first light. With a bit of luck, we get the entire bunch, especially," he pointed at the porch, "That merry bunch."

No sooner had he finished speaking when the two new arrivals returned to the BMW. Seconds later, they were gone.

"Damn!" said Roux. "We needed those guys."

"If we get the other three, Gainsford will quickly find out who they are. I'm going to talk to Prinsloo and get this thing launched. I'll ask him to update du Plessis." Meiring was gone before Roux could respond.

Once he returned, confirming everything was a go, and with the general's sanction, they sat down to decide on their next moves over the remaining hours. Prinsloo had suggested they cover the back door to the house as soon as the choppers came into view to prevent anyone escaping across the paddock. All they needed to do was position themselves. While they debated their options, the activity around the buildings was winding down, the lights extinguished as most of the men disappeared indoors. Only the floodlights remained on. They agreed to use the last hour before dawn to position themselves behind the house as best they could; relying on the darkness to cover their approach.

"You better try to get some rest," said Meiring.

Roux spent the next few hours shifting from his back to his side before eventually dozing off. After what seemed like minutes, he awoke, feeling cramped and irritable. In disgust, he sat up and poured another cup of coffee.

Meiring sat staring at the house and then crawled over to Roux. "I'm going to check out the back of the house. Stay here." He moved off, bent double.

Roux lay down on his back and stared up at the coal-black sky. Perhaps after today, this whole Mandela episode will be over, giving him and Mel time to work on their relationship. Once the man was out, and no longer his responsibility, they could take some time off and get away, just the two of them. Rian could stay with Sonja. Once Mel and he were back on track, they could talk about Rian's future. The family needed to be together again.

The return of Meiring interrupted his thoughts. "Going to be tricky, but there is what appears to be servants' quarters just behind the house. If we can get up to it and it's empty, we can move to the back door when Prinsloo arrives. The problem is we need to use the paddock to get there with no cover except the wooden-pole fence. My guess is it'll start getting light around five-ish so we need to be in position before then. We'll move at about four, so best we try to get what rest we can."

243

# Saturday, February 10th, 1990

MEIRING CLIMBED THROUGH THE large wooden poles of the paddock fence and knelt on one knee, adjusting his rucksack. On the other side of the paddock, they could see the house with a small square structure behind it.

Roux pointed at it, and whispered, "Is that the servants' quarters?"

Meiring nodded. "We need to check if they are empty. If they are, it's an ideal position. OK," he said, pulling his pistol from its holster and motioning for Roux to follow suit. "We're going to move low but quick to the paddock fence behind the house. No noise. Ready?"

Roux experienced a moment of terror when he thought he'd lost his pistol before remembering it was in his jacket pocket. Pulling it out, he clipped the holster to his jeans, hoping Meiring had not chambered a round before giving it to him, and then gave him a thumbs up.

Pistol out in front of him, Meiring crouched down. Roux copied the action, announcing his movements by breaking wind. It sounded like an exhaust backfire in the quiet night air. Meiring glanced at him, but the blackness prevented Roux from seeing the expression he could only imagine on the man's face. He grimaced as Meiring took off, not quite running, but moving fast. Roux trundled after him, and three grumbling gas emissions later, they were kneeling at the paddock fence behind the house. The back door of the house, less than fifty paces away, was visible.

"The sandwich," mumbled Roux by way of apology and justification.

"I'm going to have a look. Stay here," said Meiring. He slipped between the wooden poles, dropped to his stomach, and began slithering towards the small building. Once he reached it, he slowly rose, peering through one, then a second window, his dark shape visible against the white wall. Crouching down, he disappeared around a corner.

Minutes later, Roux made out the man waving at him. Keeping low, but not sliding along on his stomach, he joined him.

"Empty," said Meiring. "We'll wait it out here."

Roux shoved the pistol back into the holster and slid down the wall until he was seated on the ground, sweat pouring down his face. What he would give for a hot meal and a shower and twelve hours of sleep, but he knew their day was only just beginning.

They sat against the wall in silence until the first glimmers of daylight when Meiring nudged him.

"Time to get in position," he whispered, his mouth close to Roux's ear. "You need to go to the far corner facing the house, which should give you clear sight of the back door and windows. No one gets out. You ready?"

Roux grunted, struggling to his feet by sliding up the wall. He slunk along the back wall, around the first corner, and then took up position at the far corner. Dropping to his hands and knees, he peered around the corner at the back of the house. *No lights and no dogs, thankfully*. He glimpsed Meiring's face at the other end of the building, and after exchanging an almost imperceptible nod, he sat down, facing out across the vineyard. Off to his left, he could see the outline of the "hanger" in the fast improving light.

"More waiting," he grumbled, as the stale taste of cheese invaded the back of his throat when he belched. However, he didn't have long to wait. The faint, but distinctive sound of helicopters reached his ears. Looking out over the vineyard, he could see the gray outline of two Oryx troop transporters grow larger as they skimmed low across the countryside. They were minutes away. He stuck his head around the corner in time to see Meiring waving frantically and pointing at the back door. Drawing his pistol, he raced towards the door. As he neared it, a light came on in a small window to his right. Bathroom, he concluded, noting the frosted glass pane.

They were now on either side of the door. Meiring tested the handle. Locked. They both crouched low, waiting.

The first Oryx was almost at the vineyard, the noise enough to wake everyone on the farm. The second was sweeping low around the back of the "hanger," which meant it would come in adjacent to the two smaller buildings. A small Alouette III helicopter buzzed the area, the barrel of its door mounted machine gun poking down, before flying over the house and landing at the front, throwing up clouds of dirt and dust. By now, both transporters were down and offloading their cargo of operators. *It's finally happening*. He checked on Meiring.

The man was laser-focused on the door, his pistol level with his face.

Seconds later, they heard a key turn in the lock, and the door inched open. Meiring leaped up, shoving a shoulder against it. There was a cry of alarm from inside as the door flew open.

"Police! On the ground," he heard Meiring bellow.

Roux followed him into the black opening, entering what now became apparent as the kitchen. Meiring shoved two men to the ground, their hands behind their necks.

"Watch these two." He disappeared through a doorway.

The men lying on the floor were both Colored, middle-aged and dressed in tee shirts and boxer shorts.

"Which one of you is Davids?" said Roux, keeping his voice low while trying to sound menacing. The shorter of the two raised a hand. Roux nudged the other with his boot. "Akmet?" The man, overweight and sweating profusely, nodded. "OK, keep the hands behind your necks," he said. Images of American police TV shows raced through his mind. *Wish I could remember what they said in situations like this.* The only word he could recall was "freeze," and seemed a touch inappropriate, considering the situation.

"Stay where you are and no one gets hurt," was the best he could come up with, but he was quite pleased with himself, until, with a start, he realized he had forgotten to check if the pistol was loaded. *Oh crap! If they make a dash for the door, I'll have a problem.* He chambered a round, which made the two men stiffen, staring up at him wide eyed. "Faces down," he snarled. He could hear footsteps and doors opening as Meiring went through the house.

Roux shuffled backwards until he bumped against the edge of the still open door, kicked it closed, and fumbled with his other hand until he found the lever and then the key. He locked the door and pocketed the key, and then relaxed.

"Bring them to the lounge," called Meiring moments later.

"Up," commanded Roux, "and keep those hands behind your neck and walk to the lounge." He followed, keeping several paces between them and himself.

"On the floor," said Meiring, motioning with his gun. There was a couch and a single armchair on a threadbare carpet which covered less than half of the floor. He held a radio in his one hand, with a foot planted on the back of a prostrate Black man. "Delta six-one, this is Bravo two, do you copy?"

A voice responded. "Where are you?"

"In the house with three suspects," replied Meiring, "front door to the house is closed. We are in the lounge."

"Copied," said Delta six-one, who Roux assumed was Prinsloo. "One of my guys will enter now."

The door flew open and a STG man burst into the room, weapon poised for immediate use.

"Police!" shouted Meiring, raising his hands. "Captain Meiring and Colonel Roux."

The man lowered his weapon. "Morning," he said, as though passing a stranger in the park. "I'll take those three and put them with the rest." He yanked the man Meiring was guarding to his feet and shoved him towards the front door. "Up," he gestured with his weapon at Roux's captives. The two men jumped to their feet and hurried out, passing another camouflaged clad figure in the doorway.

"Well done, Marius," said Meiring, grinning. "That was Khumalo I found in here hiding behind the couch." He pointed at the two Coloreds. "Any idea who they are?"

"The old, bowlegged, short shit is Davids," said Roux. "Not what I expected. The fat guy is Akmet."

Meiring pumped his arm. "Great! We got all three then."

The entire area in and around the farm complex was a hive of activity. All the lights in the buildings were on, and groups of men were being shepherded toward a grass area next to the road. The two Oryxes, with drooping rotors, stood near the other buildings.

Roux beamed as they walked onto the porch. "Success at last. Hey! You learn all this jungle shit with *Koevoet*?"

"Yup," said Meiring.

Roux knew all about the police's anti-terrorist unit which had operated in South West. They had always been the "go to" reaction force when SB needed their intelligence followed-up on.

"Where's Prinsloo?"

Meiring squinted through the half-light. "There," he pointed toward the Alouette nestled on the grass in front of the house. The two men ambled over.

"Morning gentlemen," said Prinsloo. "Seems like we got the lot. The stop-lines grabbed a couple of squirters, but the rest were still either in their beds or only half-awake."

"Excellent," said Roux, "and I didn't hear any firing."

"Not a shot. My guys are clearing the buildings now." Prinsloo paused as one of his men walked up and handed him a coffee flask.

"Found it at the fence by the orchard," said the man before walking away.

"Um . . . ah . . . it's mine, sorry, must have dropped it," Roux mumbled with a sheepish grin. He took the flask, looking around for somewhere to dump it.

Prinsloo harrumphed. "There's a Sergeant Gainsford, and a woman constable, at the road block wanting to come up. You know them?"

"Ours," said Meiring.

"No problem, but they'll have to wait and come up with the transports when they arrive. I don't want anyone arriving or leaving the area before I know it's secured," said Prinsloo, just as the radio strapped to his chest squawked. "Go ahead Tomas," he said.

"There're some boxes here in the big building which you need to see," said a metallic sounding voice.

He looked at Roux. "You want to have a look?"

Roux nodded. A feeling of dread swept over him.

"On our way, Tomas," said Prinsloo.

The three men made their way to the building, which turned out to be a fruit packing and storage area. Packing equipment lines filled almost half of the building with dozens of empty crates and farming equipment scattered around the edges. The workbenches, car parts, and a pit at the other end suggested a vehicle maintenance area. Stacked against the far-side wall, partially covered with a yellow tarpaulin, were several long wood boxes. Someone had levered up the lids on two of them, and Roux looked in one. AK-47s. Brand new by the look of them.

A short man with pale skin and red eyebrows pointed at the other open box. "It's what's in that one that should worry you."

Roux walked over and kicked the lid aside. "Holy crap," he exclaimed, the muscles of his stomach cramping. Inside were two rocket-propelled grenade launchers, or

RPGs as everyone knew them, around which were secreted at least six grenades.

After a quick tour of the rest of the building, Roux and Meiring wandered back to the house, leaving Prinsloo to supervise the ongoing search.

"Yours, I think?" said Roux, handing Meiring the coffee flask as they walked. The captain gave him a disgusted look as he reluctantly accepted the offending object.

"I'll wait 'til Gainsford gets here, then hand Khumalo over to him. The transports can take the rest back to Compton," said Meiring. "Van der Merwe and his men are also on their way here. Do you want to go home and clean up and join us later?"

Roux shook his head. "Yes, and no. I need to have a shower and some breakfast, but then I have a date with Mr. Jonas Kani at the Foundation. Make sure Gainsford understands finding out what happened to Conradie is a priority, and who the two men in the BMW were."

"You bet," said Meiring.

They were interrupted when one of Prinsloo's men trotted up with the aerial of the radio strapped to his back waving around his head, and handed Meiring the handset.

"Compton calling you," he said.

Meiring pushed the transmit button. "Bravo Two."

"Bravo Two this is control. I have General du Plessis for Colonel Roux."

He handed the radio to Roux.

Roux hesitated. Was this just a follow up or had there been another development? He held the handset to his mouth. "Go ahead General."

"Morning Colonel, any success?"

"Yes General, we got the lot, including Khumalo, Davids and Akmet, along with a pile of weapons with at least two RPGs. Seems our so-called political activists had a lot more in mind than protesting."

"Good," there was a momentary pause. "Two things you need to be aware of. First, a visual sighting in Soweto confirms Tau is back in Joburg. Second. Our man is being released by midday tomorrow."


MEIRING TOOK THE NEWS of Mandela's imminent release with a disinterested shrug. "With Tau back in Joburg, and Khumalo and his mob detained. I don't think we have an awful lot to worry about," he said, and wandered off to check on the building searches.

Gainsford arrived with the transport vehicles and, grinning, took charge of the detainees. Roux summoned Gainsford's companion, a tall, stout, middle-aged policewoman whose mousy brown hair was shorter than Roux's, and commandeered her services to drive him home.

Using the spare door key hidden in an old paint tin in the garage, he let himself into an empty house. He called Kani to alert him of his imminent arrival, showered, shaved and changed into a short-sleeve shirt and casual slacks. As an afterthought, he added a light jacket. Two bowls of cereal and three cups of coffee later, he was on the road to the Foundation.

Jonas Kani, just as he had before, met him on the porch of his residence. The usual smile, which Roux considered facetious, was absent. Instead, Kani appeared to be all business. Roux declined the offer of coffee or tea, and the two men sat opposite each other in the lounge.

"Your visit to Waterfalls was successful?" asked Kani in an offhand manner.

"Yes. It was, thanks in part to your information. There are one or two loose ends to clear up, but we should be completed by the end of the weekend."

There was a questioning look on Kani's face. "You arrest *all* the leadership? As you can appreciate, my concern for Mr. Mandela's safety is commensurate with your own."

Roux thought he detected a touch of sarcasm in the professor's voice.

"We did. Khumalo, Davids, and Akmet, along with several other men. They're being interrogated to determine the extent of their operations."

Kani looked thoughtful as he scratched his chin. "Only those three?"

Roux peered at him. "What do you mean?"

The professor leaned back in his chair. "Allow me to provide an analogy, of sorts. Do you recall your Greek mythology from your school days? Hercules and the Hydra?"

The corners of Roux's mouth turned down. After some scratching around in his memory, he said, "Multi-head reptile?"

"Quite so," said Kani. "Hercules could only defeat the creature by enlisting the help of his nephew to simultaneously sever all of its heads. Apologies for the mythology lesson, but my point is this. You may well have chopped off one head, but is it the only head?"

Roux gave Kani a look which implied he thought he was being spun a bit of a yarn. "You suggesting Khumalo is not the leader?"

"What I am *asking,* Colonel, is are *you* sure he is? I have never met the man, but by all accounts, he is not the brightest bulb in the candelabra. A bit of a low life with no known political connections and limited aspirations who, based solely on Mr. de Klerk's speech, is prepared to alter the political landscape, and even tilt the country into a civil war." His forehead wrinkled. "I have to wonder how he gathered the financial and other resources so quickly to set up the facility at Waterfalls. Sound plausible to you?"

*Put that way, no, it didn't.* But he would not give the smug bastard the pleasure of admitting it. "We are exploring all aspects of the situation," said Roux.

"Spoken like a true copper, as they say in the UK," chuckled Kani. "I take it you are tracking down the owners of the farm?"

Roux gulped. It seemed like Kani had a better grasp of his job than he did. "Of course, as we speak."

"Good. But I digress. The MBL was not the reason I asked to meet." Kani cleared his throat, and sat in silence for a moment, seeming to marshal his thoughts as Roux waited with a sense of growing apprehension. He found the man's worried expression disconcerting. It seemed out of character.

"Colonel," began Kani, "I have a confession to make, but I hope you will take the time to consider my reasoning and apply your mind before you react." He paused.

Roux held his gaze, unblinking.

"There is someone I would like you to meet," said Kani, rising slowly to his feet. "But before I introduce you, I again urge you to show restraint, and provide me the opportunity to clarify the present situation in which I find myself." He paused again. "Do I have your agreement, Colonel?"

*How far do I trust him? By his own admission, he's lied once already.* He crossed one leg over the knee of the other and said. "Agreed. I will hear you out, but be warned, if you have in any way broken the law, I may have no option but to arrest you. Understood?"

"It will be your decision," said Kani. "I only ask you to consider the larger political picture, considering what is going to happen over the next days and weeks. But, let me not waste your valuable time." He turned and walked down the short hallway, motioning for Roux to follow.

He stopped at the last door and tapped gently. "Temba, our visitor is here." He opened the door and stepped back to allow Roux to enter.

He stepped into the darkened room. The man he saw in the bed lay deathly still. His mouth and nose were covered by an oxygen mask connected to what he guessed was a ventilator of sorts. The man's pain-filled eyes opened briefly to gaze at him for several seconds before closing.

"Colonel, I would like you to meet my brother, Temba, recently arrived in the country in the company of a small group of ANC cadres. I believe you know him better as 'the courier.'"

If the man was worried Roux would overreact, he needn't of. His mouth dropped open, and he just stared at Kani, flummoxed and wordless.

"I understand this announcement comes as somewhat of a surprise, but allow me to explain. My brother is here on a mission, a peaceful mission, with no intent to cause harm or to flout the laws. In fact, since the ANC is unbanned, he is not in transgression of the Terrorism laws. His purpose is to deliver a message to Mr. Mandela, the contents of which are known only to a very select few in the organization, including, of course, our president.

"Colonel, my brother has an exceptional memory, and it was for this reason he was asked to undertake the mission. He has committed the message to memory. No written version exists, which was deliberate, to avoid it becoming lost or discovered. However, there was one drawback. My brother's long absence from the country, resulting in the loss of his ability to converse in the local dialects, meant he would have to be accompanied by two others, both unarmed. But, as it transpires, some idiot in Johannesburg, unbeknown to the hierarchy, provided an armed escort. One man died, which I find tragically ironic, considering days later the ANC was unbanned. The decision also led to a very unpleasant experience for Temba's son, my nephew." He studied Roux for several moments before continuing.

"It was hoped, with the relaxation of the limitations on Mr. Mandela receiving outside visitors, I would find a legitimate pretext to gain an audience for my brother. This hope was dashed when the authorities became aware of his existence."

Roux looked from Kani to the brother. "Is he ill or injured?"

"The former, I'm afraid," said Kani, as he sat on the end of the bed. "My brother agreed to this undertaking, as he believes it will be his last contribution to the struggle. You see, he suffers from a chronic heart disease, a fact he hid from the leadership in Lusaka, but the opinion of various London specialists is his time is limited. The disease is terminal. His health is deteriorating fast, a situation exacerbated by his exertions while trying to evade your men. After his escape from the tavern, he made his way here before collapsing. I arranged medical treatment at our clinic here on the property, but he needs expert medical attention, which, given the circumstances, I could not arrange. However, the New York office has offered to assist and several heart specialists, accompanied by a team of lawyers, are already on route to South Africa. Until they arrive and can assess the situation, he is confined to bed in my house. No one at the Foundation knows who he is, so his identity remains a secret." A look of sadness crossed his face as he looked at his brother.

"The message remains undelivered. Your turn, Colonel."

Roux shook his head in amazement. "Holy cow," he said, staring at both men. "Can I ask why you're telling me now? Why not wait until the release and then hand over the message? I'm sure the Foundation could arrange the best medical care available here." He was on the point of adding, "even if he is Black," but bit his tongue instead. "Maybe fly him to New York."

"Three reasons. The first is Lusaka's wish for it to be delivered *before* the release, which I believe is imminent. The second is, we know APLA and the MBL are actively looking for him, and I fear they will kill him if they find out he is here. I also suspected you were becoming convinced of my involvement after you saw the photo of the Redskins jacket, which my brother was wearing the night of your raid. My compliments on your astute observation, but as a result, our situation is now rather complex."

Roux gave a wry smile. "So arresting him won't resolve anything for us. In his condition, I would imagine any form of questioning would be pointless, if not fatal. But hold on. We have him entering the country as Temba Chewitt. How can he be your brother?"

"We are brothers. My parents were both teachers at a missionary school in the Eastern Cape, where we grew up. After the Sharpeville massacre, my mother became radicalized, joining the ANC, as did my brother, much to the annoyance of my father. Unfortunately, my mother's activities drew the attention of the police, so with the help of the Missionary Society she, and my brother, fled the country and settled in Ireland. This was too much for my father, who divorced her. Several years later, she married a West Indian by the name of Chewitt. They believed a more English sounding surname would help my brother's acceptance in the country, so he adopted him.

"As to interrogating him. Any form of physical or mental abuse would only hasten the inevitable, even with the best medical care. So you would be none the wiser, and I would be robbed of the chance to spend what time is left with a man who is very dear to me." Kani paused, taking a deep breath. "I am also afraid my nephew has fled to parts unknown to either of us. He did not want to be used as leverage against his father."

Roux experienced a moment of fleeting anger at hearing of the boys' escape, but he knew deep down he could never use a child to intimidate the parents. Others might, but he could not. Besides, Kani's minor role playing exercise had left an indelible image in his head.

"Then I have to ask, what happens with the message? Will you wait until he's released to give it to him?"

"That really depends on you, Colonel."

A cynical smile played at the corners of Roux's mouth. "You're not seriously suggesting I deliver it for you? Or are you?"

The two men remained silent, their eyes locked.

Roux turned and walked back to the lounge. He heard Kani say something in a soothing voice to his brother and then close the bedroom door before following him.

"Help him Marius, he's a good man." It was as though Mel was standing right next to him as he recalled her plea.

He collapsed into a chair, running a hand through his hair. He finally had the courier and could stop him reaching Mandela. It was the last piece of the jigsaw puzzle. Tau was back in Joburg. The MBL had been stopped dead in their tracks and now the courier identified. Sure, they would not uncover the contents of the message, but it would remain undelivered until Mandela's release. Mission accomplished. He looked up as Kani sat down opposite him.

"Professor, I need an honest answer from you, please. Has your brother told you what the message is?"

"No, although I have asked him. He refused. Which does not surprise me."

Roux stared at Kani, not sure whether to believe him or assume, as he always had with Blacks, the man was lying. "Help him Marius, he's a good man."

"I assume your brother is being cared for by your clinic staff, and therefore, I have one of two options. Detain you and have your brother moved to a hospital and placed under guard, or insist you remain here with your brother until Mandela is released. The first option is the easiest for me, but, I admit not for you. I need your word that if you remain here under guard, you will not attempt to leave the premises or pass any messages to the staff until the release is complete." He paused and then said in a low voice. "It will also provide protection for your brother should the MBL or APLA find out where he is."

There was a long silence as Kani stared out the window before making eye contact again. "You have my word, and thank you. The protection would be a great relief. May I join my brother and inform him of your decision? I am sure you need to arrange the guards."

As Kani left the room, Roux ambled over to the telephone. His initial intention was to yank the connection cord out, but then thought better of it. Kani may need to call for medical help. Instead, he unplugged the handset from the device and shoved it into his jacket pocket and then went outside. Minutes later, he finished explaining to Els on the radio what he needed. Els confirmed he and his team would be on their way within the quarter hour. Roux was about to radio du Plessis, but hesitated. For no reason he could fathom, he opted to not update him. A decision he hoped he would not regret. His attempts to contact Meiring via the Control Room proved futile. They couldn't raise him but had spoken to Prinsloo, who requested they assure Roux all was progressing as planned. He returned to the lounge.

After a brief wait, Kani returned. "I will need to advise my secretary I will be unavailable until further notice." He pointed to the telephone handset in Roux's pocket. After reconnecting the instrument, he spoke briefly to two people, emphasizing he would be at the house but not contactable, and would explain everything later. He unplugged the handset and placed it on the sideboard. "Can I offer you a drink now, Colonel, as we wait for your men?"

Roux sat through a very silent and uncomfortable half hour sipping his coffee when, to his relief, he heard a vehicle pull into the driveway. Els and three men alighted from the unmarked car. It took all of five minutes to explain his instructions. No one was to leave or enter the house, nor were Kani or his brother to contact the outside world. Medical staff were to be accompanied at all times when in the house, and his men needed to be on the lookout for any suspicious characters loitering around.

The phone was to remain disconnected, unless there was an emergency, and the house checked for any other means of communication. Els was to set up a half-hourly radio check with the Control Room.

He walked back into the house, introduced Els, thanked Kani for his cooperation, and was walking to his car when his radio burst into life. It was the Control Room. They had a message from Meiring telling him to get back to the station. A helicopter was on its way to return him to the farm where he was needed urgently. Dismayed, he stared down at the radio in his hand. What the hell had gone wrong now?

HE HAD NO IDEA how long he was in the air, but as far as he was concerned, it was too long. His ingrained belief helicopters were not designed to stay in the air, and the anxiety of what awaited at the farm had his stomach in knots by the time he tumbled out of the flying machine. Arm covering his face, he dashed through the dust thrown up by the blades down draft to a group of three men standing well back from the landing zone.

Meiring and Prinsloo greeted him with perfunctory nods and then introduced him to a man in a white overall.

"Ketring from CID Fingerprint and Evidence," the man said as they shook hands. "Sorry to get you out here on such short notice, but there is something you need to see."

Roux looked at Meiring, eyebrows raised. Meiring cocked his head toward the "hangar".

"This may ruin your day, Colonel," he said, smiling without humor. "Seems the MBL are not out of the picture yet."

They walked the short distance to the building in silence. At the entrance, Ketring stopped.

"Colonel, I'd like you to cover your shoes with these plastic booties and wear gloves. Please touch nothing in the area we are going to, or approach too closely."

Roux slipped on the coverings before following the three men as they made their way toward a door in the far corner of the building. White clothed men were all over the place. The crates of weapons were still where he had last seen them.

Ketring stopped at the open door and motioned for Roux to enter. "Just a few steps inside, if you don't mind, colonel. I don't know how safe this room is."

He stepped into a nightmare. Arrayed across a wooden trestle table were glass tubes, small cooking pots, and several large plastic containers. In amongst the equipment, he saw a screwdriver, wire clippers and rolls of electric wire. Bits of what looked like a small clock were strewn across the table. On the ground were too large plastic bags; the label on one read Urea, the other Ammonium Nitrate. Two plastic bottles stood against the far wall. He did not need to see the labels to know what they contained: fuel oil, without a doubt. Instantly, he knew what he was looking at.

He turned to Ketring. "Bomb-making setup, I assume."

The man nodded.

Meiring spoke from behind him. "Chris has already spoken to de Groot at Bomb Disposal. They're on their way in by air, but there's no mistaking what this is."

"Does du Plessis know?" Roux asked.

"We were going to leave that for you, Colonel," said Prinsloo.

"Thanks, real decent of you," said Roux as he exited the small space. He waved an expansive hand, taking in the building's interior. "Your guys safe working in here with," he cocked a thumb over his shoulder, "this right next door?"

"There is some spillage on the floor, but I am confident we are looking at the contents of a bomb rather than the finished article," said Ketring. "So as long as we stay out till Kobus and his team get here, it should be OK."

Roux ripped off the surgical gloves and tossed them onto the floor, and dusted his hands off. They smelled like a baby's backside after a nappy change.

"Thanks Ketring. Tell me. Do you believe a bomb was assembled here?"

"Considering the quantity of chemicals and the amount of spillage, I believe more than one."

Roux motioned for Meiring and Prinsloo to follow him. At the hangar door, he pulled off the plastic booties.

"This is a right cock-up," he said.

"It is," said Meiring as they walked toward the helicopter. "But it explains what those three cars were doing in here. We can presume there are at least three car bombs headed for places unknown somewhere in Cape Town. Probably toward Verster."

"Christ! Just when we thought it was over. Chris, have you got direct comms with the Control Room?"

Prinsloo beckoned to a man standing a short distance away who trotted over, an aerial waving with the motion. He gave a handset to Roux.

"Control, this is Bravo, Sierra-Bravo."

"Go ahead," came a bored response.

"Please contact General du Plessis on his emergency number and ask him to please meet me at headquarters as a matter of urgency."

"Copied."

Roux returned the handset to the radioman and turned to Meiring. "Are the Murder guys here yet?"

"In the house. But I warned them to remain clear of the hangar. There's plenty in the house to keep them busy until de Groot clears the buildings. There's also a large uniform contingent on its way, which will secure the entrance, and the entire area, until the Bomb and Murder guys finish. Van der Merwe is now senior officer on scene as STG is pulling out. I'll ride back to the station with you."

"Gainsford have any luck?"

Meiring shook his head. "He had a brief chat with the three from the house but appears they are playing heroes, so he went back with everyone to be, in his words, 'somewhere he can concentrate on his work.'"

Roux pulled Meiring to one side. "Eugene, we need to find out who owns this place."

"On it," said Meiring matter-of-factly. "I asked van der Merwe to see if he could get his guys to check at the Deeds Office, but being a Saturday, it may take some time."

"Good, but right now, you and I need to update du Plessis." He shook hands with Prinsloo. "Thanks for a great job, Chris. I'll make sure the general knows about it."

Prinsloo touched a knuckle to his head in salute, "Thanks Colonel, appreciate it." He shook hands with Meiring. "Thanks for getting us involved, Eugene. It was good to be doing something constructive for a change. I'll let van der Merwe know you've left."

Roux and Meiring jogged to the helicopter. The pilot, still in his seat with the door open, glanced up as the two men approached.

"Back to Compton," shouted Roux as they clambered into the back seats.

The pilot held up a gloved thumb, closed his door, and within seconds, the whoop-whoop of the blades began as the rotor went into motion.

Roux leaned across to Meiring and shouted into his ear. "I found the courier."

Meiring's head jolted back, eyebrows almost reaching his hairline. "How?" he mouthed, as the increasing whine of the rotor blades drowned out his voice.


THE MAN CHECKED HIS watch for the third time in as many minutes. He slammed his hand against the car's dashboard, grunted, closed his eyes, and took a deep breath, holding it for several seconds, then allowing the air to escape through his nose in a slow and controlled way. This exercise was repeated ten times. He looked down at his hands in his lap, relieved to see there was no sign of tremors. Killing is what he did, but until now, had never felt as anxious as this while he waited for his targets. He was still unconvinced this hit was necessary, but orders were orders.

A quick glance in the rearview mirror confirmed the road behind him was still clear. Glancing round at the row of neat suburban homes, he spotted a couple out in their front garden pottering around, and using a watering can on small clumps of plants. His eyes narrowed. His instructions were explicit. Keep as low a profile as possible. The car, several years old, was chosen for a particular reason. Japanese designed but locally assembled, it was amongst the most popular models on the country's roads. It bore no distinguishing marks, and should anyone decide to verify the registration, it would pass a cursory check. He'd noted at least four identical models in driveways or parked along the side of the street.

The dashboard clock told him it was just past two o'clock, and he was running late. His last radio check had placed the person of interest at a complex only minutes away from the house. Once again, he studied the residence across the road. Much like all the rest in the street, a low wall with a pedestrian gate bordered it. The entrance to the property by vehicle up to the double garage was unobstructed. His line of sight to the car when it stopped in front of the garage would be clear.

As was his ritual, he pulled up the sleeve of his sweater to expose his right hand and forearm.

AT COMPTON THEY WERE informed du Plessis was waiting in Warmer's office. They got into the elevator and Roux punched the number four.

"Eugene, I need a favor, an important one. I'm only going to tell du Plessis about the courier at the end of our briefing, and I'm only going to tell him the bare minimum. Please say nothing, or ask any questions. It's imperative you remain silent. I'll explain my reasons afterwards."

Meiring's brow furrowed. "OK, no problem, but I'm interested to hear how you found him."

Minutes later, the four men sat around the all too familiar table in Warmer's office. Both senior men looked tired and irritable. Warmer fidgeted with a pen while du

Plessis played with his glasses. There was a moment of silence as Roux was scrutinized.

"You got me here, so what's the problem? The last message I got from you was everything went well. What's changed?"

Roux, in a halting voice, explained the situation at the farm, emphasizing the three cars he and Meiring had seen leaving the property.

Du Plessis blanched. "Are you telling me there are at least three car bombs, if not more, deployed in and around Cape Town, and we don't have a clue as to their whereabouts?"

Roux sat motionless for a moment, his exhaustion clouding his thoughts. He shook his head to clear his brain. "General, we don't know for certain the cars we saw were fitted with explosives, but we are assuming a worst-case scenario. Meiring jotted down a brief description of each one, color and make, but they're models commonly used throughout the city. But at least it narrows down the search."

He watched as the color on Warmer's face went from sickly white to a pale crimson and seemed happy to settle on bright red.

"Jesus holy Christ!" the general shouted, dropping his pen. Droplets of spittle spraying across the tabletop. "Where do we even start looking?"

Roux ignored him and addressed du Plessis. "Do we have any idea what time they will release Mandela?"

"No, but from what the commissioner said, I am assuming late morning. The problem is the ANC will start telling people as soon as it is announced, which means the word will spread like wild-fire, so we can expect a large crowd, with a horde of journalists, at Verster, and along the route from there to City Hall. Not ideal, but we'll have to live with it. Plain clothed men, mainly Black and Colored, and riot control units will be positioned nearby at both City Hall and Verster. The Presidential close security guys will be with him until he leaves Verster, and then the ANC will provide their own people for crowd control around Mandela." Du Plessis placed his glasses on his nose.

"But that is not my worry. It's those damn cars. We can certainly remove any vehicles around Verster, and the bomb disposal teams can comb the parking areas and side streets around the Hall, but there's still the route from Verster to City Hall. Time for some serious backup." He addressed Warmer.

"Hennie, we need to get everyone involved, including the boys in brown. Can you set up an immediate meeting with your local Command Team? Time to devise a plan to flood the city with men."

"Shouldn't we warn the ANC?" said Meiring.

Du Plessis gave him a look which made it plain no one would be telling anyone anything. He turned to Roux.

"What about the interrogations?"

"We'll check in with Sergeant Gainsford, hear if he's having any joy," said Roux.

Du Plessis leaned forward in his chair. "Roux, I don't give a rat's arse what your man has to do to find out where those cars were headed. If one or two of these MBL shits expire while in his care, tough shit! I'll cover for him. You just make damn sure within the next couple of hours, we have precise information as to their whereabouts." In a low and chilling tone, he said, "Do I make myself crystal clear, gentlemen?"

Both men nodded, then Roux spoke. It was now or never. He felt his heart rate quicken and his mouth beginning to go dry.

Struggling to maintain a neutral expression, he said, "There is some good news. We've located the courier at an old ANC house. Unfortunately, he is in a critical condition. Weak heart apparently, so in no position to be a threat, and if he is carrying a message for Mandela, he's not talking at the moment. I'm worried if we try any heavy-handed stuff, it'll kill him. So we'll need to wait. But if there is a message, it won't reach Mandela before his release."

"Damn it. Pity," said du Plessis. "But good work. Anything else?"

Both men shook their heads.

"Then piss off and find those bombs."

Back in Roux's office, Meiring closed the door. "How the hell did you find the courier?"

Roux told him everything about Kani's revelations and meeting the brother. "I know not telling du Plessis about Kani or the fact I released the boy was perhaps a mistake, but telling him wouldn't have changed anything."

Meiring had remained impassive throughout Roux's explanation.

"You were lucky the general is preoccupied with this bomb business," he said, "and didn't ask too many questions. But you did the right thing, Marius. The man is no threat to Mandela, and the message won't reach him. It would be nice to know what it is, but enough people have been hurt in this whole mess. So why punish the courier now, considering his health? Or Kani? There's no point. We know the MBL is the threat, so let's focus on them."

Relieved, Roux sat down. "Can you go check how Gainsford is doing? But I wonder if any man in the pain Gainsford inflicts is not going to end up telling us the first thing which enters his head, rather than what we need. The truth."

Meiring sighed, his features drawn and pale. "I agree. God, I'll be glad to get out of this madness."

"One more thing. Kani raised a valid question. How did the MBL finance this whole setup? I got the impression he believes there are others involved. We need to know who owns the farm."

Meiring scratched his chin. "I didn't even think of that. But it makes sense. I doubt the three guys in the house have the contacts or funds to pay for everything. I'll chase van der Merwe, but maybe we need to ask for du Plessis' help."

"Maybe, but let's see if van der Merwe finds out anything first."

"OK. I'll call you on the radio when I know more," said Meiring, as he made his way to the door. "What you going to be doing?"

Roux reached for the phone. "Let Mel know I'm OK, but Eugene, you and I need to get some rest or we're going to be dead on our feet and of no use to anyone."

"I know. But when?"

Roux pondered the options. "Check on Gainsford. If he has credible info, we advise du Plessis, and take it from there. If not, go home, get a hot meal, and try for a couple of hours of sleep. I'll cover for you. At least I got some shut-eye last night. I'll do another check with Gainsford—" He looked at his watch, "—at four, and then do the same."

After Meiring retreated, Roux dialed home. He let the phone ring for over a minute before replacing the handset.

Probably out shopping, he surmised. He rested his head on the back of his chair, looking up at the ceiling. His eyes felt sore and scratchy. The eyelids drooped. It took less than sixty seconds before sleep engulfed him.

He awoke as though a bomb had gone off in his head. He shot upright in his chair, not sure what had woken him, but a look at his watch told him he'd slept for almost two hours. It was well after four. He rubbed his still painful eyes with thumb and forefinger and then massaged his temples as he reached for the phone and called the Charge Office. Minutes later, he was holding on for Gainsford.

Gainsford was in no hurry. Roux waited for close on ten minutes before a gruff, irritated voice said in accented English.

"*Ja,* what do you want?"

Roux exploded. "Listen, you moron, this is Colonel Roux," he yelled in Afrikaans, "and if you want to stay in this force, you need to learn how to address senior officers. Fast. You hear me?"

There was a moment's silence. "Yes sir, *Colonel, sir,* what can I do for you?" the mockery in the man's tone made Roux even more angry.

"I need to know if you've found out anything I can use, or are you having too much fun?" he snarled.

"Well, *Colonel,* if you would leave me to do my job, I might find out something."

This is going nowhere, Roux conceded, forcing himself to calm down. "OK, Sergeant, what do we know?"

He heard Gainsford suck in an impatient breath.

"Khumalo is saying nothing, but I'll break him. But Davids is a chickenshit and happy to sell out the rest. He says he met Khumalo in June last year at a *shebeen*.

Khumalo had just started his new party, the MBL, and asked Davids to join and help him recruit new members, which is how Akmet got in with them. In December, Khumalo told him the MBL had been hired to go and guard Waterfalls. After they got there, Khumalo gets rid of the labor on the farm. Just after SONA, Khumalo calls him and tells him they have to hold a public meeting that night where they were to say Mandela was a White man's puppet and was secretly working for the government. Which they did. Four days ago, five Black guys turn up at the farm in three cars. They were working in the packing building, but he says he wasn't told why they were there, but from the stuff he saw being taken from the cars, he thinks they were making bombs, but was too shit scared to ask Khumalo. He says Khumalo was the only one who spoke to the men, but he overheard one or two of the conversations which were in English, but swears the men were Portuguese. All five left with the cars, but he doesn't know where they went. I'm sure the bugger knows more. I just need another couple of hours but had to stop for a while as he almost had a heart . . . uh . . . um, what do you call it *aanval?*" He used the Afrikaans word for attack.

*Too dumb to know his own language*, thought Roux. "We already know about the cars, Gainsford. What we need to know urgently is where they went!"

"I'll let him rest a bit, then I'll *bliksem* him some more until he tells me. Don't worry, man." He paused. Roux could literally hear the cogs in the man's brain struggling to rotate.

"Oh *ja*! I also found out about Conradie. They reckon the last time they saw him, he and his brother were arguing with some guys from the Crossroads gang but don't remember their names, or what they look like, or what happened to Conradie. But I'll find out."

Ignoring du Plessis' explicit orders, Roux said. "I don't want any bodies, Gainsford. I need people who can talk."

"Not what the general said," Gainsford shot back.

He was momentarily taken aback. "Which general?"

Gainsford chuckled. "Old two-plus-three, du Plessis. Came down here. Said I could *bliksem* the *kak* out of them as much as I want, as long as I get the info." Gainsford paused. "And by the way, *Colonel*, those two men you saw in the BMW. Davids says they were Coloreds. Gave me their names."

How often had he heard the expression "beat the shit out of them" from members of the security forces? And more often than not, with minimal success.

"Sergeant, just remember, dead men don't talk. When you learn something we can actually use, call Captain Meiring on his radio."

"Man," responded Gainsford. "These bloody wogs are as thick as pig shit. They don't know how to make this kind of thing happen. Someone else is giving the orders."

That was the final straw. He pulled the headset away from his ear and yelled at the mouthpiece. "I want information Gainsford, not your bloody opinions!" He slammed the phone down.

So, du Plessis had gone down to the cells to find out firsthand what Gainsford was getting. He still doesn't trust me, Roux realized with a shock.


THE MAN OPENED THE car door, stepping out into the midafternoon sunlight. Leaving the door open, he stamped around the car twice before resuming his place in the driver's seat, slamming the door shut. He glared at his watch, as though willing it to say something.

He reached between his legs for the radio when, almost in anticipation, it crackled and a soft voice said, "Target with you in ten." He thumbed the transmit button twice and tossed the radio onto the passenger side floor. Again he reached down, this time sliding his hand under his seat, emerging with a black bag from which he pulled out a set of black leather gloves. They were a tight fit, the way he liked it. Reaching back into the bag, he extracted a pistol, which he dropped into his lap. Raising his hips, he pulled a long cylindrical tube from a trouser pocket. While studying the rearview mirror, he screwed the tube onto the barrel of the semi-automatic pistol and chambered a round.

Winding down the window, he placed the silencer on the window frame. He did not need to aim. With his free hand, he turned the ignition. The engine came to life with a soft purring sound. He did a visual sweep of all the houses in the close vicinity. The couple he had seen earlier had gone inside their house, and the only person he could see was a Black gardener cutting the lawn at one house.

Minutes later, a white VW turned into the road, drove up to the driveway, and turned in, stopping in front of the garage doors. The driver got out and stood for a moment, looking back into the car.

The man slipped the manual drive into first gear and eased the car out into the middle of the road. As he drew level with the VW, he stuck out his right arm and fired four times, each pull of the trigger evenly spaced. All four bullets struck the rear window of the car. Grinning, he tossed the weapon into the gutter on the side of the road, engaged second gear, and slowly drove away. He was still in second gear when he rounded the corner at the end of the street.

ROUX SCRATCHED his upper lip. Go home? No point. Knowing his luck, he would just be stretching out on the bed and Meiring would call. He strolled into Gerda's office, and helped himself to a generous portion of coffee from her stash, reminding himself he needed to buy her a new tin. With a mug of black coffee, he headed back to his desk, sipping the scalding drink. Collapsing into his chair, he noticed a large internal envelope in his in tray with a confidential sticker over the flap. Curious, he ripped it open to find a thin sheaf of stapled A4 papers with a note attached. He recognized Gerda's handwriting on the front.

Is this what you wanted? Records weren't happy about giving me a copy, but I told them it was for the general. Hope it doesn't get me fired. Sorry, it's a photocopy of an old and tattered original, so I was told. Love Aunty.

He squinted down at the document. The front page was blank except for a single word in bold capitals which read "DESTROY." Someone had messed up. He flipped over to the next page and caught his breath. Along the top were typed three capitalized words, in a font he hadn't seen before. THE FREEDOM CHARTER.

"Would you believe it? Shit! This dates back to around 1955, if I remember."

He settled back in his chair and browsed the document. There were two centered introductory paragraphs, with the rest of the page split in two columns, each headed by a title in bold type. Turning the page, he saw more of the same. He went back to the second page and read the first paragraph heading. THE PEOPLE SHALL GOVERN! He grunted. Pure ANC propaganda was his initial thought until he read the second one. ALL NATIONAL GROUPS SHALL HAVE EQUAL RIGHTS!

His eyes went back up to the sub-heading. Leaning back in his chair, he read out loud.

"WE, the People of South Africa, declare for all our country and the world to know that South Africa belongs to all who live in it, black and white, and that no government can justly claim authority unless it is based on the will of all the people. That our people have been robbed of their birthright to land, liberty, and peace by a form of government founded on injustice and inequality. That our country will never be prosperous or free until all our people live in brotherhood, enjoying equal rights and opportunities. That only a democratic state, based on the will of all the people, can secure to all their birthright without distinction of color, race, sex or belief."

He read on as his coffee turned cold. After a third read, he alternated between the pages, re-reading paragraphs, sentences and specific words, finally settling on the first line below the italicized sub-heading—"that South Africa belongs to all who live in it, black and white, and that no government can justly claim authority unless it is based on the will of all the people."

"Well, I'll be buggered," he said out loud, tossing the document onto his desk.

He sat staring into space, his mind blank while his hands were twisting a paper clip into various shapes, when the phone rang. It was several seconds before he focused on the intrusion and picked it up. "Yes," was his terse response.

Moments later, he was tearing down the highway, heading for Groote Schuur hospital.

ALL THE CHARGE OFFICE desk had told him was the hospital called informing them a Colonel Roux was urgently required at the hospital regarding a matter involving his family. Finding a vacant spot in a no-parking area, he shoved the "Police vehicle" sign on the dashboard and ran to the Emergency Room. A gruff-looking ward sister on the third floor met him moments later.

"Follow me, Colonel," she said, her eyes conveying the urgency of the situation.

As they walked, she spoke in a low tone, firing out each sentence. "We do not know the details, as your wife was incoherent when they were brought in by ambulance. According to the medics, your son was in the front passenger seat of your wife's car and received a gunshot wound to his head. He is in surgery. Your wife, other than in a state of shock, appears unharmed, but the doctor wants to reexamine her to make sure there are no injuries. We have given her something to calm her down so she may appear somewhat disorientated and incoherent. Rest and a chance to recover from the shock is important now, so please make your visit brief."

Roux stopped, incredulity in his voice. "Shot? By whom? Where, I mean . . . where were they?"

The sister stopped to face him. "The car was at your house, so I'm led to believe. Who did the shooting? That, I assume, is what you will establish. Right now, my only concern is for your wife. As soon as the surgeon can, he will update you as to your son's condition. After you see your wife, you can wait in the family waiting room across the corridor. The surgeon will find you there." There was no sympathy in her tone. She was updating yet another grieving parent over the course of her normal day.

As they hurried down the hallway, he passed several six-person wards until he was ushered into a small room which contained only two beds, one empty, the other occupied by Mel. She was sitting up, dressed in a green theater gown, her face buried in her hands, a drip connected to her arm. Her damp hair hung across her face.

"Mel!" he called out as he rushed over to her. "What the hell happened? Are you hurt?"

He ran out of words when they stuck in his throat. Grasping her shoulder with one hand, he lifted her chin with the other, looking into blood-red, teary eyes which stared back at him with a blank expression, almost as though she didn't recognize him. Then she flung her arms round his neck, her face buried in his shoulder. Her nails dug into his shoulders. Heart-rending sobs shook her entire body. He held her, his heart thumping, tears welling up in his eyes.

"Pet," he said gently, "tell me what happened."

She lifted her face and looked at him. It was a look he would never forget.

"It's Ri-Rian," she stammered. "There was blood everywhere. I couldn't stop it. He wouldn't wake up. I tried . . . but he just sat there . . . blood everywhere . . . all over his face . . . I tried to wake him."

She uttered a cry that tore his insides to shreds. His knees shook, forcing him to steady himself against the bed.

"Your wife needs to rest, Colonel," he heard from over his shoulder. "The nurse is here with a sedative, which will give her several hours sleep. You can stay with her until she's asleep. As soon as she is in a fit state to see you, we will notify you."

A young nurse hurried in with a kidney-shaped tray in her hand and inserted a needle into the drip, emptied the contents and then left.

He sat holding her hands until her eyelids drooped, and then finally closed. Her breathing was shallow, her face etched in pain. He adjusted her pillows the way she liked them in their bed and backed out of the room into the corridor and leaned against the wall, shaking uncontrollably, struggling to remain in an upright position. His teeth tore at the flesh on the inside of his mouth. Glancing down the corridor, he spotted a door marked "Gents," and ran for it, flung open the door and only just made it to the washbasin before he threw up. His stomach heaved until there was nothing left, only spasms. Tears and snot dripped into the brown mess in the basin. After dry-heaving until his stomach hurt, he spat out the pieces left in his mouth and rinsed it. Waves of dizziness swept over him. Staggering backwards, he collapsed against a wall and slid down until he was sitting on the floor. He wiped his nose with his jacket sleeve, and then, without warning, the tears poured out. He cried like he could never have as a child. An outpouring of pain, grief and hopelessness.

When there were no more tears, he pushed himself to his feet and walked over to the basin. No amount of water was going to clean up the mess, he decided, moving to the adjacent one. Turning on a tap, he cupped his hands under the flowing cold water, rinsed his mouth out again and doused his face. Looking into the mirror above the basin, he saw a face he didn't recognize, but it was the face of a man whose sole reason for existence was on the brink of being ripped away.

It took him several minutes to clean up his appearance. He needed Meiring and to tell du Plessis. With his radio still in the car, he marched over to the ward reception desk, and after a mumbled apology to the nurse about the state of the bathroom, asked to use the phone. He dialed the Compton Charge Office to get Meiring's home number and then called him, knowing he would be waking him from much needed sleep. It took several frustrating minutes before he heard Meiring's voice.

"Eugene, someone tried to kill my family," he blurted out, not caring who heard. "I need you here, and can you tell du Plessis?"

"You got it," came the response before the line went dead.

As he turned to leave the reception area, his way was barred by a short, middle-aged, portly man with close cropped hair of an indeterminable color, thick-framed glasses and a mustache in desperate need of a trim.

"Colonel Roux?" he said.

Roux stopped and peered under arched eyebrows at the stranger.

"Captain Terblanche, CID, I've just come from—"

Grabbing the man by the arm, Roux frog-marched him down to the visitor waiting room, where he shoved him into a chair.

"What can you tell me" he said, glaring down at the man, hands on hips.

Terblanche, looking uncomfortable, reached into a jacket pocket and pulled out a pack of cigarettes.

"Now!" yelled Roux, ready to throttle the man.

"Oh. Yes. Sorry." said Terblanche, shoving the pack back into his pocket.

"What happened?" barked Roux. "I need answers."

The man fidgeted and shifted in his chair.

"Um, actually, I don't have much at the moment, Colonel. But we have several teams of detectives at the scene."

Roux sat on the edge of a chair. "So, what *can* you tell me?"

Terblanche cleared his throat and reached for his cigarettes again before changing his mind.

"From the supermarket packets on the back seat, we assume your wife and son had just returned from shopping. According to the maid next door, she heard your wife screaming for help and called her madam, who, after a quick look at your son, called the ambulance and then us. Good thing she was there. She stayed with your wife until the medics arrived.

"From what the medics told us, your son was in the front passenger seat with a single gunshot wound to the head. We are in the process of door-to-door questioning, but most of the neighbors are out. Your wife was very lucky Mrs. Meyer from next door was there. A gardener working at a house diagonally opposite says he thinks there was a car parked across the road from your house, but of course, can't be sure and doesn't remember the make or color, or if it was occupied. Problem is, there are several cars parked on the road. So no luck there."

By now, Terblanche had retrieved a cigarette from the crumpled pack and lit up, inhaling deeply. Briefing senior officers on how their child was shot was nerve-wracking work.

"I took a quick walk around the car and the area along the street. Found the weapon. Old nine-millimeter with a crudely made silencer and an empty magazine. It appears the shooter tossed the weapon as he drove off. Four holes in the back window of the car, and four nine millimeter casings found in the road. One round pierced the passenger seat headrest, hitting your son. The driver's door was open, but we don't know if your wife was inside the car, or had already got out when the shooting happened. No signs of forced entry at the house, and the car radio and your wife's handbag were still in the car, so wasn't a robbery. Other than that, Colonel, we have little. I'm sorry."

Roux had sat through the entire monologue, motionless and unblinking. Nothing Terblanche had said answered the one burning question foremost in his mind: why? Was it planned, or just some intended robbery gone wrong? He thanked the man and waved a hand in dismissal.

Mel was sound asleep when he checked on her, and until she was rested and recovered from the shock, he saw no need to harass her. The problem was there wasn't much time. If Mel, or even Rian, *were* the target, there remained the possibility of the shooter returning to finish the job. *Du Plessis will need to organize a permanent guard on his family. Maybe Chris at RTG could also arrange something? Where the hell was Meiring?*

After what appeared to be a lifetime pacing the corridor, checking on Mel, and walking to the hot drinks dispenser but purchasing nothing, Meiring barged through the swing doors to the ward. Roux, standing at the entrance to Mel's room, spotted him, rushed over and steered him into the waiting room, closing the door behind them.

"Thanks for coming," he blurted out. "Don't know what the hell happened other than Rian is in theater and Mel is an emotional wreck. A Captain Terblanche from CID was here but couldn't tell me much. Can't tell me if it was a planned attack or some horrible mistake. It makes no sense. I mean . . . you know . . ." He stopped, realizing he was rambling, and sank into a chair. "Does du Plessis know?"

Meiring flopped into a chair, his face was unshaven and drawn. He let out a long sigh.

"He does. Shit Marius, who the hell would want to shoot a woman and a kid in the middle of a White suburb? Did Terblanche have *anything* we can work with?"

Roux shook his head, relaying Terblanche's report as best he could remember it. He stopped and took a deep, shuddering breath.

A yawn followed a quick nod from Meiring as he ran a hand over his mouth. "I don't know what to say. How is your son?"

"Still in theater. Bullet hit him in the head. Why Rian? Why shoot at the car and Rian but not at Mel, who, if she was standing in the driveway, was a perfect target?"

"Unless the intention was not to kill her, only frighten her," said Meiring.

"But why? Who would want to frighten her? And why shoot Rian?" He scratched at the side of his cheek. "Maybe someone in the townships who has a problem with the work she's doing with the children?" He said, a hint of hysteria in his voice.

"Possible, I guess," said Meiring. "Maybe they intended to send a message, or maybe it's crime related. Intending to rob them when they stopped the car, but got spooked somehow and panicked."

Roux wasn't listening. "Don't you see? She's White and they don't want us Whites in the townships." He chewed at a lip. "But maybe Kani will know. I need to call him."

Jumping up, Roux took a step toward the door when it flew open.

A furious looking du Plessis stepped into the room. "Someone is going to hang for this, except if I don't get to shoot him first!" he growled.


DU PLESSIS AND MEIRING'S calm, logical assessments grounded Roux, allowing him to face the unknown: the outcome of Rian's operation and the motive for the attack. Du Plessis, with typical bluntness, commandeered a private office to confer with Warmer, ensuring the prompt deployment of uniformed and plainclothes men to protect Mel and Rian. Officers would be stationed at all access points and RTG operators positioned outside their rooms.

With Mel still asleep, Roux cornered the resident doctor who assured him she was physically uninjured, and as soon as the effects of the shock were minimized, she could return home. But she would spend the night in hospital, much to Roux's relief.

Secluded in the claustrophobic waiting room, the three men meticulously reviewed the day's events, going over each detail again and again, like a broken record. Was the shooting a message? If so, what was the message and who pulled the trigger?

Roux sucked on the lesion in his mouth, the metallic tang of blood a perverse comfort. Remembering Kani, he explained his reasoning to du Plessis, and using Meiring's radio, instructed Els to reconnect the phone at the house. He headed for the commandeered office and, minutes later; he heard Kani's voice. It did not take him long to explain the reason for the call.

"Oh, no!" exclaimed Kani, "Colonel, I am so—"

Roux cut him off. He had no time for the man's platitudes; he needed answers.

"Kani. Does any organization, gang, or person oppose what the Foundation is doing in the townships and targeting it or Mel specifically?"

There was a momentary pause.

*Come on, come on, answer you bastard*, Roux's brain screamed.

"Colonel," came the calm response. "I assure you the Foundation is a place of refuge for many of the persecuted in the townships, and is viewed as a place of sanctuary."

*That I can believe*, thought Roux, *hiding terrorists half the time.*

"If, given the extreme unlikelihood such an organization exists, why did they not target me, or the offices, why a member of staff? As to the possibility of a personal vendetta against Mel, I find it impossible to believe. The children adore her, and the parents refer to her as the 'white angel.'" Again a pause. "Trust me, Colonel, if there was any ill will toward the Foundation or any of its members, I would know."

Roux was about to ask how when it became obvious. Kani's information about Waterfalls implied he was very well connected within the townships. "Thanks." He slammed down the phone and went back to join du Plessis and Meiring.

A surgeon was standing in the waiting room when he walked in. Du Plessis made the introduction.

"This is Doctor Gregory. He did the operation on your son."

Fear gripped Roux's heart like a vise.

The doctor guided him to a chair. "Take a seat, Mr. Roux. I need to explain what his injuries are. But the good news is he is in a satisfactory condition, and coped with the lengthy procedure owing to his youth and fitness."

Roux needed no encouragement to fall into the chair. He looked up at the doctor, his eyes pleading.

"Is he conscious?"

"No. He's heavily sedated and our prognosis is he will remain in a coma after the sedatives wear off. The bullet entered his skull behind his right ear, exiting below his right eye. Fortunately, it appears to have caused only minor damage to his brain. An inch to the right, and it would merely have grazed his chin. One to the left, and he would be dead."

Roux tried to absorb what he was hearing, but the doctor's voice seemed to come down a tunnel at him. He sat staring at the floor, not knowing what to say.

"The extent of the brain damage?" asked du Plessis.

"The bullet nicked a portion of the back of his brain—I will not go into the technical explanation—but if there is any damage, there could be several consequences, but until the swelling subsides, we cannot determine the extent of the injury. All we can do is wait and monitor his progress."

"Will he regain consciousness?" asked Roux.

"I believe so," said the doctor with an encouraging smile. "The when is what I cannot answer."

"Can I see him? I just want to see him breathing and . . ." his voice tailed off into a whisper. "Hold him."

"I'll get one of the ICU nurses to take you down to his room, but the visit must be brief. If you have questions or just need to talk, let the desk know and they will page me."

The doctor dipped his head at du Plessis and Meiring, and briefly placed a hand on Roux's shoulder, before excusing himself.

Du Plessis followed him out and there was a brief discussion in the corridor before he returned. "Told him we'll be putting two RTG guys at the door of the ICU. He wasn't happy, but who gives a shit what he thinks?"

"Anything from Kani?"

Roux placed his hand on his knees and pushed himself up.

"No, nothing. He's confident neither the Foundation nor Mel are at risk from anyone in the townships. I'm going to check on her. Let the ICU nurse know where I am when she comes."

He looked down at his wife; her face contorted as though she was caught in an endless nightmare. As he reached for her hand, she groaned, rolling onto her side, pulling her hand away. Just coincidence, he reasoned.

A soft voice came from the doorway. "You ready to see your son, Mr. Roux?"

Rian's entire head, and the right side of his face, was swathed in bandages. The boy was sheet-white and frail, as though his whole body had shrunk. Roux gripped his son's hand as tears dripped off his chin onto the bedding. He couldn't think of anything to say other than "I'm sorry, my boy," which he repeated over and over until he felt a hand on his shoulder.

"He needs to sleep now, but I'm sure he's going to pull through this," said the nurse.

"How do you know that?" Roux asked, desperation in his voice.

The nurse's gentle blue eyes studied his face for a moment. There was both understanding and sorrow in them, but also a look of certainty.

"I just know," she said, leading him out of the cubicle.

Back in the waiting room, Meiring handed him a polystyrene cup of coffee and a plastic wrapped sandwich.

"All I could get from the machine," he said apologetically, "du Plessis has gone to Compton to call the commissioner and update him."

Roux lifted the lid off the cup and took a mouth-full of lukewarm coffee. He pushed the sandwich aside. They sat quietly, each preoccupied with their own thoughts. There was nothing left to say; only time, and whatever Mel remembered, could provide the answers they sought. He did not know how long they were waiting before the door opened and a nurse appeared in the crack.

"Colonel Roux?"

"Yes, me," said Roux, jumping to his feet, a wave of panic gripping him. "What's happened?"

"I thought you would want to know your wife is awake. She's still groggy, but you can go in and see her."


HE PUSHED PAST THE nurse and hurried into Mel's ward. Although still connected to the drip, she was propped up against pillows, sipping a drink through a straw. She turned to look at him as he came to the bed. Her expression asked the question.

"He's out of surgery," he whispered gently, taking her hand and squeezing it. There was no response.

"I've been down to the ICU to see him, but he's still unconscious." He gave her a rundown of the surgeon's report, but left out the part about potential brain damage. "We just need to wait until he regains consciousness."

She stared back at him as though expecting more, then looked away, a lone tear meandering down her cheek, which she brushed away with her sleeve.

"Mel, I am so sorry for what has happened. We'll find who did this. It's possible it may be connected to us making sure nothing happens to Mandela when he's released, and—"

He stopped, knowing he'd said the wrong thing.

Her head spun back to face him. "Someone is trying to kill Mandela? Why didn't you tell me?" she said accusingly. "If you'd warned me about what you were doing, I would have been more careful. Why didn't you warn me?"

She was bordering on hysteria, her voice rising with each sentence. "If I'd known, I would never have gone out. Marius, why didn't you warn me? Rian would be safe. You must have known there could be a risk to us. And you kept quiet?"

He shook his head vehemently. "No, no Pet! We don't know if he is in danger, but we have to check everything. We arrested a crowd last night who may have been planning something, but it's all under control now." He paused. "I tried to tell you what was happening the other night, but you didn't give me a chance, and then Kani turned up. Du Plessis is here and we will move heaven and earth to find whoever did this."

Her abrupt laugh was soaked in sarcasm. "You've got it under control. So if that is the case, how come Rian is in ICU?" There was anger in her tone now. "If you knew there was any chance something could happen to Rian or me, you should have told us."

"Mel, that's not fair. How could I know something like this would happen? There doesn't appear to be a link between the group we arrested and Rian's injury. It could just be an attempted robbery gone wrong. But we will find out."

She stared out the windows at the night sky. After a moment, she turned back to face him.

"I asked the ward sister to call my parents. Dad chartered a private flight and they're on their way down. I think it's best if Rian and I go back with them to Joburg as soon as he's able to be moved."

He gaped at her. "Mel, you can't. You can't just take him away like that. We've got uniform and plain-clothes men all over the hospital. No one is going to get to either of you, I promise. The house will also be guarded while you are there. It's just until we find who is responsible. So just a couple of days and things will be back to normal."

"Normal?" she jeered, her face red. "What's frigging normal any more Marius? You seem to have forgotten you promised to put this family first after South West. But as always, the frigging job gets priority. No more. My dad will speak to the surgeon. Some of the best neurologists are in Johannesburg, and Rian will get the best care there." She pushed his hand away from her face as he tried to touch her.

"You almost got your family killed today, *Colonel* Roux, because you are so wrapped up in your own importance, you have lost sight of what really matters. Go protect Mandela, and run around playing soldiers, and doing everything this stupid police force tells you to do. Rian and I want no part of it. Ever again!" Her head turned back to the window. "Go do what you think is so important."

He stood transfixed, mouth hanging open. "Mel, I tried to tell you, but things just—"

"Got in the way, as they always do," she scoffed. "Go Marius. I'm staying here to take care of Rian until my dad arrives."

She slid down in the bed, pulled the blanket up to her chin and closed her eyes. Tears escaped from the corners.

"I need to sleep."

No Mel. I'm staying here to keep you and Rian safe. Now and for always, as I promised; was what he wanted to say, but instead he said nothing.

"Marius," her voice was flat, her eyes still closed. "At least get something right for a change. Make sure you keep Mandela safe."

There were a thousand things he wanted to say, but all he could manage was to nod before he turned to leave.

"The man who shot at us was in a car in the street, an old red one, if I remember. He had his arm out of the car window with . . . the gun in his hand. I saw him shoot at us, then drive away. I think he was wearing a glove, but I saw his arm. The sleeve was pulled up." She said, her voice barely audible, her eyes still closed. She took a deep breath. "He was not a Black, Marius, I'm sure. It was a White man."

He moved back to her bed. "Are you sure? Absolutely sure it was a White guy?" He couldn't mask the disbelief in his voice.

Mel gave him a look which made it abundantly clear she was more than just sure. She was convinced and would not be dissuaded. She closed her eyes again. The conversation was over.

Roux stumbled out into the corridor. He felt numb. Mel's claim was almost beyond the realm of possibility.

There was no reason for a White man to kill him or his family. He had only been in SB a week, and there was no White man he could have upset to the extent of wanting to kill his family. Or was there?

Meiring was sitting paging through a tattered glossy magazine when Roux burst into the waiting room. "Where's du Plessis," he snapped.

Meiring yawned and gave him a quizzical look. "Said he needed to chase up Warmer with the deployment of the army engineers to help find the cars, and—"

He stopped and stared at Roux for a minute. "You look like you've been spray painted gray. What the hell has happened? You look terrified?"

"Call him," said Roux, pointing to the radio in Meiring's hand.

"It's almost ten Marius, he's probably on his way home."

"I don't care. Call him." It took several attempts before an irritated voice replied.

"I'm at home. Can this not wait?"

Roux grabbed the radio.

"General. Roux here. My wife is convinced the shooter was White. I'm still with Meiring in the waiting room. Either we can join you at the station or meet you here." He released the transmit button. The two men stared at each other as the seconds ticked by.

"I'll meet you there," said du Plessis. The radio went silent for a moment, and then, "you had better hope we are not chasing the wrong people."

Meiring leaned forward in his chair. "Talk to me Marius, what's happened?"

Roux dropped into a chair, running a hand across his face.

"Mel says the guy who shot at them was White. She saw his arm when he fired and then drive off. And no, it's not the drugs or shock. She's adamant, and I know her. When she's that sure of something, you can bet your arse she's spot on."

Meiring sat staring at Roux, his lips pursed. "White? The shooter is White? Who the hell—"

"Someone trying to get even with me, perhaps? But I can't think of any except—"

He hesitated, staring out the door before looking back at Meiring.

"What about Swanepoel? He threatened me, both of us, at the office, remember? Maybe he's trying to get even."

Meiring grunted. "Swanepoel is a vindictive bastard with some very shady friends, but the last I heard, he's in rehab. His wife gave him an ultimatum. Dry up or get out, and if you think he's an arrogant, bombastic bastard, meet her. Makes him look like a poodle. He went in two days ago, but I can check with the rehab place."

"Then who else? No one approached them, so this wasn't a robbery gone wrong. It sounds like it was a lone shooter. Pulled up in a car and opened fire. Why would some random White guy try to kill my family? It makes no sense."

"Could be Tau, but I doubt it," said Meiring, rubbing the stubble on his chin. "The PAC will have sanctioned him for his lone ranger bit, and to be honest, I just don't see APLA hiring a White gunman. Besides, he would know we would finger him as a likely suspect. It is possible it's drug or gang related. A sanctioned hit gone wrong with the shooter identifying the wrong target?" He looked questioningly at Roux.

"Really? In our suburb? All our neighbors are company employees or civil servants, for heavens sake. There's no 'drug lords' hiding in the street. And since when do we have White men hiring themselves out as hit men for Colored drug gangs? This isn't the bloody States."

"I don't know what else to suggest," said Meiring, throwing his hands up into the air. "Other than the obvious source—the MBL."

Before Roux could answer, du Plessis barged into the room. His face was dark as he glowered at Roux.

"What the hell is going on now?"

Both men stood and Roux shared the information Mel had given him, word for word, ending his monologue with the alternatives he and Meiring had just discussed.

The look on the general's face changed from annoyance to shock. "Is she sure?"

"She is deadly serious. If she wasn't, she would have said so, but there was no hesitation. She is adamant the shooter was White."

"Crap!" said du Plessis, taking a seat on the edge of a chair. The other two men sat down.

There was a soft tap on the door before it opened to reveal a nurse in the uniform of a trainee. She looked at each man.

"Is there a Colonel Roux here?"

"Me," said Roux, rising.

"There's a phone call for you. The caller says it's very urgent. A matter of life or death, I think is what he said."

"Shit! What now? Where's the phone?"

"At the reception desk," she said, backing out of the room.

Roux sprinted down the corridor with the nurse trying to keep pace. At the desk, she pointed at a receiver lying on the counter.

"That one."

He picked it up. "Roux."

Silence.

"Hello! It's Colonel Roux. You have a message for me?"

"Ah! Roux. I am sure you now know what we are capable of. This was a warning. We won't be so compassionate next time." The voice was low, but deep and guttural, unemotional. There was a long pause.

"Release our men by midday tomorrow or face the consequences. We know you are aware of the bombs, but you don't know where they will be. If our men are not free by midday, we will detonate two of them. And Roux, drop this stupid investigation you are undertaking against us. If you persist, innocents will die in their hundreds. Of that, I can assure you." The line went dead.

Roux stared at the dead phone in his hand, feeling as though he had just been poleaxed. *What the hell was that?* He replaced the receiver and hurried back to the waiting room, where he blurted out the message to du Plessis and Meiring.

"Well, clears that one up," said du Plessis. "No doubt now it's the MBL and from the sounds of it, they're not playing. I thought you had got the lot at Waterfalls?"

"English, Afrikaans, White, Colored, Black?" asked Meiring.

"Afrikaans. Could be White or Colored, difficult to tell. And no, I didn't recognize the voice."

Meiring shook his head and looked at du Plessis.

"General, I'm sorry, but this sounds to me like a B grade Hollywood movie. There's a better than even chance the shooter is White. The MBL hire him or someone else? There's something else going on here, and don't ask me why, it's just a feeling I have. I'm not suggesting we ignore the threat, but threatening to explode the bombs at midday makes no sense. I assume the reason for the use of three cars is to detonate the first two just before the release, which will divert our forces and attention away from Mandela. It will provide time for the third bomb to be placed in the ideal position to achieve maximum effect after the release. No one knows when he'll be released, so how can they fix a time to explode two of the cars? I don't buy it."

"Shit!" said Roux. "It ties in with what Gainsford said this afternoon. Reckons Khumalo and his crowd lack the intelligence or ability to put something like this together. He thinks someone else is behind it." He recounted Gainsford's report back on his interrogations, and was about to mention Kani raising the same question, but then realized du Plessis would want to know when he had spoken to him, leading to questions he preferred not to answer.

"We recruited and trained a lot of Portuguese-speaking ex-FNLA and Unita men in South West, who ended up working with some of our army units. But it would need someone with inside knowledge and authority to locate the right men to use."

"Hold on, gentlemen. This is becoming ridiculous," said du Plessis. "Are you implying there is a third force operating with Whites in command? I have worked with those units and know the CO well. There is no way he, or anyone in his units, would become involved in this. We need to focus on what we know." He took off his glasses and began swinging them around.

Meiring shifted on his feet, looking uncomfortable. "What we know for certain, General, is three car bombs are out there somewhere. The MBL guys don't seem to know much about anything, and no one has admitted Mandela is a target. The farm needed secrecy and guarding while the bombs were assembled, which the MBL provided, but were kept in the dark about what was being planned. Making a car bomb is not something you learn at Sunday school. Whoever these five Portuguese guys are, they're specialists. I have to wonder if someone else is behind this."

"Who? The PAC? A faction within the ANC?"

"Possible," said Roux, "but you've already mentioned it would be political suicide for the terrorist groups if they were discovered."

"Could there be a radical right-wing group involved?" Meiring queried.

Du Plessis' mouth opened as though to respond, hesitated, his eyes moving from Meiring to Roux.

"I grant you, there are some disgruntled Whites out there, Afrikaners in particular, and you know how the men at Compton feel about SONA, but neither NIS nor our intelligence boys have picked up anything which suggests a violent right wing backlash to the release. I just don't believe it."

He stood up and began pacing the small room, tapping his glasses against his teeth. Roux and Meiring waited. After several minutes, he stopped.

"No," he said with conviction. "I don't believe it. There is certainly opposition, but a White right-wing organization? No. I don't see it. If someone else is funding them, then it is external, or a disgruntled crowd of Blacks who do not belong to the terrorist groups, like the MBL. My money is still on them. Maybe we haven't identified the full leadership structure in the group. Perhaps Khumalo is not the leader."

"Can I make a suggestion?" said Roux. "Eugene, get on to Gainsford and tell him to question Khumalo about who really controls the MBL and where the money to pay for everything is coming from, and how did he know about the courier? But this time, he is to obey the general's orders, to the letter." He looked at du Plessis. "He'll know what I mean. Until we crack them, we are blind."

Du Plessis went a shade of red, cleared his throat, and stalked from the room.

# Sunday, February 11th, 1990

SOON AFTER DU PLESSIS departed, Meiring apologized, sounding as though he was letting the team down, but needed to get some sleep. Roux agreed, but decided he was going nowhere until he heard more about Rian. Left alone in the waiting room, he had tried to make sense of what was happening. Mel's accusations still stung. He had tried to tell her, but perhaps if he'd been more forceful, the shooting would not have occurred. But logic begged otherwise. She and Rian could not have stayed cooped up indefinitely. Besides, they had all been convinced the MBL was neutralized. Additional players in the mix would have been difficult to foresee. His only consolation was now his family was under close guard in a very public facility.

His thoughts turned to the possibility of White involvement. Although Meiring's arguments were sound, he was in two minds. He just couldn't believe it. But until they uncovered the truth, Mandela would remain in danger, even after his release. But where did he begin to uncover the truth? Ask Kani? He had hinted at someone financing the MBL, and sounded genuinely shocked at the shooting and might be more open to sharing what he knew, assuming he knew anything.

With the exhaustion and his inability to think clearly, Roux gave up tormenting himself and stretched out on the couch. Within seconds, he was asleep. When he awoke, his watch showed it was just before seven. He sat up, yawned, and rubbed his eyes. After a visit to the bathroom, now spotless, and a quick look in on the still sleeping Mel, he headed to the reception to get an update on Rian. To his surprise, he found Meiring talking to a nurse in the corridor.

"Thank you, Elsie," Meiring said to the nurse, as she hurried off. "Morning," he said, as Roux joined him. "Get any sleep?"

"Thanks, I did. I was on my way to get an update on Rian, but I didn't expect to find you here so early." Meiring looked refreshed. Clean-shaved and dressed in a sports jacket, slacks and an open-necked shirt. "You're looking better."

"Got some sleep, finally. That was Elsie, a friend of the wife's. She works in ICU and says there has been no change with Rian. Sorry."

"Thanks. Have you been to Compton?"

"I popped in and saw Gainsford. Not much more from the MBL guys, but he'll have another go at Khumalo. Davids has been admitted to hospital. I spoke to the rehab place this morning and they assure me Swanepoel has not left the premises or received any visitors. I think that excludes him. CID also got back to me on the owners of Waterfalls. It's a company called Waterfalls Winery with registered offices here, but when a squad car went to check it out, they found an empty building. Appears to be a front company and nothing more. Directors are listed as Khumalo, Davids and Akmet." He paused, looking around the reception area. "So, the day has finally arrived. Going to be a memorable one. One way or the other."

Roux snorted. "Couldn't care either way," he mumbled.

"Huh?" said Meiring, looking puzzled for a moment, then his radio crackled. Du Plessis was in the building and wanted to meet in the waiting room.

He came straight to the point as he closed the door behind him. "Anything from Gainsford?"

Meiring shared the feedback from Gainsford and CID.

"OK. I spoke to Greyling and the intelligence boys and they are convinced there is no right-wing threat. So the MBL are still in the frame, but finding those car bombs remains the priority. If one of them goes off in a crowded shopping center, or next to Mandela's car, we're all out of a career."

The fog began to clear in Roux's brain, and he decided it was now time to come clean. "General, there's something I've just remembered which supports Eugene's theory. I was at Kani yesterday," he saw Meiring's look of caution, "just to . . . uh . . . thank him for the intel, when he mentioned something which I'd forgotten." The general cut him off halfway through his retelling of Kani's mythology lesson.

"So, he also suspects there's more to the MBL than Khumalo."

"He didn't exactly state it, just questioned the logic of Khumalo being the top man, and how the MBL could find the finances or resources to set up Waterfalls. I thought little about it until now, but maybe he's trying to warn us."

"So my assumption Khumalo is not the top dog is confirmed. Gainsford needs to break him and find out who controls the group."

"If Kani knows so much, why is he not telling us everything?" said Meiring. "Maybe we need to have Gainsford talk to him rather than Khumalo. Scare the shit out of him."

Roux shook his head. "No, Eugene. You remember what happened the last time we tangled with the UN? Besides, Kani has frequently stated he is only expressing his opinion and has no information or evidence to back up his hypotheses. You arrest him, he'll clam up."

A slow sigh, in which Roux sensed defeat, escaped the general's lips. "Agreed. The commissioner will oppose it. De Klerk is hoping for international support for his reconciliatory approach, and stepping on the UN's toes now wouldn't help. Not going to happen."

He looked at Roux. "I'm satisfied with the way you handling him. Keep him on our side. As I was about to say, Mandela will be released today. No excuses. Could be as early as late morning, or by this afternoon latest, he walks out of Verster, a free man." He paused for effect.

"The scary bit is it's up to us to determine how long his freedom will last. We either stop this shit in its tracks, giving us an uneventful day, which will make the Blacks, and the rest of the world happy chappies, or we have a civil war on our hands. Captain, you and I need to get back to Compton and chase up the search for the cars. Colonel, it might be worth following up with Kani."

Roux followed Meiring out to the car park and got into his car. To his relief, he found his radio was switched off; which meant the battery was still charged. He and Meiring talked through the various developments of the past twenty-four hours, and what they could expect during the next twenty-four. History was in the making, and they were going to be part of it, possibly for the wrong reasons.

HE STROLLED THROUGH THE almost empty parking lot, waving his arms around and stretching his neck muscles from side to side. The warm breeze on his face felt good, and the exercise got his blood flowing again, helping him focus. Bugger it! He turned on his radio and headed for the hospital's main reception area. While he walked, he called Els, who responded sounding perky, which, given the circumstances, annoyed him. He explained what he wanted as he approached the main desk.

The phone rang several times before a voice said, "Who is this?"

"Who the hell do you think it is, Els? I just spoke to you a minute ago." Roux cursed silently. Sometimes the man could be a real plank. "How are things there?"

"All quiet, Colonel. I heard about your son." Els' voice dropped an octave. "I'm really sorry. Any idea who is behind it?"

"Thanks. We're working on it. Where is Kani?"

"He's working at his desk in the small room he calls his office."

"Please put him on the phone."

"Copy that. Just a sec." Els' cheeriness was irritating Roux.

Kani's voice was sympathetic without sounding patronizing. "Colonel Roux. I'm pleased to hear from you. How is your family?"

"Mel is unharmed, but still in shock. My son is out of surgery, but it's really a case of waiting until he recovers consciousness before we will know the extent of his injuries. But thank you for asking."

An awkward silence followed, then Kani said, "Your family is in my thoughts and prayers. As they are with everyone at the Foundation, but may I ask the reason for your call?"

Roux felt uneasy with what he was about to ask, but he needed answers.

"Mr. Kani, there have been several developments, and I would like to discuss them with you."

The silence was longer this time. "I'm happy to offer what help I can. Should I put the kettle on?"

"Thank you."

Twenty minutes later, he pulled into the driveway at Kani's house, and turned off the motor, but not before glimpsing a shadow ducking behind a bush not large enough to hide a child. "Amateur," he grunted. As he alighted from the car, Els appeared in the doorway.

"Jeez, Els, open a bloody window or the door, this place stinks," said Roux, as he brushed past Els into the living room.

"But Colonel, what about—"

"Lieutenant, I doubt Mr. Kani is going to make an Olympic record breaking dash for freedom considering his age and the current situation. Besides, you have that amateur trying to look inconspicuous behind a three foot high bush."

"Welcome Colonel," said Kani from the entrance to what looked to Roux like a bedroom off the passage. He was dressed in a tracksuit, looking relaxed. "If I remember, you take your coffee white with no sugar."

"Hello Mr. Kani, yes, thanks."

"Would you like to wait in my office? It's a bit cramped, but the best I can do for now. I'll get your coffee."

"How is your brother?"

"Much the same, I'm afraid, but his breathing sounds a little less labored. The doctors from New York arrive tomorrow, so I should get an informed diagnosis. Coffee won't be long."

Roux made his way into the small office and looked round. The desk and shelves of a low wall unit were covered in piles of papers, books, folders and envelopes of varying size and color; some were open, others sealed. A writing pad lay open on the desk. Minutes later Kani joined him, closing the door and handing Roux his coffee. The professor walked to a chair behind the desk, waving Roux to a lounger in the corner, and sat down, making no attempt to cover his note pad. He lifted an enormous white mug and took a sip.

"So, how do you believe I can help?"

"Professor," said Roux. "Last night at the hospital, I received an anonymous phone call, which made it clear the shooting at my house was a warning. Dire consequences would follow if we did not release the MBL men." He held up a hand, anticipating Kani's question.

"Yes, they are both under twenty-four-hour protection, but the threat remains. A very real threat to my family, which makes this all very personal. Besides the threat, we have uncovered another development which, to put it mildly, is frightening. During the raid on the farm, we learned there are three car bombs somewhere in the Cape Town area. They will probably use two of them in White suburbs as a distraction to draw off our units at Verster, while the third car is positioned to intercept Mr. Mandela's convoy. There is now a suspicion Khumalo is not the brains behind the operation, a fact you have already alluded to. I need to find out who is behind the MBL, but for reasons I cannot explain, I have limited time in which to do it."

Kani placed his mug on the desk and leaned back in his chair, looking troubled.

"Oh dear. I had a feeling it may come to this. Marius . . . do you mind if I call you Marius?"

Roux inclined his head in a single nod.

"Good. Jonas, please. Mister and professor, make me sound older than I already feel." He interlaced his fingers, placing his forearms on the table. "In answer to your question, allow me to first pose one in return. Have you found out who owns the Waterfalls estate?"

"A front company called Waterfalls Winery, with a fake address here in Cape Town. Three directors. Khumalo, Davids, and Akmet."

"Correct. Waterfalls was in fact bought for cash from the original family owners in November last year by Lyttleton Investments, which registered Waterfalls Winery as the owner. It stood unoccupied for some time. All the work on the farm stopped. They paid the old labor force off, and other than a small contingent of what I assume were caretakers, the place was dormant. Until about two weeks ago, when we noticed low-key activity at the farm. People staying for several days, boxes and other materials being moved in and out."

"Who owns Lyttleton Investments?" asked Roux.

"That I cannot answer, but my guess is it is another front company for whoever is behind the MBL. So perhaps you need to start by finding out who created it, which should point you toward the people you are looking for."

"Prof—Jonas, when we were observing the place before our raid, we saw two men arrive to meet with Davids. My initial impression was they were Whites, but in the darkness and, well . . . some Coloreds have light complexions, we couldn't be sure. Davids admits to the visit but says they were both Coloreds and gave us their names." He paused, examining his hands for a moment.

"Is it possible the men I saw *were* White?"

Kani stared over Roux's shoulder. "Marius, I believe it is very possible. My opinion is President de Klerk is walking a tightrope with the release of Mr. Mandela, but more so with the unbanning of the liberation movements. I find it difficult to accept he has unreserved support from the entire upper echelons of government, including the security forces. Logic tells me there is, and will be for some time, opposition to his efforts. The question is, how aggresive will this opposition be? If it is limited to the confines of parliament, then we will be fortunate, but I doubt it."

"Meaning?" said Roux.

"How confident are you, with your knowledge of the senior members of the armed forces and police, that *all* the apartheid hardliners are represented by the right wing opposition parties?"

Roux nodded sagely. "It's possible there are some within the security forces who still believe in separate development. But I can only speak for the officers at Compton who I know are struggling to come to terms with the situation. The very people we were tasked with uncovering and arresting are now free to move around as they choose, making it easier to attack Whites. Sure, the State of Emergency is still in place, but many feel we're trying to maintain security with one arm tied behind our backs. They fear their rights will be denied them if there is majority rule and, as some believe, forced out of the country. However, if your question is will they take up arms to protect those rights, I'm not convinced it would come to that."

"Understandable," said Kani. "I know your Black and Colored members are fearful of a backlash if there is a Black government, but we are still some way away from that. But allow me to extend your line of thought. If junior members of the security forces are concerned and confused, how are the senior members taking the shift in policy? Are they committed to supporting de Klerk irrespective of how much power he gives up, or will their survival instincts take over?" He paused, as though collecting his thoughts.

"But let's put the security forces to one side for the moment and examine what really matters. Money and power. Both of which are in the hands of the Whites. As sanctions took hold, this economy became incestuous. A small number of corporates, either directly or indirectly, own most of the economy with interests in every sector of the industry and fingers in every pie, including each other's. Blacks gaining political freedom is one thing, but without economic freedom, it is meaningless. They will want equal opportunity to own their own businesses and buy property and invest where they choose. Certainly, there are those who understand the economic devastation sanctions have brought and know this, more than anything else, is what is forcing de Klerk's hand. The country can no longer survive in its present state. The world is forcing change on the country while hoping it will be a peaceful transition to power. But, the real wealth, and the power it brings, is in the hands of a very select few.

Will those select few be prepared to give it all up, or at least share it without so much as a whimper? I am not convinced.

"In summation Marius, and again, just my opinion. You have possible discontentment amongst some senior members of the armed forces, and a select group of wealthy and powerful industrialists who have more to lose than gain with the demise of apartheid." His eyes held Roux's for a moment.

"Your coffee must be cold. Can I refresh your cup?"

"No thanks," said Roux. He leaned back in his chair, stretching his legs out in front of him, holding his now cold coffee in both hands.

"I hear you," said Roux, "and I know transition will not be easy, but if viewed from the Whites' perspective, the concerns are understandable. Many will question why they should give up everything their ancestors fought for? It's ours by right. Whites took a backward, uncivilized country, and turned it into the powerhouse of Africa. You can't expect people to just hand it all over without resentment."

Kani looked irritated for a moment before relaxing back into a more placid appearance.

"Fought for or stole? All the Whites in the early Cape Colony were colonialists. British, Dutch, German, and even some French. The land they possessed had been lived on for centuries by the San people and other African tribes who were the original inhabitants. It did not belong to the settlers. They took it by force most times, and the same happened in the country's interior as Whites migrated inland. Violence displaced Black tribes, chased off land which rightfully was theirs. How can you justify that, Marius?"

Roux bristled. "The Dutch settlers moved inland because the British at the Cape made life for them intolerable, imposing unjust restrictions and laws on them. What were they supposed to do? They left because the British abolished slavery, on which almost all the Dutch farmers relied and so robbing them of their livelihood. They imposed taxes, their culture, their way of life, but what was most unacceptable was making English the official language. Why should the Dutch-speaking farmers be forced to use a language not their own?"

"Really, Marius?" laughed Kani. "Be careful with using that argument as a justification for their land grab."

"Why? It's true."

"It may be, but consider this. What caused the seventy-six student uprising? It was the imposition of a foreign language, Afrikaans, as a medium for instruction in the schools. As your ancestors rejected being forced to accept English, the students rejected the policy of having to learn in a language which was not their natural tongue. Seems to me there's a lesson in there somewhere."

Roux was surprised to find he no longer felt annoyance at Kani's arguments, but rather curiosity. "But at the time it must have appeared to the Dutch farmers as discrimination, giving them cause to seek freedom and create their own country, free of British domination."

"So they went into the interior, driving the inhabitants off their land to achieve their goal. Is that fair?" Kani's tone was still conversational.

"Yes, why not? Black tribes were fighting amongst themselves, anyway. Look what Shaka's Zulus did. Killed, pillaged, and enslaved many tribes around them. Why is what they did acceptable but not so for the Dutch farmers?"

Kani held up his hands, palms outward.

"Let us explore history a bit, shall we? Inter-tribal wars have always been a part of man's history for centuries. But the internal squabbles in a country do not give foreigners the right to invade it, enslave the population and colonize it, and yet many of history's great empires were built by doing just that. But why did they all ultimately collapse? Because you cannot ignore the will of the original inhabitants of the countries you invade. People desire freedom, Marius, the ability to have choices, to influence their own future and development. A minority can not rule the majority, especially when the minority has no legitimate claim to the land over which they rule. Whites came to this continent as interlopers, raped it of its riches, suppressed its peoples, but were surprised when Blacks fought back. Fought for what is rightfully theirs by birth. Apartheid has failed for the same reason. At best, it's colonialism, at worst a crime against humanity."

Roux opened his mouth to voice an adamant denial, but then realized he was having trouble finding a justifiable rebuttal. He clamped his mouth shut.

"What I find difficult to comprehend is why the world allowed this travesty of justice to exist for so long? But the time for change has come," continued Kani.

"How peaceful the transition is will depend on all of us. If compromise is the approach, it will be peaceful, but if we attempt to enforce our own exclusive will on others—be it Blacks on Whites or Blacks on Blacks—there will be conflict. But, the Whites need to look into their hearts and decide if they will move with the change, or continue to resist it. A new dawn is coming, a new day, one in which Whites will no longer be the sole decision makers, the sole owners of everything, but will be part of the collective, and yes, it means being contributing citizens in a country ruled by the majority."

"But will we lose everything we have, we own, the future of our children?" said Roux.

"I do not believe so Marius. It is why I asked you to read the ANC Charter. It calls for one country in which all races, Black, White, Colored and Indian, are equal in the eyes of the law, where there is no place for racialism. A country where every child receives equal, quality education providing equal opportunities to fulfill their individual dreams. Will it be such an awful place to live in?"

"I read it. My first impression is it is too good to be true. But the question I have to ask is this. The ANC leadership may believe it, but do the people on the ground, in the townships, and the rural areas believe the same?"

"Each individual will need to decide if they can accept, compromise, and implement change," said Kani. "Our willingness to not only take, but give as well. I have faith in Tambo and Mandela, and their lieutenants, to do their very utmost to ensure the principles of the Charter are honored by all ANC members. But how the PAC and others will react, I cannot say."

Roux chewed on the inside of his mouth for several long moments. "An honest answer, please, Jonas. Do you believe Blacks can run this country? Because from what I see in the rest of Africa, Black leaders seem to be more focused on self-enrichment than improving the lives of the people. Corruption and poverty, according to the international press, is rife. African countries are amongst the poorest in the world, and they are decades behind everyone else. Nothing seems to work."

A look of annoyance crossed Kani's face.

"While there have been unfortunate events in Africa's history, there have also been notable achievements. There is no denying Africa is backward compared to other parts of the world, but the colonial powers, by limiting the development of its peoples, are entirely responsible. It's important to remember every new beginning is marked by a lack of knowledge and experience. These attributes are gained over time. As infants need nurturing and encouragement as they grow, so do new nations. The ANC will undoubtedly make mistakes, but if we, the collective, choose to support the change, it will succeed, provided we allow ourselves sufficient time. It won't be easy, and it may be especially challenging for Whites, but it is achievable. This country needs all the skills and expertise it can get, but much of it is held by Whites, so forcing them to leave would be detrimental to everyone." He studied Roux for a moment and then grinned.

"I know Marius, you were brought up to believe Blacks are ignorant, lazy and apt to steal anything not nailed to the floor. The common opinion of Whites is Blacks cannot be trusted with anything which requires intellect so confining most to manual labor. What I find curious, though, is why so many Whites leave their most prized possessions, their houses and children, in the care of these untrustworthy Blacks, while they go to work or out at night. Odd would you not concede?"

Roux threw up his hands and laughed. "Guilty as charged."

He stood up, placing his untouched coffee on the desk. "We seemed to have strayed from the reason I came to see you. The MBL." His face became serious. "From what you telling me, the MBL are being manipulated by others which could include members of the security forces or powerful business owners. Have I got it right?"

Kani stood up. "No Marius, I am not *telling* you anything. It is my opinion, nothing more, and I have no inside information or evidence to substantiate my theory. My opinion is one amongst many, and odds are even, I could be wrong, but what I am *suggesting* is you find out who is really behind Lyttleton Investments."

Roux nodded. "Point taken. Thanks. I'll give your best to Mel, and my apologies for the early visit, but it has been helpful for me." He smiled. "One day, after all this is over, I would like to continue our chat about where you see this country going in the future."

"With pleasure, but keep one thing in mind, Marius. Change is coming. It is inexorable," said Kani.

Waving a hand, Roux turned to leave.

"Oh. One last thing Marius, you may not like what you find with your inquiries into who is behind the MBL."

Roux stood for a moment, eyebrow raised, and then made his way toward the front door.

Realizing he needed to clean up and get something to eat, he headed for home. From there, he called Compton and asked to speak to du Plessis. It took several minutes before a gruff voice answered.

"This better be urgent, Roux."

He gave an overview of his meeting with Kani, and the possible connection between Waterfalls Winery and Lyttleton Investments.

"Finding out who is the mastermind behind Lyttleton and why it was created may point us at who is financing the MBL. I've heard nothing back from Gainsford, so I'm assuming he has either beaten the lot to death or no one is talking."

He could hear du Plessis' heavy breathing on the other end of the phone.

"I need some help, General, in finding out who the owners of Lyttleton are."

"OK. I'll have an answer for you asap." The connection was broken.

HE WAS ON HIS second cup of coffee when Meiring called on the radio.

"Seems we found one car."

*Some good news at last*, Roux thought. *One may lead to two and then . . . only one left to find*. "Copy. Are you still at the station?"

"Affirmative."

Roux found Meiring seated at his desk, talking on the phone. He sat down opposite him and waited until the call ended.

"That was Gainsford. Been at it most of the night, but Khumalo is not budging. Davids had a heart attack, so he's still in hospital. Serves him right."

"Doesn't surprise me," said Roux. "I had a very interesting chat with Kani earlier, but first, where was the car found?"

"Uniforms spotted it at the De Villiers shopping center in Clansfield about six this morning. When they approached it, the driver bolted. Make and color matched our descriptions and the Control Room called Bomb Squad. They are going over the car now. But sounds like what we looking for, given the description and its location."

"Let's hope. Does du Plessis know?"

Meiring's eyes went skyward. "He's together with Warmer in his office. Jonker, the boss at Bomb Squad, informed Warmer, so I assume he does."

"Save us bugging him," said Roux. "What's happening elsewhere?"

"Uniforms and army have been patrolling the center of town, but nothing as yet. Plainclothes units are in and around the City Hall with vehicles patrolling the streets in the vicinity. Verster is being watched, but more than that, not a lot we can do. All the suburban stations have patrols out checking at shopping centers, churches and any other places where the public is likely to gather. Although it's possible the other two bombs have not reached their destinations yet. Problem is, although a Sunday, once people start their weekend shopping, it's going to get almost impossible to spot the cars."

"And in the townships?"

"Local stations have been stripped of most of their men to help in the city, so if one bomb ends up there we're only going to hear about it, literally, as it goes off," said Meiring. "But to be honest, I very much doubt it's where they'll use them. My bet is once Mandela is in a car, they'll try to target a spot along the route. Warmer will get the air wing up once we know when he is due to walk out of Verster. You mentioned Kani?"

Roux explained Kani's theory, ending with his call to du Plessis.

"What he suggests makes sense," said Meiring. "You don't have free access to a property like that without the owners either being blind and naïve, or in on it. I also have to agree with his opinion on the armed forces. From what I hear there are a whole heap of very pissed off folks who feel betrayed, so scuttling the negotiation process is not out of the realm of possibility."

His phone rang. "Meiring," he said, snatching it up after the first ring. He listened and then beamed. "OK, have you informed Colonel Jonker?"

Roux could hear the caller's muffled voice coming through the earpiece.

"Good. I'm sure he'll inform General du Plessis," said Meiring. "How complex a device is it?"

Roux watched as Meiring's jovial expression changed to one of concern.

After a long silence, Meiring said, "OK, you'll need to warn your other teams." A further pause. "Got it. Keep me up to date. I'll be on the radio, Bravo Two." He replaced the receiver slowly.

"Who was that?"

"De Groot from Bomb Squad, who just returned from the shopping center. The good news is it's one of the bombs. Bad news is the initial examination shows it's a highly sophisticated assembly. Could take hours to disarm."

"Think they'll be able to handle it? It's not like they've had years of experience dismantling car bombs."

"I know," said Meiring, "but we'll have to rely on them. There are the army experts if it gets too tricky. De Groot will tell Jonker, so du Plessis will find out."

"Time to scrounge up some decent coffee from Gerda's stash and hope, like hell, de Groot's men know what they doing."

"You go ahead. I'm going to shoot down to the canteen and see if I can get something to eat. Missed my usual oats and fruit this morning," said Meiring, with a tired smile. "You want anything?"

"No thanks. I'll be in my office."

He had just returned to his office with Gerda's stash in his hand when a buzzing noise from his phone showed an internal call.

"Hello Colonel, it's the Charge Office. I have a Major Philip Roberts here who wants to come up and see you. Is it OK?"

His argument with Mel about Phil's visit flashed into view. He took a deep breath. "Yes, sure, send him up."

Moments later, Phil Roberts sauntered into his office. "Ah! Coffee ready and waiting, hey?"

They shook hands and Roux made up two cups of coffee while Roberts spoke, his voice somber.

"What the hell happened with Mel and Rian, Marius? I phoned the hospital as soon as I heard but they wouldn't tell me anything, so after I got no reply from your house, I took a chance you might be here. How are they?"

Roux updated his friend on the shooting and the current state of both Mel and Rian. "Just wish Rian would recover consciousness. At least then the doctors will have a better understanding of the damage. Mel should be up and about this morning." He felt a sudden pang of guilt. It was the first thing he should have done this morning; call the hospital.

"They have all my details," he quickly added, "so as soon as either of them wakes up, I'll know."

"Of course, of course," said Roberts as he took the coffee. "Any idea who is behind it?"

"MBL, without a doubt." He told his friend about the phone call. "But we'll get the bastard, I promise you. Then I'll tear the savage apart with my bare hands."

Roberts shifted in his chair. "Shit! This lot sound like they playing for keeps. We got briefed yesterday about the car bombs. Serious amount of activity going on and all the top military brass in a panic. Is this all to do with Mandela? Is he being released today?"

Roux nodded, lowering his voice. "Probably around lunchtime. He's going to make a speech at City Hall afterwards."

Roberts looked away for a moment, appearing to be deep in thought. But seconds later, his lopsided grin made an appearance.

"OK. I just wanted to know how you and the family are, so I'll leave you to it. Going to be a long day, but I need to head back to the barracks. We recalled my old team from their break, so I need to brief them. Any luck in finding the car bombs?"

Meiring appeared at the door, a half-eaten sandwich in his hand. "Oh sorry, didn't realize you had company."

"No problem, Eugene, come on in. This is Phil Roberts, with the Recces. We go back a long way. He came in to find out about the family."

The two men shook hands. Meiring looked skeptical for some reason.

"We were just talking about the search for the car bombs. Phil was a team leader in the Recce's until he moved to Operations." He turned back to Roberts.

"Found one this morning at a shopping center, but the guys are still trying to disarm it but turns out it's highly sophisticated." He caught a look of disapproval from Meiring out of the corner of his eye. "The bomb disposal guys are concerned—"

Meiring glared at Roux, anger in his voice, and said, "Nothing has been confirmed yet, Mr. Roberts, but the good news is we have one bomb. Hopefully, we find the others shortly."

Roux was initially perturbed, but then irritated at Meiring's interruption. He was about to continue when his phone rang.

"Roux," he answered, listened, and then said. "We both are on our way up now, General."

"His master's voice," chuckled Roberts. "Right. I'll leave you two brave souls to get on with saving our city. Oh, Marius, sorry about the clandestine visit to your place the other day. I wanted to find out how you were *really* doing, not the 'it's all under control' shit I normally get from you, and thought Mel could fill me in. Sorry if it caused a tiff."

*Assuming it was the real reason you were there.* Roux studied his friend. If there was ever a human being he trusted without question, it was Phil Roberts. So was it possible? Could Phil have been seeing Mel all these years without him knowing? He knew the man could be shallow and callous, but betray him with Mel? Dammit! He'd saved the man's life.

It had happened during Roux's first six-month stint in South West in the late seventies. Everyone had presumed Roberts dead or captured after he'd been separated from his team in Angola, but despite all the evidence to the contrary, he'd known his friend was still alive. In desperation, he had begged his father to intervene with his army contacts. The final, resultant search found Phil worse for wear, but very much alive. But now that he thought back on it, Phil had never thanked him, only heaped praise and gratitude on his father. Still. He couldn't bring himself to picture it. Mel may still be in love with the guy, but Phil would not betray him.

"Cheers Phil, talk soon." He gestured to Meiring, "Let's go."

"You guys take care out there . . . both of you, and let me know when you hear about Rian," shouted Roberts after them, "and don't worry. I'll see myself out," he said to himself.


DU PLESSIS AND WARMER were both standing at the wall map when Roux and Meiring entered the office.

"General," said Roux as they walked over to join the two senior officers.

"Ah! Roux," du Plessis said, turning toward them.

"Seems we have discovered a second bomb. Down by the refinery. It was being parked on the side of the road when one of the CID vehicles spotted it. The driver made a run for it, but a well placed round in his hips brought him down. He's been rushed to a hospital, but he's conscious and eager to talk, but doesn't speak English. Seems Gainsford was right. We're going to need a Portuguese interpreter. The Army engineers are being flown to the site to disarm it, as Jonker has his hands full with the first one. Seems whoever assembled these devices is no fool, but he's confident they'll disarm them."

He fished in his jacket pocket and came out with a sheet of paper, handing it to Roux. "This may shed some light on who is behind it."

Roux glanced down at the address on the piece of paper. His brow furrowed for a moment. Then he went cold.

"Is this the registered owner of Lyttleton Investments?"

Du Plessis nodded. "Indirectly. Bit of a long story, but a synopsis is this. The Commercial Crimes boys confirmed the farm is registered to Willows Winery, which is owned by Lyttleton Investments, as Kani said. Lyttleton is owned by Madeira Holdings. No directors listed, but it is owned by three other companies, all of them dormant. After peeling back the layers of what owns what, they got a clearer picture of where it was all leading."

Du Plessis scratched his nose. "It ultimately led back to the Company Secretary of one of the Mining Houses. Individual called Stewart. They got him out of his pool this morning, but of course he denied knowing anything about it until he heard it was an inquiry related to the Terrorism Act. Amazing how the word terrorism jogs people's memories. Claims he received a memo from the Group Chairman's office with instructions on what to do. They still interrogating him, but the short version is this. The memo instructed him to establish Madeira Holdings, and the subsequent creation of Lyttleton Investments, leading to the cash purchase of Waterfalls. There was to be no trail back to the Mining House. This all happened four months ago. The chairman of the mining house lives at the address on the paper. I have to tell you, this information spooked Greyling, who is having a rethink about the MBL and who is running it." Du Plessis sighed.

"I'm sure this is one huge misunderstanding with a simple explanation. I know this man, have done for years, and I'm struggling to believe he could be somehow involved, but we better check it out just on the off chance, so I need the two of you to get out there and interview him, and anyone else there."

"Assuming he's there," said Roux.

"Oh! He's there. I got a uniform woman to call pretending to be selling vacuum cleaners. He answered, not the house help, so he's there. Go now, and call me as soon as you know anything, and I mean anything."

"Who's house is it?" asked Meiring as they jogged down the corridor to the elevator.

"Felix Fouché."

TWENTY MINUTES LATER, THEY were tearing through the streets of the upper-class suburbs at a speed he found alarming. Meiring's driving skills were superb, but he still considered the man to be a maniac behind the wheel. He gazed out the window at the multi-million rand houses flashing past and gave a long sigh through puffed-out cheeks. It was hot, and the mid morning sun was already a searing yellow orb in a cloudless sky. He glanced sideways at his companion and guessed Meiring's choice to don a sports jacket had more to do with concealing his weapon than a fashion statement.

"I assume we don't want Fouché to know we there until he answers his front door. Du Plessis will not be impressed if the man bolts out the back gate before we get in."

"Agree. We need to surprise him, but it shouldn't be a problem."

"There'll be a security guard at the gate. How do we coax him into opening?" said Roux.

"If he doesn't, I'll ram the gates," grunted Meiring.

"I doubt it, those gates are big and heavy. You'd need a tank."

"It won't be a problem. Most of the security guys are ex-army or police."

Moments later, they pulled up in front of the high, heavy, ornate gates. Meiring hooted before both men exited the car and strolled up to the gate, looking toward the small guard house off to the left, which appeared unoccupied.

"Can I help you?" came a voice from their right as a middle-aged man stepped out from behind three small trees, pulling up the zip of his trousers. The buttons on the sweat-stained shirt of his black uniform strained to hide the hairy bulge hanging over his trousers.

Roux scrutinized the man. On his left hip, there was a hand-held radio in a holder. The weapon holster on his right side was empty. Hanging from his belt was a short silver chain with keys and a blue fob attached. It was the same gate remote as before.

"Morning," he called out. "Police. Security Branch. We're here to see Mr. Fouché on urgent police business. Please, can you open up? We are in a bit of a hurry." He kept his tone polite, but with a sense of urgency.

The man walked up to where the two sections of the gate met in the middle of the driveway. "Morning. I just need to let the house know. The boss said no one allowed in until I clear it with him." He turned to head for the guardhouse, presumably to use the phone.

Meiring, now standing alongside the hood of the car, drew his weapon and aimed it at the guard. "You move and I'll . . . shoot . . . your ear off!" he shouted, although the last three words came out more a croak than a threat.

Despite himself, Roux couldn't suppress a giggle. Meiring apparently was not an avid follower of American TV police dramas. "I'll drop you where you stand," or "I'll blow your head off," or "I'll take out your kneecaps," would have been more fitting for the occasion. "I'll shoot your ear off." Really? He struggled to stop another giggle.

He turned to the guard.

"Open the gate man, don't be stupid," said Roux. "You really want to lose your job and spend a week in our cells for obstructing the police? We're on the same side, remember?"

The man, now staring wide-eyed at Meiring, drops of sweat beginning to appear on his forehead, ran his hand along the length of the chain and pressed a button on the remote. The gates slowly opened.

As soon as there was sufficient space, Roux squeezed through and ran to the guard and pulled the radio out of its holder. "Give me the remote," the fingers of his outstretched hand emphasizing his instruction. The man unclipped the small device with a shaking hand, dropping it into Roux's palm.

Meiring, now behind the wheel, drove the car through the still parting gates. As soon as he was through, he jumped out and sprinted into the guardhouse.

"Are there any more of your people on the property?" demanded Roux.

The man shook his head vigorously, "no, it's Sunday. I'm the only one on duty."

Roux was feeling a little guilty over the mistreatment of another White man, but he knew there was no alternative.

Within minutes, Meiring reappeared. "The phone and radio are disabled. Also got the weapon," brandishing it in his hand before stuffing it into his trouser belt. He pulled a pair of cuffs from his jacket pocket and, grabbing the guard by one arm, handcuffed him to the now open gate.

Roux closed the gate and tossed the remote to Meiring. It began its slow grind, hauling the guard along with it. The two men got into the car, its motor still ticking over.

"Follow the driveway," said Roux, pointing toward the house. "It'll take us up to the front door." He glanced sidelong at Meiring, "I'll shoot your ear off? How terrifying," he said, with a broad grin.

Meiring laughed. "Sorry, couldn't think of anything else in the moment," he said, sounding embarrassed. "Problem is, if I had killed or seriously wounded him inside the gate, how the hell would we have got in?"

True, Roux conceded. Fouché getting away because they couldn't get inside the property would have been a hard one to explain.

They pulled up in front of the house and walked to the imposing front door. They could hear the chimes from the door bell echoing through the house, but it was not until he was about to push the button for the fourth time before the door slowly opened, revealing the gaunt face of the man himself.

"Oh! It's you Marius, how unfortunate," said Fouché in a soft voice. This time he spoke in English. "I suppose you had better come in. I've been expecting a call from someone, but I daresay I was expecting someone more senior."

"Why would you be expecting us, Mr. Fouché?" asked Roux, as he stepped into the house.

The old man sighed. "I am aware of your inquiries into my company's affairs in Johannesburg, and I assumed the police would have questions for me, so I have invited my lawyer to be present. I am sure you can understand?"

He pointed down the hallway. "We are in my study. You know the way." He walked off ahead of them.

As they reached the study door, Meiring's radio came to life. "I'll join you now," he said, turning back toward the lounge.

Roux followed Fouché into the familiar room and glanced around. The heavy curtains were drawn back, flooding the room with natural light. Just behind the desk, two large French doors leading onto a patio and the garden beyond stood open. A man in a dark blue three-piece suit sitting in one of the large chairs alongside the fireplace shot to his feet as they entered. He was a good head shorter than Roux.

"Morecombe," he said, walking over to Roux with an outstretched hand, "from Morecombe, Du Toit, Visser and Murray, Attorneys at Law. You are?"

Roux guessed the man was almost as old as his client. Frail face lined, and thinning gray hair hanging over his back collar. But he appeared relaxed and in control. He ignored the man's hand.

"Colonel Roux, Security Branch. We have some questions for Mr. Fouché, which he can answer here or down at Compton Square. I don't mind which. We will also carry out a search of the premises under the powers granted us by the State of Emergency."

He watched the man's face for a reaction. Other than a slight twitch in the corner of his mouth, suit man continued to look smug and confident.

"My client will not be answering questions, Colonel, so either you arrest him, or leave and get a court order to carry out a search. If not, I will have no option but to approach the courts myself. I will not allow you to—"

"Our questions relate to an act of terrorism against the State, and as you know, I don't need a warrant in terms of the Emergency Powers." Roux said, glowering down at the man. "So, Morecombe, do yourself a favor. Shut up and sit down, little man. Should we discover your firm knew of his involvement, or in some way facilitated it, you and your partners will spend tonight in a cell. Understand?"

Morecombe's eyes bulged, and his lips fluttered for an instance as he struggled for a response but instead sat down. Fouché, who had gone ashen, tottered back several steps, before collapsing into his chair.

"Good," said Roux, turning to Fouché. From the look of fear on the man's face, he was convinced Fouché knew something. *You are in on it, you bastard*, he thought. He decided to go on the offensive and see what reaction he got.

"Your Mr. Stewart has been extremely helpful in filling in some missing pieces in our investigations as to the ownership of the Waterfalls farm. He admitted receiving instructions from your office to set up various dummy companies and to purchase the farm. A farm, which until Friday, was being used by a terrorist organization who we believe is intent on the murder of Nelson Mandela, and possibly hundreds of other people, including Whites. All the members of that organization are now in custody, and everything points at you Fouché as the brain and money behind the operation, so what I need to know now is who else is involved in your little nursery school ring?"

Fouché was visibly shaking, beads of sweat forming on his upper lip. For an instant Roux feared he was going to collapse, but the old man, shaking his head, struggled to his feet and shuffled to a drinks trolley, where with a trembling hand poured a drink from a decanter. He drained the alcohol in one gulp and topped up the glass.

"That is preposterous," shouted Morecombe, half-rising from his chair. "Your accusations are groundless and I will make sure we sue the commi—"

"Quiet!" yelled Roux.

His focus shifted back to Fouché. The man appeared to have shrunk into himself. His head was shaking so violently he was having trouble getting the glass to his lips. He leaned a hand against the edge of the drinks trolley as his shoulders sagged, eyes closed.

Roux tensed, taking a quick step toward Fouché. *Don't you die on me, old man*, he screamed to himself. *Not yet*.

For a moment, Fouché steadied himself against the trolley and then staggered drunkenly over to a chair. He took another gulp, placed the half-filled glass on a side table and leaned forward, elbows on his knees, face buried in his hands.

"I know nothing of any plot to kill Mandela or anyone else," he mumbled into his hands, then raised his head. "I bought the farm as an investment for my children. How was I to know it would be occupied by terrorists? You have no proof . . . it's just a fabrication." His croaking voice tailed off. He looked pleadingly at Morecombe, whose eyes were by now the size of the morning sun. It was obvious Fouché could expect no help from his lawyer.

"Please Marius," he said, watery eyes pleading, lips quivering. "There has to be some mistake. I talk to the president frequently, and he knows he has my support. I am a business owner, for heaven's sake. I want the change, so we can open the country to new investors. Surely you see that?"

"Colonel, a moment," said Meiring from the doorway.

"You stay where you are, both of you," said Roux.

Meiring was grinning as he whispered into Roux's ear.

Roux nodded several times, grunted and walked over to glare down at Fouché.

"Seems the leader of this terrorist group, the MBL, has just signed a full confession stating he was employed by a man named Rodriquez, who told him a Mr. Stewart was providing the funding for the operation. I'm sure Stewart will be more than happy to share the blame and tie it all back to you."

Fouché shook his head. "No. I don't believe it. Why would I want to act against the party I am a member of? I have been doing everything within my power to support the president. Everyone knows it."

Roux scoffed. "You trying to tell me you did not know what was going on at Waterfalls? The MBL move in, lock, stock and barrel, and you were never told, even though you employed caretakers to look after the place? Please, we're not stupid, Fouché. We thought the MBL was a recent creation, formed after SONA. But it wasn't. You created them months ago and moved them to Waterfalls to prepare to take decisive action, including planting car bombs, if you thought the president was capitulating to the ANC. From what we have uncovered, a lot of planning went into creating the entire set-up. Money, technical support, access to firearms and explosives, trained bomb makers, all of which need money and someone in a powerful position to mastermind it. You, and whoever else is involved, have been planning to plunge the country into a civil war by killing Mandela. How stupid can you be? How do you think the world will react? Thousands would die, innocent people, Whites amongst them."

Leaning over Fouché, he spoke softly, but there was venom in his voice as he struggled to resist the urge to strangle the man.

"You even tried to kill my family, you bastard. That makes it personal."

"Easy Colonel," he heard Meiring whisper from behind him.

Fouché, his eyes pleading, spit dribbling from his mouth, shook his head violently. "I knew nothing about that!" he screamed. "It should never have happened. Believe me . . . please . . ."

"Felix. Stop it, you sound weak!" said a voice in Afrikaans from the open French doors.

The man, standing just inside the study, his expression pure hatred, locked eyes with Roux.

"Pa?"


ROUX STARED WIDE-EYED AT his father. His chest felt constricted, as though he were in a gigantic bear-hug, and a stabbing pain started in his gut and began inching its way up to his chest. It felt as if the room was swaying around him.

"Mr. Roux, why are you here?" said Meiring, in a conversational tone as he reached forward and gripped Roux's arm, preventing him from toppling over.

"Piss off Meiring," his father hissed, "you're a minnow, too young, and too junior to understand what is needed, what is at stake here. But you," he pointed at his son, "should know better after everything I taught you. How to be a proud Afrikaner prepared to sacrifice all for the sake of the *volk*, your people. But no, you finally decide its time to play hero when your focus should be on ensuring we maintain our grip on our birthright. This country is ours. Our forefathers fought and died for it. First it was the Xhosa and the Zulus, then the English, and now the Blacks again. And, as we did before, we'll teach them a lesson about civilization."

Roux's throat was dry as he tried to swallow, hoping to find his voice. He blinked several times in an effort to clear his brain.

"W-w-why are you here? Are y-you involved in all of this?" His voice cracking.

His father's face twisted into a cruel smile, then he gave a strangled laugh.

"Involved? You know me better than that, son. I *am* this! Spineless politicians and generals whine about what de Klerk is doing, but don't have the balls to do what is necessary. I took action to keep this country in the hands of the Afrikaner. The world bleats about the poor Blacks and their fight for independence and nationhood." Now there was bitterness in his tone.

"Which is exactly what we are doing. Fighting for our right to exist as a nation. Why should we Afrikaners fade into obscurity simply to accommodate millions of ignorant and corrupt Blacks who couldn't organize a piss-up in a brewery, let alone run a country like this one? South Africa is the military and economic heart of this decrepit continent and who created it? We, the Afrikaners. The Americans and British were quick to ask us to help when those red commie bastards needed to be stopped in Angola. Our boys bled for the west and now, what thanks do we get? Sanctions, political strong-arm tactics and pandering to Mandela and his sycophants." He walked into the room and stood behind the desk, hands clasped behind his back.

Meiring's radio squawked, and he left the room. A moment later, he spoke from the doorway. "Uniforms and the lab teams I called for are here. I'm going to the gate to let them in. You OK on your own?"

Roux looked at him, confused for a moment as he tried to grasp what Meiring had just said.

"Go," he said, and then he looked back at his father.

"Pa," he whispered, moving to the edge of the desk. "This is madness. How can you believe you could succeed on your own?"

"I am not alone. Powerful men, in business, in the army, police and the air force support my ideals and actions. Hundreds of them." He pointed accusingly at Fouché. "Do you think wimps like him have the stamina and guts to confront de Klerk? No. They just sit round their fireplaces and dream and talk and whine, but change nothing. So, I had to do what they were too scared to do. Stop the negotiations before it is too late. All we needed from them was their money. We will do the rest. By tonight, this country will be in the grips of violence on an unprecedented scale, and we will step in. Use all the tools at our disposal to regain and maintain control. De Klerk will be sidelined along with the rest of the weaklings."

Roux gazed at his father in utter disbelief, realizing the extent of his own naivety throughout the years. His admiration for his father wasn't based on qualities worthy of emulation; but because he and his sister were so indoctrinated by his father's bigotry and racial hierarchy, they refused to acknowledge the fact their privileged and protected lives were nothing but a sham. So blurred was their vision by false beliefs, they could not recognize the reality that the apartheid system was not only brutal and archaic; it was a house of cards. Suddenly an image of Rian's face appeared in his mind, bandaged, bruised and swollen. He felt his face redden.

"Are you talking about a military coup? It will never happen, you old fool. Despite what you believe, there are many Whites, inside and outside the security forces, who are tired of the bloodshed and isolation. They want peace. To know their boys will be safe and not forced to fight for a lost cause. Change is going to happen, Pa." His eyes narrowed.

"Did you try to kill Mel and Rian?"

His father shrugged. When he spoke, his voice was flat. "No one was to be hurt. It was a warning to you as to the consequences if you did not drop your investigation. When only the bitch climbed out of the car, our man assumed it was empty. Rian was collateral damage. Unfortunate."

For the first time in his life, Roux wished he carried a firearm. He sneered at his father. "Unfortunate? No apology or regret? Your only grandchild, who is now lying in hospital, is just collateral damage?" He was shouting. "Not only did you shoot your grandson, but you placed my wife's life in danger. A woman who has been nothing but loving and supportive of me. Not to mention her patience in tolerating your arrogant treatment of her. But as usual, you got it wrong, and your grandson, who adores you, may be retarded for life. You happy now?" he screamed.

"Loving and supportive?" his father shouted back at him. "You call sucking up to those Black turds at the Foundation supportive? Loving? How can you be so blind? Haven't you seen the way she goes all gaga when Phil is around? Flirting and giving him adoring looks. She's a slut son, its time you face up to reality."

Roux moved around the side of the desk, his fists clenched, his eyes blazing coals.

"Colonel!" Meiring's commanding voice from the doorway stopped him in his tracks.

"What?" he said, still glowering at his father.

"The CID, uniforms and technicians are here. We need to arrest these two and finish what we came here to do." He turned to Roux's father.

"Mr. Roux, we have found all three bombs, so your little ill-conceived plan will not happen. But then life's a bummer, hey! Best laid plans and all that."

To Roux's surprise, his father smiled as he sat down in the chair behind the desk. He opened a drawer, extracted something, and placed his hand on the desk. In its grip was a pistol.

Roux heard Meiring gasp as his hand disappeared under his jacket, reaching for his gun.

"Wait," he yelled, throwing out a hand in Meiring's direction. He looked back at his father.

"You going to shoot me?" he said, contempt in his tone. "Kill me, like you did *Ma*, driving her into an early grave with your selfishness and arrogance."

His father scoffed. "Your mother, like you, was weak. You amateurs think you're so smart. The bombs were never anything more than a distraction for the main event. Mandela *will* die, believe me," he said, his voice low but menacing. He raised the pistol, barrel pointing upwards. The look he gave his son was hatred personified.

"No Marius, I will not shoot you. It would be a waste of a bullet. I want you to live with the consequences of what you have done today. I want you to suffer. To live with the endless guilt of your betrayal of me, your sister, of your people. Of your God."

"Who shot Rian?" shouted Roux.

Roux's father placed the barrel under his chin and laughed. Then he pulled the trigger.

The blast deafened Roux. As he regained his hearing, he walked around the desk and looked down at his father's face with its gaping mouth and vacant eyes. Despite his attempts to conjure up feelings of remorse, or sadness, or even sympathy, there was nothing, only numbness. He lifted a hand to close his father's eyes, but changed his mind. *You created this mess, old man. Now you can see it unfold*.

The other three men in the room were motionless, as though frozen in place. Meiring's hand still on his pistol grip, his eyes the size of gum-balls. Roux had to admit it was the first time he'd seen Meiring utterly at a loss.

The office door burst open and two uniform police officers barged in, guns drawn. The first stopped just inside the room and was almost floored when his partner barged in and collided with him. He stumbled forward, grabbing at his peaked cap.

"Everyone," he shouted, "everyone stay where . . ." He regained his balance, ". . . you are." He stared at the body in the chair, then at each of the room's occupants. "Is there a Captain Meiring here?" he said, sounding rather sheepish.

Meiring returned to the land of the living. "It's all under control," he said, sounding shaky. "Get the Lab guys in here. The body is that of General Roux, retired." He stared at the body for a moment. "Permanently retired."

He never retired, just kept on fighting, but for the wrong reasons, Roux reflected.

"He committed suicide in our presence," continued Meiring, gaining control over his voice. "You men need to continue with the search of the house. We'll remove the body when the Lab men are done." He walked over to Roux, who still stood next to the chair. "You OK Marius, you want to take a walk outside?"

Roux stared out at the tranquil setting of the landscaped lawns. Anything to step out of this nightmare, even if only for a moment.

"No. I need to talk to Fouché. I need to understand what my father meant." He walked to the couch, looking down at Fouché and Morecombe. Both were in a complete state of shock. There was drool dribbling out the side of Morecombe's mouth, gasping. Fouché was doubled over, his face in his hands, his whole body trembling.

He placed the heel of his palm against Fouché's head and pushed it back. The face was white, old eyes, rheumy and streaming, stared up at him.

"Fouché, I need to know what my father meant when he said the car bombs were just a distraction. What else have you people planned? I need to know now, or I will hand you over to Sergeant Gainsford, who will beat you to death. I guarantee it," he snarled.

Roux's voice galvanized Morecombe, who, wiping his mouth with the sleeve of his jacket, stammered, "My-my client has nothing to say, and if you—"

"Eugene," barked Roux, "get this turd out of here, and handcuff him to a chair, or the toilet, for all I care. Just shut him up."

Meiring walked over and yanked Morecombe to his feet, shoving him toward the door. "Out!"

Fouché was now slumped back, his lips quivering. Light returned to his eyes as he reached for his glass of whiskey and downed the remnants. He struggled to his feet, using the back of the furniture as a support, his whole body swaying.

"I need another drink."

Roux's initial reaction was to slap the man back down into the chair, but he needed answers, and if alcohol was going to help achieve that, so be it. He helped him over to the drinks trolley.

"One drink, and then you tell me what is really going on."

Fouché filled the glass, his shaking hands spilling more on the floor than into the glass, and gulped down half the contents. Drooping against the trolley, he lifted his head until his eyes met Roux's.

"What a glorious disaster. I warned him," he pointed at the body, the pitch in his voice rising, sounding almost like a little girl's. "I warned him the whole idea would not work, but no, your father always has the answers. *Had* the answers. Marius, I'm sorry but your father was bordering on madness. His fixation on the perceived destruction of the Afrikaner nation drove him to contemplate the ludicrous." He sucked in air.

"I told him he was going too far, but he wouldn't listen. He saw himself as both the Creator and Savior of Afrikaners. He believed that without him, the nation would be massacred or evicted from the country. Killing Mandela was the only way to stop de Klerk, he said. Civil war was what he wanted. It would allow the army to take over and reinstate the *right* political leaders."

He shook his head, closing his eyes. "He couldn't accept he was alone."

"What is the plan? Who else in involved?!" shouted Roux, shaking the man, his patience at an end.

After taking several moments to steady himself, Fouché opened his eyes and sighed.

"May I sit down?"

Roux grabbed his shirt, frog-marched him over to a chair and shoved him down. "Now Fouché! I want to know. Now!"

The old man held up a hand as though to defend himself. "OK, just give me a minute to get my breath." His chest was rising and falling at an unnatural pace.

Roux stepped back. He needed to back off and allow the man to gather himself. All they needed now was for him to drop dead. He waited.

Fouché took several deep, rasping breaths, exhaling loudly. "Right. Thank you." He stared over at his erstwhile co-conspirator as though weighing up the import of what he was about to say.

"Your father had a visitor about an hour ago. I only saw him from the back. I think he was Colored, well built, wearing a jacket, the ones with the hood on, so I didn't see his face, but I overheard some of the conversation. The man told your father Mandela is to be released today and he would be speaking at the City Hall after his release, which, he said, would be the ideal location. After he left, I asked your father what the visit was about. He just laughed, told me everything was going to schedule, so I needn't worry, that by tonight, the army will be in control." Fouché stared into space, a dreamy look on his face.

"And I believed him, despite all the others pulling out. They weren't prepared to go this far. And no, there are not hundreds involved. Just nine frightened, misguided, and ignorant old men, who, like me, cannot deal with the reality of a changing world." He made a sound, like a sorrowful moan.

"It was just your father, and me left. For some idiotic reason, I still believed he would make it all happen as we envisaged it. So . . . Stupid. So . . . Naïve." He looked out at the garden for a few seconds, then turned back and held up a hand. "I know. Who are the others? Don't worry, I will tell you in due course, but for now Marius, you need to stop whatever is going to happen."

His demeanor had altered. He was the chairman again, back in control, deciding, instructing others.

"I'm no military man Marius, but I now am sure your father arranged for an assassination, and the man who will pull the trigger was here this morning."


"YOU FEELING OK?"

ROUX shrugged. "I'm not sure. Still in a state of shock, I suppose." He stared out across the rolling lawns, perfectly laid out flower beds, and manicured bushes. "If I'm honest, right now I feel nothing but loathing and pity. I know that sounds strange, but to find out my father was prepared to plunge the country into a civil war to satisfy his own ego is hard to swallow. To top it all, he takes the coward's way out." He glanced sideways at Meiring.

"I never expected affection from the man. He didn't know the meaning of the word, even with my sister. But now when I look back, I'm not sure what I expected from him. Recognition? Support?" He shook his head. "But all I appear to have been was a disappointment. Shit, his father must have been a real bastard to turn out a son like him."

"Did you ever meet him? Your grandfather?"

"No, and my father never spoke about him. Seems he died quite young. In his fifties, according to my ma. She talked about him once. Tyrant, she called him. She gave me the impression the kids were brought up on copious amounts of religion and beatings, but that was it." He gave a cynical laugh.

"And now, here we are. My father turns out to be the brains behind this whole thing and leaves me to live with the consequences. Why am I surprised? It sums up his character in one sentence. A narcissistic, egotistical maniac. But, no point in delving into the past. We have work to do, eh!" He fell silent for a moment, chewing on his inner lip. "Going to be a hard one to explain to my sister."

The two men were seated on a lounger on the patio outside the study, which was now full of uniform and white-coated technicians. Roux had stood impassively by while they examined the scene, and the body was photographed. He made no move to intervene when his father was placed in a body bag, dumped on a gurney, and wheeled out to the waiting mortuary van. The desperate need to get away from it all drove him out onto the patio where Meiring had found him.

They continued to sit in silence for several minutes before Meiring said, "What did Fouché say?"

"You'll have no problem with his cooperation. He agreed to supply the names of everyone involved, but the intriguing bit was about a potential assassin."

Meiring's head did a swift ninety-degree turn. "He said what?" He was almost shouting. "What exactly did he say?"

"Seems my father had a visitor this morning. Fouché overheard some of the conversation, and is of the opinion Mandela will be assassinated, probably at City Hall. Reckons the visitor was the shooter. Other than a Colored guy, he couldn't tell me much more about him." It sounded to Roux as though someone else was saying the words, and he was just a disinterested bystander.

Meiring, leaped to his feet, fear in his eyes. "Shit, Marius! There's a shooter at City Hall waiting for Mandela and you talk about it as though it's old news. Du Plessis needs to know. Now!"

*The man sounds on the verge of panic. So unlike him,* thought Roux. He gave a deep sigh. "Yes, I suppose we should warn du Plessis. But they can take Mandela out for all I care right now. I'm sick to death of this whole shitty situation."

Meiring pulled his radio off his belt as he rushed back into the study.

Roux sat on the lounger and gazed out over the city to what he assumed was the ocean to the south—a thin blue haze far off in the distance. *Nice one, Pa, Sonja is going to throw another of her drunken temper tantrums when she hears this one. Blame me, of course, for not helping you.* His gaze shifted down to the patio floor, where he saw a lone piece of thatch. He leaned down and picked it up, breaking it apart in his fingers. *Would I have helped you if you had asked?* An image of his father sharing his plan with him played through his mind. He sat back, tossing the remains of the thatch away. *No Pa, I would have told you the whole idea was pure fantasy. Tried to convince you of your folly, but I doubt you would have listened in the end. But of course, you couldn't take the chance, could you, because you've never trusted me.*

Meiring interrupted his thoughts, tapping him on the shoulder. "Spoke to du Plessis. Nearly crapped himself, but he wants us back at the station now. By the way, Mandela has been informed of his released today, but he's asked for time to prepare and consult with his people, so no one knows exactly when he'll walk out."

Roux looked up at him. "Eugene, what do you think is going to happen after today, assuming we stop this assassination attempt?"

Meiring seemed in two minds for several seconds before his face relaxed and he joined his boss on the lounger. "It's all speculation from now on. Let's wait and see what happens."

"You're not answering the question," Roux retorted. "What will Tambo and Mandela want, and how soon?"

Meiring thought for a moment. "They want majority rule. One-man-one-vote. A Black president with a Black government. What does it mean for us?" He stared off into the distance. "Adapt or leave, is the answer, I guess."

Roux studied his companion through hooded eyes. "And do you think it's worth staying? Are you confident in the future?"

"Right now. Difficult to say. It will depend on what the ANC says and does over the next few months, and the negotiations, of course. But the wife and I have discussed it. With me leaving the force, and the kids still at school, we agreed we need to look at things with an open mind. Once we have a better idea of what the future looks like, we can reassess our options. But strange as it may seem, Marius, I have hope. An end to the unrest, the war, and the international isolation. I want my kids to grow up in a normal society without being burdened with the guilt of what apartheid represented."

"I hear you. Mel is terrified Rian will get called-up for National Service but I suppose with his injury now it's unlikely. You know, Kani said a strange thing when I left his place."

"Uh-huh?" said Meiring, one eyebrow raised.

"He said I wouldn't like what I find when we discover who owned Waterfalls. I think he knew, but wanted me to find out for myself. By the way, I read the Freedom

Charter, have you?" he knew he was rambling but didn't care.

"I have, several times. Quite a pronouncement, if you can believe it."

"And do you?"

Meiring looked down for a moment. "I believe Tambo and Mandela, and those close to the party leadership, do. The proof will be in whether they stick to it or get blinded by the sudden elevation to government, and the chance to feather their own nests. But again, I have to believe, for now, they do."

"Do you think the Whites are going to adjust overnight? To treat Blacks as equals?"

"Not overnight. It's going to take time, and a huge change in attitude," said Meiring. "But time will tell who is prepared to compromise, and who still wants to continue the fight."

Roux shook his head. "I can't see it, Eugene. The house maid today, your equal tomorrow? Whites will find it difficult to adapt to having Blacks in the schools, on the beaches, in restaurants, movie houses, and at work. Can you imagine the reaction of the average Afrikaner finding out he now has a Black boss?"

"The real question Marius, is whether the ANC has the courage and conviction to create an equal society considering the treatment Blacks got over the last forty-odd years. I know what I would want."

"What's that?" said Roux.

"A bloody witch hunt to punish those responsible for the atrocities. It's going to take a unique leader to ignore the injustices of the past to ensure a new South Africa."

"Tambo and Mandela?"

"I sincerely hope so, for our sakes, and those of our children," Meiring replied, looking somber. "We just have to hope and prey de Klerk, and his gang, assist and provide guidance along the way."

*A month ago we were trying to put them away, but now we need to help them take over the country?* Roux pondered the thought for a moment. Maybe the time for him to change had arrived. If so, was he ready for it?

"Eugene, I have something I need to do. Probably take two or three hours. Cover for me with du Plessis as best you can." He got up. "I'll see you back at Compton."

"Du Plessis will have a fit. Where are you going?" shouted Meiring after him.


HE PULLED INTO THE driveway, honked the horn, and waited. It was not long before Els appeared at the front door, squinting at the car. Realizing who it was, he trotted over to meet Roux as he opened the door.

"Morning, Colonel. What brings you here?"

"Els. I need to see Kani. While I'm busy with him, you and your team can pack up and head back to the station. Report to Captain Meiring when you get there."

Els gave him a questioning look. "You sure, Colonel? What about the two in the house?" He seemed reluctant to leave.

"Enjoying sitting on your arses all day, are you?" said Roux with a smile. "It's fine Els. There's no longer any need to confine them to the house. You can get going."

Els seemed worried. "OK Colonel, if you say so."

"I do, but thanks for a job well done. Let Kani know I'm here."

The young man grinned, gave a mock salute, and ran back to the house. Roux followed at a leisurely pace. Once inside, he saw Kani emerging from his office, still dressed in a tracksuit.

"This is a surprise, Marius, I was not expecting to see you for a while." A momentary look of concern crossed his face. "Everything OK? Nothing happened to Mel or your son, I hope?"

Roux waved him back toward the office. "No, everything is still the same, but I need to talk to you in confidence."

A grave look appeared on the older man's face. "Oh? About what?"

Roux took a deep breath. He knew what he was about to do could end up in dire consequences, but he shook off the doubt. "What is the message? The one for Mandela?"

Kani chortled. "Really Marius? I thought I explained everything. Discussion closed."

"Even if I offer to take it to Mandela. Today," said Roux.

Kani gaped at him for several seconds before clearing his throat. "You? Take it to Mr. Mandela? Why would you do that, but more importantly, how could I trust you to deliver it? How do I know you won't use it against us?"

"You don't," said Roux firmly. "You will just need to trust me when I say I will deliver it. Today. Before the release." He paused, peering closely at Kani. "He is being released sometime today."

Kani took a step back, leaning a hand against his desk. "Praise the Lord!" he said. "Finally, we can talk about change, positive change, for everyone." He turned and stared out the small window. After several moments he looked over his shoulder at Roux. "You realize Marius, your offer could destroy both our lives. Yours, if General du Plessis finds out, and mine if you betray me."

Roux sighed, pulling out a chair and sitting down. He folded his arms and leaned back. "I know, professor. Trust me, I do." He looked away.

"I was tasked with protecting the one man who will dismantle the very foundation of what we Afrikaners have believed in for the last hundred years. A job which was a complete anathema to me. Turned my father and sister against me, but I have done it to the best of my ability. You knew who was behind the MBL, but you allowed me to discover it for myself. That happened an hour ago, and now my father is dead, but rather than face the consequences of his actions, he took the coward's way out and committed suicide. But," he drew breath, "there is still a man out there who intends to assassinate Mandela after his release. Du Plessis knows about it, and I'm sure he will warn your compatriots and do everything in his power to ensure they catch the man before any damage is done. But I am finished with this entire business. Trying to do what you, amongst many others, consider being the *right thing* by keeping Mandela alive has almost cost me my family. I'm no longer prepared to place them in further danger. There will be fallout from the arrest of my father's co-conspirators, but I want no part of the radical element they represent. I need to protect my own for a change." He stood up.

"I assure you I will deliver the message to Mr. Mandela, or a person of your choice. I know this could end badly for me if I'm discovered, but if what you said the other day about a brighter future for all is true, I have to believe the change the ANC will bring will be beneficial for my son. And if I can contribute to ensuring a peaceful transition by delivering the message, then I am prepared to take my chances. However, I do have one proviso."

"Which is."

"The message will not lead to the deaths of innocent people. I know I have no way of knowing if you're being honest with your reply, but I believe you, and your brother, are men of integrity, and if you assure me that will not happen, I have no reason to disbelieve you."

"I asked my brother the very same question this morning. He assures me it does not, and I believe him."

"Then give me the message."

Kani studied him for several seconds. Their eyes locked. "Can I make a call?"

"Sure."

He stared down at the table, making no attempt to hear what Kani was saying on the phone. He just didn't care anymore, he decided. Fate will take him where she intends.

"I've spoken to Nair," said Kani, returning to the office, "He is at Verster, and although not happy, you can give him the letter. You realize you will need to get past the police at the house first?"

"I do, but rank has its privileges." He paused, giving Kani a questioning look. "You just said a letter. I thought the message was verbal?"

Kani moved to the table and reached down, extracting a brown envelope from amongst the same papers and envelopes Roux had seen before. It was not bigger than eight by four inches. A stock standard size used by everyone to post everyday correspondence.

"Here," he said.

Roux took the envelope, staring down at it. No, he thought, I don't care what it contains.

"My brother wrote it out last night, on my insistence, on the off chance I could find a way to get it to Verster," said Kani. "It seems you have provided the way."

He waited for a response from Roux, but when there was none, he said, "I see your men have left. Does it mean my brother and I are free?"

Roux turned the envelope over in his hands. Something so small but which will forever, in his mind, be associated with tragic outcomes.

"It does, but be careful out there. Today could be an exciting, historic day. Or a very violent one. Let's hope it's the former."

How easy it would be, he thought, touching the envelope in his breast pocket as he drove toward Victor Verster Prison. Just turn around and go back to Compton. Be a hero for once in his life. He'd uncovered the brains behind the MBL, intercepted the courier's letter, and hopefully find the shooter before it was too late. He would have achieved the impossible. But he knew the reality would be different. Du Plessis would say he'd done what was expected of him, and life would move on except he would be a targeted man amongst the right wingers, and Mel and Rian would be in even more danger. He could demand protection for his family, but it would be temporary. After that, they would be on their own. His stomach churned, his chest tightened.

"What the hell am I doing?" he shouted, punching the dashboard.

"The right thing, Marius." Mel's voice in his head was as clear as the midday sun. He smiled grimly. *It's what you would want, isn't it, Pet? Would hope I would do, and maybe this time, give your unqualified support? Perhaps even be proud of me again?* He glanced at his watch and floored the accelerator.

Getting through the main prison gate was easy, but things changed when he pulled up in front of the house in which Mandela was being detained. As he alighted from his car, a welcoming group of three uniformed men approached him. The one in front, a head shorter than the two sergeants following him, looked to be only years away from needing a walker to get around. The man was wiping his face with a handkerchief, cap in his other hand. Dark patches showed beneath his armpits, thinning hair plastered to his head. He came to a stop in front of Roux, who noted, with some relief, the man's rank. Only a major. Outranking the man was a definite positive if he was going to gain entry to the house without raising too much suspicion.

"Colonel Roux," said the major between efforts to suck in air. "I am Major Smit. I was not expecting you. You're not on the list of approved visitors for today. If I approve your visit, we will need to add your details and the reason for the visit to the list. My orders, not negotiable." He placed his peaked cap on his head, trying to look confident and in command.

He had one of two options; try sweet-talk his way past this pompous relic or pull rank and bluster his way through. He decided on a combination.

"Major," he said, looking down at the man. "May I talk to you in confidence?" he said in his best imitation of a silky tone, pulling the man to one side by his elbow. "Is there somewhere we can talk privately? This is an urgent matter."

Smit's expression changed in an instant. Looking eager and conspiratorial, he said, "Oh! OK, Colonel, we can go around the side of the house. You two stay here," he instructed the sergeants.

Once out of earshot and eyesight of the sergeants, Roux stopped and faced Smit. He spoke in a hushed voice. "As I'm sure General Warmer has informed you, Major, we, the Security Branch under the direct orders of the commissioner, are, at this very moment, searching for several car bombs which we believe are intended to harm Mr. Mandela. We can't allow this to happen. To assist us with our search, I need to speak to Mr. Nair. Now."

Smit stared at Roux, his expression changing from confidence to fear, eyes wide with surprise.

"Oh, shit!" Roux swore under his breath. *He didn't know, but now he does, thanks to me.* "Major," he said, his voice taking on a firmer tone as he tried to recover from his blunder. "This is highly secret information. For your ears only. I'm sure you can understand the consequences to your career," *or what is left of it*, mused Roux, "if General du Plessis found out you shared it with anyone. Anyone." He emphasized the last word by squeezing the man's shoulder. "Do you understand, Major?"

"Y-ye-yes, yes, Colonel," the man spluttered, spraying spit into Roux's face. "You have my word," he put a finger to his lips, "Nothing from this mouth. I assure you."

*Yeah, sure*, thought Roux. *He'll either tell anyone he can find or be on the radio to Warmer.* Oh well, if he was going to go down with the ship, he might as well insist the band was playing.

"Now Major," all friendliness gone from his voice. "I need to see Mr. Nair, so I would appreciate if you would ask him to join me now and no, you will not add my name to your visitors' list. That is an order. From the Security Branch. Do I make myself clear?"

Smit stood for a moment, scratching his cheek, but then nodded and turned on his heel. Roux watched him disappear into the house. Moments later an Indian dressed in a suit, followed by Smit, who remained at the door watching Roux as the ANC man walked over to join him.

"Colonel Roux, I am Nair. I was not expecting a visit from Security Branch today. Everything OK, I hope?" he said, in a voice loud enough for Smit to hear.

Roux wondered if du Plessis had told the ANC about the bombs. *I would have.*

"Mr. Nair, thank you for coming out to meet me. Yes, everything is fine. I just need to ask you several questions." His voice was equally loud.

Nair smiled, then his voice dropped to almost of whisper. "Our mutual friend told me you would be visiting. You have something for me?"

Roux looked around. Smit was still at the door, but the two sergeants were meandering toward the front of the property, deep in conversation. He moved back behind the corner of the house, motioning for Nair to follow him. Pulling the envelope from his inside jacket pocket, he handed it to Nair.

"You have my word. I have not opened it. As I promised Professor Kani."

Nair's eyes bored into Roux's. He hesitantly took the envelope, stared down at it, turned it over to check if still sealed and then sighed; a long, shuddering sigh. He spoke, his voice filled with emotion.

"We were worried sick about this after we heard Jonas and his brother were under house arrest." He looked up at Roux. "Yes, Colonel, I believe you, but may I ask why you agreed to do this? Some may even call it treason."

Roux shrugged, not because he felt a sense of casualness, but because he himself wasn't yet sure why. "It's done now. No point in analyzing it."

"I understand. You have our eternal thanks, Colonel, and that of the Party."

Roux shrugged again and walked off. *What's done is done*, he thought. *It is what it is.*


"WHERE THE HELL HAVE you been?" said Meiring in a hushed voice when Roux walked into the SB offices. "Du Plessis is going ballistic, your arse is in a sling, my friend, and the general is winding it up to hurl it far out to sea." He chortled. "Never seen him in such a state. Everyone is in a panic over this phantom shooter, and every spare pair of boots is deployed in and around Verster, along the route to the city center, or at City Hall. What took you so long?"

Meiring appeared to be on the verge of a nervous breakdown; face haggard, eyes bloodshot, his hands fidgeting with anything within reach.

"Something I needed to do. Not a great way to spend your last couple of weeks in the force, hey!? Where is du Plessis?"

Mering pointed at the ceiling. "In Warmer's office, along with the army brass."

"Good. That means I can get out of here before he knows I'm back. Who's in charge at City Hall?"

"Chris, as far as I know. They've set up a mobile command center behind the hall. I've sent Els and his guys there, along with Gainsford and some uniform and CID constables who were sitting around picking their noses. Haveman went earlier with as many of our men as we could round up. From what I hear," said Meiring, pointing at the radio handset on his desk, "they are doing a room-by-room search of all the buildings within range of the hall. Going to take forever."

"Thanks. By the way, where'd they find the third car?"

"Army guys found it parked under a tree in the bush alongside the road from Verster. Someone either deliberately or by mistake failed to activate it."

"One less thing to worry about, I suppose. I'm going to head to the hall and check in with Chris, maybe see if I can help with the search. I can't handle sitting round waiting for something to happen. You coming?"

Meiring shook his head. "General said to stay put in case he needs something, and I was also to instruct you to report to him immediately after you arrived, so consider yourself duly instructed."

Roux smiled. "Duly noted Captain." He paused, looking down at the man he owed so much to. "Eugene, if du Plessis asks, don't screw up what's left of your career to cover for me. Just tell him the truth. You know how vindictive the bastard can be."

"You sure?"

"Yup, from the way things are going, I'll probably be joining you in civvie street when this is all over." He turned on his heel and headed for his office. "You know, it doesn't sound a bad idea," he called over his shoulder. "Please let Chris know I'm on my way. I'll be on my radio, but I need to make a call first."

First, he called the army barracks and after being passed from one office to another, he finally heard Phil's voice.

"What's up, old friend? This place is humming, units being deployed all over the city and we've been put on low-level standby. Any news?"

"Can't say much on the phone, but chaos here as well. I'm on my way to the City Hall to see If I can help." He paused. "Phil, do me a favor. Stay near a phone. I have a feeling we may need your expertise. That a problem?"

"Not at all. Write this number down. It'll come through to our offices."

Roux jotted the number down and shoved the piece of paper into his jacket.

"Thanks, pal. Hopefully talk soon."

He rang off and then dialed the hospital. After what seemed forever, Mel answered in a weak voice.

"Marius?"

His heart skipped several beats. "Hi Pet, how you feeling?"

She sighed. "Tired and stressed out. No news yet on Rian. He's still in a coma. We just have to wait it out, but my mom and dad are here so they a big help. How are things out there?"

He paused for a second before he said, "Mandela is being released today, so it's all hectic, but with a bit of luck, I'll be able to get to the hospital this evening."

"It's been on the radio and TV. Everyone here is on edge," she said, her voice lacking any emotion.

He swallowed hard, then cleared his throat. "Pet, I did something today which may get me booted out of the force. I know . . ." His voice tailed off, not sure how to go on.

"What did you do Marius?" her voice was now taking on the familiar firmness.

"The right thing, I hope. Don't ask me why, but I just felt I needed to do it. I'll explain when I see you." He considered telling her about his father, then opted to leave it until he saw her.

Her tone softened. "If it was the right thing to do Marius, the right thing for all of us, then you have my support."

A surge of emotion washed over him. How could he have ever doubted this woman? "Thanks Pet, I love you. See you later. Give Rian a hug for me."

"OK," was all she said.


AFTER NAVIGATING THREE CHECKPOINTS around the city center, he spotted a motley array of police armored vehicles, cars, vans, and army trucks in a parking area behind the hall. As he drove in, he saw the mobile command truck around which were a flurry of men in various uniforms: blue-clad policemen, RTG men in camouflage, and a smattering of brown and blue-uniformed army and air force personnel. Overhead, the buzz of helicopters sliced through the usual traffic din. He was surprised Prinsloo was in charge of such a significant operation, considering his rank, but then, du Plessis was likely overseeing things from Compton, and he trusted Prinsloo. Failing to find a vacant parking bay, he headed for the command vehicle, coming to a stop alongside.

"Hey man!" shouted a burly sergeant in camouflage. "You can't park there."

*Yes, I can,* said Roux to himself as he climbed out. "Colonel Roux, Security Branch, I need to see Captain Prinsloo."

"Hello Colonel, come on over." Prinsloo was standing in the doorway of the command vehicle. "Sergeant, find a place to park the Colonel's car."

Roux handed the disgruntled man his keys and walked over to Prinsloo. The two men shook hands. "Hello Chris, and the name's Marius, which I'm sure you already know. What's happening?"

"Thanks. Organized chaos, if you ask me. The air wing is up. They checking all the rooftops and dropping off sniper teams on the most strategic of them. We also got a company of army troopies to help with searching the surrounding buildings, but it's floor by floor, so going to take some time. Some of them are locked, so we've had to get the owners out to open up." He sighed, looking toward the hall. "I have to admit, I'm not sure what to tell the teams to look for, other than a suspicious-looking character who may be carrying a large duffel bag containing a rifle. Problem is, he could be anywhere, even in the crowd that's gathering."

"Have you any idea where a sniper would position himself?" said Roux.

Prinsloo looked bemused. "Take your pick Marius. Dozens of roof tops, hundreds of windows, trees, high ground, all of which are well within range if he's using a high-powered sniper rifle. Army snipers are of a similar opinion. Multiple spots, which means checking each one, but nothing to stop the shooter using the spot after we've cleared it. I don't have the personnel to monitor every site."

"Chris, I have a mate in the Recce's who is a phone call away if you think he can help." He handed Phil's number to Prinsloo. "His direct line. Just use my name."

Prinsloo pocketed the slip of paper. "Thanks. I may take you up on the offer."

Roux's radio ended the conversation. "Bravo, this is Bravo Two, you copy?"

He pulled the handset from his belt and thumbed the transmit button. "Go ahead Eugene."

"Our man has departed but seems he's headed to the townships to pay a visit to some friends, so not sure when he'll arrive at your location."

Shit! He checked his watch. It was gone three-thirty. Diverting to the townships complicated things, but it gave more time to find the shooter. "Thanks Eugene, you still at HQ?"

"Affirmative. I'll let you know if we get any further info. Out."

"Eugene still at Compton?" said Prinsloo. "I would have thought he'd be itching to be out here?"

"Du Plessis made him stay at the station just in case he needs something. You know he's resigning?" said Roux.

"Yes, he told me. Sorry to see him go, but he's a smart cookie, that one. Far too switched on to stay in the force when he can make good money out there," he waved an arm in the general direction of the city center. "By the way," a broad smile appeared on Prinsloo's face. "Your du Plessis got me upped to major, so he's now on my Christmas card list."

Which may go someway to explaining why du Plessis had put him in charge. He glanced at the badge free epaulettes on Prinsloo's shoulders. "Congrats man! You deserve it, but I see you not wearing the Castles yet," referring to the insignia denoting the rank of major.

Prinsloo laughed. "Not had time to get them put on by the tailor, so thought I'd go rankless today. What you got in mind Marius? You want to hang around here or join your guys over at the City Bank building? I sent them all down there about an hour ago. Some captain with a pipe is in charge."

"Haveman." *Heaven help us*, he thought. He looked towards the City Bank building, wondering if he could walk there. "Ironic isn't it?"

"What is?"

"All this to protect the one man who is going to destroy everything we know. Our very belief systems. It's a scary thought."

Prinsloo stared off into the distance. "I know. Lots of my guys are not happy at all, but times are a changing, as Dylan said."

Roux felt a nudge in his back and turned to be confronted by the STG sergeant, who, with a scowl, dropped his car keys into his hand. "Its parked by the far fence," he said as he stalked off.

Roux gave a wry smile and turned back to Prinsloo. "Thanks Chris, think I'll join my guys. I need to be doing something for a change. Too many days sitting round waiting for things to happen. I'm tired of chasing."

"Understandable. I suggest you drive there. Are you armed?"

"Nah! Can't stand the things. Make me nervous," said Roux, grinning.

With a disapproving look, Prinsloo leaned back and shouted into the interior of the control room. Moments later, a sleeveless arm passed him a black pistol. With the ease of a well-experienced firearms handler, Prinsloo ejected the magazine, inspected it, then pulled the slide back to ensure there was no chambered round. Satisfied the weapon was safe, he slid the magazine in and handed it to Roux, grip first.

"It's a new Glock, although I wouldn't suggest you get into a shootout with a trained assassin. Best to keep your head down and shout for help. Maybe put one up the spout when you get there."

He had no intention of getting into anything even faintly resembling a shootout with anyone, never mind an assassin. Carefully, he stuffed it into a trouser pocket. His trouser belt was already a tight fit, and with his luck, it would end up blowing the shit out of him—literally. Nor was he putting one up the spout, considering the angle of the barrel in his pocket.

Prinsloo stared at him in horror, as though deploring his blatant abuse of a weapon.

With a sheepish grin, Roux waved a farewell before calling Haveman on the radio.

HE PULLED UP ALONGSIDE the curb in front of the City Bank building, thankful he drove rather than walked. The bank was at the outer circle of the area being searched, which he guessed was deliberate. Prinsloo would want his best trained men combing the buildings and sidewalks closest to the City Hall. As instructed, Haveman was waiting for him in front of the building, but to Roux's surprise, so were the rest of the men, including Els and Gainsford. Intermingled with the SB men were four black uniformed security guards.

Haveman gave him a contemptuous glare and Els half a wave, accompanied by a huge grin. "The man's permanent exuberance seriously annoys me," Roux muttered, not too softly. *I need to get Meiring to have a fatherly chat with him, for his own sake. Get him to wind his neck in a bit and focus on the damn job instead of grinning at everyone.* He knew he was being unfair, but right now, he didn't care. Something he would later regret.

He stopped in front of the pipe man. "Why are you all sitting out here? I thought you've been tasked with searching the bank building?"

"Done," said Haveman, looking bored. "These guys," he pointed towards the security guards, "will stay here in front and two will guard the back entrance. We headed for the annex."

Roux found it hard to believe they'd cleared a eight story building in a matter of an hour, but didn't feel up to an argument. He glanced at the men, all of whom appeared disgruntled. Besides Els and Gainsford, there were eight other SB men, all in casual dress, which meant they were off duty when they got called in. Except for Gainsford, who carried a R5 rifle besides a pistol on his hip and one stuck in the front of his jeans, all were armed with handguns. Roux knew he would have to watch Gainsford. The man seemed to be on the prowl for someone to shoot.

"OK then, let's move over to the annex. Do we have keys?"

"I do," shouted one of the security guards.

"Right," said Roux, pointing at the man, "You first and get the front door open. Is there a back entrance?"

"There is, but it's locked, and it would be difficult to open without heavy tools."

"Open up for us and then two of you get round the back and stay there until we let you know it's time to move. Will the offices be locked?"

"No, against company policy." The guard glared at Roux as though to suggest he didn't employ him, and he'd go where he damn well pleased. But he rose to his feet, grumbling his way up to the annex front door, unlocked it and pushed the two sliding doors back.

The annex—an addition, within the last ten years, to the main bank building—boasted six levels. Once inside, the men walked toward the elevators.

"No," Roux hissed. "It'll make too much noise. We use the stairs." He glanced at Haveman. "I'll take Els with one of your guys to check out the top two floors. You and the rest of your men do the lower four. No talking or smoking, weapons ready. OK?"

Haveman pouted. "Take Gerber." He pointed to a portly, middle-aged man who already appeared to be out of breath.

Great, thought Roux, *an over enthusiastic kid paired with a soon to be geriatric. What could go wrong?* He waved at the two men as he opened the door to the stairwell. Leading from the front, he began a slow ascent to the first floor, where Haveman signaled for two of his men to break off. Just as they were about to continue upwards, Meiring came on the radio to tell him Mandela was on his way to City Hall. Roux acknowledged the call before continuing to the second level. More men peeled off at each of the levels until only Roux, Els and Gerber, by now showing severe signs of fatigue, stepped through the stairwell door to the fifth floor hallway. One look at the pale, sweat soaked face of the older man told Roux he'd gone as far as he was going.

"OK, you two do this floor. I'll head up to the sixth."

Gerber flashed him a grateful smile.

Beginning the climb to the last floor, he sympathized with Gerber. His own legs were burning and his breathing was becoming labored. He hummed to himself, somewhat surprised at how calm he felt. But then, the chances of meeting a hooded gunman were unlikely at this distance. Maybe a Phil or one of his boys could make the shot, but he doubted some bush-trained wannabe could do it. Feeling the Glock beginning to chaff the top of his thigh, he pulled it out and transferred it to the left pocket. He doubted he would need it.

The low light in the hallway caught him unawares, causing him to hesitate on the threshold. Peering into the gloom, he could see the two florescent overhead lights at the end of the hallway were out. He began moving slowly down the hallway, checking the offices on either side of him. In each case, a quick glance told him they were empty. The closer he got to the end, the gloomier it became. There were now only two doors on either side of him, all shut. Were they locked? Just in case, he fished out the Glock from his pocket, transferring it to his right hand.

With clenched jaw, he edged open the first door to his right. The room was tiny, with stacks of files and small boxes on two metal racks. Even a pixie would have a problem hiding in here, and it faced the wrong way. The next door revealed another store room of sorts. Leaving the doors open, he turned to face the two closed doors to his left. Taking a deep breath, he opened the second last door. The afternoon sunlight made it easy for him to see it was just another empty office. Through the two four pane windows, he could see the City Hall off in the distance.

*One to go, and then we done*, he thought, placing his hand on the lever of the last door. He held the Glock pointing downward in his right hand. Carefully, he pressed down, pushing the door open with his foot. The drawn blinds on two of the four windows blocked much of the sunlight, but there was still sufficient light to see. The room, although larger, was much the same as the previous one.

Except for the man leaning on the windowsill of the last window, his cheek resting on the butt of a long-barreled rifle. Roux's heart stopped for a moment. Then he felt as if his bowels were liquefying, accompanied by an urgent need to piss.

"Y-yo-you!" Roux shouted, taking several steps into the room, raising the Glock. "Police! Stand back from the window and keep your hands where I can see them." He couldn't help it but grin inwardly. Eugene and Phil would be most impressed. Then he remembered he'd forgotten to chamber a round. Again. Shit!

The man turned around slowly, moving his left arm away from his body, but as he turned face on, his right hand flew up. A pistol, with the barrel extended by a silencer, was aimed at Roux's face.

Roux gasped. Every ounce of breath left him, as though he'd been sucker punched in the stomach. The Glock dropping limply to his side.

"Phil? Why . . ."

"Aw shit Marius, what are you doing here?" said Roberts in a low voice. "How long have you been in the building?" He took a step toward Roux, his eyes narrowing. "How many more of you are there?"

Roux's lips moved without making a sound, his mind blank. He gaped at his friend.

Roberts' mouth took on the familiar lopsided grin, but the eyes were dark and cold.

"Surprised, old boy? Last person you expected to see, hey!?" He walked up to Roux. They stared at each other for a moment before Roberts reached down, snatching the Glock from Roux's hand and stuffing it into the back of his trousers. Next, he pulled the radio from Roux's belt and switched it off before tossing it away.

"You won't be needing either of those." He was still grinning. "Close your mouth, for God's sake man, you look like a drowning fish." He paused. "You've caused me a problem, friend. I have a job to do, and you're in my way. Pity you didn't send one of your Blacks or Coloreds up here. Killed them without a second thought—but you? Makes it a bit more complicated." He studied Roux for several seconds, his eyes never leaving Roux's face. Then he chuckled. "Oh, don't worry. I won't hesitate to do it, my old friend. There are more important issues at stake here than our friendship. The big picture, as the general puts it."

Roux just stared for several moments, feeling the blood pulsing in his head. Then, when he finally had his breath back, he said, "But I spoke to you a couple of hours ago. You were at the barracks, gave me your number. What . . . How?"

"Bad timing. Just managed to slip out before my CO collared me." He cocked an eyebrow at Roux. "What did you expect me to say? Sorry, I can't help as I have someone to shoot? But you barging in like this was not in my planning schedule. Damned inconvenient."

"What are you doing, Phil? This is madness," said Roux, desperation in his voice. "How did you get mixed up in all of this? Was it my father who talked you in to this? Why, Phil? For God's sake, man, use your head. What are you trying to achieve?"

Roberts stroked his chin. "Well, let's see. Maybe a civil war? Stop the ANC from getting into power? Make sure we Whites win the actual war and force the Blacks to concede to a White run country?" Only his mouth smiled. "We'll let them have their homelands, of course, but the army will run the country. Restore things to the way they should be."

Roux gave a derisive laugh. "Really? And you think the world, and the ANC, are just going to step back and let you kill Mandela and cause the deaths of thousands of people. Innocent people? You're as delusional as my pa." He stepped up to Roberts. "When did you get sucked in to this bullshit?"

"The general contacted me soon after de Klerk started making noises about change," replied Roberts, his usual cocky self. "Told me about his concerns for the future and introduced me to some very powerful, like-minded people. Influential people. In business, the security forces, and in the government. They had a plan, a logical alternative to change. The more I listened to de Klerk, the more I began to believe in what the general said. After SONA, it became necessary to act. The final arrangements were made, and everyone is in position to implement the plan." He paused. "As soon as I shoot that Black bastard," he nodded towards the open window.

Roux snorted. "For someone as intelligent as you, Phil, your stupidity amazes me. There is no plan. No one is ready to act." He stopped, and his eyes narrowed. "You've been using me this whole time, haven't you? All the meetings to 'catch up' were just an excuse to find out what we knew about the MBL." He hissed. "You told them about Conradie, didn't you, and got him killed?"

"Your fault for putting him there. He found out about Waterfalls and had to go. It's a war Marius, people get killed."

Roux shook his head in dismay, staring at the man he had trusted from the day he met him. Saved his life. And now this betrayal.

"Phil, there is no plan. We raided—"

Roberts leaped forward, jamming his pistol under Roux's chin. "Crap! I spoke to your father this morning. He confirmed everyone was on board. The army brass, the air force, special forces, all waiting for the signal once Mandela was out of the frame. Sorry old man, but you lose—checkmate."

He stepped back, a glint in his eyes. "The MBL was simply a distraction, to keep your eyes on the wrong target, and what do you know, its worked. There's still two more bombs about to go off. Send in the cavalry, save the day! And I'll finish the job." He was almost shouting now. Spit flew from his mouth, his gun hand waving in front of Roux's face. He stopped to take several deep breaths. "And you, old boy, will be lying dead on this floor. Mel and Rian will grieve for a while, but they know what a wimp you are, so they'll get over it quick enough, and of course, I'll be there to console them, as I always have." He stepped back, leaning against the desk.

Roux looked at his friend, the truth beginning to dawn on him. "You weren't concerned about my well-being, were you? You went to see Mel hoping to get back with her, didn't you? The bad news for you is she called you a 'child' and considers you a friend, only." He stopped and pointed at Roberts.

"You were at Waterfalls," said Roux quietly. "You set the whole thing up, didn't you? Waterfalls, the bomb makers, the cars. Was it you who called and threatened me? Probably not. Got one of your 'team' to do it for you because you didn't have the balls to talk to me. It was amateurish Phil. Meiring saw through it immediately. Mel saw the shooter and recognized him as White. So all it did was make us realize there were Whites behind this entire enterprise." Something about Roberts' gun hand kept catching his eye.

Then he realized. It was as if a bright light had gone off in his brain, almost blinding him. He peered at Roberts' arm, and his world collapsed.

"It was you," he gasped. "Mel saw the shooter's arm, the rolled up sleeve." He pointed at Roberts' arm. "Like yours is now. You tried to kill Mel and Rian. Why Phil, what did they ever do to you? You said you loved them. Why in God's name would you do that? If you were trying to prove a point, why didn't you have the guts to confront me? Why them?" He pleaded.

Roberts appeared momentarily unsure of himself as his eyes darted between Roux and the open window. "Slight miscalculation old boy. I didn't mean to hit Rian, if fact, I didn't even know he was in the car, but your father said you needed a warning to make you back off, and try to convince du Plessis to take you off the investigation. You and that prick Meiring seemed to be the only ones who were closing in on us. I'm sorry about that. You know I wouldn't deliberately hurt them."

"A slight miscalculation? Pa called Rian *collateral damage*, for Christ's sake! What kind of people are you?" Roux shouted.

"You OK, Colonel?" the voice came from behind him. He spun round to see Els standing in the doorway, the perpetual grin ever present. From his position, Roberts was almost entirely obscured. "I'm finished downstairs and I—"

The young man's face changed from a smile to one of confusion as a dark hole appeared just above his brow line. "Oh," was all he said before crumpling to the floor.

"No!" screamed Roux. He ran over to the prone figure on the floor. Young, brown eyes stared up at nothing. There was no need for a doctor. He knelt down and closed the eyes, imagining he could still see the smile on his face. He turned to Roberts, the pistol now pointed at him, wisps of smoke escaping from the silencer. Anger took hold of him.

"You shithead!" he yelled. "Was that necessary? I could have talked him down. There was no need to kill him. He's just a kid. Damn you Phil! What has happened to you?" He sprang up, walked up to Roberts, knocked the pistol away with one hand, and began poking his finger against the man's chest, pushing him back against the desk.

"You idiot!" he screamed. "It's all over. We raided Fouché's house this morning. The old arsehole broke down and told us everything. There is no plan, no big group of plotters, as my father led you to believe. Just nine frightened, misguided, and ignorant old men, as Fouché admitted, who, like him, could not deal with the reality of a changing world. There are no car bombs. We found and disarmed everyone of them. And the man you hero worship? He took the coward's way out. Shot himself. Right in front of me, and you know what? I felt nothing. Your influential people have disappeared and made a run for it, but Fouché will give us their names and we'll get them." He paused for breath.

"Why do you think we're here, searching the buildings? Because Fouché told us about an assassin. Everyone is looking for you, Roberts." He continued, disgusted. "For you, the traitor. This country will be a better place without my father and others like him. Including you. So no, it is you who loses Phil. Checkmate!"

He was breathing heavily, perspiration gathering on his top lip. He lowered his voice. "So give it up Phil. Let's walk out of here and end this now."

His onetime friend sagged, as though his bones had turned to jelly. "No. No . . . he wouldn't. He promised me," the voice broke. "He promised me . . ." Roberts closed his eyes, his lips a thin line, his face screwed up in pain.

Reaching for the gun in Roberts' hand, he said, "Come on Phil, give me the gun. Let's get out of here."

It was as though the man was suddenly possessed. He straightened up and thumped the barrel of the gun against Roux's chest, causing him to grunt and stagger backwards.

"Never. He would never desert me, or the cause. You can bullshit all you like Roux, but Mandela, and you, die today." He screamed, eyes blazing with hatred.

Marius Roux closed his eyes. Is this when you're supposed to see your life flash before your eyes? All he saw was Rian's disfigured face, before the sound of a gunshot deafened him.


THE BULLET WHICH TOOK Philip Roberts' life was fired from behind Roux, passing over his right shoulder and giving him a distinct feeling of warm air grazing his cheek.

He opened his eyes as he heard Roberts' gun clatter to the floor. The body of the man he thought he knew so well was lying on his back, arms flung out to his sides; a neat black hole, filling with blood, just below his left eye. Roux shook his head, trying to clear the momentary loss of hearing.

"You can stop pissing yourself now. He's dead. How the bloody hell did you allow him to disarm you?"

Roux frantically stared down at his trousers, relieved to see they were still dry. He turned, his whole body shaking, to see Gainsford, in the process of lowering his R5 rifle, glowering at him in disgust.

"Shit, bloody officers, amateurs, all of you."

"How . . . what are you doing here?" Roux mumbled.

"Du Plessis thought you would cock-up again, so told me to cover your back. It's about bloody time you looked after yourself, shit for brains. I'm not your bloody mother." He turned, pulling his radio from his belt as he stepped out into the passage.

With the smell of cordite still strong in his nostrils, Roux turned to look at Roberts. Blood was leaking from the facial wound and running down his cheek, and more blood and gray matter were pooling around the head in stark contrast to the cream-colored carpet. He thought of the countless times he and Phil had got drunk together, vowed to be friends forever, and to always have each other's back. But in the face of sudden, senseless violence, their promises had been rendered meaningless. He shook his head. *Oh, Phil*, he thought, *what have you done? Betrayed us all. For what?* As he turned to walk back to Els's body, he knew Phil's ever ready-grin, his cavalier attitude, and his loyal friendship would be what he would choose to remember of his friend. Not this.

He gazed down at Els one last time. Yes, he decided, he is still smiling.

# Tuesday, February 13th, 1990

GAZING OUT AT THE tranquil expanse of the ocean through a grimy windshield, he watched with disinterest as white crests gracefully formed and dissipated with each passing wave. However, the gathering of ominous dark clouds on the distant horizon meant the imminent arrival of the "Cape Doctor," the powerful and dry south-easterly wind, which battered the city regularly. The tranquil scene would change in an instant to one of a dark broiling ocean and stinging gusts of sand tearing at your exposed skin. It seemed, to Roux, to provide an ominous foreshadow of what lay ahead for the country. But for now, all was peaceful, which was in stark contrast to his mood.

After a long time, he got out of the car, slamming the door shut. Without worrying to lock it, he wandered toward the beach, heading for a bench on the verge of the grass where it retreated in the face of the advancing sand.

On one side of a bench, dressed in blue overalls, was a Black man, his wiry hair tinged with gray. In his hands, he twisted an old brown cap around, a worried expression on his face.

*Someone else having a bad day,* Roux thought.

"Hello," he said as he plonked himself down on the other side of the bench.

The man tensed, giving Roux a suspicious side glance.

Nodding towards the looming black clouds, Roux said in English, "Looks like there's going to be a storm."

An awkward smile appeared on the man's face as he visibly relaxed. "Oh yes," he replied. "It is going to be a big one, lots of lightning and rain. The wind will blow us over," he ended with a nervous laugh.

Roux gave a half-smile, turning to look out over the ocean. So, it was finally at an end. Mandela was home amongst his family. The drama surrounding his release was in the past, and all seemed well under control. It appeared as if everyone had gone about their business as usual, with no reported acts of violence. The international community was hailing the apparent peaceful developments with optimism. He wished he could say the same.

He'd stayed in the bank building until Els and Phil's bodies were removed. Chris had been replaced by a uniformed brigadier who heard his explanation of the past hour saying nothing. He made a few notes in a pocket notebook and then, to Roux's dismay, told him to "bugger off" home, as he was no longer needed. During the brief interview, they could hear the occasional roar of *Amandla*—or power—from the crowd in the City Hall square where Mandela was speaking from the second-story balcony. He wondered if he would be told of the sacrifice made by a young police officer to ensure he got to make his address.

Disregarding the orders to go home, he made his way to Compton to be met by Meiring in the SB office. The man looked exhausted but had the courtesy of asking if he was OK before demanding an explanation of how Els died. Roux couldn't shake the feeling Meiring held him responsible. The subsequent debrief with du Plessis and Warmer took over two hours as the generals probed the circumstances leading up to his father's death and the reasons for the involvement of a former, highly decorated special forces operative in the assassination attempt.

It was almost midnight before he'd got home. A call to the hospital from his office had left him none the wiser. The phone in Mel's room had remained answered. The house felt empty and unwelcoming. It just didn't feel like home anymore. Adrenalin still coursed through his veins, making him feel lightheaded and anxious. He had ripped off his clothes, leaving them on the bedroom floor, and wandered through to the kitchen in his underwear, and poured himself a very stiff brandy. Despite his need for a drink, he gagged on the first mouthful and spat it into the sink, followed by what remained in the glass. Turning off all the lights, he'd slumped into his favorite armchair in the lounge, begging for sleep.

He woke up on the lounge floor, his mouth tasting sour and his lower back aching. How he'd ended up on the floor remained a mystery, but one he had no interest in resolving. Heaving himself up, he'd staggered through to the bathroom. It was a normal Monday workday, and he needed to be at Compton.

The atmosphere in the SB office had been tense and somber. A small group of men stood around Haveman's desk listening to Gainsford who, by the smirk on his face, was reciting Roux's involvement in the events of the previous day. Gerda brought his coffee and muffin without the usual banter, leaving him with a whispered suggestion he remain in his office for the moment until people had cooled down a bit. Minutes later Meiring knocked softly before entering. Without a word, he dropped an envelope on his desk and walked out. It was his letter of resignation requiring Roux's acceptance. Adding his signature to the bottom of the page, he stuffed the letter back into the envelope and shoved it into his jacket pocket, realizing how much he hated letters and envelopes.

His purgatory had ended when a call from Warmer's secretary summoned him to the general's office, where he was met by Warmer and du Plessis. Anticipating at least a "well done" for stopping the MBL, his father and Roberts, his expectations evaporated when du Plessis exploded within seconds of his entering the office; demanding, at the top of his voice, an explanation as to why he'd gone to Verster on Sunday morning, and oh, by the way, what was the "something" he had spoken to Nair about. Roux confessed. Du Plessis threw a tantrum. Roux tried to explain, but even to him, his reasons for delivering the letter to Mandela sounded pitiful.

Warmer joined the fray by expressing, in no uncertain terms, his belief Roux was guilty of transgressing national security. He was summarily booted out of Warmer's office, but instead of just going as logic dictated, he handed Meiring's letter of resignation to du Plessis, who read it while his face went from dark red to a shade of purple and back to red. As he had walked out, his ears still ringing with the screamed accusations of his influencing Meiring's decision, he'd realized the general's big plans for the young captain were now nothing but dust.

Two hours later, he was re-summoned to Warmer's office to be informed by du Plessis he had two options;

either face a full disciplinary, which could lead to terrorism charges, or resign with immediate effect. In recognition of his efforts to thwart the assassination attempt, the commissioner had condescended, much to du Plessis' disgust, to allow him to leave with an honorable discharge—meaning he would receive three months of termination pay together with all benefits due to him. For the second time in as many days, he was told to "bugger off" home—but only after signing his letter of resignation waiting for him at Personnel and cleared out his office.

Most of the SB unit, still grieving the loss of Els, were pleased to see him go; Haveman making it abundantly clear he was not welcome at their colleague's funeral. Gerda, thankfully, hugged him, patted him on the cheek, shed a tear or two before wishing him well and telling him not to worry about packing up his stuff. She would do it and deliver it to his house later in the week. His only regret was the body of Conradie had still not been found.

When he finally walked out of Compton Square for the last time, he had headed for the hospital, but not before shaving off the beginnings of a mustache.

Mel had met him outside the ICU, where she appeared to have camped down, refusing to budge until Rian's condition improved. There was no hug or tearful reunion, which was not unexpected. He collapsed into a chair next to her. Without looking at him, she asked about the previous day and what was the thing he promised to tell her about.

In a flat tone, he explained the circumstances regarding his decision to deliver the letter and ended with a much abbreviated explanation of the visit to Fouché's house, his father's death, and the events at the City Bank.

Her stoic response to the deaths of the two men, Phil in particular, surprised him. He'd expected an emotional outburst when he told her about Phil, but all she said was, "It's what happens when little boys persist in playing dangerous games." After a lengthy silence, she had reached out and held his hand. "I am proud of how you handled the letter business and your commitment to ensuring Mandela survived. I know Rian will feel the same, she'd said"

Was she coming home? She'd shaken her head. "No, Marius. I am flying to Joburg with my parents once Rian can be moved. We need time and space. To heal. And then? We'll see." She'd squeezed his hand. "I know it hurts, but please try to understand how I feel."

All he could do was swallow hard and nod his head. He was given thirty minutes to spend with Rian before he left to return to the cold and empty house. On the way, he'd stopped off at his sister. The day didn't get any better. His repeated knocking at her front door was finally met by a tearful, alcohol soaked, unkempt woman who faintly resembled Sonja. She glared at him for several seconds, then screamed, "You killed *Pa*," spat at him, and slammed the door in his face.

The man on the other end of the bench eased himself up. "Have a nice day, boss," he said with an uncomfortable smile before ambling away. "You too," called Roux after him.

He looked back out at the ocean. His life had suddenly become meaningless. Every hope, dream, and everything he held dear was gone. There seemed to be no point in anything anymore. He let out a pain filled sigh as he watched the late afternoon sun dip behind the black clouds of the impending storm. His dark thoughts were interrupted when he felt a hand on his shoulder. He turned to see the face of Jonas Kani looking down at him.

"Hello Marius, Mel said I might find you here. She said it was your private moment spot." He walked around the front of Roux before easing himself down onto the bench. "But I am concerned about you. How are you doing?"

Roux shifted round to face the professor, not sure if the man's arrival was an annoying intrusion on his privacy or a welcome respite from his gloomy thoughts.

"Well, let's see," he said with a grim smile. "I got fired yesterday. My father turned out to be the brains behind an attempt to kill one of the most renown figures in the world, and my best friend was killed because he was the intended assassin. The only sibling I have accused me of killing our father and my wife is taking my son to Johannesburg, on the pretext she needs time and space before she can decide whether to return to our marriage, or end it. So, I don't have a job. I hate the house I live in, and I have no idea what to do next. So, how do you think I should be doing, professor?" He held up his hands. "But enough about me and my problems. How is your brother?"

"In a care facility. But I'm afraid his time has arrived. It will not be long now. I found Vuyo and brought him back, so my brother will at least spend his last moments with his son, who he has not seen for three years."

Roux nodded. There was nothing he could say. He shifted gear. "Are you able to tell me what the message was about?"

Kani gave a short laugh. "This is going to sound as though I am lying, but the truth is, no, I cannot. Considering you delivered it, you probably have a right to know, but my brother wrote it down while on his own and placed it in a sealed envelope. He believed if I did not know the contents, no one else could find out." A look of sadness crossed his face. "Committed to the struggle until the end."

"Probably for the best," said Roux. He really wasn't interested to know. It was just a part of a dreadful nightmare and best left unearthed.

They both sat in silence for some time, and then Kani turned to face him.

"Can I be open and honest with you, Marius?"

Roux laughed, "Please do. Everyone else seems to have been 'open and honest' with me, so feel free."

"I understand things look bleak at the moment, Marius, but unless you straighten yourself out and face up to the reality of your situation, the darkness which engulfs you will only become more intense. The black hole deeper. Until there is no way out. Mel is under tremendous strain at the moment, as are you, worrying about your son's recovery, her marriage and yes, like you, her future. She needs time to heal, and being away from here," he waved an expansive hand, "will help her. In time, as your son improves, she will take stock of what has happened over the last several weeks. Time to better understand the pressures you were placed under. The more she can relax and focus on what is important to her, and I believe her family is still paramount, the more approachable she will be. But you need to be patient. Give her the space she needs, and when she is ready, I know you two will be better positioned to begin the process of healing and reconciliation."

"I certainly hope you are right, Jonas. I just feel lost. Everything seems pointless no matter which way I look at it. It's as though I'm wandering around in a dark forest with no idea in which direction to go." Placing his elbows on his knees, his head dropped into his hands. He shook his head slowly. "Where do I start?"

Kani placed a hand on Roux's shoulder, compassion in his voice. "With what is most important to you—Mel and your son. If it means you have to move to where they are, so be it. Can you do that?"

"How? Sell the house, sure, I can do that, but I need a job to go to. Working for some wannabe security company will not provide the financial stability my family will need." He threw his hands up in the air. "All I know is how to be a policeman. I've done nothing else with my life." He paused. "Which is ironic, considering I never wanted to be in the force."

"Really? What did you want to do?"

Roux laughed. "A teacher, would you believe? But my father coerced me into joining up, not that I put up much resistance, as I'm sure Mel will tell you."

Kani stared at him, seemingly deep in thought.

"Yes," he said after a long pause. "I can believe it. You would make a fine teacher Marius, perhaps stern at times, but you are a good listener, which is what our children need now. Someone who will truly listen to what they have to share, about their experiences, and their hopes for the future, and who knows, it may well be cathartic for you. Give you hope for the future as well."

"And how do I go about doing that? I'm in my forties. Who's going to offer me a teaching job with no experience and a degree I did twenty years ago?"

"It really depends how determined you are to get your family back. What you would be prepared to sacrifice to restore your lives to some form of normality?"

"Anything!" said Roux, without hesitation.

"Well," said Kani, pulling at an ear, "with all the changes coming, London has given me the go-ahead to open a second facility. At the moment, the consensus is it should be established in or near Soweto in Johannesburg. We will need staff, welfare carers, counselors, admin folks and most definitely a teacher or two. Think you would be up to the challenge?"

Roux looked long and hard at Kani, a jumble of scenarios racing through his head. Would he be up to the challenge? It would mean working in a township, which was nothing new for him. But it would provide the opportunity to fulfill his ambition—to be a teacher. And he'd be close to Mel and Rian. Was there really a choice?

But.

"You do realize I'm still a . . . You know . . ."

"Racist? Of course. I would have been disappointed if you claimed otherwise. You grew up knowing nothing other than apartheid. Considering your father's influence, being racist would have been second nature. But it doesn't mean you have to remain that way. Does it?"

Roux hesitated. This was new ground for him. "Become color blind?"

Kani gave a disgusted grunt. "Absolutely not. I find the term insulting. If we are color blind, then we are just all boring gray individuals, which is not the case. I am proud to be Black, as I'm sure you are proud to be White. Why should we be embarrassed by our color? But, each race has its own culture, which includes our identity, traditions, and history, which are what make us interesting and unique. Color is a small portion of that culture. A 'paint job' to use an American phrase. But, although we are different, we are also similar in many ways, like our belief systems. Our need for individual freedom of choice and the right to be treated as equals and not persecuted because of our culture or race classification. To pretend we can all get along is ignoring the truth. There will be people in life with whom we just cannot get along with, irrespective of their color. There are Black and White people I dislike and avoid, not because of their color, but because to me, they are people I would rather not associate with. That is life, Marius." He placed a hand on Roux's shoulder.

"None of us can ignore the past. We have to compromise and work together to make sure it never happens again. Loved ones have been lost and the pain and grief are still fresh in our minds. To pretend it never happened and assume we can just go on as usual is only fooling ourselves. We need to face up to the past, talk about it, seek forgiveness where necessary, and work towards, first and foremost, learning about each other. Taking the time to understand we are all people, irrespective of our color. It will be the brave ones amongst us who will face up to the realities and make a genuine commitment to take the time to understand and respect each other and learn to communicate with each other without prejudices. For Whites, this may take a generation. But it is those who have young children who can begin the process now by encouraging their children to judge people on who they are. Not what they are. I honestly believe it is the youth who will begin to mend the bridges as they navigate the future unburdened by the injustices of apartheid."

He smiled. "So yes, Marius, I know you are still a racist, but with the right attitude, which I firmly believe is already there, you will learn to judge people on their merits, not their color. Working with the children will help, but I accept it will not be easy for you, or them. But I have confidence in you."

Roux nodded slowly, staring out at the ocean. He turned to face Kani and grinned, then stuck out a hand.

"When do I start, boss